THE
HOUSE
SAPHIR

ABOUT THE AUTHOR

Marissa Meyer is the #1 *New York Times* bestselling author of the Renegades Trilogy, The Lunar Chronicles series, the *Wires and Nerve* graphic novels, and *The Lunar Chronicles Coloring Book*. Her first standalone novel, *Heartless*, was also a #1 *New York Times* bestseller. Marissa created and hosts a podcast called *The Happy Writer*. She lives in Tacoma, Washington, with her husband and their two daughters.

THE HOUSE SAPHIR

MARISSA MEYER

faber

First published in the UK in 2025
by Faber & Faber Limited
The Bindery
51 Hatton Garden
London EC1N 8HN
faberchildrens.co.uk

First published in the US in 2025
by Macmillan Publishing Group, LLC

Book design by Maria W. Jenson
Printed by CPI Group (UK) Ltd, Croydon CR0 4YY

All rights reserved
© Rampion Books, Inc. 2025

The right of Marissa Meyer to be identified as author
of this work has been asserted in accordance with Section 77
of the Copyright, Designs and Patents Act 1988

*This book is sold subject to the condition that it shall not, by way
of trade or otherwise, be lent, resold, hired out or otherwise circulated
without the publisher's prior consent in any form of binding or cover
other than that in which it is published and without a similar condition
including this condition being imposed on the subsequent purchaser*

A CIP record for this book
is available from the British Library

ISBN 978–0–571–39697–9

Printed and bound in the UK on FSC® certified paper in line with our continuing
commitment to ethical business practices, sustainability and the environment.
For further information see faber.co.uk/environmental-policy

Our authorised representative in the EU for product safety is
Easy Access System Europe, Mustamäe tee 50, 10621 Tallinn, Estonia
gpsr.requests@easproject.com

2 4 6 8 10 9 7 5 3 1

FOR ERIN ARMSTRONG

I hope you like ghost stories.

GLOSSARY OF MONSTERS

AUTHOR'S NOTE: *Though these monsters are inspired by traditional French folklore, numerous liberties have been taken.*

Cheval Mallet
A magnificent spectral horse with flaming eyes. Its favorite pastime is to offer a ride to weary travelers and then throw them off a cliff.

Croque-Mitaine
Literally "crunchy mitten." A humanoid creature that likes to nibble the fingers off misbehaving children, but only the ones who deserve it.

Feu Follet
A small floating ball of light. Very pretty, until it enchants you and leads you to your death. No . . . it's still pretty, even then.

Lou Carcolh
A creature with an enormous snail shell, numerous tentacles, and a mouth lined with jagged, sharp teeth. Usually inhabits dark caves but will settle for an armoire in a pinch.

Lutin
A small hobgoblin that can be helpful or mischievous. It particularly enjoys tangling people's hair into knots while they're asleep. But then, who doesn't?

Matagot

A shape-shifting animal spirit that most often takes the form of a black cat. It can bring either prosperity or misfortune, depending on how well it's treated, or how spiteful it's feeling that day.

Salamander

A lizard-like amphibian that is as sassy as it is slimy. Most don't do anything special. Some can breathe fire.

Tarasque

Part dragon, part snake, and part crocodile, with the head of a lion and a tortoise shell on its back. There actually aren't any tarasques in this book, in part because the author did not think she could adequately describe it in a way that readers wouldn't think she was just making stuff up. Still, it's pretty great, as folklore monsters go.

Velue

Another peculiar amalgamation of a creature, sporting the head of a serpent on top of a porcupine-esque body, which is covered in long green fur and poison-tipped spines. It is often blamed for floods, fires, failed crops, and just about every natural disaster conceivable.

Voirloup

A hairy, slobbery, werewolf-like creature that is afraid of fire and allergic to silver. Created when a human sells their soul to a demon in exchange for seven wicked pleasures. (Which might sound tempting, if you forget the hairy, slobbery part. Think of your dignity.)

CHAPTER ONE

I f a young lady did not wish to be murdered, it was advisable that she not spend her evenings meeting with strangers on dark street corners.

Mallory knew this. She was an expert on *not getting murdered*—a skill she tended to value higher than, say, embroidering pincushions or playing scales on a harpsichord or the proper way of holding a salad fork. Mallory knew how to hold a salad fork, thank you very much, and it was in a tight fist while you sent those sharp little tines straight into the thigh of a would-be attacker. Or the eyeball. Or the gullet. The human body had plenty of vulnerable places to choose from, and she didn't like to limit herself.

Mallory waited, adjusting her grip on her artist portfolio. She heard the distant whinny of a horse. The grind of carriage wheels a block over. A colony of bats squeaking overhead. Though the shadows reached for her, she remained haloed in the light of the street's single oil lamp, so she would be easy for her clients to spot.

Easy to murder, a voice whispered, and in response she idly scratched her leg with the toe of her boot, feeling the handle of the dagger she kept hidden there. It might have been more respectable to keep it hidden beneath her skirts, but if she was under attack, she hardly wanted to waste time digging through layers of muslin and wool. What was she going to do? Ask her attacker to kindly pause while she searched for the weapon in her garter?

Boot heels clipped on the cobblestones as two gentlemen meandered past. She stood straighter, expecting her clients. One man was dressed entirely in black, while the other wore every color under the sun. She eyed them warily, but they merely tipped nonexistent hats to her as they vanished into the night.

The clock tower in the city square chimed the eleventh hour. Her foot tapped impatiently.

Finally, from the moon-spotted shadows, two new figures emerged on the other side of the street. Mallory studied them as they entered the lamplight. The man was light-skinned, broad and portly, wearing a stylish capotain hat and ruffled cravat. Either high society or pretending to be, in hopes he would eventually get admitted into their exclusive circles.

His companion was a petite girl in a shapeless crimson robe, the trailing hem gathering filth from the street. Her hair had been shaved nearly to the scalp, making way for the delicate tattoo of a bow and arrow above her left ear.

Mallory's eyebrows lifted in surprise. She'd had many odd characters on her tours. The scholars who peppered her with earnest questions about the mansion's history and the Saphir family's current political affiliations. (Luckily, Mallory was adept at making things up, because really, how should she know?) There were those who were intrigued by anything to do with the occult—not because it was strange or taboo, but because it was fascinating. The guests who came for a thrill, so they could proclaim drunkenly to their friends back at the tavern that they had survived the House Saphir. And then there were the romantics. The ladies who were determined to swoon and the suitors who were determined to "protect" them with needless acts of chivalry.

But a priestess of Tyrr? This was a new one.

"Welcome, Priestess," said Mallory. "You're a long way from the nearest temple."

The girl giggled shyly. "I'm only an initiate. I take the vows next week."

"My sister has decided to devote her life in service to the gods," the man said dryly. "I cannot fathom why."

The girl kept smiling, though there was an edge to her expression. "That's because you can't fathom devoting your life to anyone but yourself."

The man shrugged.

Mallory hated to admit it, but a part of her agreed with him. Devotion to the seven gods had become a popular pastime among society's elite after the fall of the veil nearly two decades ago—but she didn't see the appeal. As far as she could tell, the gods were taking no more interest in the affairs of humans now than they had back when the veil was still in place.

"This is where the tour begins, is it not?" asked the man.

"The House Saphir tour?" she said. "The one full of torture and dismemberment? Yes, you're in the right place. Though usually this tour appeals to heathens and outcasts, whereas you both appear so very . . . respectable."

The man's cheek twitched, evidently unsure if she was complimenting or insulting them.

"You must be Sophia and Louis Dumas," said Mallory, shifting her weighty portfolio to her other hand. "What brings you here tonight?"

"I feel it is my duty to introduce my sister to something of the world before they lock her up in that temple and never let her out again," said Louis.

"Priestesses are not *prisoners*, Louis. And there will be plenty of travel. One of my foremost responsibilities will be visiting townships to preside over treaties and peaceful negotiations, attending ceremonial hunts, blessing the weaponry of our great—"

"Yes, yes, what an exciting life you will lead," Louis interrupted, while shooting Mallory a *see what I mean?* look. "This is our last night in Morant. We had our fortunes told by a quaint little witch on Rue Tilance, and she suggested we take this tour before we depart. She spoke highly of the guide."

Mallory smiled thinly. That *quaint little witch* was her older sister. "I'll try not to disappoint."

"She had the most fascinating wares in her shop," Sophia said, studying the iron gate that towered above the street. "Louis bought an authentic god-relic—one of Wyrdith's golden feathers. We were guaranteed it would bring him good luck in the coming year."

"A rare treasure indeed," said Mallory, pretending to be impressed. "What did you pay for it?"

Louis puffed up his chest. "Only twelve lys."

"A bargain." Mallory turned her head so he wouldn't see her proud grin. That was well worth the cost of the gold foil and hours that Anaïs had spent figuring out how to apply it to those damned crow feathers.

She glanced up as the moon winked from behind a cloud. Her final guest, a Monsieur Badeaux, was officially late. "We are waiting for one more gentleman to join us, then we shall begin."

"You mentioned heathens," said Monsieur Dumas in a joking tone. "I imagine this tour draws plenty of unsavory characters."

"On occasion," said Mallory. "But then, you are taking the tour, are you not?"

Louis frowned. "What are you implying?"

"Only that it's rare to truly know a person's character, whether they are complete strangers or our dearest relations. Most people, if asked to imagine the circumstance of their own murder, will picture a stranger. Perhaps a random attack in some dark alley. But study enough murders, and you'll come to realize that it's far more common for the victim and the killer to know one another, sometimes intimately. It's usually the husband, but . . ." She heaved a dramatic sigh. "Murder between siblings is not unheard of."

Sophia's brow pinched in mild confusion, like she couldn't imagine why Mallory was telling her this, even as her brother sputtered in offense. Before he could defend his honor and proclaim that he did not have any intention of killing anyone (though isn't what they all say?), Mallory held out a palm.

"While we wait, the cost of the tour is six galets each, paid up front."

"Six galets?" said Louis. "That fortune teller told us—"

Sophia nudged him hard in the ribs, cutting him off. With a grumble, he dug the payment from his coin purse.

"Fabulous," said Mallory, tucking the money away. "As our final companion is running late, perhaps we will begin without him."

She faced the mansion, which sat like a crouched monster in the shadows off the street corner, illuminated by the faintest hint of lamplight and a touch of silver from the waxing moon.

The chains on the gate were an illusion. They were bulky and ominous, crafted of iron and rust, and were generally enough to deter curious passersby from trespassing on the abandoned grounds. But if anyone bothered to look closely, they would see that the padlock on the chains was broken, and had been for some time.

Mallory had absolutely nothing to do with that. She swore.

"Is it . . . *legal* for us to be here?" asked Sophia as Mallory unwound the clinking chain.

"Not to worry, I conduct these tours all the time," Mallory said, pretending that was a proper answer.

Sophia did not press further.

The hinges screamed as Mallory pushed the gate open and squeezed through. Louis made a face as the lichen-covered metal left streaks on his jacket, though Sophia did not seem to mind the same smudges on her robes.

A straight pathway led through the garden to the mansion, but Mallory walked slowly, allowing the tourists to take in the dried-up fountains. The crumbling garden walls. And—before them, the mansion. Narrow but tall, with three floors for living and entertaining, plus an attic that was mostly servants' quarters. The exterior was entirely white limestone, but soot, dirt, and trailing vines of ivy and wisteria had been doing their best to devour the façade for decades. Leaded and stained-glass windows that had been the height of fashion a century ago were now filthy, broken, or both. The massive entry doors—an arch of dark oak—were carved with medallions of demonic boar heads. A fitting welcome, Mallory thought, to the house that claimed such a sordid past.

"Let us begin," said Mallory, walking backward on the cobblestone path. "What do you know about Monsieur Le Bleu?"

After a hesitation, Louis responded, "He murdered people."

"Wives," Sophia added, her voice quietly reverent. "He murdered his wives."

Mallory tucked her portfolio beneath one arm and began her recitation.

"His name was Count Bastien Saphir, but most people know him by his moniker: Monsieur Le Bleu, thus named because his hair and beard were so black that in certain lights, they were said to appear almost blue. Of course, the surname *Saphir* may have had something to do with it as well."

She paused between two weed-infested garden beds. It was difficult to picture them as they had once been, with manicured boxwoods and colorful geraniums.

"He was born in his family's country estate outside the village of Comorre, forty miles northwest of here, and grew up an only child, the sole heir of the family winemaking fortune. For generations, Saphir's estate Ruby Comorre was one of the most expensive and sought-after wines on the market. As it is fortified with brandy, it can be preserved for years, even decades—and many say the flavor improves with time. This has made it particularly desirable with merchants who trade with countries as far as Isbren and Gai-Yin, where it is a rare commodity among the nobility. Connoisseurs also appreciate that the additional alcohol gets you drunk faster."

She climbed the front steps to the house. "But Bastien was bored with country life, so when he was twenty-one years of age, he bought this parcel of land, here in the heart of Morant, for the construction of the mansion before you. He spared no expense, as you can see from the gold-plated sundial on the south terrace and the decorative medallions that ornament the upper floors—each one unique and hand-carved by a local artisan."

"I beg your pardon," interrupted Monsieur Dumas, whose scowl had been deepening as Mallory had set the stage for her horrific tale. "Are you going to give the *entire* tour?"

Mallory stared at him. "That was my intention."

"But you . . . You're . . ." His puzzled expression turned to one of distaste. "I thought you were the secretary, or . . . You know. The one who would greet us and take our hats and coats. Not the *guide*."

Mallory's jaw twitched. "You were mistaken."

"But this tour is about . . . *murder*." He dropped his voice. "It isn't ladylike to speak of such things."

Sophia grimaced in embarrassment.

Mallory was beginning to understand why Sophia might want to run off and join an order that pledged their lives to the god of archery and war, a god who did not care if you were male or female or something else altogether. If Louis was going to make comments like this all night, she would spend her evening fighting the urge to roll her eyes.

That was a lie. She would roll her eyes without hesitation and without apology.

But it might cost her a tip at the end of the night, and no amount of chauvinism would change the weight of his coins in her purse.

She sighed. "I am Morant's foremost expert on Monsieur Le Bleu and the Saphir family, and currently the only tour guide operating at this mansion. If your delicate sensibilities would prefer to spend the evening in the gambling hall, I will not keep you. But if you wish to see inside the house, then I suggest you decide quickly so we can move on." She paused, before adding, "Also, the fee is nonrefundable."

Monsieur Dumas cast a disapproving look at his sister, as though he didn't want her getting *ideas* from such a headstrong woman, which made Mallory wonder how much he knew about the patron god his sister had chosen to serve.

"As I was saying. Once the house was complete, Monsieur Le Bleu began to spend nearly all his time here in Morant. Which is where our tale truly begins." Taking hold of the handle shaped like a sea serpent, Mallory pulled the door open with a dramatic, creaking groan. "Welcome to the House Saphir."

CHAPTER TWO

Shadows reached for them as they stepped through the doorway. The foyer was thick with the smell of dust and mildew and rat droppings. Mallory was used to it, but Sophia wrinkled her nose and Louis pulled out a handkerchief to cover his mouth.

Mallory picked up the lantern she kept on the vestibule table and lit the candle inside, illuminating the foyer. An ornate geometric pattern in white and blue tiles spanned from the doorway into the drawing room. A mahogany staircase curved upward, each balustrade carved into an ominous hooded figure. An arched doorway straight ahead guided visitors into the corridor to the dining hall and ballroom. It was a dizzying way to be received—which was quite by design. This was not a house intended to make visitors feel comfortable. It was intended to make them feel awed, honored, and entirely unbalanced.

Mallory lit the occasional candle as they passed through the ground floor of the mansion, explaining the purpose of various rooms as she went: The parlor where guests had once been greeted with a glass of House Saphir's famous wine, served ice-cold in the summer months—the epitome of luxury. The solarium where some broken pots still remained, the last vestiges of what must have been a lush jungle encased in glass. Mallory explained how Bastien Saphir had loved oranges and thus insisted on keeping a live orange tree in the center of the room, so he would always have the fruit at hand. She pointed out the empty birdcages that still hung from the ceiling, having once displayed golden canaries and melodic nightingales for the enjoyment of Saphir's guests.

They passed through the dining room with its paneled walls and ornate chandeliers that now boasted as many cobwebs as crystals, while Mallory spoke of the lavish parties, the fine soirées, the endless feasts that Saphir had hosted for Morant's elite.

"With a reputation for generosity, he was said to be the most upstanding of gentlemen. Invitations to his home were highly coveted." Mallory approached a wall where a painting was concealed behind a swath of black velvet. "He was also devilishly handsome."

She pulled back the velvet. The glow from her lantern danced across a portrait of a gentleman wearing a richly embroidered blue-and-gold cape over a matching doublet. The portrait had been commissioned when Bastien Saphir was in his midtwenties, and his features were startling in their severity—as if a sculptor had taken a chisel to his jutting cheekbones and sharp jaw. A tidy beard and mustache were as black as ink, as was the long dark hair tied at the nape of his neck. Most striking were his eyes. Even in the dim lighting, they were alarmingly blue, a distinctive family trait.

An unladylike sound filled the room—the noise of someone sticking out their tongue and blowing out air.

Mallory had been expecting it, and she tried not to cringe.

"If he's devilishly handsome," said a high-pitched, nasal voice, "then I'm the queen of Lysraux."

Mallory didn't answer. It would have made her guests uncomfortable, given that they hadn't heard a thing. Rule number one when it came to interacting with ghosts—never, ever engage with them when a living person was nearby. Do not look; do not react.

Most people already thought she and her sister were peculiar. No point making it worse.

Instead, she surreptitiously scanned the room.

Triphine was sitting at the head of the dining table, her feet propped up beside a candelabra, her slight figure dressed in a nightgown and pale blue shawl, the edges of her physical form shimmering slightly. All ghosts shimmered, their bodies trapped somewhere between corporeal and ephemeral. Triphine had been beautiful in life, and was just as beautiful in death—with the delicate bone structure of a duchess descended from Gai-Yin royalty. Her luster was only slightly marred by the blackish-red blood that covered the front of her chest, compliments of the sword that had impaled her.

"I always pictured him as a pirate," Sophia said quietly, still staring at the painting, unaware of the ghost's presence. Her voice had a dreamlike quality to it as she took in Le Bleu's secretive grin. "I thought he would be . . . rougher looking. Less genteel."

"A *pirate*," said Triphine haughtily. "Where do you find these people?"

"It's a common misconception," said Mallory. "The Saphir family owned many merchant ships for exporting their wine, and so had a lucrative trade business on the side. Though Monsieur Le Bleu did occasionally travel by ship for work, he was no pirate. Come, I will show you the ballroom."

"Oh, you're going to ignore me again, are you?" said Triphine, standing to follow as Mallory led the couple through a set of double doors. "That's exceedingly impolite, Miss Fontaine. You know I was struggling with a horrid cough last week. Could feel the sickness all through my chest. Was bedridden for days. And you're not even going to ask how I'm feeling?" She let out a stream of wet coughs to punctuate her irritation.

Mallory walked faster, hoping the clack of her boots on the ballroom's parquet floors would drown out the ruckus of Triphine's complaints. She busied herself lighting a few of the wall sconces while Sophia and Louis took in the space. There was a raised platform where musicians would have played, and heavy curtains to hide stage performers. Tall arched windows and walls lined with glittering mirrors. It would have been glorious in its day, but now their reflections were eerie and faint in the flickering candlelight, the still air dank and suffocating.

Triphine clutched her shawl against an imaginary chill. She alone did not cast a reflection. "You know, I had something important to tell you, Mallory. But if you're going to ignore me, then I won't say a word, and you're going to wish I had!"

Mallory doubted that. Triphine had her uses, but she was also a constant thorn in Mallory's side.

"What happened there?" said Louis, pointing to a corner of the room, where black scorch marks marred the floors and walls. Some of the gilded wallpaper was missing, revealing blackened wood beneath.

"Some children sneaked in years ago," said Mallory. "Thought it would be amusing to light a few candles and try to summon the spirit of Le Bleu back from the dead. Instead, they nearly burned the place to the ground. Luckily, a few neighbors saw the smoke and managed to put out the flames in time."

A thump came from overhead.

Everyone stilled, nervous gazes rising to the ceiling with its tin panels and chandeliers that had not seen candles in decades.

Mallory cleared her throat. "Well. It is haunted," she said with a light laugh.

"Mallory," said Triphine. "That wasn't *me*."

"Monsieur Le Bleu's first marriage was to Duchess Triphine Maeng," Mallory interrupted, ignoring Triphine's affronted harrumph. "Their wedding ceremony took place right here in this room. Nearly three hundred guests were in attendance. But she was not only his first wife." Mallory paused dramatically. "She was also his first victim."

Sophia shivered. Her brother, checking his teeth in one of the mirrors, did not.

"Fine, ignore me," Triphine said. "But if you're going to talk about me like I'm not even here, then you'd better at least tell them about my flowers."

"Le Bleu was the most eligible bachelor in Morant. The wedding was quite a spectacle." Mallory opened up her drawing portfolio, revealing the first page—a charcoal sketch of the ballroom they now stood in, bedecked with elaborate flower arrangements on every wall. "The décor for the event was well-documented. The florist hired to decorate the house earned undeniable fame for the extravagant arrangements made of tropical fruits and fragrant flowers, the kinds of which most of the guests had never seen before. They were brought to Morant under special glass domes to retain the heat and moisture from their natural habitats."

"They were *beautiful*," Triphine crowed. "The wedding of the century, they called it."

"Did we pay to hear you talk about flowers?" grunted Louis. "Get on with it."

Sophia smacked him on the arm.

"Fourteen months after the wedding," Mallory continued, "Triphine gave birth to Bastien the second. He was the only child Le Bleu would sire. Almost immediately following the birth, rumors began to circulate that Triphine had fallen ill. That childbirth had been too much for her. She was overcome with fatigue, eating poorly, spending weeks at a time in bed, too frail to venture into society."

"My mother always said I had a weak constitution," said Triphine. "But I was actually feeling quite invigorated after a few days of bed rest. Still, Bastien wouldn't let me leave. Kept saying I needed more rest, to be strong to raise our child." She snorted. "Manipulative bastard."

"Less than three months after the birth of their son . . . Duchess Triphine Maeng-Saphir was dead. No doctor had been called to see to her ailments. No coroner came to view the body. The sacred rites of Velos were not to be followed—no anointments or prayers, no adorning her with flowers, no preparation for a proper burial."

Sophia gasped, apparently more appalled at the lack of ritual than she was at the thought of murder.

"Bastien claimed to have conducted the rituals and buried the body himself," said Mallory. "He claimed it was out of fear that Triphine's disease was contagious and he did not want to risk the lives of his servants or the townspeople. As he was so very good at playing the part of the mourning widower, no one thought to question him."

"Lying scumbag," Triphine muttered.

Mallory let her voice drip with irony. "If ghosts could talk, perhaps Duchess Triphine could tell us the truth of what happened to her. But as it is, we are left to our own speculations."

"Oh, har har, very funny."

Mallory gestured to the ballroom's wide expanse. "Rumor has it that Triphine still haunts these rooms. To this day, you might catch a glimpse of her wandering the halls in her pale nightgown and blue shawl. They say that at times her spirit will reach out to those who come to visit." Mallory stretched out her hand, as if she would tap Monsieur Dumas on the shoulder, though he was halfway across the room. "And that she asks for one thing. The same question. Over and over aga—"

A shriek pierced the heavy air. Sophia, deathly pale, pointed at something behind Mallory.

A shadow fell across the floor.

She saw him, a figure reflected in the mirror. A man, tall and slender, with black hair and a long jacket, looming from the darkness, not two steps behind her.

Fingers grazed the sleeve of Mallory's dress.

Her mind lurched.

Intruder. Murderer. Le Bleu.

On instinct, Mallory reached behind her and caught hold of the hand. She twisted his arm, throwing her weight into the movement as she drove the figure to the ground. The floors shook as he landed with a grunt, the air knocked clean out of him.

Mallory stared down at . . . a boy.

Maybe an intruder. Maybe a murderer. But not a particularly threatening one, and certainly not the ghost of Monsieur Le Bleu.

He pressed a hand to his chest as he attempted to draw in breath.

"Who in Velos's name are you?" Mallory cried.

He wheezed slightly, then managed to suck in enough air to mutter, "Ar—er. Axel. Axel Badeaux." He coughed. "I'm here for the tour."

CHAPTER THREE

Triphine tutted condescendingly while Louis helped the newcomer to his feet. "Honestly, Mallory. How are you ever going to find yourself a suitable husband if you go around thinking every handsome boy you meet is trying to kill you?"

Mallory shot her a look. It wasn't as if she was about to take marriage advice from the woman who had *literally* been murdered by her husband.

But Triphine saw the look as a victory. "Aha! I knew you couldn't ignore me all night."

Mallory crossed her arms and waited for Axel to finish brushing himself off, trying not to feel smug at her ability to so efficiently fell this boy who had startled her. Years ago she had studied a book on ancient fighting techniques, which had been written by a great warrior, and a female one at that. Its instructions included using one's own strengths against an opponent. Speed. Agility. Skilled weaponry. And perhaps most important to the more petite half of the human race . . . the nature of surprise. Men didn't expect a woman to fight back.

The book had been an inspiration, and she and Anaïs had sometimes spent entire days practicing the techniques against each other. Sparring. Wrestling. But this was the first time she'd had cause to use those skills against a real attacker . . . even if his intention hadn't been to attack her at all.

"Are you in the habit of sneaking up on people like that?" she snapped when Axel had finished straightening his fine coat—black brocade done up in small silver buttons. She had never heard of the Badeaux family before, so she imagined he had traveled some distance, as he was either nobility or from the wealthy merchant class. Perhaps both.

"Are you in the habit of assaulting a person for no reason?" he countered.

"I had every reason. Next time, perhaps you would consider alerting us to your presence."

"I did," he snapped back. "I knocked twice at the main entrance. You mustn't have heard."

She frowned. This far into the house, and with Triphine yapping in her ear, it was possible. But she didn't want to give him the satisfaction of saying so.

Though he could not have been much older than Mallory, his posture suggested a proper upbringing, the sort reserved for those who believed themselves superior to everyone but the king himself. His scowl was made up of full lips and fuller eyebrows. The only thing about him that wasn't immaculate was the tousled, silky black hair that fell loose past his ears and one rebellious string dangling from the cuff of his sleeve. Though Mallory was certain she'd never seen him before, there was something oddly familiar about him. Something—

"Velos below," whispered Triphine, cutting into their group so that she was standing inches from Axel, staring up at his dour face. "Do you realize who he looks like?"

Mallory drew back, her attention darting between the newcomer and Triphine. They might have been related. Except . . .

The light caught on Axel's eyes, as blue as faceted sapphires.

It had to be a coincidence. Count Bastien Saphir had only one heir, and the family tree was not a robust one. Mallory knew the names of every descendant, every distant cousin—and she had never heard the name Axel Badeaux in her life.

"It's the eyes," said Triphine. "Never seen blue like that before, have you? Well, I certainly have. Once in my no-good husband, and once . . ." Her voice dimmed. "In my son. Mallory, you don't suppose . . ." She tilted her head to one side. "Ask him, won't you?"

Mallory would not. Surely the heir to House Saphir would have no interest in her silly tours. And if he did show up to one, well . . . it would probably be because he meant to have her arrested for trespassing.

The house groaned—the timbers of the floors creaking as slow footsteps clomped over their heads.

Axel glanced upward. "Very clever. Do you have someone up there? An accomplice, playing the part of a ghost?" His arctic eyes sparked with amusement. "Is it supposed to be *the duchess*?"

Mallory smiled wanly. "I've had many skeptics on these tours, but the House Saphir has a way of changing their minds."

Sophia nudged her brother. "That witch did say it was haunted."

"But it *isn't* me," said Triphine, whipping her head around. "That's what I wanted to tell you earlier. Something is—"

But Mallory couldn't listen to Triphine because Axel had started to speak again.

"—pologize for my tardiness. Please, do go on. I'm very curious about this ghost that supposedly haunts the mansion."

"Not *supposedly*," said Mallory. "She's been seen by many— ugh, never mind. You've ruined the moment." She held out her hand with a huff. "I'll collect your payment for the tour now. I don't give discounts, even if you are late."

"Mallory, are you listening to me?" said Triphine. "There is *something up there*."

She ignored the ghost as Axel handed her his coins. In this abandoned house, there was always *something up there*, and that something was usually disease-riddled rats. Even in death, Triphine was as skittish as a hummingbird.

"Where was I?" Mallory usually loved this part of the tour, when she talked about Triphine's ghost, and watched as her guests drew closer together, scanning the darkened corners of each room. Sometimes, if Triphine was in a good mood, she even played along. Though she wasn't corporeal, with enough effort she could rustle the gauzy, tattered drapes beside the stage, or thump around on the floors so chandeliers rattled and footsteps echoed through the halls, or pass through the guests to make their hair stand on end. In the right moonlight, she could even make herself appear—a hazy figure framed in the windows or gliding past the mirrors. Though most mortals could not hear her when she spoke, she could choose to wail and cry and carry on in a way that could not be ignored, even by mortal ears.

Triphine could actually be great fun, when she wasn't whining about her ailment of the week and moaning about how little Mallory cared.

It took Mallory a moment to pick up the thread of her tale. "As far as we know, Duchess Triphine was the only victim to be murdered in this house. Monsieur Le Bleu knew that if he was to continue to act on his dark impulses, the people of Morant would soon grow suspicious. So he moved back to his family estate in the country, where there was more privacy. He did not involve himself in the raising of his sole child and heir. Young Bastien was passed through a series of governesses and ultimately sent away to boarding school, while his father continued to marry—and murder—two more women over the next three years."

Mallory retrieved her portfolio from where it had landed on the floor when she tossed Axel to the ground. She brushed it off and turned to a new page, showing her guests the charcoal drawing of a massive country estate, copied from a library book she'd found on the great châteaus of Lysraux. She eyed Axel carefully as he took in the drawing, but he seemed only mildly interested.

No, she thought, *he's definitely not related.*

After showing her guests the illustration of the mansion, she turned the page to reveal a watercolor portrait of a young woman with straight black hair, crowned in pearls. For this drawing, she had not needed to copy someone else's work. Triphine had been *giddy* when Mallory asked her to sit for a portrait.

"The first wife," she said. "Duchess Triphine Maeng."

She flipped to a second portrait. "The second wife, Lady Lucienne Tremblay."

Another painting. "And the third, Lady Béatrice Descoteaux."

Her guests stared at the portraits as she revealed each page. It was different, seeing the illustrations. Triphine's sorrowful eyes. Lucienne's round, rosy cheeks. How Béatrice was so young, barely on the edge of womanhood. Suddenly, they were not only ghost stories. They were not just the tragic victims of Monsieur Le Bleu. They were real people. Real women, their lives taken too soon.

"Who was the artist for these?" asked Axel.

Mallory stiffened. "I drew them."

Axel rocked back on his heels, openly impressed.

Mallory tried not to feel smug.

"This is what I never could understand," Sophia said somberly. "Why would his later wives agree to marry him when it was so . . . suspicious?"

"He was a clever man," said Mallory. "He chose women who were deemed . . . undesirable. Lucienne was a bit of a lush—and quite an embarrassment at parties. Béatrice's family had fallen on difficult times and were grateful for an alliance to such a wealthy man. So when a handsome, respected gentleman offered his hand—we can imagine it was easy to look the other way. To see his offer as a solution to a nagging problem. It was far easier to believe his lies and to hope for future happiness than to believe his intentions could be as evil as they truly were." Mallory snapped the portfolio shut and set it on a serving table she kept dusted for this purpose. "Who wants to see where the first murder took place?"

Sophia paled. Louis muttered, "About time." And Axel startled and glanced over his shoulder—Triphine had tried to brush back a strand of his hair.

Mallory led them through the hidden panel in the wall that concealed the servants' corridor. In the kitchen, she pried open a heavy wood door, beyond which descended a narrow staircase. She stood aside so the others could peer into the impervious darkness, her lantern doing little to light the way.

"The wine cellar." She gestured to the stairs. "After you."

Sophia took a hasty step back. Her brother gulped. Axel squared his shoulders, but didn't move forward.

Mallory smirked. "Only joking."

Lifting the lantern and the hem of her skirt, she started down.

CHAPTER FOUR

The stairs were old and steep. The air damp and cool, the walls nothing but stone and mortar. Reaching the cellar, Mallory lit another sconce and stood aside so her guests could take in the cramped space. Wooden crates and wine barrels branded with the Saphir crest were stacked against one wall, and a long table stretched down the middle of the room, covered in a thick layer of dust frequently disturbed by the claws of skittering rats.

Mallory drew in a breath of stale air. "Duchess Triphine died in this room, after her husband sedated her, tied her to this very table, and drove a sword through her heart." She paused, letting these words sink in, before continuing. "And a fact unknown by the general public . . . He also cut off her finger."

Sophia recoiled, and Mallory patted the smelling salts she kept in her pocket, just in case. "A *finger*?"

"I know this because I was the one who found the finger—

well, the bones of the finger—when I first started giving tours of this house." She pointed. "I discovered it right there, between the wine barrel and the wall. We know it belonged to Duchess Triphine, as it was still wearing *this*."

She gestured to a small bell jar on top of a wine barrel, under which, on a bed of black velvet, rested a wedding ring—or at least, an imitation of one. A silver-plated band with a square of blue glass. In the dim lighting, no one could ever tell the difference, and tonight's guests were no exception, judging by their awed faces.

Once her guests had gotten a good look at the ring, Mallory grabbed a flat wooden box.

"On that note," she chirped, "we happen to offer stunning replicas for sale, among other quality goods." She opened the box, revealing rows of merchandise. Hand-painted postcards depicting the House Saphir, lead coins emblazoned with the Saphir crest, handkerchiefs that Anaïs had embroidered with the words *I survived the House Saphir*, and rings in various sizes. "Made of the finest quality silver and authentic blue sapphires imported from the mines of Dostlen."

"She's lying," Triphine sang. "Where do you find such gullible patrons?"

Mallory's smile did not falter as her guests inspected the wares. "They make a lovely gift," she said, nudging Louis. "Maybe for a special lady friend? Or perhaps you'd like to send a postcard home to your mother?"

"Not a bad idea, actually," Louis muttered, picking up a ring while Sophia studied one of the handkerchiefs. "Real sapphires, you say?"

"As real as the crown jewels."

She glanced at Axel. He hadn't said much during the tour, and he was difficult to read, but perhaps she could tempt him into a deck of Saphir-branded playing cards—as a limited edition, they were one of her best sellers.

But when she saw how Axel was studying her, the thought evaporated. "What?" she said, immediately defensive.

He drew back, startled. "Have I offended you?"

"You're staring at me."

He opened his mouth, but hesitated. Then cleared his throat. "I was hoping to ask you some questions."

She wrinkled her nose. "Fine. But I charge one lys per question. A galet if the question annoys me."

"You charge a fee for asking questions? You're a *tour guide*."

"Knowledge is priceless."

To her surprise, he reached for his pocket and pulled out a coin, but instead of handing it to her, he held it up so that it glinted in the cellar's dim light. "I am trying to find the Fontaine sisters. Are you one of them?"

It took a long moment for the question to fully register. "I . . . Who?"

"Anaïs and Mallory Fontaine of Morant. Daughters of the late Noele Fontaine. The ones who . . ." He hesitated, flipping the coin over his fingers. "The ones who have some working knowledge of witchcraft."

"Oh!" said Sophia. "Fontaine, yes. That was the name of the witch we visited. She has a darling little shop on Rue Tilance." She paused, squinting at Mallory. "I don't recall mention of a sister."

Mallory chuckled, and wished it hadn't come out sounding so uncomfortable. "Yes. My sister, Anaïs, is the talented one. But she's always been very supportive of my tours."

"From what I've heard," said Axel, "you have some unique talents of your own."

"Hearsay and hogwash. I'm afraid you'll be disappointed in the truth."

"I doubt it."

Beside them, Louis and Sophia had gone still, sensing the rising tension.

"The rumors are that you can see and speak with the spirits of the deceased."

Axel didn't sound like a heartless oaf who meant to destroy what measly reputation she had been clinging to ever since her mother had passed away, but Mallory wasn't willing to chance it.

"Don't be ridiculous." She snatched the coin from Axel's fingers. "Ghosts choose who to reveal themselves to, and when they wish to be seen. I happen to spend a lot of time in a haunted mansion. If you're lucky, you'll be seeing ghosts by the end of the night, too. That is what you're paying for, isn't it?"

She spun away from him, noting the goods in the Dumases' hands. "That will be a hundred lourdes for the ring and fifteen for the handkerchief."

"A hundred—!" Louis started. "For a replica?"

"Real sapphires," Mallory reminded him. "Real silver."

He huffed, but pulled out a reticule to pay for them both.

"Shall we return to the ballroom?" Mallory set down the box of merchandise and started back up the narrow staircase. Her voice got louder as she climbed. "There I can tell you about Gabrielle Savoy."

The others hurried after her—though Axel scowled suspiciously as he brought up the rear of their group.

"Who is Gabrielle Savoy?" asked Sophia as they gathered around the central hearth in the ballroom.

"Gabrielle Savoy was Monsieur Le Bleu's fourth wife," Mallory said. "Few have heard of her, because she is the only one who—"

"Got away," said Axel.

She shot him an irate look.

He raised a challenging eyebrow.

"Precisely," she said. "Unlike his first three wives, when Bastien tried to kill Gabrielle, she managed to outsmart him and escape. It was she who told her brothers that Bastien had attempted to murder her. Her brothers rushed to the country estate, dragged Le Bleu out to the fountain in front of the house, and proceeded to cut off his head."

"Hear, hear!" said Louis.

"Some claim that to this day Le Bleu's sinister laughter can be heard echoing through the halls of the mansion," said Mallory. "And every year, on the anniversary of his death, the fountain where he was killed runs red with blood." She took in their expressions—Sophia seemed horrified, Louis fascinated, and Axel . . . Well, if his frown was any deeper, it would be back in the cellar. "But the Saphir estate is quite far from here. We may not have wicked laughter and bloody fountains, but one death did occur in this house, and the ghost of Triphine Maeng often appears around the strike of . . ." Distantly, the clock tower began to toll. Mallory could have gloated at the sound. Some nights her timing was immaculate. ". . . midnight."

She deftly pressed her toe onto a hidden switch in the floorboard.

She heard the quiet click of the igniter. The logs on the fireplace burst into flame.

Sophia and Louis both cried out, jumping back so fast they nearly toppled over the settee behind them. Mallory and Axel also reared back—though her surprise wasn't quite as genuine.

Triphine groaned. "Are we really doing this tonight? I honestly think we ought to—"

"The clock strikes midnight!" Mallory raised her voice and stared pointedly at Triphine. "And that is when the ghost of the duchess appears!"

Behind her back, Mallory reached for a cord hidden by a curtain. She pulled, setting off a series of weights and pulleys.

In response, the entryway door blew open, striking against the vestibule wall.

"What's happening?" asked Louis, clutching his sister's arm.

Triphine huffed an aggrieved sigh. "*Fine.* But after this, we need to have a talk." With a bored expression, she paced among the group as she wiggled her fingers and muttered, "Shiver, shiver, shiver . . ."

The guests *did* shiver, each of them jumping at the uncanny sensation of a spirit passing through them.

Mallory reached for another lever and yanked it down.

Overhead, gears whirred and floorboards creaked.

"There!" Mallory pointed to the top of the staircase, as a

ghastly figure glided into view. A gauzy nightgown. A blue knit shawl. Black hair cascading down her back.

And blood. So much blood, dripping from the hole in her chest, soaking the front of her nightgown.

Mallory waited.

The ghost began to descend the steps. It stopped halfway down the staircase and said . . .

Nothing.

She shot a glare at Triphine, who groaned loudly. "I'm not in the mood for this tonight, Mallory."

Bristling, Mallory cried out, "It is the duchess! And I think . . . I think she wants us to leave!"

Triphine slumped onto the settee, inhaled a deep breath and said—in her best ghostly impression—*"Get out of my house, you scum-guzzling tourists."* She hesitated, before pointing at Axel and adding, "Except you. If you could stay behind, I'd rather like to speak with you."

Not for the first time, Mallory wished that Triphine was corporeal so she could kick her.

"Great gods," muttered Louis. "Did you hear that?"

"Who is she talking to?" Sophia said shakily. "Oh—lost spirit, allow me to guide you on your path into the afterlife."

Triphine groaned. "Ugh. The worshippers."

Despite her rule not to interact with ghosts in front of others, Mallory couldn't help nodding in agreement. "Right?"

Realizing that Axel was watching her, Mallory stiffened. "We should leave. The duchess has been known to get angry when people don't listen to her."

"Tyrr, protect us," Sophia panted, backing away. "Velos, give this spirit rest."

Triphine waved her arms in mockery of the terrifying ghost she was supposed to be—but definitely wasn't. Again she projected her ghostly voice, so that it echoed through the house. *"Get out! Leave me be!"*

"Go," said Mallory, shoving Sophia. "Go! Before she gets angrier!"

Sophia and Louis huddled by the door, their faces twisted with terror.

Then—all at once—their faces unwound.

They looked at each other.

"I've seen enough," said Louis. "You?"

"More than enough," Sophia agreed.

Mallory's brow furrowed. "Why aren't you running away?"

"For one," said Sophia, "because that is not the duchess."

With a nervous laugh, Mallory gestured at the ghost. The fake one. "Of *course* it's the duchess. Triphine Maeng was—"

"Flesh and blood," Louis said, sounding unimpressed as he scrutinized the figure at the top of the stairs. "Whereas that appears to be a couturier's mannequin, dressed up like the duchess." He scanned the mannequin from head to foot, head cocked. "Not a bad costume. The period detail is very accurate. How did you do the fireplace? And the door? Is it the same sort of trickery you and your sister use for your so-called séances?"

Mallory gasped, feigning offense. "How dare you insinuate such dishonest practices?" Drawing herself to her full height, which unfortunately wasn't much, she added, "Fine. You stay here and get murdered by a vengeful ghost. I'm not going to—"

Louis grabbed her wrist, holding her in place. "No, Miss Fontaine, you will not be going anywhere."

Mallory stomped on the top of his foot. Louis howled and drew back. Mallory squeezed her fist, prepared to punch him in the nose if he tried to grab her again—when two hands locked around her elbows, yanking her arms back.

Mallory cried out as Sophia latched a pair of iron shackles to her wrist.

Watching the scene in horror, Axel stumbled away, his back colliding with a wall.

"Something tells me," Mallory said through a snarl, "you're not really an initiate of Tyrr."

"Investigator Sophia Blaise," she said. "This is my partner, Investigator Louis Garneau. We've been tracking you and your sister for months. We've received innumerable accounts of fraudulent behavior: the hosting of fake séances, reading of fake fortunes, not to mention the selling of fake jewels, potions, and so-called god-relics."

Face red with fury as he limped toward the mannequin, Investigator Garneau tore off the duchess's wig. "I'd say this proves it. You and your sister are frauds."

"What, exactly, does this prove?" Mallory said. "Only that you paid for an entertaining tour through the House Saphir, and you got it. What law have I broken?"

"You? Perhaps none. But your sister certainly sold us a feather that she claimed fell from the wing of a god."

Mallory smirked. "Prove that it didn't."

Louis's expression darkened. "Perhaps I can't prove that one way or another. But after a short visit to the jeweler tomorrow,

I will certainly be able to prove that this ring is fake." He held up his hand, where the faux-sapphire ring sat on his pinkie.

Mallory lifted her chin. "It sounds to me like you have nothing to arrest me for tonight."

"No?" said Sophia. "How about trespassing? This is private property, owned by the Saphir estate. You have no license to operate tours here."

"Don't look so worried," Louis said as Sophia dragged Mallory toward the door. "We'll bring your sister in tomorrow, so you won't be alone for long."

"Wait."

Sophia paused.

Axel was watching the scene with dismay. His eyes bored into Mallory. "You can speak with ghosts. Can't you?"

A muscle twitched in her temple. "A little irrelevant at the moment, don't you think?"

"If the duchess is here now, ask her what she was holding in the last portrait that was ever painted of her."

"What?"

"Just ask."

Mallory glanced at Triphine, who had been standing in the center of the room, uncharacteristically speechless, though as unhelpful as ever, while Mallory was being arrested.

Louis scoffed and grabbed Mallory's elbow, yanking her forward. "This is absurd."

"Triphine?" Mallory said.

"Oh—uh. The last portrait. Right. That would have been . . ." Her breath snagged. Her eyes went watery. "My son. I was holding my newborn son."

Mallory dug her heels into the carpet, stopping Louis in his tracks. "Your son? I've never seen this portrait."

Triphine shrugged. "It showed all three of us, and was done barely a week after he was born. Right when Bastien started to spread those rumors of me being bedridden after the birth. It mustn't have been displayed much after his crimes were discovered."

"Her son. That's right," Axel breathed. "My gods, she is here." He stepped forward. "Investigators, I cannot speak to the other accusations against Mademoiselle Fontaine, but you cannot arrest her for trespassing. Not tonight."

Louis's grip tightened on Mallory's arm. "And why is that?"

"Because I am Count Armand Saphir, and she has my permission to be here."

CHAPTER FIVE

Heat rose in Mallory's face as Triphine exclaimed, "I *knew* he was a relation! Is he my grandson? Great-grandson? Wait—how long has it been since I died?"

"You're a Saphir?" Mallory breathed.

"I am." He pulled a chain from his collar on which hung a gold medallion, emblazoned with the Saphir crest—near identical to those in her merchandise box.

Armand Saphir. The sole heir to the Saphir estate.

Gods above.

"It's . . . an honor to meet you."

He scoffed. "I'm sure it is." He nodded at the investigators. "You can release her now."

They didn't—not immediately, anyway. First they had to inspect Armand's medallion and pepper him with questions to ensure that he wasn't another actor in the Fontaine scam, while

Mallory suffered the indignity of being ignored with hands bound uncomfortably behind her back.

Finally, with much grumbling, Sophia undid the shackles.

"Enjoy your freedom while it lasts, Miss Fontaine," she whispered in Mallory's ear. "We will be back."

"I love repeat customers," Mallory said, rubbing her wrists. The investigators bowed respectfully to the count—great gods, the *count*—then sauntered out through the front door, leaving it hanging open as they crossed through the overgrown garden.

Exhaling through her nostrils, Mallory considered curtsying, but . . . no. "This was eventful. Thank you for your patronage and your . . . assistance. Have a nice night."

Turning her back on him, she stomped on the hidden switch again. As soon as the flames had died down, she felt around the side of the hearth and wriggled out the loose stone. Brushing the dirt from her hand, she pulled out a small wooden box.

"What are you doing?"

Irritation growing, she did not bother to look back at Count Armand. "You can leave now. The tour is over."

She opened the box's lid, revealing a small cache of coins and a glittering sapphire ring.

"Is that . . . ?" Armand started.

Mallory started scooping the coins into her purse.

"The ring in the cellar. That was a fake."

She shot him an upticked eyebrow. "Would *you* keep a priceless artifact on full display in a glass jar?"

She reached for the ring, but another hand beat her to it.

"Hey!" She stood and wheeled around.

Armand was inspecting Triphine's wedding ring, while the ghost stood by, watching the exchange and massaging her own fingerless hand. "Still as beautiful as the day my good-for-nothing husband gave it to me."

Unlike the replica in the cellar, this ring was crafted of a white-gold band with a square-cut sapphire, heavy as a bad secret.

"Give it to me," said Mallory, holding out her palm. "I need to get home to my sister, as evidently we're going to be leaving first thing tomorrow—"

"Why?"

The words snagged on the end of her tongue. "Why?"

"Why will you be leaving tomorrow?"

"Were you not . . . Didn't you hear them? My sister and I are on the verge of being carted off to prison, and I don't know about the lifestyle of a count, but personally, I'm not suited to sharing a cold stone floor with an infestation of lice and vermin."

"You will only be arrested if they were right," he said, frustratingly calm. "If you've been conducting fake séances and . . ." He eyed the ring. "Selling fake jewelry."

She opened her mouth. Hesitated. Then straightened her spine. "You're right. I have nothing to worry about. Now give that back."

"If this is the duchess's ring, it rightfully belongs to me and my estate."

Mallory gawped at him. "Your ancestor murdered her! Then chopped off her finger! That ring would have been lost to time if I hadn't found it."

"*She* was my ancestor as much as he was. And you found it inside the home that belongs to me."

"Do I get a say in the matter?" asked Triphine. "It is *my* ring, after all."

"No," snapped Mallory. "You can't wear it and you can't sell it, so what do you care?"

Triphine huffed, but Armand's expression became curious again. "You're talking to the ghost again, aren't you?"

"You know what, I don't have time for this." Mallory finished shoveling the coins into her purse, knowing that the moment he let his guard down, she'd be able to swipe the ring from him. An elbow to the throat or heel to the knee, and she could snatch the ring away and be gone before he knew what had happened.

"Miss Fontaine, I can see you're upset about what happened with those investigators, but there's something I need to discuss with—"

The house shook suddenly with a crash, the shattering of glass, a heavy, reverberating thud.

Mallory peered up the stairwell, into the shadows of the upper floor. Gooseflesh shot down her arms.

Triphine let out a wavering cry and ducked behind the curtains, hiding her ephemeral body in their dusty folds.

"Although," Armand quietly mused, "given that the ghost of the duchess was a fake, perhaps the investigators were right to suspect you."

Mallory turned her full focus to Triphine. "All right, I'm listening. What is up there?"

"That's the thing. I don't *know*. I think it moved in last night, but I've been too afraid to go up there. It sounds *big*."

"How can you be afraid?" Mallory shouted. "You're dead!"

"Why must you always bring it up? You are the most insensitive girl I've ever met!"

"Are you talking to the duchess?" asked Armand. "What is she saying?"

"She's saying that *you* are a nosy buffoon who shouldn't ask so many questions."

He squinted at her. "I cannot tell if you are lying, and I find that very irritating."

A loud scraping sound was followed by another crash.

Mallory tucked her purse away and took hold of the mannequin, gripping it like a shield.

Armand's voice lowered to a whisper. "If this is some joke you play on people who are foolish enough to come on this tour—"

"Stop talking," she hissed. "It's probably just a rat."

"That sounds a lot bigger than a rat. Perhaps we should call the investigators back or . . . What are you . . . Is that a knife?"

Mallory yanked her dagger from its sheath and crept up the stairs, unable to avoid the creaking floorboard at the top.

"Why do you have a knife?"

She reached the landing and started for the hall. A faint glimmer of moonlight spilled through the windows that framed a sitting area at the top of the steps, but the light did not reach the depths of the long corridor. The walls were adorned in crimson wallpaper and dark wood trim. Several bedroom doors stood open between unlit candle sconces.

Mallory stopped to listen, but all she heard was her own breathing—and Armand's.

She whipped her head around, surprised to see that he had

followed her ... and somehow managed to do so without stepping on that creaky floorboard.

"What are you doing?"

He blinked at her. "If there *is* something up here, I'm not letting you face it alone."

"Do you have a weapon?"

"Of course not."

She let out a sound of disgust. "Your heroics are the stuff of epic sagas." Turning away again, she muttered, "Lots of bravado, but ultimately pointless."

"What's that?"

The pitch to his voice made Mallory tense as she squinted into the inky darkness of the corridor.

One of the bedroom doors was opening wider, hinges creaking.

A hand appeared. Long fingers wrapped around the edge of the door.

It was so dim, Mallory wanted to believe she was seeing things. But from here it almost appeared that the hand had *claws*.

It was followed by a head, peering around the doorframe. Wide yellow eyes glinted as it emerged into the hall, one clacking step at a time. The creature stood on two legs, nearly reaching the ceiling, but its back was hunched forward, its knees cocked at odd angles. Its body was covered by matted gray fur along with the tattered remains of a tunic. Its head was distinctly wolflike, with a jaw that hung open to reveal a row of jagged teeth.

Its lips twisted into a snarl that was both human and beastly.

Mallory shuddered. She took a step back, knocking Armand against the banister that stood above the entryway. He caught her, pulling her closer to him, but she wasn't sure if he meant to support her or himself.

"That," he whispered, his breath grazing the back of her ear, "is not a rat."

The beast growled, then charged so suddenly Mallory's mind went white with surprise.

It was Armand who reacted first—shoving Mallory against a wall, making a shield of himself.

The beast's jaws clamped onto his raised forearm. He cried out in pain.

Mallory lunged forward with the knife—aiming for the creature's eye, but catching its ear as it lurched backward, dragging Armand with it. Armand dug his heels into the worn carpet. Mallory thrust forward with the knife again, driving the blade into the beast's side. It released Armand as Mallory yanked the knife back from its flesh. Blood splattered across her skirt.

The beast pivoted toward her, and Mallory lifted a leg and shoved her boot into the beast's stomach, sending it hurtling down the staircase. One claw caught on the mannequin of Triphine, knocking it askew on the metal rail. The body form struck the wall. Its head popped off its neck and toppled over, bouncing down the rest of the steps into the foyer.

The sight of the rolling, bumping head brought the beast to a halt. It stared after the head, as transfixed as a dog with a discus. It leaned back on its haunches, muscles twitching, and pounced—clearing the staircase in one leap and landing on the mannequin's head with a ferocious snarl. Its teeth dug into the papier-mâché shell, cracking into it like an egg.

The real Triphine had drifted from behind the curtains, and

was partially hidden behind the parlor door, watching the scene with repugnance. "Why, of all the indignities . . ."

Mallory grabbed Armand's uninjured arm and dragged him down the hallway, throwing open a bedroom door. It was empty of furniture, but the wall sconces still held wax candles with half-burned wicks. Mallory slammed the door shut, and she and Armand stumbled over themselves to back away from it.

"Silver," Armand panted, clutching his bleeding arm. "Voirloups are repelled by silver, if I recall correctly."

Mallory gaped at him. "You recognized the creature?"

"I've dealt with my share of monsters," he snapped. But then his expression pinched with guilt. "Apologies. This is not how I imagined the night going. That was very impressive back there, with the knife and the . . ." He mimed kicking the voirloup in the stomach.

It was so comical, with his fine blood-soaked jacket and mussed hair, that a bewildered laugh tumbled out of Mallory before she could stop it. "Yes, well, luckily I had the help of a buffoon making a human shield of himself first."

"So you *do* appreciate my heroics."

A thunder of footsteps brought their attention back to the door.

"As I was saying," said Armand. "Those candlesticks aren't silver, are they?"

"Brass," she said, pulling a matchbox from her pocket. The beast crashed into the door—but the wood held. "Voirloups are also afraid of fire." With her shaking hands, it took four scratches of the match for it to light.

Another crash into the door. The wood began to splinter.

She lit one of the half-burned candles.

Armand appeared increasingly distressed. "You can't possibly think a little flame will frighten . . . *that*." He pointed at the door.

"Unless you have a silver-plated sword, I don't know that we have many options."

He glanced around. "The window."

"What about the window?"

"It might be unlocked."

She squinted at him in disbelief. "I am *not* jumping out a window. I'd rather take my chances with the evil half-dead wolf thing." She pried the candlestick from the sconce. The weak flame flickered out as she did.

The door crashed inward. They both yelped and scrambled against the far wall. The old plaster cracked and dusted their backs. Armand grabbed the candlestick from her and held it aloft, brandishing it like one might a silver-plated sword.

The voirloup snarled.

Panicking, Armand threw the candlestick, hitting the creature in the leg. It bounced off, landing on the carpet with a dull thud.

Mallory scowled at Armand, who had the sense to look chagrined.

The voirloup launched itself across the floor. Releasing a battle cry, Mallory raised her knife and plunged it into the beast's chest—but she knew immediately that she had missed the heart. Probably wouldn't have killed it anyway. Too shallow. Too not-silver. She racked her brain, trying to remember anything else about voirloups . . .

The beast reared back, taking her knife with it.

Armand gasped. "Wait! I do have something!" He dug into his pocket, and Mallory had a vision of him throwing silver coins at the beast, and wondered if she'd be able to let him do it without grabbing them for herself. But his hand didn't emerge with a coin—rather, he held a ring.

A small silver ring with a large blue stone.

Mallory released an incredulous cry. "You can't throw away Triphine's ring!"

"I'm not. This is one of your fakes," he said.

Her jaw dropped. "One of . . . did you *steal* that?"

"I was going to pay for it."

Mallory didn't know if she believed him, but in the next moment the voirloup was howling and Armand was pulling back his arm and—

"Wait!"

The ring sailed across the room, straight into the beast's maw, silencing the howl. The creature reared back, claws digging at its throat.

Mallory raised her eyebrows, almost impressed.

But then the beast coughed twice and swallowed. She imagined she could see the ring sliding down its gullet, disappearing into its ravenous stomach.

The voirloup spat a glob of saliva onto the floor and sneered at them, preparing to pounce.

"Why didn't that work?" said Armand. "You said they were silver!"

"I lied."

Expression darkening, Armand grabbed for the coin purse strapped around Mallory's waist and yanked it off, breaking the strap.

"Hey!"

"Your rings might have been fake," he said, yanking the bag open, "but I bet those coins weren't."

"Don't you dare!" She threw herself at him, trying to snatch the purse back. Too late. The money was in his hand. His hand was reeling back. "Please, don't! That's my life savings! Those coins are—"

Gone.

Armand threw every lys she had earned over the past year, the money she'd painstakingly sequestered away in preparation for the day she and her sister could leave this bloody city behind. All gobbled up by the voirloup in one slobbery gulp.

It wheezed in pain.

"I needed those!" she shouted.

Armand ignored her, using the voirloup's distraction to pry up the window sash. "Come on."

"I am *not* jumping out a window."

"Yes, you are." He tossed one leg over the sill, then stretched his hand toward her. "Take my hand."

The voirloup tore the dagger from its flesh and flung it toward Armand. He ducked. The knife struck the open window, cracking the glass and ricocheting off into the night.

The beast fixed its attention on Mallory again, fury twisting its expression.

"You cannot fight that thing!" yelled Armand. "It will kill you!"

Mallory backed away. One step. Two. Outside, there was no tree to climb, only a long fall down to certain death.

Her heart choked her. Cold sweat prickled the back of her neck.

She couldn't jump. She *wouldn't*.

"Please." Armand's voice was strained. "I'll break your fall. I won't let you get hurt."

Surprise sparked in her thoughts. Less at his words than the tenderness with which he said them. As though he meant it.

She drew in a shuddering breath. Looked at his outstretched hand. Her heart convulsed.

"I am *not* jumping."

"And I am *not* leaving you here."

Her lips parted. "Why would you care about—"

The voirloup lifted an arm, long claws catching the moonlight.

Fear took hold of Mallory as she braced for those sharp nails to dig into her flesh. She hardly felt Armand's arm snaking around her waist until it was too late.

He yanked her toward the window.

Mallory screamed. Thrashed. Felt the shift of the earth, the windowsill hitting the backs of her knees, saw the dark ground below—too far, way too far below—

The world spun. White terror swirled in her vision. Wrapped around her throat.

"Stop fighting me!" Armand cried.

Realizing that his other hand was wrapped around the dead wisteria vines that covered the exterior of the mansion, Mallory grabbed for the vines herself. The moment she took hold of them, the vines stripped free from the limestone blocks. Armand's arm tightened around her. She squeezed her eyes shut, and felt herself falling.

CHAPTER SIX

Regrets flashed through Mallory's thoughts. She would never take her sister to Verene. She would never know if the fountain at the Saphir château really turned to blood on the anniversary of Le Bleu's death. She would never tell their greedy landlady to take their rent payment and shove it up her—

She struck the ground with an impact that radiated through every bone, though it was admittedly not as painful as she expected it to be.

Whether intentional or not, Armand had indeed broken her fall.

Rolling away from him, Mallory pressed herself onto her hands and knees.

Armand's eyes were closed. His mouth lolled. There was blood on his jacket and wisteria leaves in his hair, and he was quite possibly dead.

Cursing, Mallory leaned down and pressed an ear to his chest, already wondering if she had time to forge a document willing the Saphir estate to her and her sister before anyone else found the body. All she needed was his official seal . . .

She reached for his throat and found a thin chain. But as soon as her fingers clenched around the cool metal, she also felt the pulse of his heartbeat.

"Damn," she muttered.

A thump shivered the ground beneath her. Mallory pushed herself up to her knees in time to see the voirloup—which had leaped from the upstairs window and landed on the overgrown, weed-infested lawn, effectively cutting off her path to the gate, and any hope of escape.

Mallory cast around for anything she could use as a weapon or a distraction. The beast had chased that ball—er, head before, so maybe—

She grabbed a rock. Threw it past the voirloup. It bounced into a garden bed.

The monster watched it go, before snarling at her in annoyance.

She started to scramble backward. Her hand landed on something cool and familiar. She curled her fingers around the handle of her dagger. She braced herself and lifted the knife, angling it toward the voirloup, when her attention caught on a cloaked figure beneath the yard's ancient willow tree. The drooping branches swayed—revealing a boy one moment, disguising him the next. He came closer, emerging through the trailing leaves.

Mallory's muddled thoughts recognized him as one of the gentlemen who had passed by on the street before her tour. The one dressed all in black. He wore tall boots and leather breeches, a fitted tunic, a long traveling cloak. With dark brown skin and ropes of black hair pushed back from his brow, he might have blended easily into the night, if it wasn't for the occasional streak of silver-white running through those locs, especially noteworthy given that he could not have been much older than she was.

As Mallory squinted, he reached into a breast pocket and pulled out a gold pocket watch. With a click, he flipped it open and peered down at the clockface, before flashing a devious smile.

He let out a whistle. The voirloup spun toward him.

Mallory's grip relaxed on the knife, though she expected the voirloup to spring at the figure and take both that pocket watch and the hand holding it in one hungry chomp. Instead, the boy held up the instrument, revealing a face that was not a clock at all, but more like a compass. Its needle pointed up toward the willow tree.

The voirloup hesitated. Snarled. Blood dripped into its fur, staining the remains of its shredded tunic.

"My, my," drawled the boy, in an accent Mallory couldn't place, "what big teeth you have."

The voirloup lifted its snout to the sky and howled—a deep, guttural sound that made the ground tremble.

With an impassive tilt of his head, the boy stepped to the side. "Go on, Constantino."

The second gentleman that Mallory had seen earlier appeared from beneath the willow. "Yes, Fitcher. No need to get bossy."

He was the opposite to the first in nearly every conceivable way. Still young, still handsome, but with olive-toned skin and wavy brown hair. Rather than being dressed in a sleek and simple black tunic, he wore . . .

Mallory wasn't sure what he wore. Tights of some sort. Bulbous sleeves larger than her head. And more colors than any human should ever combine into one outfit. He was also holding a longbow, nocked with an arrow, which he lifted casually. Took aim. Fired. The arrow breezed an inch from the first boy's shoulder, but he did not flinch.

It struck the voirloup in the throat. The howl was cut off, dying in a strangled gargle.

The air shimmered. The hair on Mallory's arms lifted, as if lightning were about to strike. And maybe it did strike, for there was a flash so blinding that Mallory threw up her arms to protect her eyes.

When she blinked the white spots of her vision away, the voirloup was gone. An object—small and glittering—dropped from the air where it had stood, landing in the overgrown grass with a quiet thud.

She must be imagining things. But—no. That ferocious monster had definitely been transformed into a small glass figurine, not unlike the good luck charms she and Anaïs sold in their shop.

Constantino swept the tiny bauble off the ground. "Are you all right, stellina?" he asked, dropping to one knee and reaching for her hand, which Mallory yanked out of his grip.

Stellina? She didn't know the term, but it sounded like Stivalen romantical nonsense.

A wail came from the house's upper level. "Mallory! Are you dead?" Triphine was hanging out of the open window, her blue shawl fluttering in the night's breeze. "If you aren't dead, then maybe you could clean up the mess you made in here? You can't leave it like this!"

Armand groaned, beginning to stir, but no one paid him any attention.

Ignoring the ghost, Mallory scrambled onto shaky legs. "What did you do to that monster?"

"We made it no longer your problem," said Fitcher. "This house reeks of dark magic. I guarantee these won't be the last monsters that feel drawn to it."

"Oh, for all the stinky cheeses," sighed Constantino. "Must you always be so cryptic?" He winked at Mallory. "Fitcher will never admit it, but he rather enjoys this sort of thing."

Mallory was suddenly sure that she was dreaming. There was no voirloup. She had not met the heir to the House Saphir. And these people were figments of her overactive imagination.

"Don't fret, stellina," said the colorful boy as he held out a slip of shimmering paper. "We are here for *all* your magical needs. Don't hesitate to be in touch should you require further assistance."

The way he said it made it sound like there were plenty of magical needs Mallory had but had never quite considered, and it was time to change that. She sneered as she took the paper from him.

At first she could see nothing on the card. But as she tilted it toward the moonlight, luminescent words scrawled across the surface like the fiery veins of an opal.

Fitcher's Troupe

Monster Hunters • Curse Breakers
Experts in Dark Magic and the Occult

To contact: Detail your predicament on the back of this card and entrust it to the four winds. Summons will be selected on the basis of payment and personal curiosity. (Our curiosity, not yours.) Utmost discretion guaranteed.

Mallory flipped the card over. The other side was blank.

She raised her eyes, a question perched on her tongue—

But the strangers were already gone.

"I knew you weren't a fraud."

She twisted her neck so fast it gave her a crick. Wincing, she rubbed her fingers into the muscle as she slipped the card into her pocket.

Armand gazed at her blearily. "I saw that flash of light. You cast magic." He grimaced, eyes briefly squeezing shut, before he opened them again and gave her a wry, knowing smile. "Mallory Fontaine, you really are a witch."

CHAPTER SEVEN

Mallory's sister often said that no matter how bad things were, they would always look a little better under the bright morning sun.

Obviously, this was hogwash, and Mallory had no qualms telling Anaïs as much. Mallory much preferred darkness and gloom. It was better for hiding secrets. Better for hiding unsavory curiosities. And best of all, it was better for hiding from their landlady.

"Get up! She's here!" Anaïs shouted in Mallory's ear, tearing away the worn quilts.

Mallory groaned and flopped onto her stomach. She mumbled something into the pillow, but even she wasn't sure what it was.

"Mally, don't fight," Anaïs hissed. "Up, up!"

Footsteps on the narrow staircase. Pounding at their door. Madame Cellier—the owner of their little shop and the even littler attic apartment above it—screaming in her harsh voice. "Mallory! Anaïs! I know you're in there. I'm here to collect the rent."

"See?" said Anaïs, grabbing for Mallory's arm. "You need to get up."

"Nooo," said Mallory, trying to shove her off. "Bad night. Not ready."

"We're out of excuses, Mally. Do you have the money?" Anaïs hauled her up to sitting as a key jiggled in the lock.

Damn Madame Cellier and her ring of skeleton keys.

"Invasion of privacy!" Mallory shouted, to no one in particular. "We have rights!"

"We do not have rights," Anaïs reminded her. "No rights whatsoever. Would you get—" She drew back suddenly, her face twisted in disgust. She plucked something from Mallory's hair. "Why do you have twigs in your hair? And . . ." She took in Mallory's blood-spotted chemise, which she hadn't bothered to change out of when she got home the night before. Anaïs ripped back the blankets, noting the smears of mud and flakes of dirt. "Freydon's whiskers. What happened to you?"

"Long story." The door burst open, revealing a red-faced Madame Cellier. "Tell you later."

Anaïs spun around, smiling sweetly. "Good morning, madame. We were preparing for our weekly jaunt to the creek, where we discuss our lessons on the sacred poetry of Solvilde."

Mallory muttered, "Hate poetry."

Anaïs shoved her in the side.

Mallory shoved her back. "If you're going to lie, at least come up with something believable."

Madame Cellier snarled. "I don't care what you do in your free time. I care about being paid my due, when it's due. And your rent was *due* ten weeks ago." She crossed her arms. "I'm not running a charity house. You told me you were coming into the funds, so pay up, or get to packing."

"I can pay. I can pay. With the late fee, as promised." Mallory clambered from the bed.

The landlady hissed at the ragged sight of her, then gave a disapproving shake of her head. "There's been talk lately that the two of you have been swindling honest folk from their hard-earned coin."

"Skeptics," said Mallory through a yawn. "Can't please everyone."

"You're lucky I don't double the rent on you, for all I have to deal with." She pressed three fingers to her mouth as she offered up a prayer to whichever of the gods might be able to grant her patience today. Then she spat on the floor. Mallory wasn't sure what the point of the spitting was, but she thought it might have something to do with cleansing the space. That, or Madame Cellier was a vulgar old hag. Not that the two were mutually exclusive.

Mallory knew they were already paying more than this dingy room was worth. The apartment over their shop was hot in the summer and frigid in the winter and home to a giant house spider they had named Hugo and a disgusting barn swallow that left excrement all over their dresser and refused to migrate south when it was supposed to. The room was barely large enough to hold the bed that she and Anaïs shared, Anaïs's sewing table, a couple of their mother's spell books, and Mallory's art supplies.

But at least it was a roof, which was more than some people in Morant could claim, so Mallory bit her tongue.

She suspected the reason Madame Cellier hadn't tossed them out on their rumps ages ago was out of some long-held deference to their mother, who had been the most respected witch in the entire province. People had come from miles away to hear their fortunes and purchase everything from medical tinctures to magicked charms, love elixirs to fertility potions to talismans meant to ward against evil. Though it was never talked about, Mallory suspected it was due to one of her mother's enchantments that Madame Cellier had come into the windfall that allowed her to acquire seven shop fronts on Rue Tilance, the income from which had made her one of the wealthiest women in Morant.

Their mother had been the first to let the space that had become her shop and sanctuary, where she had warmly greeted those who sought her, until the day influenza took her life. Evidently, magic couldn't cure everything, a fact that had been hard for Mallory to reconcile with all she'd known of her mother—endlessly compassionate, reliable, competent.

Mallory had been eleven when their mother left this world, and Anaïs barely thirteen. They wasted no time. Within hours of their mother's death, they gathered the same tools she herself would gather when her clients wanted to speak to their deceased loved ones. Candles and incense, wands of whittled ash and a memento—in their case, the small emerald ring that had been passed down through generations.

They had drawn sigils on the floor. Held hands. Prayed to Velos. Called their mother's name. It was their second attempt to summon the dead, and Mallory was determined that this time, they would succeed. She couldn't fail, not this time. She didn't know how to exist without her mother. She didn't know if she could.

For hours they had begged and pleaded for their mother to return to them.

But she did not come.

By the time the candle had burned out, Mallory had a plan. She did not have magic, and the only magic her sister had was . . . Well, they didn't like to talk of it, and they certainly weren't going to make any money off it.

But they were the daughters of Noele Fontaine. They had watched their mother for years. They knew the words to say. They didn't know what, exactly, went into those potions on the wall, but neither did anyone else. Mallory and her sister might be without a drop of witchcraft in their blood . . . but no one else in the world had to know that.

She'd been wrong before. Mother or no mother. Magic or no magic. She would not let them go hungry. She would not let them be cast out into the streets. She would survive.

The next day, she flipped the Open sign on the shop window, the same as her mother had done every day since before she could remember.

When Madame Cellier came to escort the two girls to the orphanage, Mallory had handed her a bag of galets instead, and the two of them had been allowed to stay.

The Fontaine sisters, purveyors of petty magic and Morant's most renowned witches.

Or so she'd thought.

It had been a good run—but as was evidenced by their dwindling income and the investigators' accusations, their luck was running out.

The tours had been going so well, too. Anaïs had thought Mallory was mad when she suggested the idea, but Mallory was convinced there was a market for tours of the House Saphir, and she'd been right. Let people judge and call her an unladylike heathen. When it came to disturbing tales of murder, everyone—lord and peasant alike—was eager to pull up a chair.

"Well?" Madame Cellier said, foot tapping on the floorboards while Mallory dug through the pockets of the gown she'd hastily discarded in her impatience to crawl into bed the night before. Only when she found her purse, buried in the folds of her skirt, and felt its surprising lightness—did she remember.

The voirloup. The coins. *Armand Saphir.*

Her heart sank.

Gripping the coin purse, Mallory faced her adversary with an expression she hoped might elicit at least a little sympathy.

Madame Cellier snarled in response. "You haven't got it."

"I *had* it," Mallory insisted. "I was set to pay this morning. I truly was. But then . . . there was this count."

Madame Cellier's gaze narrowed.

"A total kouglof, if I'm being honest. But a charming one. You know how counts can be. Anyway, we happened to run into a voirloup, and it was—"

"A voirloup," the landlady interrupted.

"Ghastly beasts. Used to be human, then sold their souls to the dark ones in exchange for seven wicked pleasures . . . but in the end they become this grotesque, slobbery—"

"Mallory," Anaïs warned.

"Right. Sorry. So . . . a voirloup dislikes silver, and this count didn't understand that I *like* silver, rather a lot, and he made the mistake of . . . feeding my coins to the beast." Her mouth puckered with a sour taste. "Every last one of them."

Anaïs gaped at her. "Who's the awful liar now?"

"It's not a lie! But the good news is that I've got a new business opportunity right around the corner, and it's going to make loads of money, and you will be paid in full by the end of the month."

A twitch had formed in Madame Cellier's jawline. "You said that last month. And the month before."

"Yes, well, I didn't realize I'd be feeding my rent to a hungry half-man, half-wolf creature, did I? Extraordinary circumstances and—"

"*Out!*" Madame Cellier screamed, so loudly that Hugo scuttled into the rafters.

"Excuse me?" said Mallory.

"I have had enough. Enough of you being always late, taking advantage of my generosity. Enough of your lies. Enough of your questionable morality." She sneered. "Never knowing what awful rituals you're performing up here. What black magic might be at work within my very walls!"

"I mostly just embroider, actually," said Anaïs, holding up an embroidery hoop with a vibrant half-finished floral motif as evidence.

Madame Cellier's nostrils flared. "I want you both out of here by nightfall. I will not deign to permit your wayward—"

A loud thumping silenced her—a knock at the front door, two stories below.

Madame Cellier jutted her finger at Mallory. "Nightfall."

She spat one more time, before pivoting on her heel and marching down the stairs.

Mallory and Anaïs exchanged looks.

"I'm sure she didn't mean that," said Mallory.

"Naturally, if you've got thirty lourdes to change her mind with. Mally, what happened? Where is the money? And why do you look like you lost a fight with . . ."

"A voirloup?"

Anaïs shook her head. "Can't you ever be serious?"

Mallory pulled her bloodied chemise over her head, quickly changing into a cleanish one, followed by the green-and-gray dress that Anaïs had made out of the tablecloth that had once covered their mother's card-reading table. She fastened the buttons of the high collar until the lace scratched her chin.

What was she going to do? She could pay half the rent now. Maybe she could start hosting séances at the House Saphir. Two galets to speak to one of Bastien Saphir's dead wives? She wondered if she could get Triphine to go along with it. If not, she could certainly coach Anaïs on what to say . . .

The second she thought it, she remembered.

Her heart jumped into her throat. "What time is it?"

"Half past nine," said Anaïs.

"And what time does the jeweler open?"

"No idea. Nine, probably. Why? Do you have jewelry to sell?" Her expression turned scolding. "You told me to stop picking pockets, you hypocrite!"

"I haven't been picking pockets." Mallory rushed to the window. A carriage stood on the cobblestone road—black lacquer and embellished with gilt moldings. It didn't *look* like something the investigators would arrest her in . . .

"Anaïs! Mallory!"

They swiveled their heads toward the door. Madame Cellier thundered back up the steps, hands on her hips as she glared at them with distrust. "You have a visitor. He claims to be your count."

CHAPTER EIGHT

Count Armand Saphir was waiting in their shop, uncorking a bottle of *True Love Potpourri—guaranteed to have you crossing paths with your soul mate within thirty days of usage, or your money back!*

He gave it a sniff. His nose wrinkled with revulsion.

Unlike Mallory, Armand had apparently taken the time to bathe since their death-defying adventure the night before. His black hair was tidied, his skin free of sweat and blood. He did not wear a jacket this time, and she wondered if the fine blue jacket he'd worn the night before had been salvageable. Judging from the bandages on his left arm, where his sleeve was rolled up past his elbow, she doubted it.

"Did you follow me?" demanded Mallory.

Armand turned toward her, startled. He blinked, examining her as carefully as he'd been examining the vials of potpourri, before he said quietly, "You have something in your hair." He pointed to his own scalp.

Anaïs, who had entered the room on Mallory's heels, plucked something from Mallory's hair and showed it to her—a delicate purple flower.

"Wisteria?" asked Anaïs.

Noticing that Madame Cellier was still loitering in the stairwell, attempting to spy on them, Mallory slammed the door shut. She turned back to Armand. "I asked you a question."

"Following you was not necessary." He set down the love potion. "That investigator said that your shop was on Rue Tilance, and here you are." He gestured to the label beside the potpourri. "This claims to have white nettle in it, but I'm pretty sure it's actually inkroot nettle. I wouldn't advise anyone to bathe in it twice weekly, as these instructions recommend."

Mallory's frown deepened. "What do you want?" She tipped her chin toward his bandaged arm. "I'm not covering any medical expenses. You signed a waiver when you purchased your ticket for the tour."

He stared at her. "No, I didn't."

"It was an implied waiver."

"That isn't a . . ." He gave his head a shake. "I don't need you to cover my medical expenses. I'm a count."

Mallory considered this, then stumbled forward, faking a bad limp as she hobbled to one of the chairs beside the table on which sat the worn deck of her mother's Wyrdith cards. She groaned as she sat down. "Actually, I was quite hurt in the fall from that window—which you definitely pulled me out of, don't try to deny it. I need a splint. Surgery. Lots of medicines. They might have to amputate. Is this a good time to discuss compensation?" She gave him a sad smile. "Given that you fed my hard-earned coin to that voirloup, I think it's only fair."

Armand opened his mouth as if to speak, but when no sound came out, he turned his attention to Anaïs instead. "You must be the sister."

His expression was dubious, and Mallory knew he was wondering if the two of them were actually related. Of the Fontaine sisters, Anaïs was the oldest and the prettiest—with her long straw-colored hair, heart-shaped face, and impish little mouth. Where Anaïs was soft, Mallory was sharp—sharp nose, sharp eyes, sharp tongue—with dull brown hair that was long and unruly and unwilling to hold a curl on those rare occasions when her sister attempted to style it.

Plus, Anaïs generally liked people. Something Mallory could hardly fathom.

"Anaïs Fontaine," she said with a curtsy.

"Enchanté. I am Count Armand Saphir. It's a pleasure to—"

Anaïs guffawed—a shrill, abrupt sound that completely ruined the grace and manners she'd established with her fine curtsy. "I'd sooner believe you were some suitor come to propose marriage to my sister."

"Hey!" said Mallory as Armand's face flared pink. "He could be desperately in love with me. Stranger things have happened."

Anaïs looked pointedly from Mallory to Armand and back again. "No, sister. Stranger things have *not* happened."

Armand cleared his throat. "I am not here to propose marriage."

"Well, good," snapped Mallory. "I would obviously decline if you did."

"Obviously," he muttered.

"So why *are* you here, Monsieur . . ." Anaïs prompted.

"Saphir."

She gave a mirthful laugh. "You're sticking with that, are you? Next you'll be telling me that the two of you battled a silver-eating voirloup last night."

Mallory leaned her elbows on the table. "Why *are* you here?"

"As I tried to explain last night, I require your help." He took the seat opposite her. "The reputation of the Fontaine sisters is well-known in Morant. Descended from a long line of powerful witches. Able to summon the spirits of the dead. Talented in the arts of dream interpretation, enchantments, and herbalism." He hesitated, glancing at the shelf of herbal tinctures with the mislabeled nettles. "Though I suppose we can't be good at everything. Still, I believe you are particularly suited to assisting me with a . . . difficult situation."

"What kind of difficult situation?"

"My great-great-grandfather, Bastien Saphir, the first, more colloquially known as Monsieur Le Bleu . . ."

"I've heard of him," Mallory muttered.

"He has returned."

Mallory frowned. Anaïs made an *oooh* noise and sank onto a settee.

"His spirit, or soul, or ghost, or . . . I don't really know what the proper terminology is. But he is back. These past seven years, he has been haunting my home in Comorre, frightening our visitors and our staff. The house and estate are falling into disrepair as I cannot keep good help. It has even spread to my vineyards. No one wishes to be anywhere near the château, and the business is suffering because of it. He is a nuisance and . . . and a danger. He has become increasingly spiteful and this past year . . ." His expression darkened as he admitted, "Increasingly violent. If I cannot get rid of him, I worry the home will need to be permanently abandoned."

Mallory's brow drew sharply down. "When do you get to the part where this has anything to do with us?"

"If I cannot purge the spirit from the house, my family's legacy will be ruined."

"And?" Mallory prompted.

Armand tensed. "I need you to exorcise him. The ghost. Using your . . ." He waved his hand in her direction. "Magic."

Mallory's eyes widened. "Of course. Why didn't you say so?" She stood abruptly. "My answer is no. You may leave now. I'm sure the investigators will be arriving soon, and I would really prefer to not be around when they do."

"Investigators?" asked Anaïs.

Armand stood, too. "You can't say no."

"I can, actually."

His mouth hung limp for a moment, before he threw up his unwounded arm in frustration. "I saw you use magic to deal with that voirloup last night. Plus, you claim to know more about Monsieur Le Bleu than anyone else alive. And also . . . you *will* be arrested if you refuse. If not for selling fake baubles or whatever those investigators accuse you of, then for trespassing. I will have you arrested myself—no matter where you run to."

"You wouldn't."

"I would."

Mallory clenched her teeth and glared at him.

He glared back for one full, ragged breath.

Then his shoulders dropped. "No," he amended sheepishly. "I probably would not. But still . . . you can't refuse. I need you. I don't know who else to ask."

"That isn't my problem." As she said it, Mallory thought of the strange boys last night. Fitcher, with the pocket watch that was not a pocket watch, and Constantino, whose arrow had reduced a terrible beast to little more than a glorified chess piece. *Monster hunters, curse breakers* . . . "Although, I might know of someone—"

"I'll pay you."

The words died on Mallory's tongue. "I beg your pardon?"

"I'll pay you. Handsomely." Armand looked beseechingly between the sisters. "I need this ghost gone. He isn't only a bother. He's . . . he's evil. He's going to ruin my entire future if I can't expel him."

"How much?" asked Mallory, ignoring her sister's aghast expression.

"How much will it take?"

Mallory thought about this for a long moment. Arrived at an acceptable amount. Then tripled it.

"Fifteen hundred lourdes."

Anaïs choked.

But Armand barely hesitated. "Done."

The breath left Mallory. "Really?"

"I am very keen to solicit your services."

She looked askance at her sister, before adding, "I meant up front. Fifteen hundred lourdes up front, and fifteen hundred when the job is finished."

Armand did not balk. "Three thousand lourdes," he said slowly. "Paid in full, *after* the job is finished. Until then . . ." He slipped the chain from around his throat and held it out to her, revealing the Saphir crest on the small medallion—two wine goblets crossed beneath a circle of blue sapphires. "You may keep this as collateral."

Mallory took the chain, watching how the stones caught in the candlelight. She knew this crest. They sold replicas in the store. But here was the real thing. Solid gold. Real gems. She estimated it was worth nearly five hundred lourdes alone.

But if she saw this through, it would pale in comparison to the final payment.

Three. Thousand. Lourdes. That would certainly put some butter in their spinach.

"May I ask a question?" squeaked Anaïs, raising a finger. "There have been rumors of the House Saphir being haunted for the past century. But you said the ghost returned seven years ago. What happened?"

Armand shook his head. "I'm not sure. You're right. Ever since the . . . the murders . . . there has been evidence of the house being haunted. Mostly by the wives—Lucienne and Béatrice. Once a year, the fountain turned red with blood, but that was all. Until one Mourning Moon, seven years ago . . . when things changed."

Anaïs inhaled sharply, and Mallory sent her a warning glare.

"The house grew cold. Shadows would play tricks on your eyes. Doors slammed. There was laughter, this cruel, terrible laughter. Sometimes there was a . . . smell. Like oranges and blood mixed together. So overwhelming it would make a person dizzy."

Anaïs pressed a hand to her throat. "Mallory, is it possible that—"

"We can help? Yes. Yes, indeed, I think we can." Mallory beamed. "When shall we begin? We will need to stay at the house, for . . . uh . . . maximum infusion of the . . . magic . . . to be most effective."

"Of course," said Armand, relief swelling through his tone. "We already have a room prepared. Can you come today?"

"Today?" said Mallory. "Well—yes. Best to get started as soon as possible."

Armand nodded effusively. "Wonderful. I can—"

"Sister, might I have a word?" Anaïs took Mallory's elbow and dragged her from the room. As soon as they were in the hall, she spun to face her. "What are you doing?"

"This is perfect!" said Mallory. "Three thousand lourdes, plus free room and board for . . . well, at least a month or two. How long do you suppose it takes to exorcise an evil spirit?"

"I haven't the faintest idea, and neither do you, because we are *not actual witches*."

Mallory shushed her. "He doesn't need to know that."

"Yes, he does! You cannot do what he is asking you to do, and this sounds serious. Plus, the timing of it." She lowered her voice to barely above a whisper. "Do you think it's possible that the return of Le Bleu has anything to do with . . . you know—"

"Don't be ridiculous. That would suggest that we successfully summoned a spirit back from the dead, and as you pointed out, we are not actual witches."

"That was *before*." Anaïs cringed and bit the edge of her pinkie nail. "If it's our fault that this spirit returned . . ."

"Pure coincidence, Anaïs. And now this count wants to pay us to deal with his spirit problem. Three thousand lourdes! We can get to Verene on that much money, traveling in the fanciest carriage we can find, and when we get there, I will buy you that dress shop you've wanted. No one will know who we are, no one will care—"

Anaïs gestured wildly. "He's never going to give us that money, because, as per usual, you don't know what you're doing!"

"As per usual, I'll figure something out. I can talk to ghosts, remember? Maybe I can . . . you know. Ask Monsieur Le Bleu to leave."

Anaïs gasped. "*Yes*. Fabulous. Positively brilliant. Do you even hear yourself right now?"

"Do you have any other ideas?" She grabbed Anaïs's hand and lifted it up, so that the ring on Anaïs's finger glinted in the dim stairwell. A gold band with a single square-cut emerald. "Would you rather we sell the family heirloom?"

Anaïs yanked her hand away. "Don't be rash."

"That's what I thought. All we need to do is act the part, get the payment, and we'll be gone before he knows it."

Anaïs scowled. "Fooling tour groups is one thing, but this ghost sounds dangerous."

"And when we're long gone, I will summon some actual experts to go help him," said Mallory, thinking of the card for Fitcher's Troupe. "Everyone wins. And best of all . . ." She grabbed her sister's shoulders. "No more Madame Cellier."

"But, Mally . . . at some point, he's going to realize that you don't have any magic. He will throw us out. Or worse, have us arrested!"

"We're already going to be arrested."

"What are you talking about?"

"The police know about us. The séances, the potions . . . Two investigators were on the tour last night. They would have taken me already if the count hadn't persuaded them not to. So either we go with him now, or we prepare to spend tonight in prison."

Anaïs paled as she took this in, one hand pressing against her temple.

After a long silence, she said faintly, "Mother's cards. Your art supplies. My embroidery kit." She inhaled sharply. "We can be ready in five minutes."

CHAPTER NINE

Mallory expected the full day's ride to Comorre to be spent in the tedious throes of pleasantry with their new employer, a drudgery she had never excelled at. But when they carried their single trunk out to the waiting carriage—relieved to see no signs of the investigators in either direction—Armand climbed up into the driver's seat himself.

Settling herself onto the plush carriage bench, Mallory frowned at her sister. "Ever heard of a count who did his own driving?"

"Perhaps Monsieur Le Bleu killed his driver," Anaïs suggested, unconcerned, as she pulled out a fashion periodical she'd swiped from Madame Cellier and started flipping through the pages.

Even without the threat of small talk, the ride felt endless. Mallory had traveled little in her life, and her body was not accustomed to the constant bouncing that made her bones feel like they would shake right out of her skin. She tried to sketch for a while, but her attempts were horrendous, and the combination of the rattling wheels and her own frustrations had given her a headache by the time the farmlands of the Lysraux countryside were replaced with sprawling vineyards.

Meanwhile, Anaïs seemed perfectly content. When she tired of the magazine, she started in on her embroidery hoop, only half minding her stitches as she took in the passing scenery, cooing over every new sight. *Oh, look! A pair of wild swans! Are those figs in that tree? What a quaint little farmhouse! Oh, Mally, they're harvesting the vineyard! And over there! A castle!* It must have been the fiftieth castle they'd passed, but Anaïs seemed every bit as delighted as she'd been with the first.

It was possible they needed to get out of Morant more often.

Eventually, Anaïs insisted that Mallory pause from her sketching to tell her everything about the night before. Mallory recounted the story as well as she could—investigators, voirloup, and all—then showed her sister the card that had been given to her by that mysterious boy.

"Fitcher's Troupe," murmured Anaïs. "This is your backup plan? When you can't actually do what you're supposed to do?"

"We," Mallory corrected her. "He believes we are both witches."

Anaïs handed back the card. "I give it three days before he sends us packing. But I intend to enjoy the luxury of the countryside while I can."

Mallory flipped back through her sketchbook, which was filled not only with portraits of Le Bleu's wives, but also a veritable bestiary of creatures she had yet to meet face-to-face (somewhat disappointingly). There was a velue—a disastrous beast with the head of a serpent and a body covered in poison-tipped spines. The croque-mitaine—a sort of goblin that liked to eat the noses and fingers off curious little children. And even a cheval mallet—a savage, spectral horse that lured desperate travelers from the road, most of whom were never seen again.

Mallory studied the illustration, then added a half-crushed skull beneath the cheval mallet's front hoof. The picture was shaky, not her best work, but the skull was an improvement.

The art kept her mind off other things, anxious things. Like how she soon might encounter Count Bastien Saphir I—not to mention his wives, who loomed as large in Mallory's mind as the murderer himself. Lucienne Tremblay and Béatrice Descoteaux. Triphine would not be there, as she seemed incapable of leaving the house in Morant, though it had never been clear if that was by choice.

"We should be nearly there," said Anaïs, pulling back the curtain. "These could be the Saphir vineyards."

Tidy rows stretched out to the horizon, vines tied up with stakes and twine, heavy with bunches of late-season fruit, the small grapes bruise-purple and drooping toward the earth.

In the distance, on the crest of a golden hill, was a château.

Mallory's pulse jumped.

It was *the* château.

She shoved her sister aside to get a better look. "There it is."

Anaïs laughed and crowded in beside her. "I knew you were excited."

Mallory had seen the house in so many paintings, so many illustrations, she would have recognized it anywhere. A sprawling château, surrounded by sloping vineyards, its stone cast in a grayish-lavender light as the sun descended over the hills. It stole her breath away.

The château was a monument of limestone walls, narrow windows with diamond leading, arched dormers set in a black slate roof, and an army of brick chimneys marching off in every direction. It was columns and pediments, elaborate modillions, and arched niches bearing statues of winged demons and mythical beasts. It was imposing and magnificent and . . . apparently, falling apart. Roof tiles were missing. Trellises set against the walls were rotting. Though the stonework had once been white, now it was smudged sooty gray.

As they neared the mansion, Armand descended to open the heavy iron gate, its detailing as intricate as fine lace. The gravel drive changed to cobblestones. Enormous chestnut trees full of spiky fruits shaded the path. They passed a series of gardens divided by tall hedgerows, which began wild and forested with dense foliage and unruly trees, but became increasingly formal as they neared the house, their geometric configurations apparent despite a proliferation of weeds and overgrown perennials. Walking paths surrounded marble fountains, boxwood borders, fruit trees and topiaries and beds of thorny roses and aromatic lavender.

After an eternity, they entered the front courtyard.

The courtyard.

Mallory's heart pounded so much it hurt.

There it was. The fountain at the center of the drive, with its iconic statue of Count Gaspard Saphir, Le Bleu's grandfather, riding a stallion and brandishing a rapier like some avenging warrior—even though, as far as she knew, the family had pretty much always been vintners and merchants. They weren't exactly war heroes. Around the horse's hooves was an impressive assortment of magical creatures—fae and kobolds, goblins and dragons, lutins and sprites, even a sea serpent entwined around the statue's base.

In this very spot, it was said, Monsieur Le Bleu was still laughing when his fourth wife's brothers took off his head.

Mallory stared at the cascading water as the carriage rolled by, and for a moment she swore the water shimmered crimson—but that was probably the reflection of the pink sunset coloring the sky.

She tore her attention from the fountain to marvel at the House Saphir.

"I don't know about you," squeaked a high-pitched voice, "but I'm not impressed."

Surprise ricocheted down Mallory's spine. Slowly, she turned to see Triphine beside her on the carriage bench, head angled to take in the full scope of the mansion.

"What are you doing here?" Mallory asked.

Anaïs jumped, startled.

Triphine peered at Mallory, hurt. "Was I not invited?"

"You . . . How did . . . I didn't think you could leave Morant."

Triphine opened her mouth, but then shut it again and cocked her head to one side. "Now that you mention it . . . I didn't either. Yet here I am. How peculiar." She scanned the carriage. "I was feeling weary this morning, so thought I'd take a nap in back with the luggage. It passed the time, but now . . . *oh.*" She made a pained face and rubbed at the side of her neck. "I've got such a terrible crick, I'm not sure my spine will ever straighten out again."

"Mallory," Anaïs hissed. "What is it?"

"Triphine," she told her sister.

"The duchess?"

"She hitched a ride."

"Is this your sister?" Triphine studied Anaïs. "She's changed a lot since last I saw her. I thought she'd be plain and awkward. Like you."

Mallory scowled. "Are you planning to stay for any length of time?"

"Where else would you expect me to go?"

"Back to Morant."

Triphine settled against the bench as the carriage clattered to a stop. "I'm beginning to think you don't want me here."

The carriage shook as Armand dismounted.

"Do you think he's in there?" Triphine said, eyeing the house again. Her voice wavered the tiniest bit. "My lord husband?"

"Yes," Mallory hissed, tucking her sketch pad into her satchel. "That's why we are here."

Triphine puffed herself up with false courage. "If I see him, am I ever going to give him a piece of my mind." But she quickly deflated. "Though I really hope I don't see him."

The carriage door swung open.

"I hope the ride was comfortable," Armand said, holding out a hand, which Anaïs accepted and Mallory did not. Alighting behind them, Triphine pouted when Armand dropped his hand to his side.

THE HOUSE SAPHIR

It was cooler here than in Morant, particularly in the house's twilight shadow. There was a breeze blowing in from the sea, which couldn't be seen from the château, though Mallory could taste the salt on the air.

"Wait here," said Armand. "I'll have someone assist with your things."

He bounded up the steps and threw open the main door, then hollered into the cavernous mansion.

While they waited, Mallory scanned the intricate façade, taking in the gargoyles perched along the roofline, the bits of crumbling stone beneath a turret, the sharp-winged barn swallows that darted in and out of their nests among the eaves. Movement in one of the upper windows snagged her attention.

Two women were watching them. Though far away, Mallory could see how their silhouettes blurred into the air around them, and the dark splotches of blood smeared down the fronts of their dresses.

"The other wives," she whispered, not sure if she was talking to her sister or Triphine. "They are watching us."

"Oh yes, I see them." Triphine waved eagerly, and the figures both slipped back into the darkness. Triphine harrumphed. "So far the famed château is not meeting expectations." She coughed. "And I'm not sure the ocean air agrees with me. Do I look pale, Mallory?"

The front door opened again, and a row of servants emerged. A butler, a housekeeper, a maid. Mallory wasn't well educated in the needs of country estates, but it seemed like a paltry staff. She wondered how many people had been employed before the spirit of Le Bleu frightened them away.

Armand trotted out after them, nervously rubbing his hands. At some point he had rolled down his sleeve to cover his bandaged arm. "Everyone, I am pleased to present Mademoiselle Mallory Fontaine and Mademoiselle Anaïs Fontaine. They will be assisting us with our . . . unwelcome guest. Please help them in any way you can."

Anaïs curtsied. Mallory made a half-hearted attempt to follow her example.

"In what manner will they be assisting?" said the housekeeper, crossing her arms.

A muscle twitched in Armand's jaw, but he addressed her with an incline of his head. "They are talented witches, renowned in the city of Morant."

One of the housekeeper's eyebrows ticked upward. "Petty magic, then." She scoffed and muttered, "This will amount to nothing."

"Manners, Yvette," Armand said warningly, before he explained, "My housekeeper is a very devout follower of the Seven and . . . skeptical of other types of magic."

"It's all right," said Mallory. "We know that witchcraft is not as exalted as god-gifted magic, but we make do with the gifts we are given."

"It is more than most of us can lay claim to," said Armand, "and I am grateful you are here, no matter where your magic comes from."

Mallory smiled thinly, wishing she could appreciate his confidence without the slightly slimy feeling of the lies in her gut.

"Julie," said Armand, "would you please find Gideon and have him tend to the horses and the carriage."

Though she'd appeared nervous from the moment she stepped outside, the maid now beamed prettily and dipped into a curtsy. "Of course, my lord," she said, before scurrying off toward the stables.

"Yvette, will you be so kind as to show our guests to their rooms while Claude brings in their things?"

"If I must," the housekeeper muttered, studying Mallory and Anaïs with unveiled displeasure.

Before she could step forward, the door burst open again and a bedraggled man in a stained chef's coat appeared, brandishing a wicked kitchen knife.

"Lord Armand," the chef cried. "There's a . . . another one. In the larder."

Armand groaned. "What is it this time?"

"A lutin, I think."

Mallory's eyes widened. "A lutin? Here?"

The chef cut her a look before returning his attention to Armand. "I was getting down the butter, and it was . . . eating the napkins."

Armand sighed heavily. "I will see to it. Thank you, Pierre." He turned to Mallory and her sister. "Monsters have been inexhaustible pests ever since the veil fell. But don't worry, most of them are more a nuisance than anything to be concerned about. And I made sure that the guest suites were thoroughly cleaned and inspected."

Mallory's nerves tingled with an unexpected thrill. She wasn't just staying in a house with ghosts . . . she was staying in one with *monsters*.

Ever since the veil had fallen more than seventeen years before, unleashing dark magic and curses and monsters into the mortal world, the existence of magical creatures had become commonplace in certain parts of the country. But until the voirloup encounter the night before, the most magical beast Mallory had ever seen was an obnoxious matagot that paraded as a black cat in the alley behind their apartment, doling out small bits of luck and misfortune to passersby based on its arbitrary whims.

But to see *real* monsters, with all the viciousness of childhood fairy tales?

She couldn't wait.

"We are the witches here, Lord Saphir. It is the monsters who should be bothered by us."

Triphine clapped giddily. "Well said, Mallory! Keep up that confidence, and he'll never guess that you are utterly useless."

CHAPTER TEN

"Here we are," said Yvette—a woman whose skin was almost as gray as her hair. "Your suite."

"Thank you ever so much," said Anaïs, smiling beatifically. It was her nature to woo an enemy with kindness, and Yvette's gruffness and distrust certainly indicated an enemy. But in this case, Anaïs's charm only made Yvette's scowl deepen.

Mallory didn't much care one way or the other if the housekeeper liked them. She was too busy taking in the details of the hallway—the elaborate wallpaper, the ornate sconces, the worn carpet with a border of belladonna flowers along its edges. She was desperate to explore the manor. The gardens. The cemetery. To see the infamous fountain run red with blood. It might not be fairy tales of godmothers and talking animals, but these were the stories that had dug their claws into her when she was growing up and had never let go. Where her sister had dreamed of princes and ball gowns and being carried off by the fairy folk to their land of enchantment, Mallory had dreamed of haunted attics and eerie cellars, specters in the windows and ghoulish laughter echoing down the halls.

But the trek through the château had been brief and hurried, with no consideration given to Mallory's abundant curiosity as she craned her neck this way and that, attempting to take in the grandeur of the house. They had bustled straight to the second story of the north wing, where the housekeeper threw open a door and stepped aside for them to enter.

The room had once been glorious, but now the pink-and-turquoise rug was threadbare in places, the taffeta curtains were unraveling at the hems, and there were signs of water damage around one of the windows.

Did Mallory care about any of that?

Not the tiniest bit.

She didn't care about the musty scent, or that the wallpaper was faded, or whether or not the writing desk in the corner was missing one of its drawers.

It was the finest room she'd ever been in, and she was in love.

"Historically, these rooms were given to the lady of the house," said the housekeeper. "But after the . . . well . . ."

"Murders?" Mallory supplied.

Yvette sneered. "They are for guests now."

A chill shot down Mallory's spine as she realized where she was standing. The very room where the wives had slept. Not Triphine, who had lived and died at the house in Morant. But Lucienne and Béatrice. Even Gabrielle . . .

"And my sister and I are to share a room?" asked Anaïs.

"Is that a problem?"

"Oh, no, we don't mind. It's only . . . the house is so big. Space can't be limited."

"Space? No." Yvette folded her hands tight in front of her apron. "But help? Very much so. Beds must be made, water brought up. And fires don't light themselves."

"And thank the gods for that," Anaïs proclaimed, trying to lighten the mood.

"Anaïs and I are happy to make our own bed," said Mallory, "for what it's worth."

It wasn't worth much, judging by the woman's expression. "Dinner is served promptly at nine o'clock in the banquet hall. I will send Julie to escort you." She curtsied and departed.

Triphine, who had followed in the wake of their little group, made her way around the room, touching the finishings while her mouth twisted to one side. "This place smells like mothballs. And why are these cushions upholstered in wool? We always had velvet cushions in Morant. I'd expect goose down, but I bet you two galets that mattress is half stuffed with straw. Hope you weren't planning on getting a good night's sleep while you're here."

While she prattled on, Mallory joined her sister at the window, which offered a view of lush, rather overgrown gardens.

"The staff seems disinclined to like us," said Anaïs.

Mallory waved a hand through the air. "We're here to make money, not friends."

Anaïs smugly settled a hand on her hip. "Perhaps, but don't think I didn't notice."

"Notice what?"

Anaïs dramatically fluttered her lashes. "We are the witches here, *Lord Saphir*."

"Excuse me?"

"That's what you said, down in the courtyard. Not Monsieur, but *Lord*."

"He is a lord. He's a count. That's . . . the official . . . Is there something in your eye?"

"He's handsome."

Mallory crossed her arms. "I thought we were here to fake-exorcise a few ghosts and take a few thousand lourdes, but if you think you can steal a wealthy, titled husband in the interim, I support you."

"Not me, you dolt." Anaïs leaned closer to flick her on the earlobe. "You!"

"Ow! And also—*what?*"

"You like him."

"I do not. He's a count."

"You've always been ambitious."

Mallory scowled, her thoughts tumbling with the rumors she'd heard about the Saphir heir over years of researching his family legacy. Armand was said to be solitary. Reclusive. Quiet. Particular. It was said that he mostly kept to himself.

It was difficult to resolve those rumors with the boy who had come on her tour. Who had held his hand out to her, urging her to trust him enough to jump out a window, promising he would break her fall.

He had been brave last night. Clever. A little reckless. Far kinder than she would expect a nobleman to be, especially to a lowly tour guide like herself. She could admit there seemed to be a goodness in him she'd rarely witnessed in her fellow humans.

And . . . yes. He certainly was handsome.

And also far too trusting.

"We're here for a job. Don't get distracted."

"Don't be so quick to write off the possibility of a romance with his lordship. Imagine—Mallory Fontaine, master of skepticism, falling in love with a wealthy count who just happens to be the heir of a grand haunted mansion?" Anaïs laughed. "That might be the greatest con of all."

CHAPTER ELEVEN

Anaïs insisted that Mallory wear one of her own colorful gowns to dinner, rather than the practical gray Mallory preferred. Too tired from their travels to argue, Mallory found herself being buttoned up into a satin burgundy gown that had once been their mother's, and onto which Anaïs had spent hours adding a conservative lace ruffle that climbed to the top of Mallory's throat, because Mallory refused to reveal any skin below her neck, regardless of the current fashions. Mallory actually liked the dress, to her own dismay, but she'd never have admitted it out loud. She even begrudgingly let her sister braid her hair and tie it with a ribbon, but only because that was the sort of detail her sister cared about. Not because she wanted to be presentable for the count.

"That will have to do," said Anaïs, inspecting Mallory's hair with grumpy dissatisfaction.

"What have I always told you?" Triphine said. "You could be

halfway to pretty with a modicum of effort." She sat in the window seat, cocooned in a quilt from the bed. "Though standards have dropped so far this past century. Back in Gai-Yin, I would never have worn my hair down for dinner. In my day, your sister would have been considered an abysmal harlot."

Choosing not to repeat this sentiment to Anaïs, Mallory stood from the vanity chair and dug through her satchel, retrieving the knife she'd stashed away at the bottom of the bag. She tucked it into her boot.

"It is only dinner, Mally," said Anaïs. "What do you need a knife for?"

"Do you really need to ask me that?"

Anaïs raised an eyebrow.

"I might need to slice some meat from a bone. Or trim wayward threads from the fine silk napkins. Also, you heard Armand mention monsters, and I was recently attacked by a voirloup, so forgive me for overpreparing."

Anaïs considered. "Fair point, but don't let our host see it. We need to be careful around Armand. If this is going to work, he must think that we're respectable witches. Like Mother."

Mallory crinkled her nose. "Boring."

"This was your idea. Try not to ruin it by being yourself."

"Embroider *that* onto a pillow, why don't you?"

A knock came at the door. Mallory glanced at the mantel clock—it was precisely nine o'clock.

"Are you coming?" she asked Triphine.

The duchess threw a wrist against her forehead. "While I do appreciate the invitation, I am thoroughly exhausted from the day's travel. Every bone is aching. And my poor head—"

"I'll bring you some dessert if you stop whining."

At the mention of dessert, Triphine noticeably perked up. "Deal."

Mallory grinned. Though ghosts rarely wanted to exert the energy required to interact with the mortal world, most of them seemed more than willing to exhaust themselves over some of the finer delights of the living—a morsel of aged cheese, a sip of brandy, the sensation of running one's fingers through soft sable fur.

Julie, the maid, stood on the other side of the door. "Good evening. I am to show you to the banquet hall?" Her eyes brightened. "Oh, my. Don't you both look lovely?"

Mallory frowned. She knew she should have said no to the hair ribbon. No one with hair ribbons was ever taken seriously.

The maid led them along a corridor, through an arched door, down a spiral staircase. Passing through a series of elegantly decorated if musty-smelling salons, Mallory couldn't help thinking of the wives who had walked these halls a hundred years ago. What had they thought when they first passed through these rooms and saw the splendor that greeted them? Had they been proud to be the mistresses of this grand estate? Had they been relieved to know that with or without marital love, they could at least enjoy their husband's remarkable wealth?

Had they had any idea what sort of man they'd married? Had they walked these halls in wonder—or in fear?

Even after the bloody business with Count Bastien Saphir I, the family had never lost their station in society. Their noble title had not been revoked. The management of the estate had been handled by a testamentary guardian until Bastien II came of age, and the family's particular brand of Ruby Comorre had maintained its popularity for the better part of the last century, as it was made with grapes that flourished only in their small region. What was a little murder when there was wine to be had?

The maid paused in front of a set of oak doors carved with entwined serpents. She gestured for them to enter.

The banquet hall was bedecked in dark wood and crystal, with stars and blue salamanders painted on ceiling beams and a fireplace that was so absurdly big, the average-sized logs burning in it looked like twigs.

Armand stood and bowed. Anaïs curtsied. Mallory—who had already curtsied once that day and wasn't about to make a habit of it—did not.

The table was large enough to seat forty or more, but they were ushered down to the far end. As they were seated, Mallory took in the place settings. Monogrammed dishes and crystal goblets etched with the Saphir crest. There were so many strange little forks and spoons. Mallory hadn't the faintest idea what a person could want with them all.

Anaïs leaned close and whispered excitedly, "I think this is real silver!"

Mallory knocked her away with her shoulder, while Claude, the butler, stepped forward to fill their goblets with deep-rust-colored wine.

"Have you found your rooms to be accommodating?" Armand asked.

"Quite, thank you," said Anaïs, smiling her prettiest smile. It made Mallory want to poke her in the ribs.

"Please let me know if there is anything that can be done to make you more comfortable," said Armand.

An excruciatingly awkward silence followed while a course of onion soup was brought out. Mallory couldn't recall the last time she'd smelled anything so delectable. As soon as they were served, she scanned the assortment of spoons, picked one at random, and bent over her bowl—only to freeze when the housekeeper loudly cleared her throat.

Armand bristled and sent Mallory and her sister an apologetic grimace. "Yvette is very devout," he whispered, before lowering his gaze. "The Seven we praise," he said softly, his expression more annoyed than reverent.

"The Seven we praise," repeated Anaïs.

Clutching her spoon tighter, Mallory shot her a disgruntled look. They'd never prayed to the seven gods in their lives.

Her sister kicked her under the table.

Mallory sighed. "Er . . . yes. The Seven. Love them. All the praise. This smells fantastic. And here I thought Count Saphir didn't know how to entertain guests."

Armand's wince was subtle, but she noticed it all the same. "It is difficult to entertain with so small a staff."

Mallory breathed in the steam, aromatic with garlic and rosemary. She dunked in the spoon and took a sip. Anaïs followed suit. They both moaned in unison. It had been a long time since they'd properly feasted.

Actually, she wasn't certain they'd ever properly feasted, but food had definitely been more plentiful back when their mother was alive.

Armand tried to conceal a smile as he started in on his own bowl, and Mallory was grateful he didn't feel the need to accost them with meaningless conversation. For a while, the only sounds were those of silver on porcelain and quiet, probably unladylike slurping.

As soon as the soup was gone, it was replaced by a course of raw oysters and boiled sea snails, served alongside slices of baguette. Mallory noted that they were each given their very own dish of salted butter, a rare luxury. She wished she'd been served twice as much.

When Mallory's wineglass was nearly empty, Armand gestured for it to be filled.

"Did you know," Mallory said, scooting her glass closer to the maid as she brought out the wine decanter, "before slashing his wives' throats, Le Bleu poisoned them with something mixed into their wine, the concoction making them slow and confused, too weak to fight back? Rather ingenious, actually."

Yvette gave a disgusted noise as she distributed the butter dishes. "This is no laughing matter."

"Yvette, please," started Armand.

"My lord, I do not see that the horrific deeds of your great-great-grandfather should make for an amusing spectacle in polite conversation."

"Perhaps not," admitted Armand, "but neither do I think it is best if we pretend it didn't happen. Those women, his victims—"

"Are *all* that anyone thinks of when they hear the name of Saphir," she interrupted. "It is only by the grace of the Seven that this household has not suffered further."

"Yes, but Mallory is something of a scholar when it comes to our family history. I'm sure it's natural for her to wish to talk about it . . . openly and without any semblance of propriety whatsoever."

"It's quite a talent of hers, actually," piped up Anaïs.

With a wry, tired smile, Armand turned back to Yvette. "Would you please prepare the third course? I'm sure our guests are famished from the long journey."

Yvette's face turned purple. "There is no third course, my lord."

"Oh. Well. Perhaps you could bring out more . . . butter, then?" He gestured meaningfully at Mallory's empty butter dish, and she wondered if maybe she wasn't supposed to use *all* of it on a single slice of bread?

Regardless, the dismissal was clear. Sucking in a sharp breath, Yvette turned on her heel and marched out of the room.

"I am so sorry," said Armand. "Yvette can be . . . Well. It isn't personal."

"Oh, we prefer that it is," said Anaïs, taking a sip of her wine. "Makes the grudges easier to hold on to."

"You seem to have a very cordial relationship with your staff," said Mallory.

A shadow passed over Armand's expression as he dug the meat of one of the snails out with a tiny fork—not, Mallory noted, the fork that she had chosen. "It is exceedingly difficult to maintain our staff here. Yvette has been with the household for more than half her life, and her loyalty has, perhaps, lent itself to some entitlements that would not otherwise be tolerated." He shrugged helplessly. "The truth is, I could never dismiss her, and she knows it."

"That is commendable," said Anaïs.

"Commendable? Bah!" said a chirpy voice, the words slightly

slurring together. "More like he hasn't the spine to show the outspoken wench to the door."

Mallory's own spine stiffened.

At the far end of the table, Lucienne and Béatrice sat together, both of them bleeding from puncture wounds in their chests. Mallory easily recognized Lucienne by her upswept blond hair, cherry-red cheeks, and elaborately embellished, if outdated, ball gown. She held a near-empty wineglass in one hand, and in the other a hunk of bread stolen from the tray when no one was looking.

In comparison, Béatrice was far more demure in a simple linen day dress, her chestnut hair falling around her shoulders in messy ringlets. She sat slightly hunched, as if afraid that someone might notice her, even though she'd spent the last century being invisible to almost everyone.

Their figures carried the ephemeral gray-tinged glow of spirits, and their arms were marked with deep slashes cut into words that Mallory could not read, though she nevertheless knew what they said. Before killing his wives, Le Bleu had carved a single word into each of their arms—*echtraus* on the left arm and *greischt* on the right.

Written in the old language, the investigators at the time had to confer with a local fae expert in order to discern their meanings: "trust" and "betrayal."

She whipped her attention back to Armand, but too late. Everyone was frowning now, glancing toward the opposite end of the table.

"What is it?" Armand asked.

"Nothing. I was just . . . admiring that tapestry. I love a good tapestry."

The tapestry behind the wives depicted a man and woman in dated finery dancing in a meadow. Mallory hated it.

But Lucienne whispered, "Nice save." Then hiccupped. Then grew excited when the butler uncorked one of the dusty bottles on the side table. "Oh, *goody*! They're opening the thirty-year vintage." She finished off the wine in her glass.

"How much have you had tonight?" asked Béatrice—her voice a meek but irritated whisper. "You're going to make yourself sick again."

Lucienne batted the comment away and stood, helping herself as soon as Claude had set down the bottle. Moments later, the butler turned around to pick up the bottle again and jolted in surprise to see that it had been moved to a different shelf.

"Perhaps we should discuss these ghosts of yours," said Mallory.

"Ooh, they're talking about us!" said Lucienne.

"There is only one ghost we find concerning," said Armand.

Lucienne sulked. "Oh, they're talking about *him*."

"Even after the fall of the veil, we were able to live in relative peace with the two wives whose spirits have been here since their deaths. But Monsieur Le Bleu is not merely a nuisance. He is . . ." Armand hesitated, searching for the right word, and finally landing on, "Despicable."

"Cheers to that," said Lucienne, raising her glass.

"Hush, Lucy," whispered Béatrice. "I'm trying to listen."

"You said he has been frightening away the staff," said Anaïs.

"In my experience," added Mallory, "ghosts can only be corporeal for short periods of time, and even then, only when they are highly motivated. Such as when they really want to sample a great vintage of wine."

Armand furrowed his brow. "Wine?"

"Just as an example. I'm curious if Le Bleu has become physically violent, or if his tactics are of a more psychological nature."

"It is violent," Armand said. "But . . . it's . . ." Again, he struggled for the right description. "It isn't *him*, so much as it is the house itself. He controls it somehow."

"The house itself?" asked Mallory.

"There was a maid who was washing a window when the glass . . . shattered. The pieces flew at her, cutting her face, her hands . . ." He swallowed hard. "One piece got into her eye. She'll never see out of it again."

"How terrible," Anaïs whispered.

"And last year, a gardener was cleaning the tools and preparing to store them for the winter when a shelf broke over his head, dropping an ax on his hand. He lost two fingers."

"Velos protect us," whispered Yvette, setting a hastily prepared platter of soft cheeses and apples down on the table before making the sign of Velos above her brow.

"Are you sure these weren't fluke accidents?" asked Mallory. "How do you know it was Le Bleu?"

"He likes to have his presence known," said Armand. "We've all heard his laughter, and it is louder when he is being cruel. And there are . . . other things, too. Illusions. Threats. I imagine you'll see for yourself soon enough."

"Has he ever attacked you?"

Armand slowly shook his head. "Only the staff."

"The more we can determine about the spirit—his motives and desires, his strengths and weaknesses—the easier it will be to exorcise him from the property."

"What exactly is your plan?" asked Armand.

Mallory moved her goblet closer for the maid to refill. "Oh, the usual."

"Which is?" he pressed.

"You know. Typical witch stuff."

His attention stayed on her, keen and curious. "I'd love to know the details, if you don't mind sharing them."

"My sister *loves* sharing details about witchcraft," Anaïs said, slurping up a raw oyster. "Could talk about it for days."

"Wonderful," said Armand. "I know so little about petty magic."

"There are many options available to us," Mallory said through her teeth, casting an annoyed glance at her sister. "It is difficult to know which . . . *spell* . . . we will attempt first. At first I thought we'd go straight for the kill. You know. Host a big, extravagant exorcism. Really make a statement with it."

Armand's brow rose. "What does that entail?"

"Oh, you know. Ritualistic dances. A ceremonial bonfire. And, um . . ."

"Sacrifices," Anaïs added.

"Yes, sacrifi—wait, no." She sent her sister a scolding look.

"Not of *people*," her sister said. "Just a drop of blood or two."

Mallory cleared her throat. "Unfortunately, that sort of exorcism can be very . . ."

"Dramatic," Anaïs said. She spread her hands above the table, painting a visual picture. "After the bloodletting, everyone present must dance in the moonlight and howl like a pack of banshees. And, oh! We'll all be completely nude. It is a sight to behold."

The room went silent as Anaïs lifted her wineglass to toast her own ingenuity.

"Which is why," Mallory said through clenched teeth, "I've determined to try some more prosaic methods first."

"Suit yourself," Anaïs sang. "If you don't want a perfectly valid excuse to lower some inhibitions and discard a few layers of clothing . . ."

The maid turned so fast that she sloshed wine from the bottle across the front of Mallory's gown.

Mallory gasped, pushing away from the table.

"Julie!" scolded the butler.

"It's fine," said Mallory, dabbing at the lace that would no doubt be forever stained crimson. Julie wet the corner of a napkin and pressed it to the fabric covering Mallory's chest. A bolt of pain lanced across Mallory's sternum, and she yanked herself away, grabbing the napkin from the maid's hand. "I can do that. Thanks."

"Was she joking?" asked Lucienne, leaning closer to Béatrice. "About the naked dancing? It sounded like a good time, if you ask me. Well, maybe not the part about the blood sacrifices."

Béatrice shook her head. "It sounds awful. So I suspect you would enjoy it very much."

Lucienne preened.

"I really am so sorry," said Julie. "I can be quite clumsy—"

"It's all right," said Armand, who had half risen from his seat and still hovered there, trying to determine what he could do to help.

But Claude intervened. "Julie, why don't you take these dishes back to the kitchen?"

Julie appeared horrified, but relaxed when Armand sat down and sent her a comforting smile. Cheeks tinted red, she bowed her head and scurried away.

As the stab of pain in Mallory's chest faded, she felt a bump against her leg. Anaïs was taking advantage of the distraction to shuffle two soup spoons and a butter knife into her pocket. "Silver!" she whispered.

"Respectable," Mallory whispered back.

Anaïs shrugged, as if a little impropriety couldn't be helped.

As the room settled again, Mallory took a long draft of her wine, emptying the goblet. As she was setting the goblet back on the table, movement at a far window caught her attention. With darkness having long descended outside, the glass reflected the flames from chandeliers throughout the banquet hall, and . . . a figure. A man in a finely embroidered jacket and lace cravat, with a trim beard and vivid blue eyes. The reflection was framed perfectly between the heavy window drapes, a dark smile playing across his mouth.

He caught Mallory staring at him.

His grin widened. He raised a finger to his lips, as if urging her to keep a secret.

A reflection passed in front of the man as the butler walked by the window, and the spirit was gone.

Mallory inhaled slowly. "When you speak of the wolf, you often see its tail," she murmured. Only Anaïs heard her, and shot her a curious look, while Yvette was still spouting apologies. Something about how the maid was young and easily distracted. How she'd been trained for tending to the rooms, but not yet for dining service, and how—

"It's all right, Yvette," said Armand. "If Miss Fontaine's dress is ruined, we will get her a new one."

Mallory startled at the realization that much of this fuss was over her and a dress, of all things. "I prefer my dresses with some stains on them anyway."

Armand smiled in gratitude before nodding at the housekeeper. "I'm sure Julie is doing her best. And as you know, we can't afford to lose anyone else."

CHAPTER TWELVE

Mallory did not care to fall asleep. She lay in bed beside her sister, waiting for Anaïs's body to sink into the mattress, for her breathing to slow and steady. Only when she was certain her sister would not stir did she slip from the blankets and pull her riding cloak over her nightgown.

"Where are you going?" Triphine asked. She had found a book somewhere and had it laid out on the windowsill so she could read by moonlight. The plate of biscuits that Mallory had brought up from the dining hall lay empty beside her—nothing more than scattered crumbs.

"I want to see more of the house."

Triphine made a horrified face. "It's the middle of the night." She lowered her voice. "Don't you realize this place is *haunted*?"

Mallory bit the inside of her cheek, certain that Triphine did not notice the irony of this statement. "I'll be fine. Watch over my sister."

She slipped into the hall, then made her way out of the north wing. As she crept down the grand staircase, she caught the unexpected aroma of ripe oranges, juicy and tangy, on the air. She froze. The walls around her seemed to pulse. Like a heartbeat, thrumming. Like lungs taking in slow, rattling breaths.

The foyer's chandelier trembled. In the darkness, Mallory thought she saw thick, dark liquid dripping down from the extinguished candles. As if they were bleeding.

Mallory blinked, and the illusion vanished.

She shivered. The scent of oranges was gone. The house fell still and silent, though there persisted the undeniable sensation that she was being watched. Followed. Studied with silent, malicious curiosity.

Mallory did not know if the house was greeting her or trying to frighten her away. She might have laughed if it hadn't felt like the air had been squeezed out of her.

She hurried through the vestibule. As she approached the entry doors, they opened of their own accord. She hesitated again. Beyond the doors, the central courtyard stretched in front of her—a circular cobblestone path wide enough for multiple carriages surrounded the courtyard's most prominent feature. The fountain—that warrior and his steed, the beasts and monsters spread out on the pedestal below.

Bracing herself, she hurried over the threshold, lest the doors try to slam shut on her, but with the air of a gentleman, the doors waited until she was off the front steps before they slowly closed in her wake.

Mallory picked her way carefully over the uneven stones. The water burbled in the darkness, the pool glistening with moonlight.

The anniversary of Le Bleu's death was mere weeks away. If she and Anaïs were still there, she would let nothing stop her from coming to this fountain's edge in the middle of the night to see the spectacle of the fountain running with blood.

She placed a hand on the edge of the stone basin, damp from the spray.

This was the very spot where Count Bastien Saphir I had been killed. Gabrielle's brothers had caught him, forced him to his knees, and took his head from his neck with one swing of a sword. As the tale went, he'd been laughing up until the end, and his decapitated head had continued to laugh for nearly a full minute before death claimed him.

Mallory listened for that telltale sign of his haunting laughter. The sounds of the night were different in the countryside—more wind, no carriage wheels. The hoot of an owl, the chirrup of crickets in the gardens. But mostly, the water striking the pool below.

It was not such a terrible place to haunt for eternity. The artistry of the fountain's sculpture was astounding. The house itself was magnificent, even in its current state.

Mallory peered up at the ornate details of the sculpture. Her attention fell on a salamander carved into the design, a plume of marble fire spewing from its mouth. There was a crack running beneath it—one of many fractures that had taken a toll on the fountain over the years. From her vantage point, it appeared as though the salamander could break off at any second . . . or with just a little assistance.

Mallory bit her lower lip. If she and Anaïs were ever able to return to Morant, that would be a terrific prop to display on her tours. A magical creature carved of white marble, taken from the very fountain where Le Bleu had met his demise. She could sell replicas of painted clay, tell her tour guests that they, too, were authentic.

She glanced back at the house, scanning the dark windows. All was still.

If Anaïs were here, she wouldn't hesitate. She could not resist a pretty bauble, and often turned little thefts into something of a game. She would point out that the salamander was such a small detail. Surely, no one would even notice it missing.

Mallory peeled off her cloak and dropped it onto the edge of the fountain, then hiked up her nightgown and stepped barefoot into the water.

She hissed. It was colder than she'd expected, the shock of it like a knife into her heel. The pool was deep enough to come to her thighs, and Mallory was already shivering when she brought in her second foot. She hastened toward the sculpture, holding her nightgown bunched around her thighs with one arm.

The sculpture was more enormous than it appeared from afar, and as Mallory reached the base of the pedestal, she realized that, even on tiptoe, the salamander was tauntingly out of reach.

She released her nightgown, letting the hem fall into the water. She hooked one arm around the head of a wyvern and pressed her foot on top of the curled tail of a sea serpent. The stone was slippery with algae, but she managed to stabilize herself as she pulled her body up. Her hand grasped the stone salamander. *Success.*

But when she pulled, the beast remained stubbornly attached to the fountain.

"Oh, come *on*," she muttered, yanking harder. It did not budge. She let out a frustrated groan. Maybe if she had a stick, she could wedge it into the crack in the stone and—

"What are you doing?"

Mallory yelped. Her foot slipped. She fell backward, her body splashing into the water. Cold accosted her, dug icy spears into her skin. Mallory cried out from the shock, but the sound exploded from her in a flurry of bubbles. She launched herself up to the surface and spun around, spluttering.

Armand was standing beside the basin, mouth agape.

"Nothing!" she cried, sloshing through the water. "I wasn't doing anything! Why would you sneak up on me like that?"

"You . . . you are standing in my fountain," he said. "You appeared to be climbing it." He tilted his head curiously. "Actually, you appeared to be defiling it."

"I would never!"

"Were you trying to break off that salamander?"

"I was inspecting the craftsmanship." She angrily climbed back over the wall, wishing that her teeth weren't chattering as hard as they were. With her sodden gown clinging to her skin, the night's breeze was a brutal assault.

Armand was grinning outright now. "An expert on my family's history, and also on medieval sculpture? I am impressed, Miss Fontaine." His gaze dipped downward, and he sucked in a sudden breath and put his back to her. "My apologies. We should get you inside. You must be freezing."

Confused, Mallory glanced down, and mortification washed over her. Her soaked nightgown was clinging to her body in ways that it definitely should not have been. She tried to pull the fabric away from her skin, but the more she struggled, the more it clung.

"Here!" Armand snatched up her forgotten cloak and held it toward her, covering his eyes with his free hand.

Mallory pulled the cloak around herself as quickly as she could, though her fingers were going numb and her movements were stilted and slow. She checked that the fabric still covered her chest and throat.

"You can turn around now."

He did so, but cautiously. "I assure you, I saw nothing that would call your modesty into question."

She snorted. "Liar."

Even with the world colorless beneath the moonlight, Mallory was certain his face went crimson. "You will never hear me admit it."

This elicited a real laugh from her, and Armand's shoulders relaxed.

"What are you doing out here?" she asked, using the edge of the cloak to dry her dripping hair.

"I often have trouble sleeping. I was going to make myself something to drink when I happened to look out the window and saw you preparing to climb into the fountain. You'll have to forgive my curiosity."

"I don't have to do anything I don't want to do. And right now—I want to get out of this wet nightgown."

"Of course." Armand bowed and stepped aside as she brushed past him. "Though perhaps you would care for some hot chocolate?"

Her steps slowed.

"It will help to warm you."

"I would not wake your staff for such a request."

"I would not either."

She turned back, noting his hesitant smile.

"I can make it for you," he said. "It's what I'd intended to make for myself."

The offer was unexpected. A lord . . . making his own hot chocolate?

When she didn't immediately respond, his smile tipped to one side. "I won't poison it. I promise."

CHAPTER THIRTEEN

Armand lit a fire inside a brick oven and pulled a stool up beside it for Mallory to sit while he prepared the chocolate. They didn't speak while he gathered a copper pot and his ingredients. His movements were precise and practiced. He knew exactly where to find the large bar of bitter dark chocolate in the larder. How much cream to pour. Where to set the pot on the stove so the chocolate would melt but the milk would not scald. He added a spoonful of sugar, then another, occasionally tasting his concoction as he went. His face was set with such focused attention that Mallory felt like she was watching an artist at work.

And then, realizing that she was staring, she promptly looked away, busying herself with a study of the kitchen instead. It was utilitarian and pristinely organized, with collections of knives, spoons, and ladles hung on hooks above enormous black ovens. A rack of copper pots shone above a stove, and a baker's table still had remnants of flour from the loaves of bread that had been left to rise overnight. Unlike so much of the house that was bleak even in midafternoon, this room had an undeniable coziness to it.

The scent of chocolate and woodsmoke filled the kitchen as Armand unhooked a ring of keys from his belt. He opened a cabinet on the wall and retrieved a glass bottle filled with thick purple-red syrup. The cork made a quiet pop as he pulled it out.

As Mallory watched, he poured a hearty dollop into the pot of chocolate.

"What's that?" she asked sharply.

Armand started at what must have sounded like an accusation. Perhaps it had been.

"Elderberry syrup." He chuckled softly. "I didn't mean to put you on guard with that poison comment. It was intended as a joke."

"I'm not on guard. I just don't trust anyone, as a general rule."

"I see." He set the jar aside. "Can that trust be earned?"

Mallory's eyes narrowed. "I'm not sure. No one's ever tried that hard before."

He seemed to be on the verge of another nervous smile. "I assure you, only the stems of elderberry plants are toxic." He paused. "Well, and also the leaves. And the berries—but only before they get ripe. Or if you eat them raw. And you have to stay away from the red varieties entirely. But when properly prepared . . ." He filled a spoon with the liquid and drank it down himself. Licking his lips, he replaced the cork in the bottle and returned it to the shelf. "It has many medicinal uses, not the least of which is helping to fend off colds. You'll feel better after you drink this."

"It doesn't prove anything that you drank it yourself," she muttered. "You could have built up a tolerance."

"Yes," he said solemnly. "I've been slowly poisoning myself for years so that my guests will never suspect me when I start to kill them off with mugs of hot chocolate."

He stirred the pot. The drink was so thick it coated the ladle as he filled two clay mugs. He handed one to Mallory and kept one for himself. Scanning another shelf, which was packed with jars, bottles, and clay pots, he grabbed a small vial with a medicinal dropper and added three drops of clear liquid to his own cup.

"And what is *that*?" Mallory asked.

"Royal skullcap. It grows wild in our forest." Armand pulled a second stool beside hers and sat down. "I used to suffer from nightmares when I was growing up. Skullcap helps me sleep."

"I suppose any child would have nightmares, growing up in a house like this."

He tilted his head, studying her. Rather than respond, he asked, "How is your chocolate?"

Mallory blew on the top of the drink, then took a small sip.

She did not want to—rather hated herself for it, in fact—but still, she moaned. "Great gods."

Armand didn't respond, but his lowered eyes and smug grin said enough.

They sipped in silence, and between the chocolate and the fire and her warm traveling cloak, Mallory felt the chill slowly leaving her body.

"What did you want the salamander for?" Armand asked. "And don't tell me you were merely inspecting the artistry again. I know you were trying to steal it."

She blew out a breath. "I thought it would make an interesting showpiece. For my tours."

Armand's face turned incredulous. "You couldn't have asked for a cobblestone? Or a monogrammed candlestick? Or . . . I don't know. The sword he used to kill his wives?"

Mallory perked up. "You still have the murder weapon?"

"Of course. It's hanging in one of the parlors." He started to laugh, but it died out quickly. "Though I find it unnerving how eager you looked when I said that."

"It's an important historical artifact," she said, luxuriating in how warm the clay mug felt between her palms. "Nothing strange about that."

"Some might disagree." At least he was smiling when he said it. "Please don't steal it. When you think of some other prop that would add authenticity to your tours that does not require defacing my family estate, it will be my honor to obtain it for you."

Mallory scowled. He seemed earnest, but . . .

"Why would you want to support my tours? It seems as though it would be better for you if everyone just . . . forgot what had happened. Clearly your housekeeper feels as much."

"Yvette has been with our family since long before I was born, and she seems to think it is her sacred duty to absolve our family name of Bastien's evils. She doesn't like anything that could be seen as a deviation from the path of the Seven, and unfortunately, many believe that Bastien practiced dark sorcery himself."

"The sacrifice theory," Mallory murmured.

He nodded solemnly.

Though many suspected that Le Bleu was a wicked man with

an insatiable taste for violence, others believed he had even darker intentions. That his murders were in service to some unholy spell. But for what purpose? It was anyone's guess.

"I suppose I might be distrustful of witchcraft myself, given the circumstances," Mallory confessed.

"There are times when it horrifies me to think that I could be descended from such a monster," said Armand. "But I can't help being curious, too. When I was growing up, my aunt never wanted to talk about the murders, and forbade the staff from discussing them. But . . . the story isn't only about Le Bleu, is it? I am descended from Bastien Saphir, but I am also descended from Triphine Maeng, and . . . I would like to know more about her. About all of them. Lucienne. Béatrice. Even Gabrielle."

Mallory sipped her drink to keep from telling him that Triphine had recognized him on the tour and was even now lounging about the upstairs suite. The kind thing, Mallory thought, would be for her to offer to facilitate a conversation between the two of them, so Armand could ask his questions and Triphine could get to know her great-great-grandson.

But she knew Triphine, and that sounded like an exhausting ordeal.

Maybe she'd broach the subject tomorrow.

"How long ago did your aunt pass?" she asked instead, which seemed a more polite way than asking how long he'd been relatively alone in this enormous, drafty, haunted house.

"Just over a year ago," he said.

"Were you close to her?"

"She raised me as well as she could, but she did not have

children of her own, and I think she preferred it that way. She was not the matronly sort."

Mallory was well-versed in the clinical details of Armand's childhood. A mother who died in childbirth. A father who died of tuberculosis when Armand was still crawling. Raised by an aunt who was tolerant of the child, if not particularly affectionate.

"But I had a number of governesses and tutors I cared for a great deal." He tilted his head. "Why do I feel you already know this?"

"You're the one who called me a scholar of the Saphir family," she said, then took another sip of her chocolate. "Is that why you came on the tour? Because you were curious about your family history, when talk of Le Bleu has been prohibited from this house for so long?"

"I came on the tour to meet you," he said, sounding as if he thought she should have realized this already. And perhaps she should have. He had been so insistent when he asked if she was a Fontaine—one of the famed witches of Morant.

"You could have come to the shop. Why attend a tour first? Why *pay* for it, when the house belongs to you?"

"I hoped to determine what sort of person you were before I made my business proposal." He scanned her wet hair and cloak with some amusement, making it clear that any hope he'd had for professionalism had vanished when she fell into that fountain. "A few months ago, a constable in Morant sent a letter to tell me about a local entrepreneur who had been caught breaking and entering at the mansion, conducting sensationalist tours for curious patrons."

Mallory clenched her jaw, remembering the night a police constable had noticed her lantern light in the windows of the abandoned mansion and had come in to capture the intruder. Mallory had been conducting the tour with only one client at the time—a gentleman who had made his career studying the history of the region's renowned winemaking families—and she had barely managed to sneak him out through the back door before she was caught. She was kept in a jail cell for the rest of the night before she was allowed to get word to Anaïs, who had shown up an hour later with empty pockets but maximum charm. Mallory had been released with a stern talking-to. She'd hoped that was the end of it—but clearly not.

"You could have stopped me from giving the tours at any time," she said. "Sent a cease and desist. Had me arrested."

"I could have. But when I mentioned the incident to one of our distributors in Morant, I was surprised that he knew your name. He asked if the Miss Fontaine who had been arrested for trespassing was the same who had been caught"—he hesitated—"conducting unsavory business in the house many years before."

"Witchcraft," she said darkly.

"Your reputation precedes you."

"For the record, not all the stories are true."

"No?" His lips twitched. "I would very much like to know which ones are."

Her body prickled with unexpected warmth, even though the chocolate was beginning to grow cold and the flames on the fire had died down to low-burning embers.

"I did not expect to come face-to-face with a voirloup that

night, and I certainly did not expect to witness you using your magic," Armand said, softer now, as if afraid that speaking the words too loudly would send her scurrying away. "But I am glad that I did. It confirmed all I needed to know. I understand that you are reluctant to trust people, when your occupation must arouse a fair amount of suspicion and distrust from others. But you have nothing to fear from me, Mallory Fontaine."

The way he said her name sent a shiver along her spine. Though the nightgown beneath her cloak was still damp, she was no longer cold. If anything, her skin was starting to burn.

"You don't know anything about me."

"I know that you are not afraid. Not of ghosts. Or dark magic. Or monsters."

"Are you joking? I was *terrified*."

"Yet you acted more bravely than any person I have ever met."

Her mouth ran dry, the remnants of the chocolate still coating her tongue, lying heavy in her stomach. The luscious sweetness had begun to turn bitter.

She wanted to admit that he had been every bit as brave as she was, but she didn't.

"I can't explain how I know it," said Armand, "but I know you can help me. And I feel you might be the only one who can. As though . . . as though we are already connected, somehow."

A shadow appeared on the wall behind Armand. A figure looming over the copper pots, a hand stretching toward Armand's throat. Mallory gasped, standing so suddenly her stool toppled over. She rounded on the intruder—but there was nothing there.

Though Armand scanned the shadowy corners of the kitchen, he seemed unsurprised by Mallory's sudden unease.

"Monsieur Le Bleu," he said. It was not a question.

The warmth Mallory had felt vanished at once, leaving her shivering. "Thank you for the chocolate, but I think I ought to be getting to bed. I have a lot of work to do tomorrow."

CHAPTER FOURTEEN

When Mallory awoke the next morning, Anaïs was gone and Triphine wouldn't stop scratching her neck and calves, convinced that the house had fleas.

After dressing and devouring a few pastries off the tray of morning tea that had been left at the foot of the bed—by the maid or housekeeper, she guessed, certainly not Armand—she grabbed her sketchbook and, after much contemplation, bravely invited the ghost to join her in venturing off to explore.

But Triphine barked a laugh. "Do you want me to have fleas *and* leprosy?"

Mallory wasn't sure how a house might give her leprosy, but sensing there was more going on here, she perched on the edge of the bed. In the gentlest tone she could manage, she said, "You can't stay in this room forever."

"Why not?"

Mallory considered this for a long, long moment.

Then she shrugged. "Actually, I suppose you can. All right, then. See you later."

"Wait!" Triphine crossed her arms. "It's just that . . . *he's* out there. Somewhere. And I . . . I had hoped to never have to see him again."

"What happened to giving him a piece of your mind?" Mallory asked.

Triphine pouted. "I'm working up to that."

Understanding struck Mallory, along with a vexing touch of sympathy. Triphine might have been murdered a century ago, but some wounds never fully healed. Of course she wouldn't want to risk encountering her murderer if it could be avoided.

She was tempted to point out that, as a ghost himself, Monsieur Le Bleu could as easily come into this room as anywhere else in the mansion, but she didn't think that would be useful information.

"He can't hurt you again."

"No, he can't *kill* me again. We ghosts can absolutely hurt each other."

Mallory frowned. The House Saphir was one of the few properties she knew about that was inhabited by multiple spirits. She'd never considered that ghosts could cause each other pain and harm as easily as people could, but she supposed it made sense, even if their interactions with the mortal world were limited.

"Why did you come with us," she asked, "if you were so afraid of him? Why not stay in Morant?"

Triphine looked at her, apparently confused. "I had no choice. One moment I was at home and the next I was in that carriage, among your luggage. I don't think I would mind, though, if I wasn't afraid of encountering Bastien. It was awfully lonely back in Morant."

"You know, his other wives are here. Lucienne and Béatrice. They've found a way to coexist with Le Bleu's spirit, so I'm sure you can, too."

"Have you met them? Are they . . . kind?"

"I saw them briefly at dinner last night. I shall endeavor to arrange an introduction, if you think that would help?"

Triphine tightened her grip on her shawl, a grateful smile playing at her lips. "You're a good friend, Mallory Fontaine." Then her brow twitched. "Except for all those times you've been a lousy friend. Don't think I've forgotten."

Mallory chuckled and ventured off to explore the House Saphir.

She felt like she should have already been intimately familiar with its halls and the great expanse of rooms, having studied everything from blueprints to personal accounts of dignitaries who had been invited to stay as guests generations before. But she soon discovered that descriptions of its grandeur paled in comparison to reality. Decrepit as it may be now, Mallory could easily envision what it once had been.

The second story of the home was composed mainly of guest rooms and salons for recreation. A billiards room was followed by a parlor filled with card tables and high-backed chairs. A trophy hall was lined with the heads of stags and wolves and even a grizzly bear that watched her pass by with dead black eyes. She descended to the ground floor and discovered a gallery of sitting rooms, each with a grand fireplace, an intricate painted ceiling, dark wood paneling, and elaborate wallpaper. Though morning sunlight was streaming through the east-facing windows, the rooms never exuded the bright airiness one would expect from a country manor. This was a mansion built for shadows and secrets and quiet conversations by firelight.

Mallory loved it.

She pictured herself giving tours here, recounting what gruesome tales might be resurrected from these walls. She imagined visitors following in her wake as she pointed out the desk where Lucienne wrote her scathing complaint letters to Lysraux's king over unequal usage of the royal hunting grounds. Or the sofa where Béatrice had spent whole afternoons reading the latest gossip rags. Or the solarium where Gabrielle had tended to the caged birds Saphir enjoyed having shipped in from Dostlen and Sarogi.

And here, in this salon, the sword. The *actual* sword that Le Bleu had used to kill his wives, now reduced to ornamental décor, just as Armand had said. It was exactly the sort of disturbing detail that Mallory lived for.

She moved on, discovering the music hall, a study, a—*ooh*, the library. Mallory's feet stalled as she took in the massive room that was filled with the comforting smell of leather and parchment and ink. The shelves towered up to a second level, where a narrow balcony provided access to yet more tomes, many accessible only by rolling ladders. A large desk sat in the center of the room, and a couple of damask-upholstered chairs had been placed beside the enormous arched windows. The room was warm and intimate, with whole cases of books protected behind leaded glass cases.

A painting on one wall caught Mallory's eye. She drew back— sure it was a portrait of Le Bleu, his blue eyes studying her with cruel curiosity.

But when she caught her breath, she realized her mistake.

It was not Le Bleu at all, but a much more recent portrait of Armand. Tamping down her nerves, she approached the painting, which was much too small for the ostentatious frame that surrounded it. Armand had been depicted in the gardens, framed by topiaries and the trailing branches of a weeping willow. His pose was regal and stern. Too regal and stern. It was almost difficult to see the boy who had posed for this painting as the same who had made her hot chocolate the night before. Here, he really did look like his great-great-grandfather, just as Triphine had said when he came on the tour. The comparison went beyond the arresting color of their eyes. It was the pitch-black of his hair, a little too long and too unruly to fit contemporary trends. The edges of his jaw. The full lips, almost unnaturally red—severe in this portrait, though she recalled how pleasant they were when he smiled, a smile that never expanded across his face, as if he wasn't entirely sure he was allowed to smile at all.

If it were not for his clean-shaven jaw and the distinct shape of his eyes, passed down from Triphine's lineage, it would have been nearly impossible to distinguish him from the murderer.

Murmured words drew her attention to the doorway. Mallory listened, picking up on the stern, clipped tone of the housekeeper, Yvette. And a moment later, Armand, though he was more reserved, almost hushed.

Mallory crept closer to the library door and cracked it open a few inches. She could see Yvette with her back to the door. Beyond her, Armand was bent over a writing desk, messy stacks of papers spread before him, one hand buried in his hair.

"—strangers into this house," Yvette was saying, "as though it were a museum of *oddities*."

"They are talented in petty magic," said Armand, sounding exasperated. "I have witnessed Mallory's abilities for myself. She can help us."

"Oh, *bah*. I have a cousin in Morant, and do you know what people say about them? That they are frauds. Swindlers who prey upon the gullible and desperate."

"People are always willing to vilify that which they do not understand, but I have seen what they can do. Mallory vanquished a monster right before my eyes."

"Nothing but trickery, my lord. I do not trust them."

Armand sighed, irate. "You've given your grain of salt, but you needn't concern yourself with this. I'm not afraid of looking like a fool. I'm far more afraid that Monsieur Le Bleu will murder again—and this time, the blood will be on my hands." His voice wavered. "I need help, and I do not know who else to ask." Picking up a stack of papers, he loudly thumped their edges on the desk to straighten them. "If you will excuse me, I must attend to the accounts."

Yvette let out a snort of derision. "Two more bodies on the payroll is hardly going to help with *that*." She stomped toward the library.

Mallory spun away, pretending to be inspecting a shelf of books when Yvette entered and came to a hasty stop.

"Oh, good morning!" said Mallory, practicing the startled, doe-eyed expression Anaïs excelled at.

"You were eavesdropping," she said sharply.

"Eavesdropping?" She feigned insult, pressing a hand to her

chest as Armand appeared in the doorway. "I have been doing nothing of the sort. I've merely been admiring this wonderful collection of books."

Yvette threw out a frustrated hand. "You see, my lord? She is a liar and a sneak!"

"I would rather consider her a scholar," Armand said mildly, studying the shelves in front of Mallory. "Is it engineering, agriculture, or geography that interests you most?"

Mallory scanned the book spines. *The Great Aqueducts of Otellien. The History of Sheep Herding in the Ruckgrat Mountains. How Stivale Tamed the Ocean.*

She barely refrained from gagging as she muttered, "I have varied interests."

Yvette let out a disapproving grunt, then gathered her skirts and marched in the other direction.

"Are you feeling well this morning?" Armand asked once she was gone.

"I am, thank you. The elderberry has done its job."

"I'm glad to hear it."

"Actually, I'm glad to run into you. As I concoct a plan for how best to deal with your ... problem ... I thought perhaps you could tell me more details about the hauntings."

"Of course. Why don't we go out on the terrace? My aunt always said that sunny days are not to be taken for granted."

Mallory typically avoided anything to do with being outside—sunshine and fresh air were entirely overrated—but she nodded anyway. "Lovely."

CHAPTER FIFTEEN

Mallory and Armand found Anaïs already on the terrace, having made herself quite comfortable on a cushioned settee, a parasol overhead and a book in hand. She beamed when she spotted Mallory, marking her page with a finger.

"Mally! I expected you to sleep until the afternoon." She sighed dreamily as she sank into an assortment of pillows. "Good morning, Count Armand. What a very fine terrace you have. It's positively sublime."

"Thank you," said Armand, a little stiffly—perhaps at being so informally addressed. "As you know, we've had few guests lately. I am glad to see the terrace being properly enjoyed."

"Château life suits you well." Mallory dove into the shade of a potted tree. The terrace stretched the full length of the back of the house, and led to symmetrical staircases that curved down toward the formal gardens.

Or what had once been formal gardens. Despite how unkempt

the gardens had become, the breathtaking intention was still apparent in the patchwork of lawn, the geometric borders, the tidy rows of topiaries.

"I hardly knew such luxury existed." Anaïs held her book up toward Armand. "I hope you don't mind if I borrowed a book from your library."

Mallory read the title on the fabric cover—*The Maiden and the Marquis*. Typical.

"Not at all. I hope you will make yourself quite at home while you are here," said Armand. "You and your sister have very different tastes in literature. She was fascinated by the Otellien aqueducts earlier."

Anaïs laughed. "Usually you can't interest her in anything other than dark fairy tales. Well, and the occasional gothic romance."

Armand's eyebrows rose. "Romance?"

"Oh yes," Anaïs went on. "Haunted châteaus, dark forests, a handsome lord with a secret . . ."

Armand glanced at Mallory, intrigued and . . . blushing?

"Not to mention the angst and the pining. She'll never admit it, but my sister is a romantic."

"She's lying," Mallory deadpanned. "I would sooner impale a handsome lord on my dagger than kiss one."

Lips twitching, Armand looked away. "I will keep that in mind."

Mallory's insides twisted. Why had she mentioned *kissing*?

She shot a glare at her sister, who ducked back behind her book.

A giggle drew their attention to the corner of the terrace, where the maid—Julie—was polishing a stout marble statue of a goat-horned satyr that stood at the edge of a raised garden bed.

"I certainly don't feel that way," she said idly. "I'm rather fond of handsome lords myself."

She cast a look at Armand that was part suggestive and part embarrassed, before hastily returning to her work.

Armand's expression was nothing short of horrified as he choked back a cough.

"I did mean to ask, my lord," the maid went on, "that these were the sculptures you wanted polished?"

"Er—yes, I think so. Thank you, Julie. Would you let Claude know you're finished? We are having them relocated."

"Of course."

"By the way, Lord Armand," said Anaïs, "I took the liberty of doing a fortune reading for you." She set her book aside and waved her hand at the stack of Wyrdith cards on a small table. The cards that had once belonged to their mother.

"Fortune reading?" asked Armand.

"I hope you don't mind. Whereas my sister is skilled at communing with the dead, my talents lend themselves more to divination. And I must say, this reading was *very* illuminating." Anaïs flipped over the top three cards, fanning them out. Mallory knew immediately these had not been selected by chance—and certainly not by magic. Anaïs had chosen these three specifically. The Forked Road. The Witch. The Lover's Moon. "It would seem you are being pulled in two different directions," Anaïs went on, summoning her dreamy fortune-telling voice. "But there is a new magical presence in your life, one that might lead to . . . *romance*."

Armand's posture went rigid.

While Julie, leaning against the statue in an attempt to better see the cards . . . accidentally pushed it off the pedestal.

The statue crashed to the terrace. A cloven hoof broke off in shards.

Julie jumped away, pressing the polishing cloth to her mouth. "Oh! I . . . I'm so sorry!"

Armand shut his eyes. "It's all right, Julie. Just . . . work on the others. Please."

Biting her lip in mortification, Julie stepped over the fallen statue and scurried to the next pedestal.

Armand forced a smile at Anaïs. "Thank you, but I am really far more concerned with the ghost of my ancestor than I am with, er . . . romance."

"Suit yourself," said Anaïs, shuffling the three cards back into the deck. "But I am available if you would like further guidance."

Biting back her mortification, Mallory pulled out her sketchbook. "Should we get to work?"

"Yes, *please*." Armand grabbed a small iron table and dragged it into the tree's shade, followed by two chairs. "I am yours to command. Whatever I can do to assist you, I will."

"My first order of business is to determine what sort of spirits we are dealing with." Mallory found her charcoal pencil and selected a blank page in her sketchbook.

"A murderous count," said Armand.

"Right. Got that. But there are different . . . identifications of ghosts. Apparitions, phantoms, poltergeists, revenants . . . and each one requires a different tack when it comes to their exorcism."

Mallory could sense both her sister and the maid listening, but she kept her attention on Armand, searching for any hint that he suspected she was entirely making this up. Mallory had spent nearly half her life with the ability to see and communicate with ghosts, and had educated herself on a compendium of magical beasts and creatures besides. As far as she knew, a ghost was a ghost was a ghost.

But Armand believed her to be an expert, and she had to impress upon him that exorcising the spirits from this house would be no easy task if she and Anaïs were to enjoy his hospitality for as long as possible.

"I suggest we begin with the wives. What can you tell me about Lucienne?"

Armand ran the tip of his pinkie finger across his lower lip as he considered, then began to recount his own experiences, since childhood. A figure in a large ball gown occasionally seen drifting through the halls. Countless tales of bottles of wine being moved, or half-full glasses suddenly empty. A boisterous giggle and the clinking of goblets, as if she were always in the midst of a lavish party.

Unlike Béatrice, who was shy and quiet, moving like a whisper through the house. Armand had only caught a glimpse of her once, when he walked into the music room and saw a girl in a gray dress slink off in the other direction. He had heard her plenty of times, though. She had a passion for the pianoforte in life, and her somber melodies could often still be heard drifting through the corridors.

Mallory pretended to be taking notes, but while he spoke, she found herself distracted by the line of his jaw. The swoop of a defiant lock of hair. The elegant fingers that tapped out a pattern on the table whenever he stopped to think.

Julie had stopped polishing. The maid was craning her neck

to try to see the sketchbook, but as soon as Mallory caught her snooping, she turned away and rubbed harder at the statue.

"Does that help at all?" asked Armand.

Startled, Mallory looked up from the portrait she'd idly started to draw of Armand, half-finished. "Yes, that's very helpful. And . . . Monsieur Le Bleu?"

His expression darkened. "As I said before, his presence has only been felt here these past seven years, and it has brought about a horrible change in the mood of the house. He is . . ." He swallowed. "He is cruel. Not to me, necessarily. But the way he taunts people. Makes them see things. Dark things. Corpses hanging from the ceiling. Heads removed from their bodies. Linens soaked in blood . . ." He grimaced. "I am sorry. This is not pleasant to talk about."

"We are not delicate maidens who swoon at the mention of bloodshed."

"No," said Armand. "I know that. I apologize. I don't think I've ever met a lady quite like you before." He glanced at Anaïs, before amending. "Ladies like you, I should say."

"Oh, I don't enjoy the discussion of bloodshed half as much as my sister," said Anaïs, turning the page of her book.

Mallory added a final touch to her sketch—thickening the line of lashes around Armand's eyes. Only when she'd finished did she realize he was watching her again.

She cleared her throat. "I have many ideas for how we might go about removing these unwanted spirits from the estate."

"To be clear," said Armand, "I do not mind the wives. I do sometimes wonder if they would prefer to move on and be at peace in Verloren, but I see this as their home as much as mine.

It is only Le Bleu that absolutely must be dealt with. Le Bleu . . . and the monsters."

"Monsters. Such as the lutin?"

"Yes. Well, we gave the lutin some cheese and transferred it to the pantry, and it seems content for the time being. But we are constantly dealing with some new, strange creature, and they are not all as amiable." He gestured toward the forest. "We had a cheval mallet that was tormenting travelers on the road behind our forest for weeks."

"Really?" Mallory brightened. "Can I see it?"

He looked at her like she'd just asked for a tour of the necessaries. "Er . . . no," he said. "It moved on, thankfully."

Mallory sat back, disappointed.

He massaged his temple. "I hired a trapper a while back to help get the monsters under control, but they keep coming back. Thank Eostrig, most of the beasts are more annoying than harmful, but still—do you have any idea how mortifying it is to invite a wine merchant to visit the vineyards, only to hear that he turned around and left because some demonic horse would not let him pass? Or for half the season's grape harvest to rot on the vine because the farmhands are afraid that a fox-matagot is going to bring misfortune on their families? Sometimes I wonder if I should move to the city and be done with it all."

"Why don't you?" Anaïs said, lowering her book.

Mallory wanted to throw the pencil at her. If Armand decided to abandon the house, he'd have no need of two fake witches at all.

But Armand shook his head. "It is not so simple. Our business is tied to this land."

"The grape varietal only grows here," said Mallory. "To make the Ruby Comorre your family is known for."

He nodded. "To abandon this estate would be the end of our heritage. My family has worked this land for generations—long before Le Bleu tarnished our name."

"Winemaking must be quite a passion," said Anaïs.

In response, Armand bellowed a dry laugh. "Gods, no. I hate it. I don't even like Ruby Comorre. It's so sweet, and that syrupy aftertaste? I can't understand what the fuss is about. But . . . but I do not wish to be the Saphir who ruins everything, after all these years."

"Your great-great-grandfather is the one ruining everything," said Anaïs.

"Even so," said Armand, "this estate is my responsibility. I know we keep a meager house staff, but we have many more employees in the vineyards and winery. Dozens of people are relying on me to maintain the family business. And the income that is brought into the town of Comorre itself because of our exports . . . it's quite significant." He hesitated before adding, "I also feel some remorse for Lucienne and Béatrice. They deserve nothing of their fate. I would not abandon them here, with him."

Mallory's pencil hovered over the curve of Armand's upper lip. She had not considered how the return of Le Bleu seven years before might have affected the two wives who had died here and haunted the place in relative peace for nearly a hundred years.

"Oh, *my*. You are . . . most talented, Miss Fontaine."

Mallory slammed her sketchbook shut and glared over her shoulder. Julie shrank away—even as her expression took on a fierce protectiveness.

With a noncommittal huff, the maid started for the edges of the terrace, dusting every surface within reach.

"Is everything all right?" Armand asked.

"Fine," Mallory snapped, wishing she wasn't embarrassed at having been caught sketching the count's features. But it wasn't her fault that he was uncannily handsome. Any artist would have found him irresistible.

To draw. Irresistible to *draw*.

Armand's voice went quiet. "Julie is fairly new here, and she is . . ." He trailed off, embarrassed.

Mallory could imagine how easy it would be for a young lady to become infatuated with the lord of a great country estate. It surprised her that Julie would be so forward about it, but as Armand seemed incapable of drawing boundaries between himself and the staff, she supposed it wasn't that astonishing.

"It is truly none of our business," Mallory said firmly.

This only seemed to make Armand more uncomfortable, but then he fixed his gaze on her and asked, "What do you plan to do?"

The question, so earnest and direct, caught her off guard.

"Yes, Mally," said Anaïs, using a finger to hold her place in the book while she stood up to stretch. "What do we plan to do?"

"Well," Mallory began, feigning confidence, "as I said last night, there are numerous methods available to us. We shall begin with the simplest and work our way into the more complex spell work."

"What is the simplest method?" asked Armand.

Mallory searched the depths of her imagination. "That is . . . to be determined," she finally concluded. "I would like a chance to walk the grounds and . . . perhaps communicate with the spirits firsthand, before I decide on the best course of action."

"Yes. I'll gladly accompany you—"

"No! No, thank you. I need space. To think. And to talk with them. The ghosts, that is. To . . . sense. Things."

"Sense things?" asked Armand.

"Spirity things."

Anaïs smirked. "My sister is a genuine authority on the subject of spirity things." She winked at Armand. "You are in good hands with the Fontaine sisters."

Armand nodded slowly, and only the smallest pinch in his brow suggested he was a bit skeptical.

Mallory peered around the terrace. "It's a shame you don't have any land here that has been dedicated to the Seven. Hallowed spaces tend to be best for conducting séances and exorcisms."

"Like a chapel?" asked Armand.

"Precisely. A chapel or an altar or—"

"We have a chapel."

She froze, her mouth open with an unfinished thought. She'd never heard of a chapel on the Saphir estate.

"My aunt had it built and consecrated by an acolyte of Freydon," he added, "perhaps thirty years ago."

"Of course she did. We will certainly make good use of that information."

"Fantastic," said Armand, beaming at having been useful. "Then I shall leave it in your capable hands."

CHAPTER SIXTEEN

"You should tell him that we can't do anything until the Mourning Moon," Anaïs said, who had read through six novels in as many days—each one involving a combination of pirates, rogues, and nobility, and sometimes all three in one. "Or better yet, the winter solstice. You could buy us months without him being any the wiser."

"It might come to that," Mallory said, fingers skimming along the tops of the book spines on an upper shelf in the library.

"What are you looking for, anyway?"

"I'm not sure. A manual on how to exorcise spirits for the magically uninitiated?"

"If he had that book in his possession, one would think he'd have already tried it."

"I don't need a book on how to exorcise spirits," said Mallory. "I need something that makes us appear . . . knowledgeable. That suggests we are trying."

The frustrating thing was that Mallory and Anaïs *were* knowledgeable. Magic or no magic, they were still their mother's daughters, and had grown up surrounded by charms, potions, and spell books. As a child, Mallory had loved the lyrical quality of the spells written out in various grimoires. She had been especially fascinated by those in the old language, the way the unfamiliar syllables danced on her tongue. She'd memorized so many of them in her youth. A talent that was utterly useless to her now.

She wondered what their mother would have done, if hired by Lord Saphir. Which spell would she have used? There must have been some ritual to lure, to bind, to banish . . . but Mallory certainly didn't know what it was.

At least the situation didn't seem as dire as Armand had first made it out to be. She'd barely seen evidence of the ghosts that haunted the mansion since that first night at dinner. A maudlin piano tune played in the middle of the night. Footsteps on the stairs. Whistling down the corridors. The painted eyes of gloomy portraits watching as she moved through the halls. Rooms that never warmed, despite roaring fires in the hearths. Candle flames that were snuffed out with no hint of a breeze. Pages mysteriously turned when she left her sketchbook sitting out . . . though that could have been Triphine, who was still holed up in the bedroom and liked to look at the pictures.

It seemed to be a fairly mild haunting, but given what Mallory knew of Le Bleu, she wondered if maybe he was biding his time. Waiting for something . . .

But what?

"Oh, *look*," said Anaïs. She had discovered a world atlas and had it open to a double-page spread detailing some of the most populous cities in Stivale. Anaïs traced her finger along a hard-painted scene of Caprietti, a city of floating buildings, green canals, small boats, and arched stone bridges. One drawing showed half a dozen party-goers dressed in flamboyant gowns and bejeweled masks, prepared for one of Stivale's famed masquerades. Anaïs sighed longingly.

With renewed determination, Mallory refocused on the bookshelves. She reminded herself that she didn't actually have to rid the house of the ghost—she only had to play to Armand's sense of goodwill. He was a count. He had money to spare. As long as he believed that she and her sister had done all they possibly could, she would doubtless be able to talk him into rewarding them for their efforts.

Once that money was in her pocket, she would take Anaïs anywhere in the world she wished to go. Mallory would give her sister elaborate gowns and take her to sparkling festivals and watch her dance with masked men beneath star-studded skies. The entire world would be theirs, along with a freedom they'd hardly dared to dream about.

Mallory's fingers paused on the spine of *Herbal Remedies for Common and Not-So-Common Household Ailments*. She pulled the book out and flipped to the table of contents. She scanned the page, stopping at chapter nine: "Aromatics for the Cleansing of Bad Fortune and Unclean Energy."

"Close enough," she said, slamming the book shut.

WHEN MALLORY ASKED YVETTE WHERE SHE MIGHT BE
able to find pennyroyal, viper's bugloss, and madderwort, she was

given a suspicious scowl before being directed to check the kitchen gardens. Failing that, she might try the conservatory, where there was a fine collection of herbs and plants, and—if that should still not yield anything—there was an apothecary in the town of Comorre, six miles to the south.

"The conservatory?" Mallory had asked, unable to keep the intrigue from her voice. "The same one where Béatrice was murdered?"

Yvette had let out a scandalized groan and stomped away.

Hoping she would not have to go into town, Mallory hitched her drawing satchel onto her shoulder and set off for the potager. When she arrived, she quickly discovered that she preferred it to the formal gardens off the terraces. There might be fewer flowers, but the plants here were abundant with late-season produce—turnips and onions, squashes and beets, cabbages and lettuces of every variety.

Thankfully the plants were labeled with slate plaques, otherwise she wouldn't have known what many of them were. She paced along the path, reading the unfamiliar names aloud. *Gooseneck squash. Snake gourd. Saltbush. Skirret.*

She walked around the garden three times before she was certain that what she needed was not there.

She headed for the conservatory next—a palatial structure of glass walls and decorative iron. As she opened the doors, she was greeted by a wall of warm, humid air, at striking contrast to the autumn chill outside. Knowing that one of the wives had been killed here, Mallory had expected the greenhouse to be dismal and unkempt, as neglected as the rest of the gardens. Instead, she found it flourishing with plant life in every corner. Wooden tables and benches overflowed with countless flowers and exotic greenery tucked into an assortment of clay pots. Fuzzy stems, prickly leaves, flowers with voluptuous petals, and others that had strange needlelike teeth, plants with purple berries and vines with jagged thorns, shrubs with bulbous black-tinted fruit and blooms redolent with the scents of licorice or vanilla or pepper or pine. The aromas clogged her lungs as she wound through the jungle of growth, searching for the neatly written labels like those in the potager, but here there was nothing. Every pot, every plant, was a mystery.

An even bigger mystery was the boy spritzing a feathery vine in a suspended planter with water from a small glass perfume bottle.

"Armand?"

Startled, he shoved back a lock of hair from his face, leaving a smudge of dirt high on his cheek. It was not possible that he was more surprised than she was, because he was dressed like one of the vineyard farmhands in simple trousers and a loose linen shirt that gaped indecently at the throat. A belt at his waist held his ring of iron keys.

"Mallory," he said, setting down the perfume bottle. "Hello."

"What are you doing?"

He glanced around, almost guiltily, but also apparently confused as to what he ought to be guilty about. "Tending to the plants. Were you looking for me?"

"No. I was . . ." But she couldn't remember what she'd come for. Her brain was too wrapped up in seeing the heir to the Saphir estate wearing the clothes of a common peasant. Clothes that revealed the hollow between his clavicle bones. The golden skin at the top of his chest. "What do you mean you're tending to the plants? Don't you have servants for that?"

"We used to," he said, wiping his hands on his pants, leaving filthy smears behind. The table in front of him was littered with dark soil and an assortment of clay pots—some sporting baby plants, others empty and waiting. A tray of seedlings rested beside it, along with a collection of knives and scissors and small shovels. "But I prefer to do it myself."

She gaped at him. "You're a *gardener*."

He chuckled awkwardly. "Hardly. I assist in the formal gardens from time to time—we have only two gardeners, who come but once a week. It's far too much for them to handle alone. But these are mostly medicinal plants, some from Lysraux, but many more from around the world. It's . . . fascinating. To learn what parts of a plant can do to help us, or heal us."

"Or hurt us," she added.

He smirked. "Ever the contrarian. But yes, a fair number of poisons could be made from these plants, too." He shrugged. "Sometimes I wonder if I might have trained as an apothecary, if I didn't have to run a wine empire." He picked up a watering can and gave a drink to the newly filled pots.

Mallory found herself inspecting the lush landscape of foliage with new appreciation. She could not name any of these plants, and doubted she had seen half of them before in her life. One vine in particular caught her attention, for along its length blossomed a series of unusual flowers. Long, amethyst-colored petals curved like a pinwheel in one direction, while at their center, a second layer of speckled blue-and-white petals twisted the opposite way. It was beautiful, but almost made her dizzy to look at.

"Do you know what all of these are?" she asked.

"I do," he said, without pride. "That is a pinwheel crown. Most of the plants in here I keep for practical uses—medicines, tinctures, and so on. But that one . . ." He smiled a bit whimsically. "I just always thought it was pretty."

He quickly looked away.

"Perhaps you can help me." Mallory walked to the opposite side of the long table, tenderly brushing her finger along a wide leaf that appeared to be as soft as peach fuzz—and was. Her hand strayed curiously to its neighbor.

"Don't touch that one."

She retracted her fingers.

"That's impweed. Its sap is extremely toxic. To get any on your skin can cause blisters and a stinging sensation that lasts for days. I touched it by accident once. It made for a terrible week."

"Why do you have it?"

"It flowers in the spring, and the nectar it produces is used to treat seizures, among other things."

Mallory grinned, awed by this information.

Sensing her interest, Armand went on, "I have some books in the library you might like. One on carnivorous plants, too."

"Carnivorous?"

"Yes. I have one here." He picked up a shallow bowl, where a gangly plant was steeped in wet soil. Its serpentlike heads each had little mouths with needlelike teeth, open wide. Except for the one that was closed, and when Armand held it closer, she could see the wings of a moth sticking out.

"Is that plant *eating* an insect?"

"In a manner of speaking," he said, setting the bowl down. "You said you needed help?"

"Oh. Oh, right." Mallory racked her brain, trying to recall the herbs she'd seen listed in the book, wishing she had written them down. She slowly ticked them off on her fingers. "I'm in need of juniper, baby's breath, viper's bugloss. Um." She squeezed her eyes shut. "Something-wort. Maidenwort?"

"Never heard of maidenwort," said Armand. "Milkwort maybe? Or madwort?"

"Madwort." She snapped her fingers. "That sounds right. And there was one more. Pennyroyal, I think."

"That's quite a list." He started working again, filling a pot with soil from a barrel beneath the table, then tenderly transplanting one of the tiny seedlings into it. He handled each one like it was a precious thing, even though the seedlings themselves were rather ugly little plants—droopy and spiny with an unhealthy gray pallor. Moving on to the next seedling, he asked, "What are you planning to do?"

"I told you we'd begin our exorcism with the simplest method. This is it."

He considered this, and Mallory was surprised that she recognized the expression he made when he was thinking through new information. The tiny line that formed between his eyebrows. The dirt-encrusted fingernail mindlessly tracing the shape of his lips. "Is this a common spell?"

"It doesn't get much more common than this."

He regarded her uncertainly as he watered the new plants, then brushed the dirt from his hands.

"If you're sure. It's only . . . Pennyroyal is dangerous. When distilled to an oil, it can cause fatal organ failure."

Mallory digested this information. "Which is why I'll be burning it."

"Ah." His expression relaxed. "I've never heard of any dangers from pennyroyal smoke. So . . . yes, I have what you need."

It took a few minutes for Armand to collect the specimens she requested, and he even helped her tie them into neat bundles, his hands plucking away dead leaves as Mallory knotted the twine.

"What exactly is this supposed to do?" he asked, tidying up the stray bits of stems and leaves that littered the worktable. Mallory could not help being impressed, as he had run down the list of ingredients that she needed, not only knowing precisely where to find each plant within the labyrinth of the conservatory, but also having an encyclopedic knowledge that rivaled her own expertise in murder and mayhem. Which parts of the plant could be eaten, which were poisonous, and which were poisonous but could be eaten if prepared to precise (and in Mallory's opinion, not-worth-the-risk) specifications.

"The smoke should create a pathway for the spirits to follow into Verloren, and they will find the aroma too alluring to resist its call."

He laughed.

When she didn't even crack a smile, his laughter abruptly cut off. "Really?"

She tapped the bundles against the table, feeling like it was silly to even pretend such a thing could be the undoing of a spirit like Monsieur Le Bleu.

Mallory had made her living off of pretending silly things, and she wasn't about to stop now.

"It is only the first step. If it proves to be ineffective, I have many more tricks up my sleeve."

CHAPTER SEVENTEEN

Mallory lit the first bundle of herbs as soon as she stepped out of the greenhouse, and spent nearly twenty minutes spreading their smoke around the edges of the formal gardens before approaching the house itself. She entered the main vestibule, trying not to feel ridiculous as she encouraged the smoke to waft over the fine furnishings and behind the heavy drapes, into the chimneys and beneath the tables. Despite the book's assurances that this method would cleanse the home of bad fortune and unclean energy, she was quite certain the spirits of the House Saphir would not be deterred. The only people who were likely to be affected by the aromatic smoke were those who were very much alive and found themselves wiping their eyes and coughing. She powered through more than one coughing fit herself.

But Mallory had a job to fake, and she was not a quitter.

She went slowly, winding her way through parlors and galleries, leaving a trail of ashes wherever she went. Each bundle burned slowly, as if the herbs knew they had a lot of space to cover.

After completing the first floor, she moved on to the games and billiards rooms on the second, the bedrooms and suites on the third. It took her a while to discover the stairwell that led up to the northern tower—the highest point of the château—and the smoke must have been getting to her, because her head pounded with every step she took up the spiraling limestone staircase, her satchel, heavy with her drawing portfolio banging against her hip.

At the top of the steps, a short ladder finished the journey through a trapdoor cut into the floor of the tower's uppermost room. Mallory was sweating as she kicked the trapdoor shut so she wouldn't accidentally fall through it.

She paused, swishing the herbs in front of her—though the smoke was almost immediately blown out through the room's arched openings. Unlike most of the château, with its centuries of luxury displayed in marble statues, carved pediments, and frescoes, this room was . . . simple. Rustic. Unfinished.

Mallory couldn't tell what the purpose of the tower was. Perhaps a watchtower to protect against invading armies. Or maybe there had been an expectation of converting the space into a falconry or dovecote.

Whatever the plan had been, the tower now felt like a forgotten space. A floor of dusty clay tiles. Cracked and broken plaster between the beams of the domed ceiling. In some distant past, vines and birds had decorated the wooden trim, but open air had faded the paint to a hint of what it had been. With no glass in the arched openings, bird droppings coated the banisters, while the dried-mud remnants of barn swallow nests hung among the rafters. The only furniture was a small iron table and a few wooden chairs, gray and worn from being exposed to the elements.

As Mallory stood there, a swallow landed on one of the rails, its blue-pointed wings folded back and its copper-red face tilted suspiciously as it eyed the intruder in its midst.

Mallory approached the banister. The bird cocked its head to one side, then—after a hesitation—spread its wings and flapped up to a nest above Mallory's head. A little gray cocoon crafted of mud and straw.

A light caught Mallory's attention. She blinked, startled at the sight of a tiny glowing ball, no larger than a galet coin, floating among the rafters. Mallory's lips parted as the sparkling sphere bobbed closer to her.

As she stared, mesmerized, a second appeared, then a third, emerging from the shadows of the tower's ceiling and floating leisurely toward Mallory. They surrounded her like curious cats. She held her breath as they brushed through her hair, skimmed down her arms. Mallory lifted a palm, and one of the balls of light hovered above her hand, shimmering in shades of yellow and green.

"Feu follet," Mallory murmured, hardly able to believe the words from her own mouth. These creatures were said to inhabit the deepest forests of Lysraux. She'd never believed she would encounter them herself.

As soon as she'd spoken, the feu follet danced away from her hand, drifting toward the stone rail that surrounded the tower. Mallory's feet followed of their own accord, her hand reaching out, drawn to the creature's gentle, pulsating light. There was something about their soft presence that filled Mallory, coursed through her veins, warmed her soul. She felt light. Unburdened by the pressures of paying the rent, providing for her and her sister, searching for an escape from the misfortunes that had plagued their lives. She had no responsibilities. She had no worries.

Her heartbeat slowed. Her breaths deepened.

The feu follet bobbed over the rail, continuing beyond the edge of the tower.

Mallory's thigh hit the protective balustrade as she reached for the creature, wishing to grasp it and pull it back to her. But it was barely out of reach. She stretched forward, yearning to keep it close.

The barn swallow dove at her head with a screech, tiny talons scratching her scalp.

Mallory gasped. Her center of balance shifted. The world came into focus. Her attention dropped from the feu follet, down to the gardens below.

The air left her lungs.

The gardens were so very, *very* far below.

With a shriek, Mallory stumbled back to the center of the tower.

The light of the feux follets dimmed, as if with disappointment. Then together they flickered and twirled out of the tower, disappearing beyond a distant gable.

The calm that Mallory had felt vanished as if it had never been there at all—replaced with barely tempered panic. She pressed her back to a wooden column and struggled to take in breaths. She sank down to the floor, grasping for the soothing comfort of stable ground. Her head spun. Her stomach felt hollow, as though the sensation of falling had really happened, and not been entirely in her mind.

"Feux follets," she said through a groan. "Pretty little things . . . until they try to kill you." She buried her face in both hands, feeling utterly foolish for falling prey to such a well-known tactic. She knew that feux follets were as dangerous as any monster, but she had underestimated their powers of enchantment. She had been taken in far too easily.

She squeezed her eyes shut and knocked her knuckles against her skull. "Do not trust pretty things. You know better."

Her thoughts raced back to the night she'd met Armand at the House Saphir in Morant. When he had wrapped his arm around her as he hauled her out the window. She knew, logically, that he had been trying to rescue her, but every fiber of her body had rebelled at the idea of leaving the safety of the house and letting herself fall.

Do not trust pretty things.

Only when the room had stopped spinning and Mallory's breaths had grown even again did she open her eyes.

The barn swallow was perched on the rail, cleaning its feathers, ignoring her.

Mallory pulled herself back to her feet. One hand pressed against the pillar as she peered over the Saphir estate. The feux follets were long gone, but the view remained. And it *was* glorious, even if her aversion to high places kept her from fully enjoying it. The distant forest with its wash of gold and red leaves. The perfect symmetry of the gardens. The vineyards in their neat, endless rows. The rolling hills on the horizon. And—there, far in the distance, a haze of blue.

The ocean.

The air left her in a startled breath. Mallory had never seen the ocean before.

She grabbed her satchel and pulled out her sketchbook. She pushed one of the weathered chairs to the center of the tower, giving herself enough distance from the ledge that her pulse wouldn't become erratic or her mind dizzy.

She started to draw.

Lost in a fount of inspiration, she did not know how long she'd been sitting there, trying to transfer the exalted beauty of the world before her onto the pages of her portfolio, when a feminine voice intruded on her privacy.

"She's rather good, isn't she?"

Mallory's fingers unwittingly snapped her charcoal pencil.

Lucienne and Béatrice were watching her.

CHAPTER EIGHTEEN

"Béatrice!" Lucienne scolded. "You frightened her!"

"I didn't mean to," Béatrice said meekly.

"She must be ghost-sensitive," said Lucienne. "You know how some people are."

Mallory tucked the broken pencil back into her satchel. The interruption made her realize that she'd been bent over her book for so long, her upper back had become cranky and stiff, and she used the excuse of rolling out her neck to steal another glance at her company.

Lucienne was swirling a glass of honey-colored wine while Béatrice perused a month-old edition of the *Royal Gazette*. Unable to hold up the publication for long, she had it laid out on a dusty table, using her corporeal energy to occasionally flip to the next page.

"What is that putrid odor?" asked Lucienne, waving her free hand in front of her face. "The house smells like a funeral parlor today."

"I believe it's from those herbs she was burning," said Béatrice, in a wisp of a voice. Not looking up from the paper, she added, "I do believe she may be trying to get rid of us."

"With some foul-smelling foliage?"

"It's familiar, isn't it? Like the exorcism spell Gabrielle used to cleanse the house."

Lucienne let out a bellow of a laugh. "Perhaps we'd be more inclined to follow the smoke into Verloren if it didn't smell like horse dung."

Mallory bit her lip, hard, and found a blank page in her sketchbook.

Lucienne and Béatrice stared at her. It was hard to resist the urge to stare back.

Losing interest in Mallory, Béatrice turned another page of her periodical. "It sounds like the Harvest Ball was well attended this year, but the duck liver foie gras was disappointingly bland. And *oh*, listen to this. Prince Torben and Princess Bernadette called off their engagement." She clicked her tongue. "Is that the second or third betrothal he's backed out of?"

Lucienne swirled her glass. "I don't know how you keep any of these royal families straight anymore."

"They're saying that without that alliance, Tulvask may be on the verge of civil war." Béatrice turned another page and made a face. "Oh, dear. Madame Couturière claims that metal codpieces were quite popular at the hunting festivals in Mara this year. I would think that is a trend we could do without."

"So . . ." Lucienne said, still eyeing Mallory. "She is a witch? Or is not a witch?"

"Madame Couturière?"

"No, *her*. Armand's guest. I'm fairly certain she's a fake. Or at the least, she is pathetically incompetent."

Indignant heat shot up the back of Mallory's neck as she sketched the scene before her. The vaulted tower ceiling. Two figures framed beneath an arched opening, haloed by the gloaming light.

"If she *is* a witch," said Béatrice, "perhaps she could help us?"

"Gabrielle was a witch," said Lucienne, "and she couldn't help us. Just up and ran away the first chance she got."

Mallory sketched out Lucienne's exquisite ball gown, the apples of her cheeks, the bloodied hole in the bodice of her gown where Bastien had stabbed her.

Béatrice's features were more youthful—big eyes and hair that trailed limply around her shoulders, the words that Bastien had carved into her forearms vivid red on her porcelain skin.

"I think we should try to get rid of her," said Lucienne. "Just in case. You could start haunting the mirrors. A bloody reflection always spooks them."

Béatrice pouted. "It's so *cold* in the mirrors."

"It wouldn't take long. You saw how those feux follets got to her. She isn't as tough as she's pretending to be."

The tip of Mallory's pencil snapped off. Scowling, she pulled out yet another.

"All right," Lucienne continued. "How about this? You take the mirrors, and I'll sneak into her room in the middle of the night. No one likes waking up to a spirit over their bed."

Béatrice sulked. "Can't I be the one to hover over the bed this time?"

"You're not scary enough."

"I can be scary."

Lucienne scoffed.

"I *can*. But I don't see why we have to frighten her at all. What is she going to do?"

"She's been hired to get rid of us."

"Perhaps, but she isn't likely to succeed, is she?"

Mallory stood suddenly, crossed the tower room, and dropped her sketchpad onto the floor between the wives—open to the sketch of two women chatting to each other. She had done quite a fine job, if she did say so herself, perfectly capturing Béatrice's anxious sulking and Lucienne's nonchalant slouch. But that was not what would have drawn the attention of most people. Most would immediately have noticed the swaths of black blood drenching their fronts.

The wives stared down at the drawing for a long, long moment.

When they finally looked up, Mallory said, "Hello. My name is Mallory Fontaine, and I'm not to be trifled with."

After another long silence, Lucienne's confused expression broke into a wide grin. "Ooh, that was very menacing. I like her better now." She took a giddy swig of her wine.

Mallory scowled. "I can hear you."

Lucienne's eyes widened. "You *can*?" She leaned toward Béatrice and loudly whispered, "You know, she may be a witch after all."

Béatrice jumped out of her seat and ducked behind Lucienne. "She *can* see us! I had wondered before. Oh, dear."

Mallory pulled a face. "Why are you hiding?"

"Yes," said Lucienne. "Why?"

After a moment, Béatrice poked her head over Lucienne's shoulder, peering shyly up at Mallory. "I don't entirely know. It's just . . . it's been quite a long time since I had to meet anyone new."

"Was it my imagination," said Lucienne, "or did we not see another ghost with you when you first arrived?"

"That's Triphine. Duchess Triphine Maeng."

They both gasped.

"The first wife!" said Lucienne. "You don't say! Wherever has she gone off to? Why hasn't she introduced herself?"

"She's . . ." *Frail. Reclusive. Dyspeptic.* "Shy. Like you, it's been some time since she's met new people, and I don't know that she's ever met any other ghosts. This has been a difficult transition for her. But if you were to introduce yourselves, I think that would be well received."

"Is she kind?" asked Béatrice.

"Is she fun?" Lucienne added.

"Triphine? She's the *greatest*." And, Mallory thought, it would be especially great for her to have someone else to cling to for a while. "You'll adore her."

"How nice," said Béatrice. "We can put together a welcome package."

Mallory sat down on the dusty floor, ignoring the white splotches of bird excrement. "While we're on the topic of . . . well, *you*, there are some things I'd like to discuss."

CHAPTER NINETEEN

Lucienne and Béatrice were laughing. They were laughing so hard that Lucienne had spilled her wine and Béatrice was pressing the folded gazette to the hole in her chest in an effort to stanch the gush of blood that came out with every guffaw.

Mallory was not laughing.

"Go ahead," she muttered, though they weren't listening to her. "Get it out, so we can talk about this like *adults*."

They laughed harder, tears glinting at the corners of their eyes.

Mallory picked up her sketchbook and slammed it shut, shoving it into her portfolio.

Wheezing, Lucienne reached over and grasped Béatrice's forearm. "Just go to Verloren, she says! Just . . . cross the . . . the bridge!" She devolved into another burst of cackles.

Béatrice pressed a hand to her face. "Why didn't we think of that, Lucy? What do you say? Would you care to join me in the afterlife?"

"Why, yes! What an idea! Off we go now!"

They bent their heads together, giggling and gasping for breath until finally—*finally*—their chuckles subsided.

Mallory cleared her throat. "Now that we've gotten through that—"

Lucienne snorted. Squeaked. Took a drink and coughed. "Yes, yes, do go on."

Sighing, Mallory scooted closer. "I am being paid to remove the spirits from this property, and it would be *most helpful* if you would decide to . . ." She splayed her fingers. "Leave. Hilarious as that may seem."

While Lucienne burst into another fit of giggles, Béatrice brushed away her tears. "It is hilarious because what you ask is impossible."

"It is not impossible. I have met dozens of spirits in my life, and seen many of them cross the bridge into the land of the lost. You only need to make the decision and call on the grace of Velos and—"

"You are mortal," Béatrice said, her soft voice returning. "You are alive, Miss Fontaine. You do not know of what you speak."

"I know that with some willpower and courage, you can—"

"We cannot," said Béatrice, almost firmly. But then she shrank back and chewed her lower lip for a moment, as if ashamed of her outburst. "Do you truly believe that Lucy and I have never wished to quit the entrapment of our afterlife? To leave this house—a house that was never a home? The house where we both were killed, most brutally, by the man who had vowed to care for us, to protect us? Do you not believe we'd like to forget that heinous betrayal and spend an eternity instead in a land of beauty and peace?"

Lucienne gaped at her friend. "Goodness, Béatrice. I don't think I've ever heard you speak so eloquently on any topic beyond the lurid love lives of the ruling classes."

Béatrice looked down, fidgeting.

"Actually, now you mention it," Lucienne continued, "I'm not sure they have wine in Verloren, so I really don't want to go until I know for certain. Either way, it hardly matters. Velos has summoned us. They have been summoning us for nearly a hundred years. But we cannot go, no matter what we do."

"What do you mean?" asked Mallory. "Have you tried?"

Lucienne sipped from yet another goblet of wine—Mallory had no idea where she had procured it from. "What's the use? Thanks to Bastien, we are in limbo. Trapped until . . . until his dark magic is complete."

Mallory frowned. "Dark magic?"

Lucienne released a heavy groan. "Bastien was not just a murderer. He did not kill merely for sport. He was a very powerful sorcerer, and he was trying to accomplish, well, something."

"And that something is . . . ?"

Béatrice shrugged, her whole body shrinking as small as she could make it. "We can speculate, but we believe only Gabrielle figured out his true ambition. She knew things."

"But what does that have to do with you *not* haunting this château and instead passing on to the afterlife?"

"The magic is holding us here," Béatrice said, as if this should have been obvious.

"Great gods above," said Lucienne, rubbing her temple. "You are the worst at explaining things. Do you realize how out of practice you are when it comes to civil conversation?"

Béatrice blushed—though her ghostly cheeks became more violet than pink. "At least I can carry on a conversation when I'm still sober."

Lucienne tapped the side of her glass. "This is my better half." She turned to Mallory. "We do not know the particulars, but we do know that Bastien was attempting some awful spell. One that required five sacrifices. The blood of five wives, to be specific. Something about the vows that tied our spirits to his made us acceptable fodder for this particular magic. But obviously, he never finished the spell. He sacrificed only three wives before his death."

"And as he never finished the spell, the magic was left incomplete," said Béatrice. "And now we are stuck here. Bound to this place where our bodies were sacrificed and our blood spilled."

"Literally," said Lucienne, pointing to a spot on the floor. "I was standing right there, enjoying an afternoon cordial, when he stabbed me." A shadow crossed her expression as she rubbed at the scars on her arms. "He didn't even wait until I was fully dead before he started carving the words into me."

"I'm so sorry," said Mallory, wondering if the dark stain on the wood was from Lucienne's blood. "I know you're stuck here . . . forever?"

Lucienne hiccupped. "Not in this tower, specifically, but on the estate, yes."

"Don't feel too bad for us," said Béatrice, noticing Mallory's horrified expression. "It isn't so terrible. Or at least, it wasn't. Until . . ."

"Until Le Bleu returned," Lucienne murmured. "Seven years ago."

"But what was it that he was trying to accomplish?" asked Mallory. "What was the spell meant to do?"

The wives blinked at her, then—in unison—shrugged.

Mallory tapped her pencil against her lips. Five wives. Five sacrifices. A dark spell left incomplete. And now he was back. What did it mean?

Armand had made it clear that there was only one ghost causing trouble at the château. One spirit who needed to be eradicated. She could pretend to be making progress on the wives, while focusing her energy on the real troublemaker.

"I am going to try to help you," she said, and though she wasn't sure if she meant it or not, in that moment, she wanted it to be true.

"How?" said Lucienne. "In order for the spell to be fulfilled, two more women must be sacrificed. *After* marrying the brute. Good luck with that."

"I'll think of something," said Mallory. "I always do."

Lucienne made an unconvinced sound in her throat, then took another sip of wine.

"In the meantime, will you do something for me?"

The wives said nothing.

"I need Armand to believe I'm capable of ridding the house of Bastien's spirit. Is there some way that you could convey that you recognize me as a powerful ally? Perhaps even that Bastien is afraid of me?"

"Bastien? Afraid of you?" Lucienne's lips twitched.

Mallory raised a hand. "Don't start laughing. It doesn't have to be true, I just need Armand to believe it."

Béatrice picked at the dried blood beneath her fingernails, though after nearly a hundred years, she had to know they would never come clean. "I suppose we could try to think of something . . ."

"Thank you," Mallory said, grateful she hadn't received an outright refusal. "Now. Where can I find Bastien?"

Béatrice frowned. "He is always near. He is . . . in the house. The walls. The floors. Every closet, every chimney—"

"I get it," said Mallory. "But if one were to go searching for him, where might one want to start?"

Lucienne bit her lip. "I cannot recommend going there, but . . . it would have to be the cellar."

"Oh, don't do it," said Béatrice, wide-eyed. "He is very territorial. Going down to the cellar is the surest way to anger him. We stay as far away from it as possible."

"And yet, alas," said Lucienne, "the cellar stairs are right next to the cupbearer's room, so a visit from time to time cannot always be avoided." She lifted her glass—now empty—and pouted. "If you *are* going that direction, perhaps you could bring me a refill?"

CHAPTER TWENTY

In the servants' halls, Mallory passed the linen room, stocked with towels and napkins and tablecloths. The butler's pantry, with its monogrammed porcelain stored tidily in mahogany and glass cabinets (disappointingly, no sign of the lutin). The kitchen, where Armand had so tenaciously stirred the simmering pot of chocolate. The cupbearer's room, stacked high with dusty casks and bottles of wine.

Stepping around a corner, she crashed into Julie. An armful of linens scattered across the floor.

Julie gasped, her arms still outstretched. "Gracious! You are in a hurry, Miss Fontaine."

"I'm sorry." Mallory scooped the linens into a messy lump and tried to pass them back to the maid.

Julie smiled thinly, then took a hand towel off the top of the stack and folded it neatly. "Quite all right." She took a bedsheet, whipped it straight, folded it corner to corner. "What are you doing in the servants' halls, m'lady?"

Realizing that the maid intended to refold every piece, Mallory cast around for another place to set the work, but there were no tables in the corridor.

"Just trying to be thorough in my search for wicked spirits."

Julie hummed in acknowledgment as she studied Mallory, eyes narrow with suspicion. Maybe Yvette had persuaded her not to trust Mallory and her witchcraft.

Noting a sprig of small white flowers tucked into the maid's pocket, Mallory said, "Lovely bouquet. Are you warding off dark spirits yourself?"

Pink flooded Julie's cheeks as she pressed delicate fingers over the flowers. "I don't think they have magical powers. Other than making me smile. Perhaps that is magic in itself." She finished with a towel and set it on the stack. "You would know better than I."

"They were a gift?"

Julie's blush deepened, but she didn't respond. Confirmation enough. The girl had a beau.

"I hope you're being careful."

Julie paused halfway through folding a pillowcase. "Careful?"

"With whomever is wooing you." Mallory shifted on her feet. The linens were growing heavy. "You can't always tell which ones are monsters until it's too late."

Julie let out a peal of laughter. "Oh no, Miss Fontaine, he is the sweetest, most thoughtful man in the world." She set down the pillowcase, pressing out its corners. Her expression took on a dreamy quality.

"Right," Mallory mused. "And no wolf ever donned sheep's clothing."

Julie clicked her tongue. "You sound as though you've been jilted in love, Miss Fontaine."

"I've had enough sense not to fall in love to begin with."

The maid's shoulders seemed to relax. "I am relieved to hear it."

"Relieved?"

Eyes going wide, Julie giggled uncomfortably. "That is—I'll be relieved when you change your mind, Miss Fontaine. Surely you won't be so staunchly opposed to love when it finds you. I daresay, there's no avoiding it." She shook her head. "I wasn't looking to fall in love, and yet . . . it was inevitable." She stiffened. "But perhaps I shouldn't be speaking so forwardly. And Yvette will be wondering what's keeping me."

She hurried through the rest of the pile—three towels, two pillowcases, another bedsheet. Mallory folded the final dishcloth herself.

"Sweetheart or not," said Mallory as Julie bustled away again, "I'd still be careful."

The maid paused. "You're kind to worry, miss. But I assure you, he wouldn't harm a—" She screamed suddenly, jumping back. The tidy pile of laundry tumbled from her arms onto the floor again. "Salamander!"

Mallory spotted a reptilian tail as it disappeared beneath a baseboard.

"Oh, what *is* it with this house?" cried Julie. "It's becoming an infestation. I'm going to find a broom." Lifting her skirts, she stepped over the linens and rushed down the hall.

Mallory crouched down and peered along the baseboard. Glowing yellow eyes peered back.

She had loved catching salamanders as a child. There had been a pond near their family home that had overflowed with them every spring—so many that she could fill entire jars with their squirmy, slimy bodies. She could watch their tiny toes scramble against the inside of the glass and their slick bodies writhing in one confused mass, before inevitably dumping them back into the water, where they scattered beneath the grime-covered surface.

She reached a finger forward. "Don't be frightened. I won't hurt—"

A spit of fire burst from the salamander, singeing Mallory's finger.

She yelped and recoiled. Her elbow struck a rack of drying herbs, sending lavender buds and twigs of rosemary scattering across the floor. She stuck her burned finger in her mouth.

Not just a salamander, then. Mallory knew about the fire-breathing creatures, as revered by the kings and queens of Lysraux as wyverns and dragons were elsewhere in the world, though it struck her as a peculiar comparison. She supposed when it came to mythical creatures, people took what they could get.

This house got better and better.

The salamander darted out from its hiding spot. It was longer than Mallory's hand, with a flat, slimy body, deep red with yellow splotches along its back. As it skittered through the mess of herbs, it paused suddenly, reared back on its hind legs, and sneezed—which released a rope of flame nearly as long as a candlestick.

It glared at Mallory, as if it sensed that the dried lavender was her fault.

"Oh, wait!" Mallory dug through her pockets, retrieving the last bundle of herbs from the greenhouse. She crouched down and held out the bundle. "Would you mind?"

The salamander cocked its head.

Not to be outwitted by a creature who was 80 percent slime, Mallory pinched a pile of purple flowers and flicked them at the little beast.

It sneezed again and spat another flame at her. Mallory intercepted it with the herbs, which promptly caught fire. She stood up, delighted. "Thank you."

The salamander flicked its tongue at her, then dove beneath the kitchen door.

Julie reappeared at the far end of the corridor, wielding a broom. "Where is it?"

"That way." Mallory pointed not to the kitchen but the pantry, then stepped aside as the maid charged through.

Gripping her smoking herbs like a magic wand, Mallory headed in the other direction—toward the cellar.

This corridor was colder than the others, a gentle yet frigid breeze blowing in from a stairwell that was cut into the hall, leading down beneath the house. It was narrow and easy to miss, the shadows at its base impenetrable.

Mallory stood there for a long time, letting the smoke wind its way like a serpent around her body. The smell of the herbs became repugnant.

She had never before known such a soul-deep dread as when she stared into those shadows. Every instinct told her to run away. To pretend she had never seen this place. To never, ever come back.

Something evil was down there. She knew it with as much certainty as she knew Anaïs's favorite gemstone was all of them, and that Triphine had never broken a bone in her life, though she still sometimes limped and complained how her leg had never healed right. She knew it with as much certainty as she knew that Le Bleu was still haunting this house and it might—possibly—be her fault.

She took a candle from a wall sconce, brandishing it in one hand and the pathetic bundle of herbs in the other. Her weapons against whatever evil lay below.

There was nothing particularly interesting about the stairwell itself. Stone walls. Stone steps, worn smooth. And that bone-seeping cold coming up from its depths.

Mallory took one, two, three steps down, but halted when she saw a smear of red staining one of the risers.

Blood?

She crouched, lowering the candle toward the mark. And . . . no, she did not think it was blood, but more likely . . . wine?

Of course. It was a wine cellar.

The shadows peeled back from the flickering candlelight, and she could make out an arched wooden door at the bottom, hung on ornate black hinges. A wrought-iron handle sat above an ancient keyhole.

Her heart pounded as she took the final steps. The candle flame wavered, and she feared it would go out, but it held strong. The incense curled beneath her nose, filling up every corner.

She set the herbs on the base of the candlestick and pressed her palm to the door, telling herself that it was only a door—the ancient wood rough beneath her touch.

Beyond it, only a cellar. There should be nothing within but crates of apples and onions. Casks of wine. Rat droppings and cobwebs.

And possibly a very angry, very murderous ghost.

Everyone knew what had happened beyond that door. After killing Lucienne and Béatrice, Bastien Saphir had dragged their bodies down these stairs. Cut the ring finger from each of their hands. Hung their bodies on metal hooks like a butcher might hang a carcass of swine.

She imagined what Gabrielle Savoy must have felt to open this door and see the mutilated corpses of the wives who had come before her. Very few things, no matter how gruesome, truly upset Mallory, but now, standing here, the terror was stifling. This was not some cautionary tale. The suffering here had been real.

Her stomach twisted. She knew she should turn away. Leave this place.

Instead, she reached for the handle.

She pulled—but the door stayed firmly in place. Locked.

A new scent filled the air, more pungent than the herbal incense. The sweet citrus smell of fresh-cut oranges.

A skeletal hand emerged from the wood, reaching for her throat.

Mallory screamed, launching herself backward so fast she tripped on the bottom step and sprawled across the stone staircase. The candle fell and extinguished.

The hand disappeared in a wisp of black smoke, leaving Mallory to wonder if she'd imagined it.

Then a low voice purred against her ear. "I wondered when you would come to see me, little witch."

Mallory sat up and spun around. Her foot hit the candle, sending it rolling across the stone floor.

Before her, framed in the pale light from the corridor above, stood Monsieur Le Bleu.

He was dressed precisely as she'd seen him in the banquet hall, smiling the haughty smile she recognized from the portrait in Morant. Tall and lithe, with hair so dark it gleamed navy blue when the light flickered across it. A trim beard on a striking face. Even in this shadowy stairwell, his eyes shone like cut sapphires.

She pressed her back to the door, knowing better than to be fooled by the charm that rose up from him like mist on a moor.

"I do believe you dropped something," he said, making a show of inhaling deeply. Though the herbs had fallen with the candlestick, they were still burning. The bundle was halfway gone, but the smoke was thickening inside this narrow space, seeping into Mallory's lungs. Until Le Bleu sauntered down the steps and crushed the brittle stems beneath his boot. He smirked. "Did you believe that a bit of smoke would be enough to drag me back there?" He clicked his tongue and reached for her, his fingers brushing beneath her chin—the touch an icy breeze. Mallory tried to draw back, but there was nowhere to go. "Sweet, sweet Mallory Fontaine. Look at you, all grown up into such a fine young lady."

Strangely enough, these words served to shake Mallory from her terror. No one would ever think to call *her* a fine young lady, and she certainly wasn't *sweet*.

"I didn't realize we'd already had the pleasure of meeting," she said, voice straining with indignation.

"Should I be wounded? Surely I am not so easily forgotten." He smiled knowingly. "How have you liked my gift?" His thumb traveled down her neck, ice-cold through the fabric of her dress. The lace collar that never stopped itching, but she refused to go without.

Bastien's thumb lingered at the base of her throat. Then pressed down, hard.

She gasped at the pain that seared through her. White light flared in her vision. She cried out and pushed back against the door, but there was no escaping.

He released her.

Tears had gathered at the corners of Mallory's eyes, and she panted with the lingering remnants of agony. The ember burning in the dip of her clavicle.

"This is no gift," she growled. "You cursed me."

Bastien made a shushing sound as his voice dropped to a whisper. "No, no, child. You asked to be like your sister. To share the same magic. Isn't that right?"

"That's not what I . . ." She gritted her teeth. "You twisted my words. You manipulated me. You stole my magic from me!"

"Stole your magic? I resent such an accusation." His smile widened as he mimed turning a key in a lock, right over her heart. "Who would not give up petty witchcraft in exchange for a gift from the gods?"

"You are not a god."

He chuckled. "True. I am far more generous with my gifts than they have ever been. Death magic, little witch. How are you not grateful, when I owe you so very much?" He clicked his tongue pityingly. "You opened the door for me all those years ago, and I am never going back to Verloren. Not even if Velos themself should come for me."

Mallory clenched her jaw, trying to think. She reminded herself that he could not kill her. Could barely touch her.

But that pain had been real enough.

When Le Bleu pulled away, she braced herself, but he merely stooped to pick up what was left of the incense.

She inhaled sharply in surprise. The herbs did not weigh much, she told herself. Triphine could have picked them up, too.

But only for a moment—and she would have complained about it.

"Clever little girl." He stroked a finger along the edges of his beard. "You do not resemble her, you know. But your sister . . ."

She snarled. "I don't know who you're referring to."

"I think you do." He appeared downright nostalgic as he tucked the bundle of herbs into his pocket, like a knight might save a posy of wildflowers from his lady.

He drew close again, until she had to crane her neck to hold his gaze. Until she could feel the cold nothingness of his body tickling the hairs on her arms.

He was different from other ghosts she'd seen. Not cast in a silver-gray light that emanated from the inside out. Rather, his figure was part man, part shadow. The edges of his body bled away into inky blackness. Of all the ghosts Mallory had seen over the years, this was the only ghost who glowed not with iridescent grayish light, but with the blackness of impenetrable shadows, wearing them like a shroud. She had seen this living darkness once before.

She had hoped to never see it again.

Monsieur Le Bleu lowered his head, pressing his cheek to hers. Mallory cringed at the sensation of his rough beard against her skin, and his breath—unexpectedly warm—on her ear.

She couldn't just see him or hear him.

She could *feel* him.

For the briefest of moments, he was solid. He was alive.

"You are already in my snare, little witch. Gabrielle may have gotten away from me, but you and your sister will not. And I have you to thank for it."

He pressed his lips to her neck, where her collar met skin—and Mallory felt like there were cockroaches skittering beneath her flesh.

Gathering her courage, she tried to shove him away—

But her hands met only shadows.

Monsieur Le Bleu was gone.

CHAPTER TWENTY-ONE

Nearly three full days had passed since Mallory had encountered Monsieur Le Bleu on the cellar stairs, and while she had heard nothing else from the ghost, she still found herself moving hesitantly through the house, half expecting to be met with the apparition around every corner.

But the days had been blessedly uneventful. She'd even heard Julie musing to herself about how quiet the hauntings had been since Mallory had spread around her witchy-herbal-smoke stuff. Mallory had been eager to accept the praise of her skills, but she knew those bundled sticks had not deterred the spirit.

His silence unnerved her. It was as though he were plotting something. As though he were waiting.

But for what?

Lucienne and Béatrice had indeed introduced themselves to Triphine and welcomed her into their little circle of the murdered and mutilated. Triphine complained about them when they weren't around—"All that Béatrice wants to talk about is which prince is courting which princess and which queen is pregnant with her ninth child, and on and on, as if anyone cares about such things. No wonder Lucienne has spent the last century drinking herself into a stupor. I'd probably take up the bottle, too, after spending so much time with the two of them. That is, if I could trust that the wine here wouldn't give me hives."

Despite her whining, Mallory had the sense that Triphine rather enjoyed having new company.

Meanwhile, Mallory and Anaïs spent their days immersed in faux witchcraft. While Mallory waved chicken bones into dark corners of the house (checking for evil vibrations . . . or something like that), Anaïs conducted fortune readings in every room, as if she could tell the fate of the house itself. They burned candles in the parlors and chanted nonsense rhymes. Demanded that every hearth be lit nonstop for a full day and night, in order to drive out the wicked spirits with sweltering heat. Scattered flower petals into the courtyard fountain and prayed loudly to the seven gods . . . in case Yvette was watching.

But their ruse seemed largely inconsequential, as they were in the midst of the fall harvest, and Armand was too busy meeting with farmhands, vintners, and merchants to pay much attention to their efforts. He was rarely around to listen to Mallory's lies or witness her half-hearted attempts to eradicate the ghosts using scrying mirrors, tea leaves, and the bones of small rodents. Only Yvette watched her with focused contempt, which compelled Mallory to keep up her subterfuge, but it wasn't much fun without Armand around to marvel at her antics.

Mallory was trudging through the house, sprinkling pure god-blessed water (that most certainly was not left over from her own washbasin that morning) in the doorways when she was stopped by Yvette, wearing her signature scowl and scanning Mallory's dress, as if searching for stolen goods tucked into her pockets.

"Good afternoon," Mallory said. "Did you want some purifying?" Without waiting for an answer, she dipped her fingers into the jar and flicked the water onto Yvette's apron. "That's Solvilde's best, right there."

Yvette screwed up her face, evidently not sure if she should be offended. "Have you seen Julie while you've been sneaking about? She was supposed to help me with the rugs."

Refusing to acknowledge the *sneaking about* comment, Mallory confessed, "I haven't seen her since breakfast."

Yvette sighed. "That girl is more easily distracted than a butterfly." She pushed past Mallory. "By the way, Lord Armand was asking for you."

With this statement, she let the door swing shut, dividing them.

Mallory's pulse jumped. She'd thought Armand was away in the vineyards. What could he want? Had something raised his suspicions? Had he uncovered evidence that she was not the witch she claimed to be?

She forced herself to take a calming breath as she made her way through the house. Armand had said nothing to indicate he doubted her abilities. He likely just wanted an update on her progress. And if he did start to grow suspicious, she would simply claim that her magical attempts to banish the spirits had exhausted her, and retire to her bedroom for the rest of the day. She'd learned a thing or two from Triphine over the years and was very good at faking a splitting headache when necessary.

"Mallory, there you are."

Mallory froze halfway up the main staircase.

Plastering on a smile, she faced Armand. He stood in the vestibule, a large square basket hanging from one arm. He was slightly out of breath, like he'd been in a hurry.

"Were you looking for me? I had no idea."

"Yes. I . . ." He cleared his throat. "It's been a few days since we spoke. I was curious to know about your progress?"

Her shoulders relaxed. Nothing to worry about at all.

"Everything is going according to plan." Already her mind was racing with the list of all the little charms and imitations of spells she and Anaïs had conducted these past days.

But Armand didn't ask for more details. Instead, as he switched the basket to his other arm, he said, "I'm glad to hear it. Are you busy?"

Mallory stared at him. Was she busy? If she said no, would he think she wasn't trying hard enough to complete the task?

If she said yes, would he think she was hiding something?

Opting to play it safe, she said merely, "Am I busy? Now?"

"Yes. I don't mean to disturb you if you're . . . working." He peered at the jar of water in her hand.

She looked down. She'd forgotten about the water.

"Yes! Yes, in fact, I am quite busy. With . . . this priceless . . . holy water." She gave the jar a shake, and pointedly ignored the water that sloshed over the sides.

"Oh." Armand sounded disappointed. "I thought perhaps you'd be hungry, and was wondering if . . . That is, I thought we could discuss your progress over . . . a . . . picnic." His enthusiasm faded the further into the statement he got.

"A picnic," Mallory repeated. Her first thought was of her grumbling stomach and the potential for a fresh-baked baguette and soft, creamy cheese. Her second thought was of ants and sunburned skin. "You mean . . . to . . . eat food? Outside? On purpose?"

After a long silence, he set the basket down and kicked it off to the side. "You're right. Overrated." He hesitated, scratching his ear. "We also have boats."

"Boats?"

"Rowboats. On the lake." He frowned. "You do know what a boat is?"

"Yes, of course. Those little vessels that require manual labor so one can float out into the middle of nowhere, far away from safe, dry land. I don't see the appeal."

He pressed his lips tight together, straining against a laugh. "Sometimes people also like to catch fish."

"I understand that even less."

This time, he did laugh. "All right. No picnic. No boats."

Mallory wrinkled her nose in fake apology. "Perhaps we can discuss my work another time."

His smile faded. "Of course."

She turned away and was nearly to the top of the stairs when Armand asked—even more tentative now—"Unless you would like to see the cemetery?"

Her hand clamped on the rail. She glanced back, side-eyeing him. "The cemetery?"

"It's out in the forest. Overgrown. Damp. Admittedly not well tended to. A haven for small, terrifying creatures. Generally speaking, it's a horrible place to spend any amount of time." His eyebrows lifted. "Might that interest you, Miss Fontaine?"

CHAPTER TWENTY-TWO

They passed Julie on their way through the gardens. She was humming cheerfully to herself, but froze when she saw Mallory and Armand. She blinked at the two of them, startled, as if she'd been caught doing something much worse than gathering an armful of nearly spent blossoms.

"Armand!" she gasped, then grimaced and curtsied. "I mean . . . Lord Armand, that is."

He nodded politely, showing no offense at her slip.

"I believe Yvette wanted you," said Mallory. "Something about rugs."

"O-oh." Julie was having a difficult time pulling her gaze from Armand. "Yes. I'll . . . be right there."

"Thank you, Julie," said Armand. "When you're finished, would you remind Yvette about those pieces stored away in the attic?"

Her forehead creased. "Attic?"

"The artwork."

Her mouth parted. She looked at Mallory, who could not understand why Julie suddenly looked so upset. "But where are you two going?"

Armand drew back, surprised.

Immediately realizing the impudence of such a question, Julie lowered her gaze. Then, with a huff, she dropped her armful of flowers right into the middle of the pathway. "I mean—certainly. Whatever you need. *My lord.*"

She stormed past them, fingers strangling her apron as she went.

They watched her go, bewildered.

"I cannot decipher half the things that girl says," said Armand. "It's like she speaks another language entirely and gets frustrated when no one has any idea what she's saying."

"Don't be dense," said Mallory. "She obviously likes you."

"I should hope so. I try to be a good employer. Yvette would say I'm too—"

"Not like that," said Mallory as they continued down the path again.

It took Armand another beat before horror eclipsed his expression. "I—well. If that is the case, then it is not mutual." He frowned deeply. "I hope she hasn't misinterpreted my actions for . . . interest. I would feel awful."

Mallory could easily see how a girl could be swept away by Armand's simple kindnesses, but she didn't want to make him feel worse than he evidently already did. "I'm sure it's only a passing fancy."

Though the gardens had once consisted of many acres of

hedgerows, boxwoods, and tidy plant beds, it did not take long for them to reach the portion of the property that had been taken over with wild seedlings, scraggly trees, and a proliferation of weeds. Most of the estate was surrounded by vineyards, but the gardens to the north eventually gave way to a forest—what had once been the Saphir family's personal hunting grounds.

She supposed it was still, technically, Armand's personal hunting grounds, but when she asked about it, he appeared revolted. "My father enjoyed the sport, but I never developed a taste for it." He paused suddenly. "But look!"

He pointed at a fallen log and Mallory hoped to see one of those small, terrifying creatures he'd promised her, but instead she saw . . . nothing, actually. Just a log.

"What?"

Armand trudged through some shrubs and crouched down. "Emerald brittlegills."

"You mean . . . those mushrooms?" Mallory eyed the large fungi with shiny green tops that grew from the side of the log.

"Not just mushrooms. These can help with a host of indigestion issues. They're also highly valued for being a powerful aphrodisiac." As soon as the word was out of his mouth, he flushed scarlet. "Not that I . . . I wouldn't know . . . I've just heard rumors."

Mallory put a knuckle between her teeth, fighting every instinct to keep from teasing him.

Lowering his head, Armand pulled a napkin and a small knife from a pocket, and there was a moment when Mallory wondered if she should be concerned that she was being led out into the forest with a boy, barely more than a stranger, who was secretly carrying a knife.

But when he cut the mushrooms from the side of the log and wrapped them up in the napkin as tenderly as one would wrap up a piece of cake, she found it impossible to be afraid.

Besides, he probably didn't know about the knife she was carrying, either.

The path became more neglected the deeper into the forest they went. Armand stopped every few minutes to forage for nettles, berries, mullein, even mustard greens—plus more varieties of fungi than Mallory knew existed. He ran out of pockets and was immensely grateful when Mallory offered to carry the mushroom that resembled a rotting brain.

There was something about his enthusiasm that was unexpectedly endearing.

No, not just endearing. Mallory couldn't quite fathom why, but she had never been so attracted to someone as when Armand waxed poetic about the poisonous properties of oleander.

"You do this often?" she said.

Armand paused from gathering a handful of wild violets. "Er . . . not as often as I wish. But I'm slowing us down. I promised to show you the graveyard."

"I'm in no hurry. What do those do?" Mallory asked, nodding to the flowers.

"Oh—nothing at all. They just look nice." He smiled crookedly. "I try to come foraging when I can, but managing the winery has taken up so much of my time this year. I missed the spring mallow harvest entirely."

"Not the spring mallow harvest. How will you survive?"

"Oh, don't worry," he said, eyes brightening. "There'll be another opportunity at the end of fall." He picked a few more stems, tucking them into his fist. "The herbs were helpful the other day?"

"Herbs?" She was thinking of purple-red syrup and hot chocolate, wondering what he might have tasted like that night . . .

When Armand gave her a peculiar look, she hastily shook the thought away. "Oh, those herbs! Yes. They were very helpful. They may not have eradicated the spirits in question, but they did . . ." She swirled her hand through the air in search of the right words, exuding confidence like a snail exuded slime. "Encourage the ghosts to consider secondary afterlife options."

Armand blinked.

"It's a process," said Mallory, grateful when he did not press further.

They had not gone much farther when Mallory spotted the cemetery gate through the trees. It was hung in a stone archway that connected to a high stone wall, slick with moss and sprouting an entire hierarchy of mushrooms. A statue of Velos greeted visitors. A wren was perched on the carved lantern that hung from the god's hand, trilling a discordantly cheerful song.

The gate screeched when Armand pulled it open.

Inside, the cemetery was everything a graveyard should be. Ancient and serene, smelling of earth and autumn winds and coming rains. The graves themselves were mostly marble slabs above the ground, carved with names and dates. Some were succumbing to moss, others to ivy. A patch of brambles was doing its best to creep in along the edges of the wall, stretching its thorny fingers for the nearest stones. There were tombstones with sorrowful poetry. Statues of winged fae and kneeling demons. Patches of tall grass that had recently gone to seed between the plots.

It was the most exquisite place Mallory had ever seen.

She scanned the stones as they meandered down one of the paths. Armand had been respectfully quiet since they'd entered, but now Mallory peered over at him. "I thought this was your family cemetery, but I do not recognize any of the names."

"Most of these graves belong to the staff. Some choose to be buried in the cemetery outside of Comorre, but many prefer to be interred here. A lot of these are vineyard workers, but there are household and garden staff as well. My first governess is there." He pointed to a stone that had been carved into the shape of an open book. "As for my family . . ."

He indicated a series of tall mausoleums in the distance.

"Will you show me?" she asked, starting toward them.

He pointed out the crypt that held the remains of his parents, and the one that contained the aunt who had raised him. She died the year before and was laid to rest beside her husband.

Finally, he paused in front of the largest mausoleum—a tomb of white limestone blocks and a grated iron door, covered in rust. Small winged demons with sneering faces loomed along the cornices, so lifelike it was hard to believe they had been carved from stone.

"Is Bastien in there?"

Armand shook his head. "Bastien is not inside the cemetery. Though he was the one who commissioned this mausoleum to be built. For . . . his wives." He hesitated, before asking, "Would you like to see inside?"

He didn't wait for her to answer before he pulled out the ring of keys. Intrigued, Mallory noted the largest key—dark brass, with intricate scrollwork around the edges.

"What does that one open?" she asked.

Armand stilled. He weighed the key in his palm, and she had the sense that it was unusually heavy. "The wine cellar," he said simply, before stepping up to the door of the mausoleum and inserting a different key into the lock. She heard the telltale clunk of the internal mechanism, then they were stepping inside.

Though the mausoleum was large, there was barely enough space inside for the two of them. To the left were two narrow altars—one for Velos, the other for Eostrig, each ornamented with candles that had long ago burned down and bouquets of flowers that had decayed nearly to dust.

Facing the altars, three stone crypts, covered in dust and cobwebs, were laid side by side. Carved onto the top of each crypt was the reclining likeness of the entombed woman, her body cast in still, cold marble. The statues wore beautiful gowns, jewelry, and headdresses, and their hands were clasped demurely over their hearts. Though Mallory knew the statues were intended to honor the dead, she couldn't help feeling that they did nothing to capture the essences of the women she had met. Lucienne's boisterous cackle. Béatrice's quiet earnestness. Triphine's biting wit.

Engraved marble plaques on the wall held a series of dates beside three familiar names.

Triphine Saphir née Maeng
Lucienne Saphir née Tremblay
Béatrice Saphir née Descoteaux

There were platforms prepared for two additional crypts, and two marble plaques remained blank.

Armand divided the wildflowers he had gathered and laid a small bouquet on each of the three crypts.

"He claimed to have had the mausoleum built for Triphine," he said. "That as the mother of his first child, she deserved to be laid to rest in a palace fit for a queen. That's why it's so large. Of course—later, it became clear that he had never intended for her to be alone in here."

"And the artisans who built it didn't suspect something strange?" Mallory said. If she were tasked with burying three wives in a crypt with two additional vacancies, she would have had questions.

"I'm sure they did," said Armand. "But I'm also sure they were grateful for the work, and I have no doubt they were well compensated. Feeding one's family can be a powerful motive for silence."

Mallory's own gut twisted with memories of too many missed meals. "I thought Triphine was buried in Morant."

"She was, initially. But once this crypt was completed, her body was exhumed and brought here."

As Armand used his sleeve to brush dust from the surface of the graves, Mallory's focus drifted to the two empty slabs.

Five total.

She suspected one of them was intended for Gabrielle Savoy—the wife who got away—but it would seem that Bastien had not intended for her to be his final victim. Lucienne and Béatrice had been right. His goal had been five sacrifices. But to what end?

"Have you spoken to them?" Armand asked, his voice deferential.

She swallowed. "I have."

"What do they look like?"

"Look like?"

"I've seen their portraits, of course. And I'll occasionally see their silhouettes in a window or moving through a hall, but they always disappear so quickly. I've always wondered if their spirits were . . . different somehow. If death changed them."

"Ghosts look more or less as they did at the moment of their death. The same clothes. But they have a particular appearance. Ghosts are . . . faint at the edges. It's never quite clear where their bodies end and the air around them begins. They can be corporeal, when they want to interact with the world—in a physical sense—but it requires a lot of effort. If they wish to do much more than turn the page of a book or . . . or take a sip from a glass of wine . . . it quickly tires them."

He nodded slowly, taking this in.

"And they still have their wounds, the ones that caused their deaths. There is a lot of blood, and . . . they are still bleeding. It never stops."

Armand winced. "That's terrible."

"But they are not in pain, I assure you."

"I'm glad. I've felt their presence my entire life. Heard their whispers, occasionally even their laughter. Sometimes objects will move, and you are never quite sure if you imagined it."

"Were you frightened, growing up with ghosts?"

"No. Never." Armand flicked a dead beetle off Lucienne's crypt. "They felt more like guardians than ghosts. I always knew they were benevolent. As if they were watching over me." He chuckled to himself. "Ask anyone, and they will tell you that I am uncannily lucky at dice games. Always have been. It wasn't until a year ago when it occurred to me that Lucienne was known for gambling, and that perhaps I am so lucky because I have a cheater on my side."

Mallory's cheek twitched. "And Béatrice?"

"Her presence isn't as obvious. But I'm sure you've heard her playing the pianoforte?"

"I have."

"You can tell her mood from how she hits the keys. She is usually melancholy, but every now and then, the songs will be almost cheerful, and it makes me smile." He scratched his neck. "She's very talented."

"It sounds as though you're fond of them."

A long moment passed before he spoke again. "It was lonely growing up here. I had my governess, my tutors, a few children of the staff to play with, some farmhands . . . but I liked knowing that I was never truly alone."

A pang of sadness struck Mallory's chest at this confession and, perhaps aware that he'd revealed a vulnerable spot he hadn't meant to, Armand straightened his spine. "That is enough about me. I am curious what it was like for you, seeing ghosts as a child. Was it very odd to discover that not everyone sees them as you do?"

Perhaps Mallory should have expected such a question, but it nevertheless caught her off guard. So when she blurted out, "Actually, I could not see them growing up," she immediately regretted it.

Armand started. "Really? I assumed you were born with such a gift. That it was a part of your . . . magic."

"Oh . . . it is," she said. "But it developed later."

"How old were you then?"

Mallory weighed her answer, debating the benefits of truths and lies. But seeing no reason to fib, she answered, "Ten."

"Still quite young."

Yes, she had been young. Too young to know what she was doing. Too young to understand what she was giving up—and what she was asking for in return.

CHAPTER TWENTY-THREE

Two little girls sneaked into the abandoned house, long after nightfall on the Mourning Moon. Dressed in too-large cloaks, they held hands as they crept through the shadows, past the empty birdcages and cold fireplaces, until they reached the ballroom. Moonlight drifted through broken windowpanes. Cobwebs clung to elaborate chandeliers. To be in the center of the massive room felt too vulnerable, too exposed, so instead they sat cross-legged in a corner, and set a mirror between them, one they'd stolen from their mother's boudoir while she was giving a card reading in the shop. On top of the glass went a candle in a pewter candlestick. It took three attempts to light the wick, but it finally crackled to life, illuminating their round faces.

"It's going to work," said Mallory, copying the sigils from the book in her lap directly onto the wooden floor, using a stick burned to charcoal on the end. "If Mother can summon the dead, then so can we."

Anaïs tugged at the ends of her blond hair. "I don't think magic works that way. At least, mine certainly doesn't. And Mother says that death magic is not to be trifled with."

"Your magic *is* death magic."

"Yes, and I despise it."

Mallory paused from her sketches to place a hand over her sister's. "After tonight, things will be different. You'll have the same magic as I do, and you'll never have to hide it again. I promise. Gabrielle will be able to help us."

"How can you be sure? Mother couldn't change it."

Mallory scowled, though she didn't want to look resentful. "Mother didn't want to change it. She thinks you're special."

With a great shudder, Anaïs pulled her knees into her chest. "What if no one answers?"

"She will answer."

After a long silence—"What if she is not the only one?"

"Who else do you think will come? The duchess?" Mallory giggled and wagged her fingers in mockery of the ghost who was said to haunt this very house—though Mallory sought out the apparition every time she walked by and had never seen anything but rats and spiders. "All right, that's the last of them. Are you ready?"

She expected Anaïs to argue again, but, chewing on her pinkie nail, her sister merely nodded.

Mallory had spent days memorizing the incantation, even going so far as to convert the spell into a simple song so that the words would be as fluid as gossip from the baker's wife. It was far more complicated than the petty magic spells she'd worked in the past. But then, summoning a spirit from the dead was a much more complicated matter than dyeing a bully's teeth green or making an enemy's breakfast sour in their stomach.

Still, Mallory knew she could do this. She was going to be a powerful witch someday, like Mother. And Grandmother. And—long ago—Gabrielle Savoy. The greatest witch of them all.

After this night, she and her sister would be the same. No more god-gift. No more curse.

She used the blade of a bone-handled knife to draw blood from her finger, letting three drops fall into the circle.

They reached across the circle and took hands, framing the candle between their arms. Mallory kept her eyes on the candle flame as she chanted the spell—her small voice wavering as she sang every word of the unfamiliar language.

Anaïs remained silent, her grip on Mallory's hands slowly tightening.

An odd screeching gave her pause. Wings flapping in the chimney. Only a bat trapped inside.

She kept going. She was halfway through the fourth repetition when the flame changed color. From orange and white to bluish black.

The candle tipped over—but at the moment it should have clattered to the floor, it instead vanished into the nothingness that yawned open between them. Anaïs gasped and tried to pull away, but Mallory held tight.

Gabrielle, she thought. *I wish to speak to Gabrielle Savoy. Please grant our wishes, that my sister and I might share the same magic. That she will not be ashamed of who we are and what we can do. Please, Gabrielle . . .*

But it was not Gabrielle Savoy who emerged from that bottomless void. It was a shadow, curling and shapeless at first, with hands like claws. It emerged from the depths to grasp at the floor by Mallory's knees. It climbed onto sharp elbows, a hiss and a gurgle coming from somewhere in that writhing mass. It lifted its head—what must have been its head, for there were two eyes glowing like gems, staring straight at her.

Mallory screamed. She let go of her sister's hands, hoping that would break the spell and send the thing back to Verloren, or whatever lay beyond that black pool.

But the creature kept coming. First onto hands and knees, then drawing itself upward with agonizing slowness, towering nearly to the ceiling.

"Sweet little witch . . ." it seethed. It lifted one long arm, pointed a clawed finger at the base of Mallory's throat. She wanted to scream, but her fear had her voice in clutches. "I shall grant your wish . . . in gratitude for your troubles."

It continued to speak, but Mallory did not recognize the words that followed. The mellifluous cadence of the old language, punctuated by the creature's rasping hisses. Then, blinding pain tore through her, and she thought the monster had killed her—driven a knife straight into her throat.

The last thing she heard was whistling—a strangely jaunty tune—before the world faded away.

When Mallory returned to consciousness, Anaïs was trying to put out the flames that licked at the wallpaper from their toppled candle.

For a long moment, Mallory couldn't talk. Something was wrong. On the inside. Something was wrong with her.

She pressed a hand to the base of her throat, flesh burning where the demon had touched her. "It . . . it's gone," she whispered.

Anaïs spun toward her, startled. "Mallory! You're awake! Quick, use your magic to put out these flames."

Mallory gaped at the smoldering wallpaper. Horror swept over her. She knew the words well enough, but when she spoke them, the flames did not die down. "I . . . I can't. It's gone. Sister. It's *gone*."

Ultimately, Anaïs ruined both of their cloaks putting out the fire—a loss that hardly registered when they told their mother the next day, because what were a couple of cloaks when her youngest daughter had just had her magic stolen from her by some dark creature that had crawled up from the underworld? Their mother had mourned the loss of Mallory's magic, but never as much as she mourned for it herself.

As for the new ability the demon had given her? The death magic that was now burned into the center of her chest?

Mallory did not notice it until the fire was put out. Only then did she see the third person who stood in the room. Who had, perhaps, been there the whole time, clutching a bloody blue shawl and glaring at her with quiet distaste.

For the first time in her life, Mallory could see ghosts.

"It's a good thing you're alive," said the duchess in her tart, nasally voice, "because I was about ready to tell you to go find your own mansion to haunt."

"MALLORY?"

She snapped back to attention, surprised to find herself in the mausoleum. Armand had a hand on her elbow, gently squeezing. "What's wrong? Are you cold? You're shivering."

"No. I—I'm fine."

"I'm sorry," he said. "I didn't mean to pry. If you don't want to talk about your magic—"

"N-no. I don't mind. Being able to communicate with ghosts is a wonderful gift, one that is uncommon even among witches." She tried to smile, but knew that it was as fake as it felt. "I wouldn't trade it for any—"

Armand grabbed her arm suddenly, silencing her. "Do you see that?"

He was staring at Lucienne's crypt, and the hand that was emerging out of the statue of the reclined woman. The spectral hand that was followed by an arm, a head, a ball gown, all shimmering in the dim light.

"Y-yes," said Mallory. "But how are *you* seeing it?"

A second figure followed, emerging out of Béatrice's tomb. Béatrice herself appeared, though far less dramatically than Lucienne, who now stood on top of her own crypt, posed like one of the angelic statues outside.

Lucienne's wide eyes fell on Mallory as she spread both hands to the side. "Oh, most magical one! We hereby beseech you!"

Armand cursed in surprise and drew back, pulling a stunned Mallory against the altar. "What . . . ? Who . . . ? Is that . . . ?"

"Lucienne," she said. "And Béatrice."

"Please, help us," Béatrice said, her voice a squeak compared to Lucienne's boisterous plea.

"Why can I see them?" Armand asked. "Why can I *hear* them?"

"You are the only one who can free our beleaguered souls, oh powerful sorceress!" bellowed Lucienne.

"Witch," said Mallory. "Not a sorceress. It's a totally different . . . never mind. Uh, *yes*, poor, helpless ghosts. I shall help you. I am here to guide your souls to their eternal rest." She waved her hands around in a gesture that she hoped implied spellcasting.

Béatrice frowned at her. "This is all just a tad melodramatic, don't you think?"

But Lucienne, who apparently loved nothing more than a bit of melodrama, fell to her knees and grabbed at Mallory's skirt. It only made the fabric wave for a moment, but Mallory felt it was a nice touch.

"Your presence at this house has already done much for us," said Lucienne. "Our lord husband, Monsieur Le Bleu, fears your powers most—erm."

"Fearsomely?" Béatrice suggested.

"Fearsomely! So long as you are near, I know you shall protect us from his wicked ways!"

"Soon, I shall vanquish him entirely," said Mallory, "and Monsieur Le Bleu shall be no more!"

"Thank you. Thank you." Lucienne's voice was growing weak. Mallory knew from having Triphine interact with her tour guests that it was exhausting for a ghost to communicate with most mortals, and she had far exceeded Mallory's expectations. "We will be forever indebted to you . . . Mallory Fontaine." Her voice became whisper thin as she faded away, slipping back down into her crypt and disappearing.

Mallory and Armand both looked at Béatrice.

"Oh! Yes. We are in your gratitude." Béatrice curtsied, then blinked away into nothingness.

The mausoleum was once again still and silent, except for Armand's ragged breathing.

Mallory beamed as she faced him. If that wasn't a glowing validation of her skills, she didn't know what was. "So. Now you've met the wives."

CHAPTER TWENTY-FOUR

Days and nights ticked by, steady as a metronome. Mallory found that she could relax after the wives' visit in the cemetery. Their performance had worked like a god-blessed charm. If Armand hadn't been thoroughly convinced of Mallory's talents before then, he certainly was after. All the rest of the day he'd looked at Mallory with a sort of awe that left her both flustered and, if she admitted it, a tiny bit guilty. She started to dread the day when he would discover she was nothing but a fraud. How would he look at her then?

Oh well. She'd known what she was doing when she agreed to this job. It was nothing to lose sleep over.

What *was* worth losing sleep over was the fact that every night—sometimes multiple times during her slumber—she awoke to the uncanny sensation that someone else was in the room. Watching her.

It happened again, five nights after the visit to the cemetery.

The curtains around the bed fluttered. A floorboard creaked. The smell of summer oranges drifted past Mallory's nose, pulling her from a dreamless sleep.

Her eyes flew open.

This time, she saw him. A figure at the foot of the bed. Blue eyes glinting in the darkness. Lips twisted into an insidious smile, revealing pearl-white teeth. An orange was in his palms, his fingers digging into the skin, slowly stripping off its flesh.

Mallory jerked upward with a cry. Her hand reached for the knife beneath her pillow.

Beside her, Anaïs gasped and yanked the blankets up to her chin. "What is it?" she said sleepily, sitting up.

But Le Bleu was already gone—leaving behind merely a wisp of smoke, the smell of citrus, and a low chuckle that made gooseflesh prickle on Mallory's skin.

"Mally?"

Mallory clutched the dagger, shaking. "N-nothing," she said. "A bad dream."

Anaïs peered at her in the darkness. After a long silence, she flopped back down on the pillow with a groan.

Mallory stayed sitting up, her body tense. She searched for Triphine, but the duchess wasn't there. Perhaps she was visiting with the other wives.

The night was impenetrably dark. A windstorm was rattling a glass pane somewhere in the house. Gusts crooned through the chimney. The fire had gone out in the night, and Mallory found herself shivering as cold replaced the rush of adrenaline.

Somewhere deep in the endless corridors and salons, music began to float through the halls. Béatrice was playing the pianoforte again. Mallory did not recognize the song, but it was dramatic and brooding, all minor chords and thundering crescendos.

"Maybe that's what woke you," grumbled Anaïs. "Why must she play in the middle of the night?" She rolled onto her side, pulling the blankets over her head. "I thought you said ghosts can't touch things in the mortal world."

Mallory's gaze fell on a strip of something on the edge of the blanket, colorless in the dark. When she stretched forward to grab it, she realized it was the waxy peel of an orange.

She shuddered and threw it onto the floor.

"They can touch things," whispered Mallory, "but it's not easy for them."

Anaïs grunted. "I guess she really likes this song, then."

The music faded into the background as Mallory remembered what Le Bleu had said on the steps to the cellar. *You opened the door for me all those years ago.*

She tried to tell herself that this changed nothing. So what if Anaïs was right, and she really had summoned Monsieur Le Bleu back to the world of the living? It was an innocent mistake. Certainly no one could expect her to take responsibility for it now. She was a child then. They both were.

Over the music, a noise intruded on her tumbling thoughts. She held her breath, ears straining against the creaks and groans of the house.

There—somewhere in the hall. Whistling.

The hairs lifted on her forearms.

Anaïs went taut beside her as the slow, ominous tune grew louder. Soon it was accompanied by plodding footsteps. The creak of the hallway floor.

Mallory reached for her throat, where her scar was searing, a lingering effect of the dream.

The sound came closer.

"Mally?" Anaïs whispered. She reached out to squeeze Mallory's hand.

The whistling stopped—right outside their door.

Mallory shuddered, her entire body braced for whatever came next.

When nothing happened, she pulled together her threads of courage and swung her legs over the side of the bed. She fumbled for the candle on the bedside table. The wick caught and flared.

Mallory pulled herself from the bed, holding the candle aloft.

"Mally, *no*."

Ignoring her sister, she went to the door and yanked it open.

The hallway was empty. Quiet.

Sticking her head out, Mallory peered in both directions. There was no sign of Le Bleu. No sign of anyone or anything.

Until—distantly—a rumble of laughter disappearing into the shadows.

"You know," she shouted after it, "as far as I can tell, the scariest thing about you is that you can't carry a tune!"

She slammed the door shut and threw the deadbolt with a resounding thunk. She immediately felt silly for it, though. A lock wasn't going to keep out a ghost.

At her shouting, the piano music ceased, too. She sighed.

"That's just grand," said Anaïs. "As if it wasn't already hard enough to get a decent night's rest in this house, now we've got a murderer prowling around our door."

Mallory frowned. "You haven't been sleeping well?"

Anaïs snorted. "Between the musical ghost and the sister who likes to pace around our room, plotting her next move at all hours of the night? That can't be a surprise."

"I'm sorry. I'll try to keep my pacing to a minimum." Mallory lit another candle, hoping in vain to chase away some of the darkness. "Armand has an herb that helps him sleep. Maybe he can make you up some special tea."

Anaïs shrugged. "Maybe. It isn't so bad. Though . . . you should know that I did see him yesterday." Her voice wavered the tiniest bit. "Le Bleu."

Mallory's lips parted. She had seen countless ghosts over the past seven years, but to her knowledge, her sister had never seen any.

"I went to the orangerie, and when I was returning to the house . . . I saw a figure in one of the upstairs windows. Watching me. At first I thought it was Armand, and I waved. But he didn't wave back, and I noticed that he had a beard, and . . ." She gulped. "I didn't realize until later that it was our window he was standing at. That window."

"He was only trying to frighten you."

"No. I don't think so."

Mallory frowned.

"I think he's curious about us," Anaïs said. "From what we've been told, he could have done much worse to us than he has."

"Perhaps." Mallory sat on the foot of the bed. "But he clearly did not want me going into the cellar."

"The cellar?"

"That's where the took the bodies, after he killed them."

Anaïs shuddered.

"He recognized me. He said . . . he said that he should thank me.

For opening the door for him, all those years ago." She bunched the fabric of her nightgown in her fist. "He insinuated that it's because of me that he escaped from Verloren, and he doesn't intend to ever go back."

"Great gods." Anaïs drew her knees in closer. "I *knew* it. When Armand told us about the timing, I knew it couldn't be a coincidence. I went along with your séance, and now . . ."

Mallory became more insistent. "We still don't know exactly what happened that night. We were children."

"It would seem we released a murderer that night."

"Maybe. But . . . it was an *accident*."

Anaïs reached forward. Only when she'd removed the candlestick from Mallory's hands did Mallory realize she was shaking. Anaïs returned it to the nightstand.

"This doesn't feel right, Mally," she said softly. "Armand is a good person. A little awkward and unsocial, perhaps, but also . . . kind. He is doing the best he can by his staff and his family legacy . . . and here we are, mucking it up."

"Le Bleu isn't our fault," Mallory said forcefully.

But Anaïs's expression was sorrowful, even complacent. "Actually," she said sadly, "it would seem that he is very much our fault."

Mallory tightened her jaw.

"No more games, Mally. We have to find a way to make things right." Anaïs inhaled sharply. "It's what Mother would have done."

Mallory huffed. "Don't bring Mother into this."

"It's true, isn't it?"

When Mallory turned away, Anaïs pressed, "People came from all over Lysraux to ask Noele Fontaine for her help. And she would help them. Whether she was preparing fertility potions or medicinal ointments, reading fortunes or conducting séances . . . everything she did was to help people. To bring them comfort, closure, even joy." She picked idly at a loose thread on the blanket. "Sometimes I wonder if she would be horrified to see what we have become in her name."

"Don't say that," Mallory whispered, surprised at the prickle she felt behind her eyes. She could not remember the last time she had cried. "We have done what we had to do."

"And now," said Anaïs, "I think we have to help Armand. Really help him."

"That's what we're here for, isn't it?"

"Is it? Because I thought you were here to cheat that poor count out of his money."

"Say that a little louder, why don't you?"

"This is serious."

"I'm being serious!"

"How? You wave around your herbs and sprinkle bathwater on the floor and pretend like you know what you're doing, and in the meantime, there is a violent ghost on the loose and we have absolutely no idea how to stop him." She lowered her voice to an insistent whisper. "I feel compelled to remind you, once again, that you are not a real witch. Not anymore."

Drawing in a slow breath, Mallory lifted her pointer fingers. "True. *Except* . . ."

Anaïs groaned.

"Le Bleu has been relatively docile since we arrived. Everyone has been saying so. Something about our presence seems to have mollified him. So maybe . . ."

"What? Maybe what? Are you going to move in? Live here forever, with your count and your gaggle of murdered women?"

"It only sounds ridiculous when you use that tone of voice."

"No, Mallory. It sounds ridiculous because it *is* ridiculous. You need to tell Armand the truth. Stop wasting his time and give him a chance to find someone who can actually help him."

Mallory dug her fingers into the blankets. "Let's not be hasty."

"Mallory!"

"I have a plan."

"Your plan isn't working."

"Another plan. A new plan."

"You always have a new plan, and honestly, it's usually worse than the last one." Anaïs threw her hands into the air. "You know what? I'll tell him."

"No, wait! Listen." Mallory went to the vanity and dug through the drawer. It was easy to find the stark white card in the darkness— the paper almost glowed. "Fitcher's Troupe. Remember?"

"Oh, I remember. Honestly, Mally—"

"I've seen them work. I saw them capture a voirloup with magic, actual magic."

"Con artists can be very convincing, as you well know."

"They were the real thing." She examined the business card. "If we start to feel like we're in over our heads, I'll contact them and offer to split the profits."

"We are already in over our—"

Anaïs cut off abruptly.

Mallory heard it, too. Footsteps in the hall. Floorboards squeaking. That quiet, steady shuffling.

Again, it stopped outside their door.

With a growl, Mallory stormed toward the door and threw back the deadbolt. "You are not half as scary as you—"

She opened the door.

Julie cried out and threw herself against the corridor wall, nearly dropping the lantern she carried. "I'm sorry! I wasn't meaning to frighten you."

"What do you want?" asked Mallory. "Has something happened?"

"No, no, nothing! I . . . I heard voices. My bedroom is just above here, you see." She pointed toward the ceiling. "And I thought you must be awake, and I was going to offer to make you some tea . . ." She trailed off, her face pinching with guilt. "Oh, that's a lie! I came for an entirely selfish purpose. Forgive my terrible manners, but I've been wanting to ask ever since the first day you came."

"Ask what?" Mallory tensed, prepared to defend herself or her sister against any accusation that was lobbed at them by the curious maid.

But Julie's eyes were shining with emotion as she said, "I was wondering if you would read my fortune."

Mallory stared. "Your what?"

"My fortune. You are . . . You do that sort of thing. Don't you?"

Anaïs climbed from the bed and threw a robe over her nightgown.

"I . . . well . . . yes. My sister does, anyway. But what . . ." Mallory turned back to the maid, and the question evaporated from her thoughts as her attention fell on Julie's hand, clutching the lantern—and the sparkling blue stone on her finger. Far bigger and *far* more brilliant than she would expect for a housemaid.

Her eyebrows shot upward. "Is that an engagement ring?"

Julie clasped a hand over her fingers, hiding the jewel. "It's nothing special."

"Nothing special?" said Mallory. "That rock could sink you to the bottom of the ocean."

Julie bit her lower lip. "I suppose perhaps it is a little special."

"You have a beau," said Anaïs, shouldering beside Mallory. She reached forward and took the lantern away so she could properly admire the ring. "A very generous beau," she added, dragging the maid into the room. "Is that what you want a reading for?"

"Yes, miss. It started so of a sudden, and my mind is quite aflutter over it all. You know, things like this don't usually happen to plain nobodies like me."

"Nonsense," said Anaïs, leading Julie to the table by the window. "Everyone deserves to find true love, no matter their station in life."

"Do you think so?" Julie took the seat offered to her. "It's been feeling all a bit too good to be true. But . . . oh, I do so desperately want it to be true."

"But . . . I thought you liked Armand!" Mallory said.

The maid looked at her, eyes wide. "A-Armand?" she squeaked.

"You blush and giggle every time you see him," said Mallory.

To which Julie . . . blushed. And giggled. "Well, the lord *is* rather handsome, isn't he?"

"But he isn't your beau?"

Julie bit her lower lip again. "I would really prefer not to say. I've never been one to keep secrets, and this has been the hardest of my life. But my beau, as you call him, said it would be best if we waited until everything was settled before we tell anyone. And I do very much hope all will be settled soon."

"Do not worry," said Anaïs. "Keep any secrets you like. The cards will guide you regardless."

Mallory crossed her arms impatiently. "But when did you have time to meet anyone? You live here, you work here . . ." She gasped. "Is it the stable boy?"

"Mally!" Anaïs scolded. "She already said that she would prefer not to say."

Mallory sulked, her curiosity getting to her. But she held her tongue as Anaïs opened her traveling case and pulled out their mother's cards, wrapped in the delicate handkerchief she kept them in.

"Do you have a specific question," Anaïs asked, "or do you wish the cards to offer general guidance on your engagement?"

Julie fidgeted with the ring on her finger. "Not an engagement, miss. I . . . I married him. Last week."

Mallory and Anaïs both gaped at her.

"Well, then, what are you needing us for?" Anaïs said.

Julie shied away. "It's only that . . . he's been acting odd ever since we said our vows, and I wonder . . . I'm worried I may have made a mistake." Her voice trailed into a desperate whisper, thickening with unshed tears. "I love him so desperately. But I am not sure if he truly loves me." Clearing her throat, she said, "I don't expect any charity. I can pay you for the reading tomorrow, if that's all right? I'll bring some coin with your breakfast." Her smile thinned, weighted with desperation. "It won't be too great a hardship, not if . . . if the reading is favorable. As you said. My . . ." She fumbled for a word. "My husband is quite generous. Now that we are married . . ." She pressed a hand to her heart, almost as if she couldn't believe her words. "I shall not need for anything ever again."

Biting back a pessimistic response, Mallory nodded at her sister.

Anaïs shuffled the cards.

CHAPTER TWENTY-FIVE

The deck of Wyrdith cards might have been battered and worn around the edges, the designs faded from time, but they were still beautiful. Forty-nine cards in total. Thirteen moons. Seven gods. Four seasons. And the twenty-five enigmas, their meanings as murky as their names and the symbols hand-painted in intricate detail. *The One-Eyed Swan. The Tinkerer. Six Unlit Lanterns.*

When their mother read the cards, it was as if they were speaking to her. She knew things, things she shouldn't have known. She made uncanny predictions and was not surprised when they came true. Mallory and Anaïs had hoped that perhaps some of her magic was still inside the cards. That perhaps a bit of her spirit remained in the faint smell of clove oil she dabbed onto her wrists before each reading.

They had hoped their readings would be true.

They weren't.

To Mallory and her sister, the cards were pretty pieces of paper, with no meaning beyond what a person imposed upon them.

Mallory had come to realize that it didn't really matter anyway. No one came to have their fortune told—their real, undeniable, unavoidable fortune.

People wanted happy untruths. They wanted hope, encouragement, advice.

Together, she and Anaïs had crafted a collection of scripts, interchangeable based on what a client wanted, and most people wanted the same things: Wealth. Success in some endeavor. Children. Health. And always the easiest to predict . . . love.

There was no doubt what Julie had come for that night.

Anaïs spread the cards before her, fanning them across the table. "Choose four," she instructed, "and place them face down into my palm."

Julie fidgeted nervously as she pored over the cards. Her slim finger trailed over their faded backs, occasionally hesitating. Slowly and thoughtfully, she selected four cards and handed them to Anaïs.

Anaïs scooped up the deck and set it aside, then flipped over the four cards with a flourish—laying them across the table in a tidy cross.

Perched on the cushioned window seat, Mallory craned her head.

The Silver Stag.

One Empty Coffin.

The Untouched Feast.

Velos—god of wisdom and death.

The scar at the base of Mallory's throat burned, sharp and sudden. Words rose unbidden in her mind. *A false marriage. A coming betrayal. Death. Get out, get out, get—*

She gasped, pressing her finger against her throat. Even her pajamas were high-necked, and the cotton was soothing as the pain slowly ebbed.

"What is it?" said Anaïs, concerned.

"Nothing," said Mallory. "Just . . . something in my throat. Go on."

Anaïs's expression was dark. They both knew it was an ominous spread, but that was coincidence. Meaningless paintings on paper. Nothing more. Julie was a paying customer, and Anaïs's job was to give her what she paid for.

"It's bad, isn't it?" Julie said, a tremble in her voice as she hovered over the cards, inspecting each one.

"Not at all," said Anaïs. "In fact . . . this is quite promising." She pressed a finger onto the first card, a majestic depiction of a stag with enormous antlers. It stood in a forest glen speckled with foxglove flowers and moonlit briars. "This indicates your past—your life before. A resignation, so to speak. You were not searching for love . . . would, perhaps, have been content to go on as you were, despite bouts of loneliness, and a yearning to find connection. But here we see a change in your path."

As Anaïs pointed to the second card, Mallory exhaled a slow breath, relieved that her sister was following the script for the romantics. The Empty Coffin was a good omen, Anaïs said, lying through her teeth. A symbol of hope and love everlasting. The Untouched Feast suggested desires unfulfilled—but that would surely be changing now that she had such joy. And Velos?

In this reading, it referred to the god's dominion over wisdom, for surely this marriage was a wise decision . . . and an inevitable one.

Mallory knew the predictions so well that she had to bite the inside of her cheek to keep from mouthing the words along with Anaïs, as she talked about a love that was pure, a union fated by the stars. And so on and so forth.

By the end of it, Julie was enthralled, grasping at every word.

"I made the right choice, then?" she said once the reading was finished. "In marrying him?"

"Were you in doubt?" asked Anaïs.

"Well . . . no. But also, a little. He is such a good man, and can be so thoughtful at times. But other times . . . so distant. I'd hoped it would change, after the wedding, but . . ."

"Did you really?" Mallory said. A warning was ringing in her thoughts now, despite the sludge her sister had spoon-fed to this girl. Inconstancy was a telling character flaw, as far as she was concerned. One that suggested dishonesty at best—and cold depravity at worst. "I've never known marriage to change a man as much as most women would like to think."

"Oh, I don't wish to change him. Truly, I don't. It's more . . . our situation. But the heart wants what the heart wants. And the cards . . . they have comforted me. You have comforted me." She beamed at Anaïs—but faltered when she looked beyond Anaïs. "What is that?"

Mallory and Anaïs followed her look to a wardrobe, the doors propped open. Dawn was approaching, painting the room in pale gray light, barely illuminating a piece of cloth that dangled out from the armoire's shadows.

Anaïs stood. "No doubt a ribbon left unfastened. Mallory never did learn how to properly hang up her—"

She froze.

The ribbon was moving. Writhing and flicking along the carpet.

Anaïs stepped back. "Not a ribbon."

Julie stood abruptly. "Another monster? I've been chasing around lutins and matagots and salamanders all week."

Mallory shook her head. "That is no salamander."

The cabinet doors shifted, and the not-ribbon wriggled farther into the room. It reminded Mallory of a snake, but as wide as her arm, and much, much longer, as it reached for the floor and extended toward the fireplace.

Not a snake. A tentacle, she realized, as a second one appeared, emerging from the depths of the cabinet.

The door squeaked open, and the light hit the creature. Thick gray tentacles, as long as Mallory was tall, dotted with wiry hair and excreting an oily substance. They writhed along the carpet, originating from a giant snail shell, covered in clumps of fuzzy lichen. As the tentacles pulled the shell from the cabinet, it landed with a thud on the floor and tipped back, far enough for Mallory to glimpse a gaping black mouth lined in two rows of jagged teeth.

A lou carcolh.

Julie screamed and stumbled away, putting her chair between herself and the creature. Then, abruptly and without warning, the color drained from her face and she fainted onto the carpet.

Mallory and Anaïs gawped at the maid's limp form, then at each other, then at the creature.

With a screech, the lou carcolh shot three of its tentacles forward. They wrapped around Julie's leg and started dragging her body across the floor. Its shell raised up, revealing that horrifying maw, the unearthly rows of jagged teeth.

Anaïs screamed and dropped to the floor, locking her elbows beneath Julie's arms, trying to fight against the monster's strength—though the maid's body was so small, Mallory worried her entire body would be torn in two.

"What do we do?" Mallory yelled.

"Don't ask me!" Anaïs yelled back. "What even *is* that thing?"

"A lou carcolh."

"A *what?*"

"Think giant man-eating snail with tentacles."

Anaïs shot her a disgruntled look. "Well, I can see *that*. What other useless information can you tell me before it eats us?"

A fourth tentacle joined the battle, ripping the maid from Anaïs's hold. She scrambled forward, but the mouth was opening wider, preparing to clamp around the girl's ankle.

Mallory grabbed the fireplace poker and smashed it into the top of the creature's spiraling shell. The impact resonated up her arms as if she'd struck steel. She stumbled back, teeth aching from the jolt.

Undeterred, the creature had started to close its jaw around the maid's foot when Mallory took the end of the poker and jabbed it into the nearest tentacle instead.

The lou carcolh released a piercing shriek. It took all Mallory's willpower to keep from dropping the poker and covering her ears. Instead, she lifted the weapon again, preparing to impale another tentacle—when a fifth tentacle appeared from beneath the shell and lunged toward Mallory with whiplike speed, snatching the poker out of her hand and tossing it at the window. Glass shattered. Frigid air and wind rushed inside, tearing at the curtains.

Another tentacle took hold of Mallory's arm. She grabbed for one of the bedcovers. As pain lanced up her arm, she tossed a blanket at the creature, fully expecting it to shove the fabric away. But it hesitated, its free tentacles inspecting the fabric instead.

The distraction was enough for Mallory to lower her head and bite down on the tentacle holding her. Slime oozed into her mouth, tasting of sour mucus. The creature screamed and let her go. Mallory reeled back, spitting.

With one hand still holding the corner of the blanket, she launched herself over the creature, pulling the cover over and around, tenting the monster within the ballooned layers of fabric.

"Ha!" she announced victoriously, once it was trapped beneath. "You should know that I *love* escargot, you disgusting, slimy little—"

A rip. A tear. The distinct sounds of chewing.

Anaïs made a face. "Is it eating our linens?"

"Better the linens than us. We need another weapon. Do you see my dagger on the nightstand?"

Suddenly Anaïs's eyes lit up. "What about smelling salts?"

"Honestly, I think she's better off unconscious for now."

Anaïs sprang away from Julie. "Not for her. This thing is part snail, isn't it? Salt is like poison for snails!"

"I'm pretty sure smelling salts don't contain any actual—"

Ignoring her, Anaïs raced from the room, hollering, "I have an idea! I'll be right back!"

"What? Get back here! Don't leave me here to deal with

this—" She yelped. A tentacle had slithered through a hole in the blanket and grabbed Mallory's thigh. It yanked her to the floor. Mallory kicked, her feet getting tangled up in the fabric, her arms burning against the carpet as she was dragged toward the creature's mouth, barely visible through the gash in velvet and lace. The scene was so absurd Mallory would have laughed if she hadn't been scared out of her wits. Instead she flailed around for anything she could grab.

She threw a chair at the creature. It pulled her closer, indifferent.

Flipping onto her stomach, she spied Anaïs's sewing box and threw that—only afterward realizing that the scissors inside could have come in handy.

There was a slipper discarded on the carpet. She grabbed it and took aim, waiting until the creature's mouth had opened. A vicious gate of glistening teeth, an oozing tongue—

She threw the slipper in.

The creature didn't release her, but it hesitated, its tongue exploring the shoe, pushing it from side to side. There was a slurping sound as it devoured the shoe whole.

"Here!" Anaïs stood in the doorway, hefting a linen sack with blue letters stenciled on the side. *SALT.*

Stomping forward, she upended the bag and started dumping the contents onto the lou carcolh's outstretched tentacles in a great, salty waterfall.

"I really don't think . . ." Mallory started, but stopped when the beast released a tortured scream. The skin on its tentacles began to shrivel and hiss.

The lou carcolh pulled its tentacles away from the salt, then limped to the broken window. It lifted itself out, lowering itself down by outstretched tentacles before crashing onto the terrace below. Wounded and hissing, it slid and hobbled into the gardens.

Mallory and Anaïs watched until it had disappeared behind a hedgerow.

"All right," Mallory said in disbelief. "Good thinking."

With a shivery breath, Anaïs dropped the empty bag to the floor. She sank to her knees beside Julie and bent over her.

Julie's chest lifted in a spasm.

"Oh! Excellent!" said Anaïs. "She's not dead. *That* would have been difficult to explain."

As the adrenaline seeped from Mallory's limbs, she crawled over to the mess of salt on the carpet, where the monster had left slimy trails, and used her finger to draw shapes into the salt. A pentagon. A star. Fake runes that meant nothing at all.

"What are you doing?"

"Magic," said Mallory. "If anyone asks, *this* is how we got rid of the beast."

"Mally, please. We almost died. If we keep pretending—"

"I'm not pretending anything. We battled a lou carcolh, and we won."

"Barely! And certainly not with . . . whatever those drawings are!" Anaïs gestured at the salt drawings. "Is that a snail? Did you draw a snail in your fake spell to get rid of a giant snail?"

Mallory scratched out the snail. "No."

Anaïs puffed up her cheeks and blew out one vexed exhale.

Julie stirred, her head swiveling from side to side. "Another one . . . a monster . . . upstairs . . ."

Anaïs laid a hand on the girl's arm. "The monster is gone."

With a cough, Julie squinted open her eyes. "Gone?"

Mallory crossed her arms. "We dealt with it." She fixed a warning stare on her sister. "With magic."

Anaïs huffed, but didn't refute her. Even still, Mallory knew from Anaïs's expression that she had to figure something out, and soon.

And one of her sister's most annoying traits was that she was usually right.

CHAPTER TWENTY-SIX

"*Entrust it to the four winds,*" Mallory murmured, reading the glittering text of the card from Fitcher's Troupe. "What in the name of Wyrdith is that supposed to mean?"

She stood in the center of the tower, ignoring the numerous barn swallows that swooped around overhead, darting in and out of their nests. She did not doubt that the two gentlemen who had captured the voirloup and given her this card were very powerful magicians, but these instructions felt intentionally confounding.

At least she could feel a strong breeze here, blowing in from the sea to the west. That seemed promising.

Sitting on the floor of the tower, she pulled the quill she'd taken from the bedroom writing desk and dunked it into the small pot of ink. She'd spent all morning planning out what she would say, but she still hesitated before pressing the brass tip to the back of the card.

A bird trilled. She glanced up. One of the barn swallows was perched on the rail, head cocked, watching her.

"No," said Mallory. "I really don't know what I'm doing." She refocused on the card. "But that's never stopped me before."

She started to write, attempting her best penmanship.

> *Your assistance is requested at the House Saphir in Comorre to expel ghost of known murderer summoned from Verloren seven years previous. Offering 500 lourdes upon satisfactory removal. Ask for the Fontaine sisters upon arrival.*

She set down the quill and read over the note. According to the troupe's card, they selected their summons based on "payment and personal curiosity."

What was more curious than a murderous ghost?

"I didn't like them," said Triphine.

Mallory yelped. "Triphine! How long have you been standing there?"

The ghost floated to the rail, and the way the barn swallow tilted its head had Mallory wondering—not for the first time—if animals could perceive spirits where humans could not. After a moment, the swallow chirruped and darted upward, disappearing into its nest.

"Long enough," said Triphine, taking in the gardens below. "I don't understand why you want them to come here."

"Curse breakers and monster hunters? Yes, it's quite the mystery."

"You're hiring these men, and yet what do you really know about them? That one of them wears far too much color, and the other, not nearly enough. That there seem to be only two of them, and yet they call themselves a *troupe*. Everyone knows you need at least three people to make a troupe."

"I know they destroyed a voirloup," said Mallory. "One arrow transformed that bloodthirsty monster into a cake topper."

"Which I find to be *highly* suspicious behavior."

"You don't trust anyone."

"Neither do you! Which is why I can't understand why you would ask them for help. You never ask anyone for help."

"That's not true. You used to help me all the time when you would scare the tourists during my tours."

"Until you built a mannequin to replace me!"

Mallory frowned as she twisted the lid back onto the inkwell. "I wouldn't say it *replaced* you . . ." She stood up, pinching the card between her fingers. It fluttered in a gust, but she held tight. What was she supposed to do? Let go? Trust that the *wind* would carry it to its proper destination? What if it didn't work, and the card got stuck on one of the trellises that climbed the side of the house, and a gardener found it and gave it to Armand and then he would know—

She sighed, lowering the card. "I don't like to admit this, but I need help. In case you haven't noticed, I am not making very much progress on *dehaunting* this mansion, and there are more monsters every day. A lou carcolh was in our bedroom last night!"

"I heard about that." Triphine shuddered. "I hope you gave the carpet a good scrubbing afterward, or that slime will never come out."

"Some slime in the carpets is the least of this house's concern."

"And of course I've noticed that you aren't making any progress on this job you've been hired for. But I don't think Lord Armand has noticed. Which is also suspicious, don't you think?"

"It's fortunate," said Mallory. "He's been too busy with the grape harvest to mind what I'm doing, but eventually he's going to start asking questions, and I'm not going to have answers for him. But if this Fitcher's Troupe can take care of the problem for me, well . . . everybody wins."

She hoped they could make quick work of the whole situation. Some spellcasting, a touch of wizardry, a few of those fancy arrows fired at the right targets, and voilà, Mallory would have fulfilled her obligation to Armand, dealt with the ghost that she may or may not have summoned from the afterlife when she was a child, and best of all—she and Anaïs would get the money Armand had promised them.

Most of it. If she had to share a few coins with those two magicians, she would make do.

With any luck, everything would be taken care of before Armand figured out her ruse.

And before Le Bleu killed them all.

"Do you think it means 'the four winds' in a literal sense?" Mallory said, eyeing the swallows flittering in and out of the tower. "Maybe I'm supposed to tie it to a bird, like a carrier pigeon?" She huffed. "These instructions count for plums."

"I don't trust him," said Triphine.

"Fitcher? Or his friend? Either way, they're the best hope I've got right now."

"Both," said Triphine. "But I was talking about Armand."

Mallory wrinkled her nose. "Armand?"

"If that Ruby Comorre wine is so special, why is this house in such disrepair? Why doesn't he have nicer things? His chef served *parsnip soup* last night, Mallory. That is peasant food."

"I like parsnip soup."

"That's because you don't know any better."

Mallory rubbed her temple. Between the winds and the birds and the ghost, her head felt like it was about to implode. "He cannot keep a full staff," she said slowly, "because of the *killer ghost* who won't leave his house. And he can't get rid of the killer ghost because he unwittingly hired a *fraud*, a problem that I am trying to fix, so that someday I might actually get paid."

Triphine yelped suddenly and jumped up onto the rail. "I just saw a rat!"

Mallory raised an eyebrow. "How are you possibly still afraid of rats?"

"They're horrifying," said Triphine. "And they carry diseases. You know I have a delicate constitution."

Mallory spied a long, thin tail as the creature dove behind a pillar. She peered around the side.

"Oh," she said, surprised. It wasn't a rat at all, but another salamander, skin shining wetly.

Its eyelids blinked—one first, then the other. It was unlikely that this was the same salamander she'd seen by the kitchen over a week ago, and yet, if she wasn't mistaken, it seemed to recognize her.

"You're saved," she said dryly. "It's only a salamander."

"A salamander!" cried Triphine. "That's even worse."

Mallory read the instructions on the card again, though she had long ago committed them to memory. "*Entrust it to the four winds,*" she murmured, then sighed. "If you say so."

She waited for another breeze to blow through the tower. Bracing herself for disappointment, she held the card out over the ledge, exhaled, and let go. As soon as it was out of reach, she stepped back from the ledge.

The card started to fall, fluttering down toward the distant ground. But then it stopped and hovered, buoyed upward, dancing on the wind.

Mallory held her breath, waiting.

The card began to transform. The corners folded in on themselves. Again and again. It happened so fast, a blur of transformation. Mallory barely blinked and then—it was no longer a card, but a tiny shimmering moth, crafted from folded pearlescent paper.

Mallory's lips parted. It was magnificent. The prismatic calligraphy winding around its elegant body. Sunlight catching on fluttering wings. It was alive but not alive.

It was magic. Or sorcery. Or witchcraft, beyond anything she'd ever seen her mother do. Beyond anything—

A stream of yellow flame appeared from the stone rail, shooting straight at the paper moth.

The paper ignited in a brief fiery orb, then burned clear away. A trail of black ash drifted skyward on the wind.

"Well," said Triphine, "that was tragic."

Mallory gaped at the empty place where the moth had been.

Slowly, she turned her appalled glare toward the salamander.

It alternately blinked its immense yellow eyes, then flicked its tongue, as if asking what she planned to do now.

Red splotches invading her vision, Mallory launched herself at the creature.

It darted along the length of the rail and threw itself down to the floor, running right through Mallory's ankles, and through the trapdoor that led down into the house.

Mallory shrieked and leaped after it, shoving her arm through the gap in an effort to catch the little beastie. "Get back here, you slimy, web-footed, baby dragon impost—ah!" A face loomed at the bottom of the ladder, startling her.

Mallory lost her balance. Grappled for the rungs of the ladder and missed. She heaved forward, down through the trapdoor.

Armand yelped, barely catching her as she collided into him and sent them both sprawling across the wooden landing.

"We really ought to stop meeting like this," he muttered, groaning as Mallory rolled off him. "What were you yelling about?"

It took a moment for Mallory to catch her breath and gather her wits. "Oh. Just . . . there was a salamander." Her face was flushed with fury as she sat up, but she stilled her tongue before she could recount the travesty of the paper moth. "I was, er . . . trying to catch it, before it set the house on fire." She glanced around the stairwell, but the salamander was gone.

"Wily creatures," said Armand. "And more clever than they look."

Mallory guffawed. "This one is nothing but a menace." She quieted, noticing a basket that had spilled across the floor when they'd fallen—some bundled plants, fabric, a couple of small glass bottles. And on Armand's sleeve . . . a reddish-brown spot. Blood? "What's all that?"

Flustered, Armand started putting the basket to rights. "I heard about what happened, with the lou carcolh."

She didn't respond. It felt like a trap.

"I was worried you might have been injured. You . . . or your sister. Or Julie. I wondered if you needed any medicine? I have calendula for any pain or swelling you might have and valerian root if you need help sleeping. I also had a bit of a tussle with a barberry bush, but lived to tell the tale, and the poultice will help with infection." His chuckle was charmingly self-deprecating as he indicated some scratches on his wrist. "Doesn't look as bad as your arm, I guess."

Mallory straightened the arm that the lou carcolh had grasped. Red welts and bruises had appeared where the tentacles had wrapped around her.

Armand seemed to take the movement as an invitation. He scooted closer and gently took hold of her wrist, his studious gaze raking across the wounds.

"Similar to a burn," he said. "I think the lavender oil will help."

"Do you see what I mean?" said Triphine, still loitering on the upper floor of the tower. "What sort of count knows about lavender oil and calendula? He's very peculiar."

Mallory bit back a smile. She didn't disagree—he *was* peculiar.

"Is it painful?" Armand asked.

"Nothing I can't handle."

"That sounds like a yes." He pulled out a small jar of ointment and dipped his fingers into the salve.

If it bothered Armand that they were standing in a dusty stairwell, where any servant could happen by to see the lord of the house tenderly applying a pale pink salve to the bruised arms of his hired witch—he did not show it.

After a minute, it stopped bothering Mallory, too. The salve tingled, and his fingers were both sure and gentle, massaging the ointment into her arms from her wrist to her elbows. His expression always the picture of gentlemanly studiousness—a scientist inspecting a specimen. If it wasn't for the touch of pink that had risen on his cheeks . . .

He put the lid back on the ointment and retrieved a length of gauze, winding it around Mallory's injured arm. "It may not be fashionable," he said, "but it will give the salve time to seep in and do its work."

When he was finished, he put his things away into the basket and met her eyes for the first time since he'd begun.

His cheeks darkened further, and he immediately looked away. "Does your sister . . . ?"

"She wasn't hurt."

"I'm glad. No one was expecting a lou carcolh in the house. Lutins and salamanders come in from the fields when the weather starts to change. But something that vicious?" He shook his head. "It's almost as though they're being drawn here."

"You said the house has always attracted monsters."

"Yes, but not usually this many. And nothing like that."

He spoke so earnestly that Mallory felt captivated. And then his gaze was on her again and she felt suddenly weightless. He was so close to her. Her heartbeat quickened.

He was most peculiar indeed. And she . . . she liked him. In spite of it. Because of it.

She more than liked him. She *wanted* him, in ways she couldn't recall ever wanting anybody before.

She had only realized this positively unacceptable reality when they heard the screams.

CHAPTER TWENTY-SEVEN

She raced toward the sound, Armand at her side. Down the stairs, through endless corridors, infinite parlors and galleries. The screaming stopped, but it was still ringing in Mallory's ears. Was it Julie? Yvette? Anaïs?

"Where was it coming from?" she panted.

"The north wing," Armand said. "I think."

They barreled beneath an arched doorway, between two marble columns, over worn carpets, past ancient clocks and soulless statues.

"What in the name of the Seven was that?" bellowed Pierre, appearing at the bottom of a stairwell, his apron stained with grease.

Neither responded. They kept running—until they emerged into the hall of trophies. A black-and-white marble floor stretched in front of them. The walls were lined with the heads of every imaginable creature, hung on polished wooden plaques, watching as Mallory and Armand arrived.

A group of people were gathered at the far end of the hall.

Yvette was sobbing into Claude's shoulder. Anaïs stood with a hand pressed to her mouth, her expression tormented.

"What happened?" Armand asked. "Who was screaming?"

"It was Yvette that screamed," Claude said quietly. "She's the one who found her, sir."

"Found her? Found——" Armand drew up short. Yvette and Claude had shifted aside enough for them to see what was beyond them.

The head of an imperial stag had been mounted on the far end of the hall—a glorious beast, with at least twenty points on antlers that grew like the branches of a regal oak. Sprawled across those antlers was a body.

Julie.

Her arms and legs hung limp, her head tipped backward, her long hair a tangled cascade. A spot of blood reddened her blue-tinted lips. Her eyes were open but dull and unseeing.

A sword had been driven through her chest. Blood dripped down the blade, onto the face of the stag. A dark puddle was spreading across the tiled floor.

Mallory was the only one who moved. Her shoes clipped harshly in the otherwise silent room—even Yvette's sobs had quieted with their arrival.

Nothing seemed real as she approached the body, taking in every gory detail. The maid was in her uniform, but her feet were bare—no shoes, no stockings. The sapphire ring was gone—the entire finger cut clean from her hand. Was theft the motive? No—she didn't believe so. This was too staged. Too dramatic. The killer wanted to send a message.

A warning?

And there were the words. She knew them without having to read them. The same that had been carved into the arms of Bastien's victims.

Echtraus. Trust.

Greischt. Betrayal.

Mallory had read news articles detailing various diseases, asphyxiation, bludgeonings. Coroners' reports that spoke of poisons and stab wounds. She had devoured the details of murder investigations as voraciously as she'd devoured that morning's croissants.

Mallory knew a thing or two about death, and she was not afraid of it.

She reached toward the body, pressing her knuckles to Julie's cheek, then brow. Not warm, but not yet cold, either. She felt her arm, her elbow, her wrist. The muscles were beginning to stiffen.

"I would guess she's been dead for an hour, maybe two," she said, her focus going to the hilt of the sword. "Does anyone recognize the weapon?"

There was a long silence before Armand said in a strained voice, "It's Bastien's sword. It's hung in the indigo salon for ages."

He didn't say it, but Mallory knew. This sword had been used to kill before. Mallory scanned the room. Other than the blood directly beneath the body, the floors were spotless—no trail of blood, no muddy footprints. A feather duster lay forgotten beside a taxidermy fox.

She wondered if the murder had happened here. The killer could have sneaked up on Julie while she worked. Taken her by surprise. Or if it had been her secret beau—her *husband*—he would not have had to sneak up on her at all. She would have welcomed seeing him.

Mallory looked from shadow to shadow, dead creature to dead creature. There were no open windows. If the killer was human, they would have had to leave via one of the doorways at either end of the hall.

Perhaps most interesting, she saw no sign of any ghosts. Not Monsieur Le Bleu. Not his wives. And not Julie.

Had her spirit gone to Verloren upon her death, guided by Velos's lantern? It was the natural way of things, and yet, this death had been anything but natural. Le Bleu's first three victims had been trapped on the mortal plane after their brutal murders.

But what if Le Bleu had not been the one to kill her? As far as anyone knew, Le Bleu had only killed—or attempted to kill—his own wives. But Julie was a maid, not . . .

Mallory's pulse thundered in her ears.

How? Bastien Saphir may have been charming, but not even he could trick a mortal girl into falling in love with him, *marrying* him. Not when his violent crimes were so well-known.

"I wish to speak with the staff individually," she said. "No one is to communicate with each other until I do."

"Whatever for?" asked Claude.

"To determine who has an alibi, and who might have had a reason to kill her."

Yvette let out a frustrated wheeze. "We all know who did this, Miss Fontaine. It was that monster, Monsieur Le Bleu!"

"That is an easy assumption to make," said Mallory, "but I do not know of any ghost who is capable of this."

"He is not a normal ghost," snapped the housekeeper. "He has hurt people before. Now this poor girl has become one more of his victims."

Mallory thought of mirror shards lodged into eyeballs. She thought of an invisible force shoving a victim down the stairs. She thought of how easily Bastien had lifted the burning incense. How he had pressed his thumb to her throat, sending a bolt of pain through her chest.

Yes, Le Bleu was capable of a lot. He had shown signs of being corporeal, of having strength unlike any spirit she'd seen.

But *this*? To not only impale Julie on a sword, but then to position her body in such a way? It would have been difficult for anyone to accomplish. She doubted any ghost could have done as much, not even Monsieur Le Bleu.

"Perhaps you're right," she said. "But I think it's best we know for sure, don't you?"

Yvette rounded on her. "You dare to accuse someone in this household of such a heinous act?"

"I'm merely pointing out that most ghosts are not capable of such strength, no matter how depraved they are."

"Well, then," said the housekeeper, "I shall point out that of all the people in this house, only two of them are relative strangers." Her sharp gaze bored into Mallory, her insinuation clear. But it didn't bother Mallory. She was used to being mistrusted, and she would sooner suspect Anaïs of being a finger-eating croquemitaine than a murderer.

"My sister," said Anaïs, with unusual severity, "knows more about death and dark magic and the occult than everyone else in this room put together. I would urge you not to doubt her instincts in this matter."

Mallory's insides warmed at the vote of confidence, but it was short-lived when Yvette laughed dryly. "Forgive me if I do not find her knowledge of *the occult* to be a comfort in such a situation. For if this was not the work of Le Bleu, then who else but a witch would be suited for such a vile act?"

Anaïs tensed. "Julie did have a beau."

"She what?" snapped the housekeeper.

"She was in love," Anaïs continued. "She asked to have her fortune told, after she . . . after they eloped. Secretly, and quite suddenly. She wanted to know if she . . . if she made the right decision . . ." Anaïs trailed off.

"If that is true, then no doubt your magical predictions informed her of her impending doom." Yvette gestured at the body. "Surely your impressive abilities indicated what was about to happen? Perhaps even suggested who the murderer would be?"

Anaïs shied away, but Mallory snapped, "Of *course* the cards predicted this—*a disastrous end to the romance*. I was there for the whole thing, and those were her exact words. But clearly, she was too late."

Anaïs pressed her lips together and said nothing.

"For all we know, Julie planned to dissolve the marriage after hearing her fortune," continued Mallory, "and it led to a quarrel that got out of hand. It wouldn't be the first time. Plus—her ring is missing." She swallowed painfully. "Along with the finger that wore it."

"The finger?" Yvette shrieked. "It could only be Le Bleu, and Julie has said nothing to me of a wedding. Not even a courtship."

"What about the stable hand?" asked Mallory.

"Gideon?" barked Claude, one arm still holding Yvette. "You cannot be serious."

"I haven't met him," Mallory confessed.

"If you had," Claude went on, "you would know that he is as harmless as a dove. He could not have done something like this. And for him to be making promises to our Julie? Bah!" He threw his other hand dismissively toward Mallory.

"That may be, but I would like to speak to him."

"If you honestly believe this was anyone other than my ancestor," said Armand in his quiet, measured voice, "then it would be prudent to summon the police."

Mallory inhaled sharply. "That won't be necessary."

Armand's expression turned sympathetic. "This has nothing to do with you and your sister. It's unlikely the Comorre constable will have had any contact with those investigators."

"Investigators?" asked the housekeeper. "What investigators?"

Mallory crossed her arms. She didn't need any more reasons for the housekeeper—or any of the staff—to distrust her or her sister, and admitting that there might be a warrant out for their arrest was unlikely to help the situation.

"If this was done by the ghost," she said, "then there is nothing the police can do. But if it wasn't him, we cannot waste any time. It will take too long for help to arrive, and the killer could be destroying evidence or preparing to run even as we speak."

"This is absurd. Of course it was Le Bleu," muttered the housekeeper. "To suggest otherwise is despicable."

"What of her family?" asked Anaïs. "What will you tell them?"

Yvette shook her head. "She does not . . . did not have any. Raised by her grandfather, who passed last spring. She's lived here in the château ever since."

The words hung heavy in the room. Mallory scraped her

attention over Julie's pale face again—the open eyes, the blood at the corner of her lips.

Le Bleu had chosen his victims carefully. Women with few connections, or whose families would be relieved to be rid of them.

"Anaïs," she said, "I would ask you to gather everyone. I will conduct my interviews in the indigo salon."

"I can do it," said Armand. "I should be the one to inform the rest of the staff, those who don't know yet."

"No," said Mallory. "Not you."

He frowned. "Why not?"

She lifted her chin, unblinking.

Realization slowly crossed his face. Armand took an unsteady step back. "Surely you don't think I could have done this?"

When she didn't respond, hurt swept over his features. Then irritation. A muscle jumped in his jaw, but he inclined his head. "The indigo salon it is."

CHAPTER TWENTY-EIGHT

To Mallory's consternation, the interviews were almost entirely useless.

She could admit to herself that she'd hoped it *was* the stable hand. That Gideon, when subjected to her questions, would be so unnerved he would dissolve into a blubbering, guilty confession.

No confession came.

Instead, Gideon—a ruddy-faced boy of sixteen—seemed genuinely horrified to learn what had happened to Julie, and even more genuinely horrified at Mallory's suggestion that he might have had anything to do with it. When Mallory asked if he and Julie had a romantic relationship, he'd stammered that he was quite in love with Théo, the son of Comorre's blacksmith. They had been courting since the Harvest Festival, as anyone in town could have told her.

Mallory believed him. It was highly unlikely that a stable hand could have saved enough money to purchase that sapphire ring, anyway.

The rest of her interviews were just as frustrating. In the hours prior to Yvette finding Julie's body, everyone had been going about their daily business. Yvette had been cleaning the floors in the game room. Claude had been in the study, writing a letter to a local glass artisan about fixing the window in Mallory and Anaïs's room—the one the lou carcolh had thrown the fireplace poker through. Pierre had been in the kitchen, chopping vegetables for a stew. And before he'd come up to the tower, Armand had been in the greenhouse, gathering medicinal ingredients for Mallory's wounds. He appeared rather put-out as he told her this, still resentful that she could suspect him.

Perhaps Julie had a lover in town—a possibility that Yvette thought unlikely, given how rarely the maid left the estate. But Mallory was willing to grasp for any alternatives.

She didn't want to suspect Armand. The very idea of it churned her stomach and left her reeling with memories of his hand outstretched to her; the way he'd softened her fall when the voirloup was after them; his soft, knowing smile as he handed her a mug of hot chocolate; the dirt that collected beneath his fingernails when he'd spent a morning in the greenhouse.

Surely he could not be a murderer. Surely.

But who else might Julie have been so smitten with? The stable hand aside, she could not picture the young maid being taken with the elderly butler or gruff chef. Only Armand was handsome, sweet, charming when he wanted to be. And wealthy. A vast estate, a wine empire, a noble title. What girl—orphaned maid or otherwise—wouldn't be swept up in a dreamy romance to such a man?

The more Mallory dwelt on it, the more her insides squirmed.

Not *her*, obviously. She knew better than that. She'd heard too many stories of foolish girls taken in by the charms of affluent, cruel men. She would far prefer to believe that a ghost had somehow gained the strength necessary to continue his murder streak.

Armand, or Le Bleu.

Le Bleu, or Armand.

Neither added up. Nothing seemed right. She was missing an important detail—some possibility not yet considered.

"The sword was missing late last night," said Béatrice, who was sitting on the piano bench, idly dragging her fingers along the ivory keys. There was a faded spot on the wallpaper above the mantel, in the exact shape of the sword that had been plunged into Julie's chest. Evidence that it had hung there, untouched, for years. "I noticed it when I was playing the Gloaming Nocturne."

"What time was that?" Mallory asked.

"Oh—midnight? A little later? I don't pay much attention to time."

"But you didn't see who took it?"

Béatrice shook her head.

"And we didn't see who killed her, either," piped up Lucienne, "as I'm sure you're about to ask." She was playing both sides in a game of chess while Triphine pouted on the nearby settee, having insisted that Lucienne was a lousy cheat and she would never play anything with her ever again.

Mallory *had* been about to ask. "You didn't hear or see anything suspicious?"

"Everything around here is suspicious, in case you hadn't noticed," said Triphine, glaring as Lucienne captured (and lost) the white queen.

"And yet, this is the first murder to occur here in a century," Mallory pointed out.

Béatrice felt around the hole in her chest. "She was stabbed, like we were?"

"Yes. And had the same words carved into her arms."

"That certainly sounds like Bastien," Lucienne muttered.

"Ah, you did it again!" Triphine hollered triumphantly, and grabbed the black rook off the game board. "You can't do that. You're even cheating against yourself!"

"So what if I am?" said Lucienne, trying to grab the piece back. When Triphine held it out of her reach, Lucienne sniffed and pinched her hard on the arm.

"Ow!" Triphine dropped the chess piece. "I bruise easily, I'll have you know."

Mallory rolled her eyes. Their arrival at the House Saphir had not lessened Triphine's infinite list of imagined ailments.

Although—as the duchess rubbed the spot on her arm that Lucienne had grabbed, it did seem that a bruise was already blossoming above her elbow. A reminder that ghosts existed on a different plane from humans, from mortals. They could touch each other. Embrace each other. Soothe each other. And—hurt each other.

Mallory shuddered, grateful on behalf of these women that Bastien rarely strayed far from the cellar, and when he did meander about the house, he seemed more intent on harassing the living than the captive spirits.

Harassing the living and . . . murdering them?

"But how could it have been Bastien?" Mallory whispered to herself. "I've never known a ghost to remain corporeal long enough to kill a person. If he was capable of it, I'm sure he would have killed me in the cellar that day. Unless . . . he's somehow getting stronger." She'd been taking notes, and now tapped the charcoal pencil against her mouth. "Also, if it was Bastien, wouldn't her spirit still be here? Tethered by the same dark magic that keeps the three of you unable to pass on to Verloren?"

The ghosts stilled, considering this.

Béatrice finally murmured, "She makes a fair point."

"I know," said Triphine. "Such a rare occurrence."

"Well, I say, good for her if she managed to escape this bloody place." Having captured the black king, Lucienne started resetting the board. "Though it would be handy if we could talk to her."

If we could talk to her . . .

Mallory sighed. "Yes. It would."

"You're sure she had some mysterious lover?" said Lucienne with an approving smirk. "It does explain some of her sneaking about, though I wouldn't have expected it from her. You never know with the shy ones."

"What sneaking about?" asked Mallory.

"She would be out of bed at all hours some nights," Lucienne said. "She liked to go for midnight walks in the gardens. Would disappear when she was supposed to be finishing the laundry or helping to polish the floors. A few nights ago, she went into town to pick up some things from the couturier and didn't come back until after dark. Said she lost track of time. I'm sure Yvette would have fired her, except she didn't want to throw the girl out on the street—and if it wasn't so hard to keep help around here in the first place."

"I'll have to search her room. Maybe something there will indicate who gave her the ring."

Mallory jotted a few notes about Julie's comings and goings into her sketchbook, while Béatrice launched into a dramatic piano melody that made the sconces tremble on the walls.

THE SERVANTS' QUARTERS WERE ON THE TOP FLOOR, peeling off from a dimly lit corridor. Julie's door was unlocked. The room was tidy, the furnishings simple. Linen drapes hung over a dormer window, where a sewing kit sat beside a wooden stool. A narrow bed was dressed with two faded quilts and a single pillow, where a few dark strands of Julie's hair clung to the pillowcase. A small table held a nub of a candle. A wooden trunk sat at the foot of the bed.

Mallory fell upon the trunk first, digging through another maid uniform and apron. Wool stockings. A plain dress. A small tin full of hairpins. When the trunk held nothing of interest, Mallory moved to the nightstand, with its single drawer.

Inside were a couple of handkerchiefs, a green hair ribbon, nine copper lys—Mallory hesitated for only a moment before tucking them into her pocket, as Julie never had paid for her card reading. There was also a tiny book—*Psalms of the Seven* printed upon its cover.

As soon as Mallory picked up the book, something fluttered from between the pages. A pressed flower fell to the floor.

She picked it up, holding it toward the pale sunlight from the window, twirling the stem in her fingers.

Though the petals were faded, as delicate as ancient papyrus, she recognized the flower. Its unique blue and purple petals, curved in alternating rings. The pinwheel crown. Precisely like those in the greenhouse.

Armand's greenhouse.

CHAPTER TWENTY-NINE

Claude quit the next morning. According to Yvette, he had a daughter in Comorre who was with child, and though he had served the Saphir family dutifully for near twenty years, he wasn't about to risk the wrath of Le Bleu before he held his first grandchild in his arms.

Mallory didn't blame him, though she didn't really believe he was in danger from Le Bleu, whose victims fit a particular mold.

Armand didn't try to stop him, either, and gave him use of his finest carriage to take him into town. Mallory watched from a ballroom window as Claude said his goodbyes to the remaining staff, and Armand pressed a parting gift into his hand. Coins? Jewelry?

Mallory's insides stirred with envy, a reminder of why she was here. Not to solve a murder, but to get rid of a ghost. To get paid—more money than she'd ever dreamed she would see in her lifetime. To take her and her sister far away from Lysraux. To start a new life.

The carriage rolled away, and the staff returned to their work.

Mallory stayed at the window, watching the gardens, the skies, the birds swooping in and out of the house's eaves. Armand had told her that Monsieur Le Bleu would laugh and whistle and stomp around the house when he had been cruel, ensuring that everyone knew what he had done. But he had been quiet since Julie had been found.

"I knew there was something wrong when I saw her cards."

Mallory hadn't seen her sister come in, but now Anaïs stood at the next window, staring blankly out at the same gardens, the same sky.

"I lied. I told her what she wanted to hear, even though . . . I knew that isn't what the cards were saying."

"You can't read the cards, Anaïs. You don't have petty magic."

"Magic or not, they were trying to tell us something." Her voice rose. "The Empty Coffin? The Untouched Feast? They were bad omens."

"We don't know that."

Anaïs threw her arms up, exasperated. "For all the—! She drew *Velos*."

"Who is the god of wisdom. It doesn't always mean death."

"I think it's safe to say that this time, it did."

Mallory sighed. "There's nothing you could have said to change what happened. There was no way for either of us to know. Besides, she'd already gotten married, even before she asked for a reading. You couldn't have prevented it."

"Yes, but married who?" Anaïs asked. "We could have asked . . ."

"I did!" Mallory reminded her. "But she didn't want to say, and you didn't want to press her—"

"So you do think it's my fault?"

"No, of course not!" Mallory thought of that perfectly pressed flower tumbling from the pages of Julie's book. And how angry and hurt she'd been on the terrace overlooking the gardens. The way she'd swooned and joked about kissing a lord, right in front of him.

A naïve girl. A secret wedding. And the lord of the manor, who had such a genuine smile it did not seem possible he could be harboring a taste for brutality.

A smile so genuine it had even made Mallory forget herself.

Anaïs deflated. "I could have told her something. Something true. She saw it in the cards. I know she did. But I lied through my teeth, and she believed me."

"Because she wanted to believe you. That isn't your fault." Mallory leaned against the windowsill. "We need to do something, before he figures out that we have no idea what we're doing."

Anaïs looked at her, incredulous. "Are you really concerned about tricking Armand into paying you right now?"

"If Le Bleu killed Julie, then getting rid of him solves two problems, doesn't it?"

Anaïs drummed her fingertips on the windowsill, studying Mallory. "But you don't think it was him."

"It's the only thing that makes sense."

After a beat, Anaïs asked, "Is it?"

Mallory swallowed. "What about protective wards?"

"Protective what?"

"Mother used to go to people's houses and draw symbols on their doors. It was supposed to create a barrier against evil spirits and dark magic. We could do that."

"You think a few doodles are going to frighten away Monsieur Le Bleu?"

"Of course not, but so long as Armand thinks we are useful, he is more likely to keep us around, and give us a chance to determine what is really going on here."

Mallory knew she would need to tread carefully. If Armand was so cruel and manipulative as to be the real murderer, she had to stop saying anything that might reveal her suspicions.

"All right," said Anaïs, sounding doubtful. "Any idea what those protective wards looked like?"

Mallory didn't respond. It had been many years since she'd believed she would ever need to know the shapes of magical runes, but . . . yes. She still remembered them as clear as crystal.

Anaïs let out a tired huff. "I'll find some chalk."

MALLORY SPENT TWO HOURS WALKING AROUND THE house marking the doors with elaborate designs inspired by those she recalled from her mother's books. Runes to call on favors from the gods. Runes to protect. To banish. To . . . well, she wasn't entirely sure what, but they certainly made all this magic business *feel* legitimate. A constellation of stars. A two-headed snake. A ring of brambles and roses.

She needed Armand to witness her putting these protective wards on the house. There was no point if he didn't notice. He had to believe that she had her sights fully and entirely focused upon his great-great-grandfather, and she was more determined than ever to send him back to the land of the lost.

Besides, she wanted to believe that perhaps the ghost *was* still the biggest threat within these walls. If she should miraculously succeed in banishing him, or at least making Armand believe that she had succeeded . . .

Three thousand lourdes. A new life. Travel to far-flung places. Everything she could ever ask for.

But those fantasies were tainted now. Julie had married *someone*, and Mallory didn't think it was a hundred-year-old ghost. *Someone* had driven a sword through Julie's chest and had the strength to lift her onto those antlers.

Much as she wanted to believe otherwise, she could only see one possibility. But if Armand was as devious as his ancestor . . . then why bring her and Anaïs here under the ruse of needing their help?

If Mallory found evidence that he had killed Julie, then . . . *poof.* No more payment.

But if she found evidence that it *wasn't* him . . .

Then what?

She was back at the beginning. Still no witchcraft. Still no ability to do anything practical in this situation. And a new, uncomfortable certainty that Monsieur Le Bleu was a far more powerful ghost than she'd ever encountered before.

Mallory's thoughts churned in never-ending spirals as she sketched wards on the threshold of the greenhouse, which was dark and quiet inside.

She warded the steps of the garden terrace. The wall surrounding the orangerie. A potting shed.

She warded the library, the study, the banquet hall, and every salon on the ground floor.

The guest rooms. The stairwells. The tower ladder. The ballroom floor.

She finally dared to make her way to Armand's private suites. She hadn't been to this part of the house yet, but she knew from poring over plans of the house that it held a private library, study, bedroom, and the largest bathtub on the property.

The air smelled different here—more earthy, as if Armand had brought the aromas of the greenhouse with him.

She pulled out her chalk and started drawing sigils on the arched wooden door, making sure to be *very loud* about it.

When Armand didn't immediately come to investigate, she drew even more elaborate symbols. So elaborate that she was running out of ideas and had resorted to doodling an assortment of random gravestones along the base of the door when it finally opened.

Armand stood before her, bewildered.

Bewildered and . . . *shirtless*.

Bewildered and shirtless and . . . was that blood on his hands?

Mallory jumped away, her back colliding with the wall of the corridor. A painting trembled, threatening to fall. The chalk clattered to the floor and split in two.

Pink rushed into Armand's cheeks. "Forgive me. I thought you were—I thought maybe Claude had changed his—er. One moment."

He shut the door.

Mallory stood, unable to move while her heart knocked around inside her rib cage, making it difficult to breathe. A practical part of her mind signaled that seeing blood on Armand's hands was a very bad thing.

The rest of her mind noted that seeing him half-dressed was . . . less bad.

When the door swung open again a few seconds later, Armand had thrown on a linen work shirt and was rubbing his fingers with a damp towel. "Miss Fontaine. What can I . . ." He hesitated, noticing the drawings on the door.

Mallory looked, too. She had gotten a little carried away, she supposed. The door was as cluttered with random symbolism as the ceiling of one of Solvilde's temples.

"What's all this?"

"I'm warding the house against evil," she explained in a tone that suggested this should have been obvious. "It isn't the strongest magic, but after what happened yesterday, it felt like we could use a little extra protection."

He opened his mouth. Closed it. Opened it again and pointed at the door. "Is that a seahorse?"

Her hand curled into a fist, before she shook it out and rubbed the chalk dust on her skirt. "An ancient symbol of strength," she lied.

"Seahorses? Really?"

"Are you hurt?" she asked, trying to shake the image of his bare chest from her thoughts. No—not true. She wasn't trying to shake anything. "Are you bleeding?"

The color in Armand's cheeks deepened. "I'm fine."

An obvious lie. He was also more unkempt than she'd ever seen him. Hair uncombed and a shadow of facial hair gracing his jaw.

She stepped closer, craning her head. A bandage was poking out of the collar of Armand's shirt, across the left side of his throat.

"Were you attacked? Was it Le Bleu?"

Armand blinked in surprise, and she could admit she sounded a bit too hopeful. But if Le Bleu could wield a knife . . .

Armand grimaced. "No. It was . . ." He made a disgusted sound in his throat. "This is mortifying."

He spun away and marched back into his room, leaving the door hanging open.

Which was almost an invitation. Close enough for Mallory, anyway.

She stepped inside, marveling at the suite's sitting room. Black marble around the fireplace, veined with copper and cream. Damask wallpaper of blue and gold. Brass chandeliers dripping with crystals. Every surface covered in elaborate moldings and gilt details.

Armand had disappeared into the next room. Mallory saw a four-poster bed hung with cerulean velvet curtains and trimmed in thick golden tassels. Armand himself was standing in front of a mirror that hung above a washbasin, where the bowl, the pitcher, and even the soap dish bore the crest of the House Saphir. He was peeling back the bandage to apply some sort of salve from a jar. When he was finished, he scowled at his reflection, angling his head back and forth and running his fingers across the bit of dark scruff on his face.

She craned her head further, noting the ebony armoire, the leather reading chair, the stacks and stacks of books messily strewn into every corner. She spotted the ring of keys that Armand usually wore on his belt, now hung on a hook beside the bed.

Cursing, he leaned back on his heels and dragged both hands through his hair. "It won't stop growing. I don't understand it."

It took Mallory a moment to realize he meant the facial hair—the barely there shadow of a beard creeping across his jaw.

"You're growing a beard?"

"Not intentionally," he said, sounding frantic. "People already say that I resemble him. And now, this? It's a nightmare."

"Some women find a full beard quite fetching," Mallory said.

He cast her a withering look.

"That isn't helpful," she conceded. "But surely you can shave it off."

"That's what I was trying to do. But I used to have a valet for that, and Claude took over the job months ago, and now . . ."

She tried to bite back a snicker. She really did.

But *honestly*.

"You nobles. So spoiled," she said jokingly, well aware that few nobles would be willing to make their own hot chocolate. "Is that why you're bleeding? You cut yourself? *Shaving?*"

He leaned forward to inspect the wound in the mirror. "I thought I hit something important. It was bleeding a lot a minute ago, but it's stopped now."

Mallory crossed to the vanity. "Show me where you keep the razors. I can do it."

Mallory had never held a straight razor before, but she was no stranger to sharp objects, and the dusting of hair on Armand's jaw could hardly qualify as a beard. It would only take a moment.

Armand looked dubious at her proclamation—but not, perhaps, as dubious as he should have been. "You?"

She grinned. "How hard can it be?"

CHAPTER THIRTY

Despite her confidence, Mallory was still surprised when Armand pulled out a drawer on the washstand, revealing a collection of small tools organized into open boxes. There was a round brush with a puff of badger hair bristles attached to a crystal knob, and a puck of tallow shaving soap settled inside a porcelain mug. Inside a long wooden box was a folding straight razor with a bone handle and a dreamy steel blade, its edge perfectly sharpened and glinting in the light from the window.

Armand started to unbutton his shirt.

Mallory's eyes widened. "What are you doing?"

His hands froze, his expression more alarmed than ever. "Sorry. Should I keep it on? I always . . . before . . ."

Great gods. "Right. Yes. Carry on. I'll just . . . find some towels." She darted into the washroom and gathered up an armful of towels, ignoring the one streaked with blood that had been thrown into the bathtub—which truly was enormous. She wondered how many buckets had to be carried up from the well to fill it.

When she returned, Armand was seated in the vanity chair, his head leaned back against the bowl of the washbasin.

Shirtless, again.

She tossed the entire armload of towels at him. He caught most against his chest, though a few scattered across the floor.

"In case you get cold," she said. Her voice squeaked only a *tiny* bit.

As he draped a towel over himself, Mallory examined the shaving instruments. She could feel Armand's attention upon her as she picked up the silver blade.

"You have no idea what you're doing, do you?"

She clenched her jaw. "Do you want my help with this or not?"

"I'm honestly not sure."

Mallory bent over him, inspecting the tiny hairs beneath his left ear, planning her attack. Armand's cheek twitched. "Usually Claude puts a damp towel over my face, then uses the brush to add the soap."

"I know that."

She did not know that, but as she dunked a towel into the basin—still lukewarm from Armand's botched attempt, she sensed him starting to relax. His eyes even twinkled with a hint of amusement.

And . . . trust.

Far too much trust.

"I'm not telling you what to do," he said.

"Hush. I'm focusing."

She squeezed the water from the towel and handed it to Armand, who pressed it to his jaw.

Mallory dunked the brush into the water next, before swirling it around the soap, building up a lather that smelled faintly of peppermint.

The lump in his throat jumped as she spread the lather down the length of his neck.

She reached for the razor and flipped open the blade with a satisfying click.

"Be careful," he whispered. "It's very sharp."

"I thought you weren't telling me what to do."

Armand didn't even flinch as she pressed the blade along the side of his cheek. It made a quiet scraping noise as she slid it along his skin, hair and soap gathering against the thin metal edge.

After each swipe, Mallory dunked the blade in the washbasin, where suds and bits of hair floated together. She briefly stilled, squinting at the tiny specks of hair on the surface—not black, but as blue as the sea itself.

Her movements were careful and steady, passing systematically from cheek to cheek, the bow of his lip to the line of his chin. Armand was so still, she wondered at times if he was breathing at all.

She made the last couple of sweeps up his neck, careful to avoid his previous wound. The blade glided above his carotid artery. She tried to ignore how he was watching her, his gaze uncannily piercing, inhumanly vibrant, as if he were seeing straight into her thoughts. Which at this moment, would be very bad indeed.

His lips parted, the tiniest bit. "Mallory . . ."

In her suddenly nervous state, Mallory could have sworn he'd said, *Marry me* . . .

She gasped. The blade dug in. He winced. At first, there was nothing. Then, slowly, a line of blood beaded up on his skin and dripped toward the towel.

"I'm sorry!" Mallory dropped the razor into the basin and grabbed another towel, pressing it to the wound.

She could feel her world upending. One hand remained pressed to his throat, feeling his warmth through the towel, the fluttering thumps of his pulse. This felt like a lover's caress. How she might touch him if she woke up beside him in the morning. If she could curl her body beside his, lift herself onto an elbow, smile down into his sleepy eyes, be met with his drowsy grin. If she could run a thumb along the edge of his jaw. Dig her fingertips into the hair at the nape of his neck.

Armand was watching her, his breaths a tiny bit erratic, his brow lightly furrowed. Still entirely too trusting, too vulnerable. She could do anything. Kill him. Kiss him. He was at her mercy, and yet—he did not seem afraid.

"Mallory," he whispered again, more uncertain now. "What's wrong?"

Her body was electrified. Her knees were barely keeping her upright.

"Nothing," she managed. "Why would anything be wrong?"

Armand leaned forward in the chair, but keeping pressure on the wound was the only thing Mallory knew for sure she should be doing, even while her thoughts surged with a thousand things she was quite sure she *shouldn't* be doing, so she clung to that one insignificant task. She did not pull away. Not when his eyes darkened a shade and dipped downward. First to her mouth. Then to the collar of her dress, buttoned all the way up her throat. Even when his gaze filled with wanting and Mallory thought she would burst into flames from the heat pooling in her stomach. Still, she did not let go.

"I didn't mean to," she said.

He flashed a soft, barely there smile. "I know you didn't." His hand found hers, helping her hold the towel to his throat. "Were you finished?"

She scanned his face. Though some hints of soap remained, she saw no sign of the blue-tinted facial hair. "I think so."

"Thank you."

He threaded his fingers through hers. The towel dropped to the floor.

A resigned curse whispered in her thoughts.

She didn't bother to look at the cut, to check on the bleeding. Instead, she bent forward, dug her other hand into his hair, and kissed him.

He inhaled sharply in surprise. It was the most delicious sound.

She came to herself half a second later and jerked back, horrified. Not so much at the impropriety, but rather her utter lack of control. "I'm sorry. I wasn't thinking—"

"Please, don't be," he breathed, his skin mottled rouge and his eyelids half-lowered, half-pleading.

His arms encircled her waist. Suddenly she was in his lap, kissing him again, and he was kissing her, and no—no, *this*, the quiet moan in the back of his throat. That was certainly the most delicious sound.

His fingers cradled the back of her head. His tongue hesitantly touched her bottom lip. Her breath caught, and she welcomed every touch, every exploration. Fingers pressing into her hips. One hand twisting the hair at the nape of her neck. Armand's mouth left hers, and then he was burying his face into the cotton fabric at her throat. His teeth nipped at one of the buttons.

"These dresses you wear," he said, his voice rough, "have been driving me positively mad."

"Ar-Armand," she gasped, fingers splayed across his chest, where she could feel the drumming of his heart. "We should . . . we shouldn't . . ."

"You started it," he teased, pressing a kiss to a patch of bare skin beneath her jaw.

Mallory didn't know what sound she made, but she didn't think it was entirely human.

Armand stilled then, his hands hot on her back. Slowly, he drew away, his expression pained. "But of course . . . if you wish to stop . . ."

Somewhere in the back of her thoughts, a tiny voice of reason knocked at her consciousness. Reminded her that he might be a murderer. Reminded her that she knew so little about him. Reminded her that falling in love was dangerous.

She told herself this wasn't love, before sliding her arms around his neck and kissing him again. She did not know when her body had begun to crave him, but she couldn't deny that she had wanted this for a very, very—

The chair tilted backward.

They both cried out as they toppled over, Mallory's head barely missing the edge of the washbasin.

Armand laughed as he rolled them off the broken chair, his

hands tenderly running along Mallory's side. "This is becoming a bad habit," he said. "Are you all right?"

She nodded. "I'm fine."

One finger lightly traced the top of her collar, and though he didn't undo a single button, the very suggestion of it made her spine curl toward him. He bent close and placed a kiss at her temple.

Mallory let out a trembling gasp. The sound prompted Armand to flutter a collection of kisses on the soft, sensitive skin along her jawline, his teeth lightly catching her earlobe—

But it was not the kiss that had prompted the sound.

Lying on the carpet, half tucked beneath the washbasin, Mallory could see an iron hook hung on the underside of the vanity. On it were four rings cast in shades of silver and gold—including a delicate gold band with a deep blue sapphire cut into a perfect oval.

She planted her hands on Armand's bare chest and shoved him away.

He rolled onto his elbow, startled. "Did I hurt you?"

"No. No. I just . . . I just remembered."

He frowned. "Remembered what?"

"I have to go."

He opened his mouth, but said nothing as Mallory hauled herself to her feet.

"Mallory?"

She hurried for the door, straightening her skirts, combing fingers through her knotted hair.

"Mallory, wait—"

She slipped out the door and slammed it shut behind her.

CHAPTER THIRTY-ONE

She ducked into an unused guest room, the furnishings covered in ghostly white cloths, to compose herself.

Mallory sank against the door and buried her face in her hands, still scented with the shaving soap. The pleasure that had shivered at the end of her nerves now felt cold and traitorous.

She spent an entire minute trying to convince herself that she'd been mistaken. It wasn't Julie's ring. It was only something similar. Surely other girls had sapphire wedding rings. Surely Armand couldn't have murdered her. Surely . . .

Nothing she told herself made any difference.

All the signs were there. The way Julie had talked about her beau, like a knight coming to rescue her, like he was too good to be true. The pressed flower in her prayer book. The ring hidden beneath Armand's vanity.

She had to go to the police. Tell them everything. Have Armand imprisoned before he could harm anyone else.

She shuddered.

For the first time, she felt like she could truly begin to understand what had compelled Bastien's wives to choose him, despite all the signs that he was a man to be avoided. What had Julie said?

The heart wants what the heart wants . . .

Right now, her heart wanted away from this place. Away from Armand, and his manipulations, his lies, the way his uncertain smiles seemed crafted entirely for her . . .

Crouching over her knees, she stuffed the hem of her skirt into her mouth and screamed. The fabric muffled her frustration and anger and betrayal, but didn't lessen it.

Gods alive, she liked him. She liked him *so much*. His curiosity. The way he flustered so easily. His bravery in the face of monsters. His willingness to believe *her*, no matter how many times she lied to him. The way he'd kissed her, as though she was both fragile and dangerous at the same time.

Breathless, Mallory let the fabric fall from her mouth. She stared balefully at the floor as her pulse gradually slowed.

She had to be sure.

She had to be absolutely, without-a-doubt, cannot-possibly-be-wrong-about-this *sure*.

She stood, forcing strength into her legs. Smoothing her hair away from her face, she dared to step back into the hall.

She found Anaïs in their room, embroidering a border of fortune's wheels onto a handkerchief, a full cup of tea on the table beside her. She startled when Mallory came in, pricking herself with the needle.

"I was beginning to worry about you. Have you learned anything?" She must have seen something in Mallory's face, because she sat straighter as she popped her jabbed finger into her mouth.

"I need your help."

Anaïs watched her a long moment. Swallowing, she set the embroidery aside and picked up the teacup instead. The china clattered in her shaking hands.

She turned back to the window and took a sip.

"Please, Anaïs." Mallory dropped onto her knees beside the settee, pleading with her. "You know I wouldn't ask if I didn't have to."

Inhaling sharply, Anaïs glanced at the sky. Dark clouds were rolling over the vineyards. "I knew you would," she whispered. "From the moment I saw her body."

"Anaïs—"

"Just as I knew that you shouldn't have to. Maybe I should have offered to do it from the beginning. But . . . I'm scared, Mally. It's unnatural, and dangerous. And . . . what if it happens again?"

"It won't."

"You don't know that."

"We can hardly summon him twice."

Crossing her arms, Anaïs settled deeper into the cushions, studying Mallory. "Who do you think it was, if not Le Bleu?"

She didn't want to say it. Saying it out loud would make it too real, too . . . *plausible*.

The words came out brittle. "I'm afraid it was Armand who killed her."

Mallory had hoped for a gasp. Some shock. A whispered, *no, surely not Armand.*

To her disappointment, Anaïs nodded. "I fear that as well."

JULIE'S BODY HAD BEEN TAKEN TO THE CHAPEL TO AWAIT the final rites and burial ritual—an initiate of the Seven had been sent for but would not arrive for at least a day, given the distance to the nearest temple. Until then, her body was not to be disturbed.

The chapel stood apart from the house—in a clearing in the western gardens, surrounded by ash trees. A domed roof was covered in moss and debris. Vines clung to the white stone walls. Like so much of the château, it was uncared for, its former beauty rotting with the passage of time.

A pair of oak-and-iron doors faced the château, greeted by a meandering cobblestone path.

Mallory pushed them open and instantly wrinkled her nose. The air inside was musty and stale, full of mildew and decay and death—though someone had tried to perfume over it and the result was so cloyingly false it turned her stomach.

Anaïs peered stoically ahead, her expression resigned.

A splatter of rain started on the path as they slipped inside. The door shut behind them with a resounding thud.

The building was octagonal with a high, vaulted ceiling. The door took up nearly a full wall, and the other seven each boasted a massive stained-glass window depicting one of the seven gods.

Straight ahead reigned Eostrig, the glass flourishing with spring flowers and vibrant hues, suggesting that this chapel was built primarily with the happier purpose of weddings in mind. Six benches stood facing an altar, three to each side of an aisle that was littered with dried leaves and puddles that had gathered from a leak in the roof.

Julie's body had been laid on a plank on top of the altar. The sword had been removed, and her arms rested at her sides, but her blood-soaked clothing would remain untouched until the temple acolyte could cleanse the body.

The rain now drummed down on the roof. Mallory studied the glass portrayal of Solvilde, whose tears were said to bring the rain. But in this depiction, the god of the sea and sky looked merry and aloof, framed by two waves curling over their head.

The shuffle of feet could barely be heard over the gale as Mallory and her sister approached the altar. Holding a lantern aloft, Mallory went to stand at Julie's left shoulder—Anaïs to her right. A full day had passed since she had been found in the trophy hall. Someone had closed her eyelids, but otherwise the body seemed unchanged.

Too unchanged, Mallory thought. There shouldn't be any color in her cheeks. There should be some sign of decay—a smell. Evidence of maggots feasting on the flesh. Mallory knew enough about decomposition to recognize it was not normal for a body to appear merely asleep nearly two days after death, as if she were held in some sort of unholy stasis.

Anaïs was even more pale than the corpse between them.

Mallory barely breathed, listening to the pounding of the rain. The hiss of the lantern flame. The wind knocking tree branches against the windows. She reached into a pouch at her hip and pulled out a small hourglass. She set it on the altar above Julie's head. The sand crystals inside glistened like snow.

"Are you ready?"

A muscle jumped in her sister's jaw. Mallory worried she would change her mind.

But then Anaïs reached forward, the movement quick and decisive, and wrapped her fingers around Julie's hand.

Mallory flipped over the timer. Five minutes.

The lantern extinguished, plunging them into darkness.

The storm bellowed outside, as if Solvilde were screaming from the heavens.

And Julie's eyes flew open.

CHAPTER THIRTY-TWO

Julie dragged in a rough, crackling breath that wheezed into the hole where the sword had impaled her. She tossed her gaze from the ceiling to Anaïs. Anaïs to Mallory. Mallory to the window that depicted Velos, god of death.

She started screaming.

"Julie!" Mallory cried, pressing a hand to the girl's shoulder. "Julie, calm down."

She did not calm down. Ripping her arm from Anaïs's grip, Julie threw herself off the altar, landing in a heap at Mallory's feet before Mallory could think to catch her.

Julie paused long enough to take in a breath, then screamed again—the sound coming in shrill, short bursts as her limbs flailed on the stone floor. She scrambled forward, crawling on hands and knees until she reached the first bench. She scuttled behind it. The scream cut off, replaced with shaking, erratic breaths.

"This was a mistake," Anaïs whispered. "I shouldn't have . . . I'm sorry . . ."

"It's all right," Mallory said, not sure if she was trying to comfort her sister or the dead girl. "Julie, it's us. Mallory and Anaïs. You remember us, don't you?"

Julie choked and whimpered and coughed. Finally, she poked her head up high enough that she could see them over the top of the bench.

Her voice was thick with disdain. "Of course I remember you. I've only been dead a short while." She peered around at the gods, the rafters, the altar—all cloaked in shadows and barely visible without the lamplight. Though it was dusk, the wailing storm made it nearly as dark as the witching hour. "How did I get here? What did you do to me?"

"We need to talk to you," said Mallory, stepping carefully around the altar, afraid of frightening the girl if she moved too quickly. "To ask you some questions about what happened."

Julie's enormous eyes blinked at her. Her expression changed then, as swift as pulling a curtain across a sunlit window. Snarling, she launched herself to her feet and pointed her finger—first at Mallory, then Anaïs, then back again. "You lied to me! You said all those pretty things about love and commitment and . . . and happiness!"

Anaïs whimpered. "I am sorry, Julie. I am so—"

"You wouldn't have listened to her," Mallory interrupted, "even if she had told you the truth!"

Anaïs stilled. Julie, too, looked taken aback by the proclamation, but Mallory planted her hands on her hips and continued defiantly, "You were in love. You were already married. You wanted us to tell you it would all work out, regardless of the truth. Tell me I'm wrong."

With a huff, Anaïs pressed her fingers to her temple.

But Julie's anger faded into something like anguish. She said nothing.

"Someone wanted you dead, Julie, and they went to great lengths to ensure you fell into their trap."

Her lip trembled. "But *why*? What did I do . . . ?"

"We are trying to figure that out." Mallory sat down on the bench and draped her elbow over the back, taking hold of Julie's hand. She gave it a gentle squeeze. "We need to know who murdered you."

Julie pried her hand from Mallory's hold and curled it into a fist. "You are more dense than a month-old kouglof," she said, with ire on her tongue. Glancing down, she pressed a hand to her chest, the front of her uniform dried black with her blood. She felt around for the wound, searching the edges of the hole in the fabric, before sticking her finger inside. Up to the first knuckle, the second, then all the way in. "One would think it would keep hurting, but I don't feel anything now. It hurt *so terribly* when it happened." She moaned and pulled her finger out.

"Who was it, Julie?"

"My lord husband." She snorted derisively. "I suppose I should have known better than to fall in love with a Saphir."

Mallory shuddered. She didn't want to hear it. But she had to know . . . "Which Saphir?"

Julie looked perplexed by this question. "Which do you think? Oh, but I know it isn't *my* fault. He was ever so thoughtful at times. So awfully convincing, with his promises and his sweetness.

When he ignored me other times, I thought it was for propriety, that things would change after we said our vows. How naïve I was, to think a count . . . a real count . . . could ever . . ." Her body swayed like she might collapse beneath her heartache. Her voice sounded wet with tears as she whispered, "Why did you bring me here? This was cruel, Miss Fontaine. Utterly cruel."

Her movements were becoming stiff as she marched back to the altar and crawled up onto it. Barely a pinch of sand remained in the top half of the glass timer as Julie stretched out long, adjusting her skirt primly around her before lying on her back, nearly a corpse once more.

"No—Julie," Mallory said, pressing a hand into her arm. "Which Saphir? Which count? Was it Le Bleu? Tell me it was Le Bleu."

"Le Bleu?" Julie's tone carried a tinge of revulsion, even as weariness passed across her face. "You really do not know." Her lips began to tremble. Her voice became paper thin. "It was Armand who married me. Armand who killed . . . m-me . . ."

The life left her with an exhale that came churning through the chapel, a cyclone that grabbed at Mallory's hair and clothes, dragged the dead leaves from the floor, before silence descended again with the darkness.

Mallory had thought she'd prepared herself for the truth, but with Armand's name still ringing in her ears, it felt like a physical blow. Usually she loved to be right. Not this time.

Armand was a murderer. He had manipulated this girl into marriage. He had taken her life.

Why?

Scholars of witchcraft talked about the power of vows, like

those pronounced in a marriage ceremony. The power of symbolism inherent in the rings, the flowers, the food served and music played. The power of giving yourself over to another person—of relinquishing your heart with complete and total trust.

Bastien Saphir's marriages may not have been love matches, but still—there was power in a trust betrayed.

Could Armand be attempting a similar spell, like the one his ancestor had begun? But if so, why had he brought Mallory and Anaïs to this place? Was he competing with Le Bleu for the magic? Was there some other reason he needed his ancestor gone? And why ensnare Julie—an innocent maid? Remembering how Julie had blushed and stammered from the moment she and Anaïs had arrived, Mallory had to assume this seduction had started before they had gotten involved.

"We have to leave," said Anaïs.

Mallory studied Julie—a corpse once more. She adjusted the placement of her arms. Pressed down her eyelids. Brushed back the wisps of hair from her face.

"Mally."

"Yes," she breathed. "You get our stuff. Mother's cards. My sketchbook. Meet me in the stables."

They gathered up the timer and lantern and slipped out into the storm, separating on the garden path. It was so dark, Mallory lost her way twice, among the never-ending, twisting labyrinth of garden paths, tree limbs grasping at her hair.

She did not relight the lantern until she had ducked into the stable, her skin slick, her hair plastered to the sides of her neck.

The stables were large enough that they might have housed a hundred horses in the day of Bastien Saphir I, but now there remained only a team of six. Mallory took the first two she saw. It had been years since she had cause to ride a horse, and her movements were clumsy as she worked to get on the bridles, the pads, and the saddles. Sensing her agitation, the horses whinnied and ducked away from her unfamiliar hands, but she managed to have them tacked and ready by the time the stable door opened again, the wood grumbling as it dragged across the stone floor.

She turned, expecting her sister.

Fear seeped into her bones.

Armand stood in the door. Strands of dark hair dripped rainwater across his face. His shirt—that linen work shirt he favored in the greenhouse—clung to the planes of his chest and shoulders. His bare feet tracked muddy footprints across the hard floor.

His expression spoke of bewilderment. Disbelief. Hurt.

"Armand . . ."

"You're leaving. In the dark. You're . . . running away."

She swallowed, trying to clear the lump that clogged her throat.

"I . . . I'm going for help," she said. "I am not strong enough to banish Le Bleu on my own. I need assistance."

"Assistance from who?"

"There is a witch who lives not a half day's ride from here. I'll be back before tomorrow's dinner, and we will put this spirit to rest."

He stepped closer, and it took all of Mallory's will not to press back against the horse. Armand paused an arm's length from her, and she watched, breathless, as a drop of water slipped down a lock of hair, over his eyebrow, dripped down into his lashes. He blinked it away.

Even now, knowing what she knew, her fingers tingled with the urge to twine through his hair. Even now, she would have clung to any reason to believe she was mistaken. Her body wanted to be pressed against him again, to feel the thrum of his pulse, the pounding of his heart a reflection of her own. Her mouth yearned to kiss the rain from his.

Traitors, all.

"You're afraid of me."

"N-no. I'm not afraid."

His focus dropped to her mouth as she said the words. She did not know if it was disgust or desire that stoked in her belly.

But then Armand smiled, his mouth pulling to one side. His eyes darkened into something taunting. If desire had been kindling inside Mallory, it now hardened into icy fear.

He dipped his head closer to her. She tried to draw back, but his hand caught her elbow, pulling her close as his brow pressed against hers.

"You should be," he whispered.

A shudder engulfed her. Armand spun her around. She yelped in surprise—then went still as one hand wrapped around her neck, his other arm shackling her against his body.

"Miss Fontaine." His voice had become a low growl, hot breath brushing against her ear. "You cannot leave yet. Not when there is still work to be done."

She cast around for a weapon. Her knife was in her boot, but she couldn't reach it. The lantern was hanging from a hook, also out of reach. A row of shovels lined the wall by the door.

Armand squeezed her throat—just a little at first, just enough to make her wince, to send terror clawing its way into her thoughts.

"I am so very glad that you came," he murmured. "I had thought I would need another wife, but no . . . not if I can have you, or your sister. With that precious Savoy blood."

With fear and adrenaline scorching through her veins, Mallory almost didn't register his words. *Savoy blood.*

Her insides knotted. He knew. How did he know?

"Though, between you and me, I would not have minded one last proposal."

He pressed a kiss to her earlobe. She shuddered so hard her teeth rattled.

Both hands met around her neck, fingers digging into her flesh. She tried to remember how to fight back, all the soft, vulnerable places on the human body, but she had no air, and she was afraid and confused, and her knife . . .

"Thank you for your sacrifice," he breathed, his voice tender, almost loving.

Grinding her teeth, Mallory lifted her knee and stomped down, hard, on the bridge of his foot.

He howled in pain. His grip loosened enough for her to throw her elbow into his gut. Armand stumbled back.

Mallory swung around to face him—and saw the wide, flat head of a shovel floating above Armand's head, seconds before it fell onto his skull with a clang. Bits of manure scattered across the floor. Armand's body crumpled.

Anaïs gripped the shovel's handle, breathing hard, a pack slung across her shoulders.

Their eyes met and they shared a single breath of stillness and horror. Mallory could still feel the raw burning in her throat where he'd started to choke her. It hurt almost as bad as the ache in her chest where, for the briefest of moments, she'd felt what it might be like to be treated as if you were as precious as sapphires.

"Sorry it took me so long," said Anaïs, dropping the shovel beside Armand's prone body. "I stopped to grab a few more spoons." She jangled the bag on her hip, suggesting it was full of much more than spoons. "Figured we could sell the stuff along the way."

CHAPTER THIRTY-THREE

The horses were anxious after the fight in the stables, and Mallory could sense their tension as they made their way down the drive—the clomping of their hooves almost painfully loud in the otherwise still night.

The iron hinges of the gate were squealing like a banshee when Mallory heard a voice calling her name.

A pale figure was racing down the road, bare feet and bloodied nightgown, her blue shawl trailing behind her in the howling wind.

"Mallory Fontaine!" Triphine cried. "Don't you dare leave me here!"

Mallory drew back on the reins. It took Anaïs a moment to realize she had stopped.

"It's Triphine," she explained. "She wants to come with us."

She surveyed the house, trying to discern if an alarm had been raised. If anyone other than the duchess was coming after them.

The mansion was a looming ghoul in the distance, as imposing as a fortress, lit by a few sparse lanterns that flickered behind leaded windows. When the clouds parted and the moon struck the limestone façade, it transformed the mansion into a specter of itself.

Mallory did not expect the cascade of remorse that befell her. She had known, logically, that she would not solve the problems of the House Saphir. She would not send Monsieur Le Bleu back to wherever he had come from. She would not banish the spirits of the wandering wives. She had hoped, briefly, that she might give justice to Julie . . . and perhaps she still could. When they were far away, she would pen a letter to the local constable, tell him about the strange happenings at the House Saphir. Tell him that Count Armand Saphir was a murderer, as his great-great-grandfather had been.

The cool air felt brittle with each breath, stabbing her lungs. She felt as if one powerful exhale could shatter her.

From the branches of an oak that towered behind the estate wall, a barn swallow crooned a sad, almost frightened song, then fell quiet.

Triphine paused on the drive and bent over, breathing hard. "Don't . . . you . . . dare . . ."

"Fine," Mallory snapped. "You can come, just stop yelling before you draw the attention of Le Bleu and every monster from here to Chablac."

Rewrapping the shawl around her shoulders, Triphine darted toward the gate. "You won't regret this, Mallory. I'll—"

Triphine vanished. One moment she was passing through the gate, and the next she was gone.

Mallory gaped, hands tightening on the reins.

"What?" said Anaïs, her voice pitching higher. "What is happening?"

Mallory's lips parted, but . . . she wasn't sure how to answer.

Her attention lifted to the house again. Perhaps Triphine had been doomed when she set foot on this estate. Perhaps, like the other wives, now that she was here, she could never leave again.

It was the last sadness that her heart could take. With a painful ache tearing at her chest, she steered the horse away from the gate as tears welled in her eyes.

"Nothing," she said. "Let's go."

They headed east. They would not go into Comorre, where they would be too easy to track, in case Armand chose to seek them out . . . wanting their *Savoy blood*.

Slowly, the events of the night settled in her thoughts. He knew. He knew that she and Anaïs were descended not only from witches, but from the very witch who had escaped Bastien all those years ago.

Gabrielle Savoy.

Had that always been his intention? To drag her and her sister to the château, fool her into thinking he might actually feel something for her, so as to lure her into a sinister trap? All because she and her sister were the last descendants of Gabrielle Savoy, the fourth wife of Bastien Saphir. The wife who got away.

But why? What did that matter? Why would Armand care?

By morning, Anaïs believed they should reach the town of Grevinny, where they could trade the horses for fresh mounts and sell off the treasures she'd stolen from the house. They would need coin for food and lodging. A few pieces of silver wouldn't get them far, but Mallory still had the collateral Armand had given her when he hired them.

The Saphir crest imprint upon a solid gold medallion, studded with sapphires. It may not be worth the full three thousand lourdes she'd hoped for, but it would be enough to get them far away from here, so long as she could find a dubious enough jeweler who was willing to melt down estate jewelry that had almost certainly been stolen. She didn't think it would be too hard. And afterward, they might be able to book passage across the sea, into Tulvask, or south to Stivale. Anaïs had always wanted to travel to somewhere new, a place where she could set up a nice little dress shop in the heart of some grand city.

Mallory didn't know what she would do in a dress shop, but at least her sister would be happy.

They had been traveling for nearly two hours. Occasionally she spotted a small bird darting in and out of the vineyards, or maybe a bat squeaking above the fields, no doubt feasting on midnight grubs. But eventually the vineyards gave way to a rocky path up to a flat plateau. The rain had eased and tall grasses were painted silver by a trickle of moonlight. A thick copse of trees lay ahead, rising up from a swirl of dewy mist—the start of the Mairmont Forest, if her geography served her.

They were halfway across the plain, the fog gathering around their steeds' legs, so thick she could no longer see the ground beneath them, when Mallory heard a snuffle. It was followed by a horse's whinny. Not her own ride, and not Anaïs's.

Their horses slowed, then stopped altogether.

"Who else would be traveling this time of night?" Anaïs

whispered. Mallory knew her sister's thoughts were filling with the same threats hers were—bandits, murderers, and monsters.

Her hands tightened on the reins.

Under the distant tree cover, she could see a pair of red eyes glowing in the darkness. The beast moved forward, emerging slow and agile from the woods.

It was a horse. Riderless and entirely white from mane to hooves, its coat shimmering like mother-of-pearl. All but the eyes, which burned like lit embers.

Fear stiffened Mallory's spine. There was something otherworldly beautiful about it. Tall, muscled, and graceful, its silver-white mane cascading to the ground, floating on the heath's gentle breeze.

Her own mount had begun to tremble. It took a step back, and Mallory could tell it was getting ready to bolt. She laid a hand on its neck, knowing that it could sense her own fear. And she was afraid. Though resplendent in its beauty, this other horse radiated an unmistakable threat. Her body instinctively recoiled, even as her mind filled with wonder.

"Cheval mallet," she murmured, hardly able to believe it. The creature was every bit as glorious and horrifying as she'd imagined. "The horse spirit that haunts the wildlands of Lysraux, attacking travelers in the night. They say it likes to lure travelers onto its back and then . . ." She glanced at the edge of the plateau, where limestone cliffs dropped hundreds of feet to the valley below. "Throw them off cliffs."

"You know, sister," Anaïs said, "your knowledge of monsters is rarely as helpful as you think it is."

The cheval snorted. Its hot breath steamed the cold air.

One hoof stamped at the earth.

"All right," Mallory whispered to her steed, tugging the reins to the left, keeping the other horse in sight while they turned back. "We'll find another route. Nothing to worry about . . ."

The cheval reared back on its hind legs and let out a bellowing whinny.

Mallory's and Anaïs's horses squealed in terror and launched themselves forward, scattering in two directions.

Mallory hunkered over her steed's back as her horse drove forward, sprinting straight toward the cliff's edge. She clutched the reins. Never had she ridden a horse at this speed. Her heart was in her throat. The horse's mane whipped across her face.

She dared to look back—the cheval mallet was chasing her. She held tighter, leather cutting into her palms. She yanked the reins to the side, but the horse was done listening to her.

Her mount let out a terrible scream and reared up on its hind legs. Mallory cried out as she was tossed from the saddle. She hit the ground so hard she worried her teeth had been jarred loose. Rocks scraped her elbow and knees.

Her horse fled at full gallop across the field, heading back to Comorre.

Somewhere, her sister screamed her name.

Mallory flipped onto her back, body aching, flesh torn. The cheval mallet was bearing down on her. Demonic eyes and frothing mouth.

It would trample her.

She pushed herself back, heels scraping into the dirt as she scrambled for purchase. She hauled herself to her feet and ran— but she hadn't gone thirty feet when she skidded to a stop. She'd reached the edge of the cliff. The world before her was a landscape painting—a moon-streaked river winding its way through silver fields, a cluster of farmhouses on the horizon, windows blazing orange.

The cliff face was a sheer drop. The sight made her insides feel scooped out. Her vision spun.

She turned to face the cheval, forcing back her nausea. Every instinct roared at her. The cliff was not an option. She would not jump. She would not fall. She would not let herself be thrown from this height.

She fumbled for her boot and pulled out the dagger—that small, useless blade—gripping it in both hands as she faced the beast.

It did not slow, its hooves tearing up the dirt as it drove toward her. It was gargantuan, at least ten hands larger than any natural horse.

Anaïs screamed her name, over and over again, but Mallory dared not take her focus from the beast.

She gritted her teeth. Planted her feet.

She heard a roar and thought it was the cheval. Then a shape emerged from the mist—as silver-white and enormous as the cheval itself—and charged. It was a blur of speed and fur and teeth. An angry roar. The beast landed on the cheval with horrifying ferocity. Razor claws dug into the horse's flesh. Fangs flashed as they clamped down on its neck.

It appeared to be a bear, but this was not like any bear she'd seen before.

The cheval managed to kick its hind legs into the beast's stomach, sending it flying onto its back. The horse spun, crashing down upon the bear with its massive hooves. The bear slashed, leaving a bloodied gash on the horse's foreleg. The horse pawed at the ground, preparing for its next attack while the bear rolled onto its side, tried to get back up—

Something whistled through the air. The cheval screamed and reared. Mallory glimpsed an arrow jutting from its side. A flash blinded her. She squinted against the burning light.

The cheval mallet was gone.

In the distance, a figure was tromping through the tall grass. Mallory had to search her memory for his name, though she recognized him instantly. Not Fitcher . . . *Constantino*, with the quiver on his back and a bow on one arm, overdressed for this wild landscape in colorful silks and layers of garish stripes and harlequin diamonds.

She saw no sign of Fitcher himself. No sign of Anaïs.

A snarl drew Mallory's attention back to the bear as it climbed to its feet and stood at full height, towering over her. Its snout and paws were as black as its fur was white. Able to catch her breath, she realized it was an ice bear—native to the frigid tundras and glaciers of Isbren, thousands of miles to the north. Far larger and far more dangerous than the mild black bears that wandered their mountains.

Mallory shrank back, hoping that Constantino had another one of those arrows. She listened for the telltale pluck of the bowstring as the bear dropped back onto all fours, shaking the earth.

It gave a snort, steaming the air. Its muscles undulated as it crept closer.

Tightening her hand around her dagger, she searched for Constantino, wondering what was taking so long. Why hadn't he shot the bear as well? He did know she was here, didn't he? About to become this bear's dinner?

"Nice bear," she whispered, lifting the knife again, knowing it would do nothing. Louder, she called out shakily, "A little more help, please?"

The beast growled, low and ominous, eyeing the blade in her hand.

Then it huffed and sat back onto its haunches with an ungraceful *kerflumpf* and started licking its wounds.

Mallory gaped at it, distantly wondering if her heartbeat would ever slow down after the night she'd had.

Constantino appeared beside the beast, approaching without a hint of concern. He wasn't even holding the bow anymore, but had it tossed onto his back. He kicked at the ground with the toe of a gold-buckled boot, then stooped to pick up a small rock.

No—a delicate glass figurine, about the size of Mallory's thumb. A horse, rearing back on its hind legs.

Constantino tucked it into a pouch on his belt, before holding out a hand toward Mallory. "Buona sera, stellina. I had hoped we would meet again."

CHAPTER THIRTY-FOUR

"You have a pet bear," she muttered in disbelief, waiting for her legs to stop shaking before she could trust herself to accept Constantino's assistance.

Constantino guffawed, and as soon as Mallory was securely on her feet, he gave the bear a jovial whap. "Hear that? You're my pet now."

The bear made a disgruntled noise, then went back to licking the gash on its arm.

"Suppose he's difficult to recognize under that mangy fur," said Constantino, "but this here is the boss. Come along. We caught up to your sister by the tree line. She's probably worried sick for you. Let's get back to the caravan and put on some coffee."

Mallory had stopped listening after *the boss*.

As Constantino headed back to the trail, the bear stood, too, and plodded alongside him on four legs.

"You mean . . . that's *Fitcher*?"

"The one and only. You remember him, right? All stoic and serious." Constantino lowered his voice to a deep rumble. "And he is especially handsome when he says cryptic things in that smoky voice."

She could have sworn the bear rolled his eyes.

"Yes, I remember. Why is he a bear?"

"It's a curse thing. Happens every full moon." Constantino gestured to the horizon, where a hazy gray light suggested the approach of dawn. "He'll be back to normal when the sun rises."

Anaïs was waiting on the road, not far from where they'd been separated. She screamed Mallory's name and charged for her, wrapping her into an embrace. "How many times can you escape death in one night?"

"I hadn't meant to make it a habit."

Constantino led them off the road, where animals had pressed the grasses into a path that continued through the woods. They had not gone far before they reached a meadow, in which stood the largest stagecoach Mallory had ever seen. The exterior was painted amethyst purple and accented in copper and gold. Ornate moldings framed numerous windows of various shapes and sizes, each with drawn crimson curtains. Metal boxes and traveling trunks in every color teetered in precarious stacks on the roof. A team of baukhauv—oxen-like beasts imported from Tulvask—grazed in the meadow, with no apparent interest in meandering off.

Constantino bounded into the stagecoach, leaving the door wide open. Far too enormous to fit through the narrow door, Fitcher stayed outside and started setting logs around a fire pit with his massive paws, creating a ring of makeshift benches. The logs would have taken two people, at least, to move them, but as a bear, he made quick work of the job.

Mallory glanced at her sister and found her staring back. They both knew it was unspeakably rude to barge into someone's home without an invitation, regardless of whether or not that home was on wheels. Especially when one of those hosts happened to be a gigantic bear.

So Mallory was glad when Anaïs's curiosity got the better of her first. With a giddy shrug, she lobbed herself into the coach. Mallory followed close behind. She heard Fitcher make a surprised grunt, but what was he going to do? Eat them?

The moment she stepped inside, Mallory was hit with an overwhelming wave of nostalgia. The air inside the stagecoach was warm and perfumed with cinnamon. It was dim, the curtains blocking out the impending daylight, though an array of colorful pillar candles ornamented every available surface.

It reminded her of the shop, back when their mother was the most admired witch in the entire province.

Two hammocks hung on one wall—one right above the other. Two traveling trunks were tucked beneath the cots, each one strapped shut with leather bands. An assortment of ornately patterned carpets littered the floor. Constantino was bustling in the back, digging a copper pot out from a cabinet so crammed full of porcelain dishes, it was amazing the pieces hadn't shattered during their travels.

Other than the hammocks, traveling trunks, and makeshift kitchen, every inch of the space was lined with curio cabinets, each shelf protected by leaded glass.

The floor swayed as Mallory approached the cabinets, scanning the assortment of peculiar objects inside. A porcelain box full of tiny white teeth. A carnival mask accented with inky-black feathers. A small mirror with a tarnished handle and shattered glass— one shard missing. The skull of a small creature, its eye sockets shaped like diamonds. What might have been an average ball of yarn if it hadn't, evidently, been made of shimmering gold.

She spied a small painting, framed in ebony, that presented seven symbols in red ink. An arrow. A wheel. A compass rose. A stalk of wheat. A sprig of lily of the valley. Another wheel, this one more ornate. And an hourglass.

Seeing them together, it wasn't difficult to tell which symbol related to which of the seven gods, and her skin prickled as she studied that final symbol. An hourglass—through which the sands of time slipped by. The symbol of Velos.

Her chest burned, right beneath her collarbone. Mallory pressed her fingers to it, feeling the sore spot beneath the fabric of her dress, and told herself it was her imagination.

Yanking her gaze away, she scanned the top of the nearest cabinet, which was cluttered with random, less precious ephemera: tattered books bound in leather. Scrolls of parchment wrapped in fraying ribbon. A branch of witch hazel in a clay jar. A wooden bowl overflowing with crystals. As Mallory studied their rainbow of colors, Anaïs reached out and deftly swiped one of the prettier ones, tucking it away into a hidden pocket, before casting a guilty grin in Mallory's direction.

Ignoring her sister's propensity for theft, Mallory asked, "What is all this?"

Constantino took in the shelves, almost like he'd forgotten the assortment of bizarre objects was there. "Fitcher calls himself a collector. Though what any of it does, I haven't the faintest."

Mallory's attention landed on a red lacquer box on top of the cabinets. She reached for it, undoing the latch. Inside, the box held a tray neatly divided into twenty-five satin-lined pockets, a handful of which contained a glass figurine of a different monster, precisely like the figurine of the cheval mallet that had dropped into the grass on the moor. She recognized the voirloup and a salamander.

The box was deep. Mallory lifted the tray to see a second identical one beneath, then a third and fourth—though most of the compartments were empty.

"Though it's rather against my nature to suggest that two beautiful ladies *leave* my sleeping quarters," said Constantino, holding a crowded tea tray, "I think it's best if we take our coffee by the fire. In his current state, Fitcher doesn't quite fit in the coach."

Outside, a pile of kindling had been expertly constructed in the fire pit, but Fitcher was growling at a box of matches, too small for his massive paws. Constantino set the tray down and gamely lit the fire, before putting the copper pot into the coals. While waiting for the water to boil, he added ground coffee beans from a dented tin, followed by a heap of sugar. "This will be a minute."

Fitcher perched on one of the logs, looking very much like a bear trying to convince everyone else that he was a civilized nobleman with exquisite manners.

"How did you find us?" Anaïs asked, perching on one of the logs and dragging Mallory down beside her even though the wood was slimy and damp from the rain. "I thought for sure that horse would kill my sister. When you showed up, it felt like a miracle."

"No miracle," said Constantino. "We were hired by some merchants in Grevinny to deal with their little equestrian problem. Evidently, that horse has been disrupting their business for months now. We've been camped here for a few days waiting for the cheval mallet to target some passersby. As soon as we heard your screams, we knew it was close." He leaned forward, grinning. "Who would have thought the night would bring two bounties?"

"Two bounties?" asked Anaïs.

"Don't you know? You two have a sizable reward on your heads." Constantino opened a pouch on his belt and pulled out a piece of yellowed parchment, handing it to Mallory as he stoked the fire.

She unfolded the note. A sketch showed their faces—the resemblance quite good, actually, though the artist hadn't quite gotten the shape of Anaïs's chin right. *Anaïs and Mallory Fontaine of Morant wanted for fraud and thievery. 50 lourdes offered upon capture.*

"Only fifty lourdes?" griped Anaïs, affronted. But after a moment, she admitted, "Actually, that sounds about right."

"I spied this flyer two days after we caught that voirloup," said Constantino, opening the lid on the copper pot to check the coffee. The steam that wafted out smelled both sweet and bitter. "Sounds like there are a good many people who aren't happy with the way you've been conducting business."

Mallory considered denying it, but quickly realized it would be pointless. She passed the flyer back to him. "You can't please everyone."

His teeth glinted as he refolded the parchment and tucked it

THE HOUSE SAPHIR

away. "I like a challenge." He wrapped a towel around the pot's long handle and pulled it from the fire.

"I tried to contact you," Mallory said, "using the card you gave me before. But I had a mishap with a fire-breathing salamander."

"Troublesome pests," said Constantino. "What were you contacting us for?"

"My sister and I were hired to evict a dangerous ghost from the House Saphir. When we failed, I thought perhaps you could assist us."

"The House Saphir?" Constantino whistled in appreciation. "I got my hands on a bottle of their Ruby Comorre once. Quality stuff."

Fitcher made a snuffling sound, drawing their attention. He gestured in annoyance at Constantino, who frowned.

"What?"

Fitcher waved his paws through the air.

"Ah—right. Does this job come with payment? We are not in a position to offer services on charity." He poured the coffee into four cups, added a splash of milk to each one, then handed two to Mallory and Anaïs. He even gave a cup and saucer to Fitcher, who settled it on one of his massive paws, then proceeded to glare down at it like he wasn't quite sure how to enjoy the coffee in this form while still maintaining his dignity.

"I'll make you a deal," said Mallory. "If you don't turn us in, you can have the Saphir job all to yourself. Count Saphir himself offered us three thousand lourdes in payment for banishing the ghost of Monsieur Le Bleu, infamous serial killer. You can have it all—far more than you'll get for having us arrested."

Constantino rubbed his chin. "Or we could take the job and

also collect the reward for your capture. Though it does make one wonder . . ." He tossed his booted feet up onto the stones ringing the fire. "If you were due to receive three thousand lourdes, what were you running for?"

Again, Mallory considered lying. But there was something about this boy—and something about Fitcher's keen gaze, copper and amber, watching her. Something told her she would not fool anyone.

"The lord of the manor tried to kill me."

Fitcher's cup wobbled. He reached for it, but the massive paw bumped it instead, sending the cup crashing onto the ground.

"Fitcher! That was my mother's set!"

Fitcher gave him an unamused scowl, to which Constantino cupped a hand to his mouth and whispered loudly, "It was not my mother's set."

Anaïs grabbed Mallory's arm so quickly that coffee sloshed over the edges of both their cups. "Mother's cards! And your sketchbook. And the silver! It was all in our packs." She hunched forward. "On the horses."

Fitcher snuffled and tossed a paw toward Constantino.

"You think I wasn't going to do that?" He pressed a hand to the front of his blue-and-yellow-and-lavender tunic. "The lady is in distress. Of course I will retrieve the ponies." Spinning toward Anaïs, he grabbed her hand, cupping it in both of his and looking at her with such intensity that Anaïs nearly toppled backward off the log. "Fear not, mademoiselle. I shall return with your treasures, or I shall perish in the effort."

Fitcher grunted, perhaps rooting for the latter.

Glancing up at the sky, Constantino grabbed a cloak from a

hook on the side of the stagecoach and tossed it into Fitcher's lap. "Sun's coming up," he said to Fitcher, before taking off down the road, a jaunty bounce in his step. Apparently in no hurry.

He had just vanished into the woods when a swirl of starlight wrapped around Fitcher's humongous body. In the next breath, he was human again, still seated on the log and entirely naked judging from his bare chest and shoulders, though Mallory was grateful that the positioning of the cloak on his lap prevented them from seeing much else. Still, she and Anaïs both awkwardly busied their attention elsewhere.

Fitcher cleared his throat and wrapped himself neatly in the fabric, before standing with an impressive lack of embarrassment and walking to the coach. "If you will excuse me."

Mallory and Anaïs traded bewildered looks as they sipped their coffee and waited.

Fitcher emerged two minutes later, fully clothed in black boots and breeches, a black tunic, and the same black cloak Constantino had thrown at him, buckled at the throat with a silver clasp. Mallory wondered if it was her imagination or if there was an extra streak of white in the black ropes of his hair.

Pulling out his pocket watch, Fitcher glanced briefly at the face before he shut it with a loud click and tucked it away again, one side of his mouth twitching. He swished his cloak to the side and returned to the log like a prince settling upon his throne, trying to appear unflustered.

"That's a very nice watch you have," Mallory said. For even in that momentary glimpse, she could tell it was quality—more fit for a duke than a traveling magician.

Mallory knew from having seen it in Morant that it was not

really a watch at all—at least, not like any watch she'd ever seen. She recalled the single golden arrow, more like a compass, though she didn't think it was any normal compass, either.

"It is," he said, his tone lacking arrogance. "It is the only one like it in the world. Handcrafted by a Tulvaskian princess."

It sounded like something she would say to someone she was trying to swindle.

Anaïs giggled, but when Fitcher's expression remained stoic, she caught herself. "Really?"

Fitcher poured himself a second cup of coffee, thick with the dregs from the bottom of the pot. "I believe you were saying that Count Saphir threatened you?"

"He tried to murder me. After he killed one of the servants. A housemaid."

A bird swooped down from nowhere and landed on the log Constantino had vacated. It peered at each of them in turn before releasing a stream of fierce twitters.

Fitcher grunted in surprise. "Constantino must have been feeding the birds again," he muttered, taking a sip of his drink. "You say it was the current lord of the manor that tried to kill you. Not the dangerous ghost?"

Mallory shook her head. "It was Armand. Though . . . the ghost has threatened me, too."

"Friendly place," Fitcher said. "Sounds like a joy to visit."

"Look, if you don't want the job for yourself, we can still make a deal," said Mallory. "If you can take us to the nearest town, we'll pay you double the reward."

"In what coin?"

Though Mallory's instincts withered, she reached into the

pouch at her side and fished out the medallion Armand had given her when he hired them. She handed it to Fitcher.

He inspected the family crest, examining it from side to side. He put it into his mouth and bit down, hard, then held it up to the sunlight with a grunt.

"Worthless." He tossed it back to her.

Mallory fumbled to catch it. "What?"

"It's a fake."

Mallory stared at him, anger rising in her chest. Was he trying to con *her*?

"It is not a fake. Count Saphir gave this to me himself. It is the family crest—likely two hundred years old and of significant historical value, not to mention the value of the stones themselves."

"He gave you a fake."

"Let me see that." Anaïs snatched the medallion from Mallory, repeating the same tests Fitcher had conducted. Her eyes widened. "He's right, Mally."

"What?"

"It was likely crafted using the same methods we used for the replicas you sold on the tours."

Mallory's thoughts whirled. A *fake*?

"It's hardly surprising," said Fitcher. "The Saphir estate has been suffering financial difficulties for years. As I understand it, competition has increased in the wine business, and merchants are happy to take their business to . . . less troubled vintners."

In fact, Mallory had caught wind of such rumors, too, but she'd always assumed it was nothing but hearsay. Armand himself had been well-dressed. Had arrived in a fine carriage. He owned four hundred acres, for Freydon's sake.

And he'd offered her three thousand lourdes without hesitation.

Acid burned in her gut. Maybe he hadn't hesitated because he'd had no intention of ever paying her that money. Money he didn't have to give, even if he wanted to.

His carriage had been of the highest quality, but Armand had driven it himself. He didn't have a coachman, or a team of footmen like one would expect a lord to keep. No valet. A paltry staff to maintain such an enormous estate. He claimed it was because the ghost was frightening away the servants, but maybe it was because he couldn't afford to keep the help.

And while he may have worn fine clothes in Morant, she'd never seen him in another suit—only clothes such as the farmers wore. Was Yvette really polishing the silver for storage, or had she been selling it off? And the statues on the terrace—Armand said they were having them *relocated*. But to where? An antiquities dealer? Maybe the same one he'd sold the original authentic family seal to?

She felt her world splintering. He'd seemed so earnest. So trustworthy. But he had lied to her about *everything*—taken her for every kind of fool.

All this time, she'd thought she was conning him, when really, she'd been the mark all along.

Mallory tossed back the last of her coffee, ending up with a bitter mouthful of grounds.

If she ever saw Armand Saphir again, she was going to murder him.

CHAPTER THIRTY-FIVE

Mallory was still fuming when they heard the melodic clomping of horse hooves. Constantino appeared in the brush, riding Mallory's steed, while leading Anaïs's by the reins—beaming as if he'd obtained the crown jewels.

"I return victorious!" he bellowed, stopping the horses a few feet from the fire. He dismounted and unstrapped the saddlebags. But rather than giving them to the sisters, he tossed them to Fitcher.

"Hey!" cried Anaïs, slipping to her feet. "Those are our things."

"And you shall have them back," said Fitcher, opening a flap to dig through the contents. "After we claim our reward. You wanted to negotiate, yes?" He pulled out a silver jewelry box, considered it, then set it aside. "If you can pay us in enough goods to equal the reward on your heads, we won't turn you in."

"Seems fair," said Constantino. "Don't suppose you have any of that famed Ruby Comorre?"

Anaïs fisted her hands on her hips. "What was all that about damsels in distress?"

"I've reconsidered." Constantino untacked the horses, letting them graze with the baukhauv. "I recognize a damsel when I see one, and the two of you seem far too competent to fit the description."

"Are these yours?" Fitcher pulled the stack of Wyrdith cards from Anaïs's pack.

She crossed her arms. "Do you think I stole them?"

"Like you stole everything else in here? Yes, I think it's likely."

"Well, I didn't. They were our mother's."

"Do you know how to read them?"

Still glaring, Anaïs said, "Five galets if you want a reading."

"Perhaps another time." Fitcher studied Anaïs and Mallory. "You wouldn't happen to know anything about god-blessings, would you?"

Mallory stilled. The air around them crackled with a new infusion of energy, like lightning waiting to strike.

When Anaïs said nothing, Mallory stepped forward and held out her palm. "One hardly needs a god-gift to read fortunes."

"Perhaps." Fitcher gave the deck to her. "But these cards suggest a connection to Wyrdith. I only ask as anyone with a legitimate god-gift would be far more valuable to us than a mere fifty lourdes."

"I did not realize blessings could be bought and sold like common commodities," Mallory said. "Unfortunately for you—"

"It isn't Wyrdith," said Anaïs.

Slowly, Mallory turned to face her sister. "Anaïs."

"What?" she snapped. "This was *your* backup plan, remember?

Bring in the monster hunters to solve the problem. You were going to trust them before, why not now?"

"You know this has nothing to do with trust."

"With you, Mally, it never does."

Exasperated, Mallory gestured at the two boys. "They are threatening to turn us in for reward money!"

"They are offering a chance to negotiate. If it's true that god-gifts are valuable, we may have something they want." Ignoring Mallory's harrumph, Anaïs turned back to Fitcher. "It is not Wyrdith's blessing, though. It is—"

"Death magic," Mallory interrupted. "I am gifted by Velos."

Anaïs's jaw tightened, but she didn't correct her. Mallory knew how her sister despised her gift, and would avoid using it at any cost. Seven years ago, Mallory had hoped that in summoning their ancestor—Gabrielle Savoy herself—they could have Anaïs's curse transformed into the same petty magic that Mallory and her mother had.

But things hadn't worked out that way.

"God-gifts do have value," said Fitcher. "At least, they do to me." He nodded at Constantino. "Show them."

"Yes, my lord," said Constantino, though he didn't sound as annoyed as he might have at what was clearly a command. With much flourish, he unfastened the cuff of his diamond-patterned sleeve and rolled the fabric up to his elbow—revealing a tattoo of an arrow down the length of his forearm. It shimmered like molten gold etched across his tan skin.

"The mark of Tyrr," Anaïs breathed.

Mallory swallowed as Constantino's magic began to make sense.

According to legend, centuries ago, the Seven had erected a veil to separate the world of mortals from that of ghosts and demons and dark magic. The veil had fallen, when Anaïs was a baby and Mallory not yet born, and the magic that had sustained it was dispersed into the world. Some of that magic latched onto babes and children, forever marking them with god-blessings. Gifts that were more powerful than any amount of petty magic, though they were limited in that the power they bestowed was very specific. Such as being able to return a corpse to life for a brief five minutes. Or transforming magical beasts into tiny blown-glass baubles with the shot of an arrow.

"I have been searching for those with god-gifts," said Fitcher. "The blessing of Velos would be an asset in our group. We can offer you transportation. Shelter. Food."

"Payment?" Mallory asked, ignoring the disgruntled glare Anaïs gave her. Anaïs despised her god-gift. She had always seen it as unnatural, vulgar, and disrespectful to the deceased. She would never have used it to resurrect Julie if it had not been necessary. Mallory knew she would want nothing to do with helping Fitcher, not if she had to abase herself by bringing more corpses to life.

"The payment we receive for our work is divided equally among us."

"How much does curse breaking and exorcism run these days?"

Fitcher's mouth pressed into a thin smile. "Enough."

"But you must not be very good at it if you can't even break your own curse. Unless you enjoy parading about as a bear every four weeks."

If she'd hoped to induce irritation, Fitcher's reaction was unsatisfactory. "Different curses have different requirements," he said simply.

"What does breaking your curse require?"

"The magic of all seven gods."

Mallory leaned back in surprise. "Oh. And so far, you have . . ."

"Only Constantino, blessed by Tyrr." Then he added grumpily, "Thus far, my choices have been limited." He leaned his elbows on his thighs, steepling his fingers. "It is true that I would like to be free of the curse that binds me, but it is far more complicated than that. This is not a selfish request. If I fail, many lives will be lost."

"Really? Whose?"

"Innocent people. People who should not be punished for my failures."

Mallory smirked at Constantino. "He's doing that cryptic thing you mentioned."

"You get used to it," he said. "Can I see your tattoo? Or is it someplace where we'd have to get to know each other better first?"

Mallory swallowed hard and reached for the high collar of her dress.

"Mallory," Anaïs breathed. "You don't have to show anyone. It is none of their business."

But maybe she did. It was proof, anyway.

Proof that, this once, she wasn't lying. Not *entirely*.

She undid the top three buttons. Hands shaking, she pulled down the collar to reveal the pale skin of her clavicle.

Constantino hissed in surprise. Fitcher did not, though his gaze darkened with curiosity.

Mallory had not looked in a mirror recently, but she had some idea of what they were seeing. A mark reminiscent of an hourglass, smaller than a wasp. It was not gold like Constantino's arrow . . . or the hourglass that had appeared on the nape of her sister's neck the day the veil fell.

Mallory's mark was different. Blackened like charred flesh. Wet, shiny, bloody. A festering wound. She assumed it had gotten worse since the last time she'd seen it, as the cool air made it sting more than usual.

"What's wrong with it?" Constantino asked. He looked to Fitcher. "Are we sure that's Velos's mark?"

"Of course it is," Mallory said, hastily buttoning her collar up to her throat. "You think I would do that to myself?"

"But why is it—"

"Corrupted," Fitcher said, sounding suspicious. "How did you receive this blessing?"

"I didn't steal it if that's what you're asking."

"You aren't telling us something."

Anaïs studied her own interlocked fingers. No doubt reliving that night, and the horrors they'd seen.

"What do you care?" Mallory snapped, growing irate. "The mark doesn't need to be pretty. It is the mark of Velos, and because of it, I can see and talk to ghosts. Do you want it or not?"

Fitcher hesitated. "I do."

Mallory's mind whirred as she considered all the ways this could work to their advantage. Fitcher's Troupe would take them far away from Comorre, perhaps out of Lysraux altogether.

Travel. Shelter. Money. And when she and Anaïs were safe, they could vanish into some busy city, Fitcher and his curse be damned.

"Well, then," said Fitcher, stoking the fire. "This is convenient. We will not need to return to Morant. Perhaps we shall next investigate those rumors of a bog witch who is kidnapping children in the Stivalen countryside."

"Ah, my old stomping grounds," said Constantino, with fake wistfulness. "Wonder if I know her." His tone darkened. "Sounds like someone who would get on with my brother."

A shrill birdsong cut across the crackle of the fire. The barn swallow from before had been pecking for grubs in the ground, but now hopped back onto the log and flapped its wings, yammering at them. Mallory wondered if they'd set up camp in its favorite breakfast spot.

"We don't have enough supplies to get to Stivale," said Fitcher. "We'll need to find paying work on the way."

"Shouldn't be so difficult." Constantino smirked. "We've got witches now. Every town loves a traveling caravan with witches and fortune tellers."

"I wouldn't say *every* town," Fitcher muttered.

Mallory didn't respond. Petty magic was appreciated in some parts of the world, but in others it was considered borderline blasphemous.

The swallow dove for the tray and knocked over the sugar dish.

"Hey!" said Constantino. Standing, he shooed the bird away with his hand. It took to the air and circled a few times before dropping onto one of the discarded saddles. Its chirps became more frantic as its wings flapped erratically.

Then it ruffled its feathers and fell silent and brooding, scowling at Mallory with one black eye.

"I could be mistaken," said Fitcher, "but I don't believe that's a bird."

They leaned closer, curious, as a curl of smoke appeared above the swallow. Mallory thought it might be an ember that had fallen onto the grass—or steam from the kettle. Until the shape grew, hazy and silvery in the morning light—slowly solidifying into the figure of a woman.

She had a scruffy tangle of short yellow-blond hair and eyes as round and dark as the bottom of a well. She was entirely naked, and seemingly unashamed of this fact—though her nakedness did reveal the way her bones jabbed beneath her skin, and the raw scars scattered across her body. A slash of a wound on her chest. Faint words scrawled down her arms. She was holding a long black-and-white feather in one hand, and she shook it at Mallory as she spoke.

"You cannot leave! You must return to stop Bastien!" Even her human voice carried the uncanny warble of a barn swallow.

"Welcome, madame," said Fitcher, standing to greet the woman. He removed his cloak and held it out to her, though she seemed more annoyed than grateful, even as she snatched it away and wrapped it around her body. Fitcher bowed, as if he were addressing a foreign dignitary. "Perhaps you would care to introduce yourself before chastising my guests?"

She huffed and bobbed her head, birdlike, a couple of times, before going still. "I am Gabrielle Savoy."

Mallory and Anaïs both gasped—in a way that drew the curious attention of the others.

"A pleasure to make your acquaintance," Fitcher said coolly.

"Yes, lovely, fabulous," said Constantino. "For clarification . . . who is Gabrielle Savoy?"

She tittered in annoyance, flapping her arms in a semblance of furious wings.

It was Mallory who answered, "She was Bastien Saphir's fourth wife. The one who escaped. And she is also . . ."

She looked at Anaïs, who had paled. "Our great-grandmother."

CHAPTER THIRTY-SIX

The tale of Gabrielle Savoy was the stuff of epic family lore, as delectable as the adventure novels Anaïs loved. An unwanted betrothal. An eerie château on a windswept coast. A husband with a cruel smile, mysteriously widowed three times over. A stolen key. A cellar with a bloody secret. A magic spell. A daring escape.

Gabrielle Savoy was often referred to as the wife who got away—but few knew how she had done it. Some thought her brothers arrived and stopped Bastien moments before he slaughtered her. Others said she had tricked her husband by decorating a statue in the château's western tower to make it appear that she was sitting in the window praying to Velos on the eve of her expected death, and while Le Bleu sharpened his sword, she fled in secret. Had she taken a horse? Slipped out through secret tunnels beneath the estate? Had she convinced the staff to help her? There were many theories, but they were all wrong.

Gabrielle Savoy had pleaded with her husband to be allowed

to pray to the Seven before he claimed her life. Whether he was feeling generous or he merely wished to cruelly draw out her terror, Bastien Saphir granted the request. What he didn't realize was that Gabrielle Savoy had magic of her own.

When she reached the top of the tower, she recited a powerful incantation and took a literal leap of faith. It worked. Transformed into a bird, Gabrielle flew away to safety.

Mallory knew the story was true because she'd found the very incantation in one of her mother's spell books, written in Gabrielle's own hand. As a child, Mallory had memorized the strange, melodic words. Practiced repeating them to herself, while she imagined soaring over the roofs of Morant in the guise of a majestic hawk. But it was always that last step that kept her from actually attempting the spell. Even back when she had petty magic, there was no way she was ever going to trust it enough to take that final leap.

Gabrielle eventually changed her surname to *Fontaine*, fearful that the sordid history with her dead husband would someday return to haunt her. In Morant, she gained notoriety for her witchcraft, developing a small but lucrative business selling spells and tinctures, assisting in childbirths, and conducting séances for mourning loved ones. Though she refused to ever marry again, she did have a child, who inherited her talent for petty magic.

According to the tales Mallory's mother had told them, Gabrielle waited until her daughter was full-grown and able to manage the business on her own. Then one night, she kissed her daughter goodbye and changed herself back into a bird. She flew off into the night and was never seen again.

Of course, that was decades ago.

Of course, she was long dead.

At least, that's how the story went.

But this woman before Mallory did not have the customary crackling, hazy edges that ghosts had. Rather, she was as colorful and lifelike and solid as any one of them gathered around the fire.

Plus, it was clear that they could all see her.

"You will return to the house," Gabrielle said, punctuating the statement with a jab of the feather and a shrill tweet. She coughed, clearing her throat. "You must finish what was started."

"What was started?" Mallory asked.

"You came to rid this world of Bastien, did you not?"

Mallory pulled a face. "I came for three thousand lourdes. And all I've gotten are some bruises on my throat and nightmares that will haunt me the rest of my life."

Gabrielle scoffed, as if ashamed to hear such nonsense from her weakling descendant. "Coward! Where is your sense of duty?"

"Duty?" Mallory glanced at her sister, but Anaïs was gaping at their suddenly alive ancestor, speechless. "Armand tried to kill me! And if he can't kill *me*, he'll go after Anaïs next. We're not going back there."

Gabrielle shook her head, sending her short, wispy hair flinging against the sides of her face. "He did not try to kill you. I've been watching, and Armand is a sweet boy. Likely the kindest soul to ever come out of that accursed family."

"He tried to strangle me! After he put a sword through Julie's heart!"

"Nonsense. That was Bastien."

"It was not Bastien." She ground her teeth, furious to have to explain herself when Gabrielle, of all people, should have been entirely on her side. "It was Armand. He tricked Julie into marrying him, then he came after me. Because of *you*, by the way. He knows we have Savoy blood. Also, I saw Julie's ring in his room, and she had a flower from the greenhouse and—"

"You were in Armand's room?" Anaïs asked, not trying to hide her intrigue.

Gabrielle fluttered the feather like an irate symphony conductor. "I am telling you, it was Bastien."

"And I'm telling you it was Armand."

"Because Bastien is possessing him!" Gabrielle screamed this, then burst into a series of frustrated chirps. She pressed her hands over her mouth, but even still, it took a few moments for her to stop what appeared to be a reflexive response.

Mallory reeled back. "What did you say?"

"As far as I have gathered, he has been doing so for years," said Gabrielle, peeling her hands away. "Possessing Armand's body when it suits his needs to do so. It was he who wooed that poor maid, he who married her, though he wore Armand's skin like a cloak as he did it." She bounced on her toes—hopped side to side a couple of times. "I believe Armand keeps no memory of the times in which his mind is not his own. He likely has no idea that Bastien has been using him to complete the spell he started when he killed Triphine Maeng."

Mallory stared at her, dumbfounded.

Armand was *possessed*?

"What spell is this that he wishes to conclude?" Fitcher asked.

Gabrielle snatched a stick from the fire, charred on one end, and drew a circle in the dirt. Around the circle she spaced five smaller rings. "Five wives. Five wedding rings. Five vows of trust and protection—broken through the ultimate betrayal."

"Murder," Anaïs whispered.

Gabrielle's head bobbed. She drew X's through four of the five rings. "Powerful dark magic. If the spell is completed . . ." Her entire body shivered.

Fitcher scratched his bottom lip, displeased.

"What?" asked Mallory. "What will happen?"

"His spirit resurrected and made immortal," said Gabrielle.

"Immortal?" Fitcher said. "Are you sure he has that power?"

"He was a skilled sorcerer in life, and has become stronger with death."

"But . . . but he didn't manage to kill you," said Mallory. "What are you even still doing here? Why aren't you dead? And why are you a bird?"

Gabrielle squawked once, then grimaced. "I took the vows that bound me to him. When he spilled my blood, it tied me to his dark magic, and to my wedding ring, forever."

"Your wedding ring?" Mallory grabbed her sister's hand and lifted it up—showing the simple gold band and emerald that Anaïs had worn every day for years. "This wedding ring?"

Gabrielle nodded. "Where the ring goes, the spirit goes. I can never travel far from it, and can never be free until the spell is finished—or he is expelled from the mortal world."

"Where the ring goes, the spirit goes?" Anaïs said. "You mean . . . the bird that lived in the apartment with us. That was you?"

"Yes," said Gabrielle. "I have tried to watch over you, as well as I could. As I have watched over every generation since my dear daughter was born."

"Watched over us?" said Mallory. "You could have turned into a human this whole time! Why have you stayed a bird? So many things you could have told us, explained to us. The séance. My magic..."

"I must choose carefully how much time I spend in this form," said Gabrielle, her expression more fierce than regretful. "When I am human, my body ages, but I learned long ago that to stay a bird is to remain between worlds, not alive and not dead."

"How long have you taken that form?" Anaïs asked gently.

Constantino muttered, "Too long."

Gabrielle whapped him with the feather, but . . . it was just a feather, and didn't do much beyond amuse him.

"Besides," Gabrielle added, snapping her focus back to Mallory. "I have helped you! I saved you from those feux follets. You would have been smashed thin as a crêpe if you'd thrown yourself from that tower."

Mallory shuddered. "That was you?"

"That was me," Gabrielle affirmed. "You are welcome."

Grumbling a chastised *thank you*, Mallory studied her ancestor. Bird. Witch. The one who got away. Her heart thumped as she sorted through Gabrielle's words.

You must finish what was started.

Bastien is possessing him.

Where the ring goes, the spirit goes.

She thought of the ring that had been discovered on a dismembered finger behind a wine barrel. She thought of Triphine, who had not left the house in Morant for more than a hundred years, suddenly appearing in the carriage on their way to Comorre. She pictured the hook she'd seen beneath Armand's vanity—holding Triphine's ring along with the others. It was because he'd taken the ring out of Morant that Triphine had been forced to come with them to the estate deep in the countryside.

Her thoughts were a blizzard, and she found it impossible to wade through them. Armand was being possessed by a wicked spirit. Gabrielle Savoy was alive. Le Bleu needed five sacrifices to become immortal. Armand might be a liar and a thief, but maybe he hadn't tried to kill her after all.

"Triphine," she whispered, counting off on her fingers. "Lucienne. Béatrice. Julie. And . . . you." She squinted at Gabrielle. "Except he didn't kill you."

"No, but he married me. Which is why sacrificing either of *you*"—she bobbed her head at Mallory and Anaïs—"would suffice. You carry my blood."

"Or he could marry someone else," said Fitcher. "Find a new sacrifice."

"Yes," said Gabrielle. "But it will take time to woo another into marriage."

"Will it?" said Anaïs, smirking at Mallory. "How long would it take for him to seduce some unsuspecting young lady, do we think? Reasonably speaking?"

Mallory flushed. Armand—no, *Bastien*—hadn't needed to get her to marry him. He'd only needed her to trust him enough that he would have the opportunity to kill her when he was ready to. How long had that taken?

Not nearly long enough.

"If you ask me," said Constantino, gathering the coffee cups and returning them to the tray, "the fact that this ghost specifically wants one of *you* seems like a valid reason to never go back there again. I say—onward to Stivale!"

"No," said Anaïs, horrified. "If we don't put an end to this, Le Bleu will find another victim. He will use Armand to woo and murder some other innocent girl. We can't let that happen. Can we? Mallory?"

Mallory scrunched up her shoulders. "I don't know. I guess innocent girls shouldn't be so easily taken in by a pair of pretty blue eyes."

Anaïs punched her in the arm. "You hypocrite."

"Oh! Hold on one moment," said Constantino, setting down the tray and eyeing Mallory with renewed intrigue. "Precisely how *taken in by his pretty blue eyes* were you?"

Mallory glowered. "How about you tend to your own onions?" She turned to Anaïs. "You too, for that matter!"

Anaïs and Constantino exchanged knowing looks.

Mallory stood and stomped through the drawing of rings that Gabrielle had made in the dirt. She started pacing through the dewy grass, wishing Armand was there so she could throttle him. Then kiss him. Then throttle him again because how was she ever supposed to know if she was kissing *him* or his evil, manipulative ancestor?

She thought of all the times Armand had seemed so thoughtful, so genuine. His eagerness to show off his plants. The way he instinctively caught her when they fell down the tower steps. The hurt that had flashed across his face when she'd pushed him away after that kiss . . .

That kiss.

Gods help her, but she still wanted him. She wanted to know, intimately, the texture of his lips and the crush of his arms. She wanted to witness his sleepiest grins. She wanted to know if he snored at night or talked in his sleep and what he dreamed of, and when she awoke from her own nightmares, she wanted him there, beside her, so they could dissect the dreams until they were nothing more than bits of nonsense and stories to tell around a summer fire. She wanted to spend afternoons by his side, foraging in the trees and grinding mysterious herbs into oblivion so he could transform them into tinctures or ointments or whatever he did all day. She wanted to spend evenings reading about unsolved murders by the fire and knowing that she could tell him all the goriest details and he wouldn't be appalled by her fascination.

Just thinking it made her dizzy. What was wrong with her? Never in her life had Mallory believed she wanted love. Love made people weak. Love got you killed.

She didn't dare to let down her defenses. Not for anyone. And certainly not for a Saphir. Especially now, when she knew it might have been Bastien all along. Perhaps he had seen a weakness in her that Mallory had tried so hard to smash into dust. A yearning for connection, for someone to see her and appreciate her. To chuckle at her dark humor. To listen to her talk about decaying bodies and slimy monsters and not shrink away in disgust. Maybe Bastien had known exactly what sort of boy would attract her, and it had been nothing but a manipulation. A killer pulling her into his trap . . .

She stopped pacing. If they didn't put an end to it, he would find another victim. One last bride. One last sacrifice.

She squeezed her eyes shut. To return would be to put both her sister and herself in enormous danger. And besides . . .

She faced Gabrielle. "I'm not like you. I'm not a witch. I have no petty magic. Not anymore."

"You are not helpless," said Fitcher. "You are touched by Velos."

"I can speak to ghosts, but I don't see how that will help us. Most ghosts are only helpful when they want to be, and that's almost never."

Gabrielle stomped up to Mallory and wrapped her bony fingers around Mallory's arms, squeezing tight. Her expression unflinching.

Then she shoved her backward. Hard.

Mallory stumbled, barely catching herself before she fell. "What was that—"

Gabrielle shoved her again. "Foolish girl! Do you think that I do not know what you did? What became of your magic?"

Mallory stilled.

"I was there!" she shrieked. "I was there that night. I watched it all, and could do *nothing*!"

Mallory shook her head. "No. No . . . I called to you, but you didn't answer. You didn't come. It was only . . . it was only that monster. Bastien. Le Bleu—"

"You were trying to summon the dead. Of course I did not come to you as a *spirit*. I am not dead! But I was there, trying to get in, trying to stop you."

Anaïs gasped. "In the chimney. We thought it was a bat."

"When you opened that door to Verloren, I could not answer, because I was not in Verloren. But Bastien saw the opening and took advantage of it."

"I know," Mallory whispered. "I know. I'm sorry. I didn't mean to. I just . . . I wanted to help my sister. I thought, if I could talk to you, you could tell us how . . . how to get rid of it."

"Get rid of what?" asked Fitcher.

It was not her secret to tell. She glanced at Anaïs, who had her arms tightly crossed. But then, resigned, Anaïs straightened and brushed her hair to one side, revealing the hourglass mark on the back of her neck. Smaller than Mallory's and perfect, shimmering gold.

"They are *both* marked by Velos?" said Constantino, gaping. "What are the odds of that?"

"No," said Mallory. "Only Anaïs was marked by Velos. And she hates it, always has."

"It is not a gift," Anaïs said, her voice wavering, "but a terrible, vulgar curse. Mallory and our mother, they could do such beautiful things. Things that helped people. Things that had value. So Mallory thought we could bring Gabrielle back and ask her to help us . . . make the trade. My god-gift, for the same magic that was supposed to run in my blood. I wanted that so badly. But instead . . ."

"It was supposed to be easy," Mallory said. "Our mother had conducted dozens of séances over the years, helping those who were grieving their lost loved ones, who needed closure. I memorized the words from one of her spell books, and we waited until the Mourning Moon, sneaked into the Saphir mansion in Morant, and then . . . tried to summon Gabrielle. But instead, we let Bastien out of the underworld. And he did grant our wish. He made us the same. He corrupted my witchcraft with death magic, and . . . I've seen ghosts ever since."

"You were children," Fitcher said. "You were attempting to summon a spirit who was not dead. It is not surprising that Bastien slipped through the opening you gave him. And as Gabrielle said, he was a skilled sorcerer."

"He was more than that," said Gabrielle. "I believe he also had the blessing of Velos. But this gift had been corrupted by his use of dark magic, limiting his abilities. It was this corrupted death magic that he forced upon you that night, and it has been at war with your natural witchcraft ever since." Her expression turned fervent. "But while he may have transferred that mark to you, witchcraft is still in your blood. He cannot have taken that away." She grabbed Mallory's shoulders. "Your mother was powerful. I know that you are as well."

"Maybe I could have been, but not anymore. It's gone. I've tried everything I could think of to get my magic back. For seven years I've been trying, but . . ." Mallory threw up her hands, breaking her contact with Gabrielle. "It's no use, unless you're going to wave that feather around and grant me another wish."

"Do I look like a fairy godmother?"

Mallory examined her. The bottomless eyes, the shaggy hair, the unabashed nakedness, the feather wand. "A little bit, actually."

Gabrielle wrinkled her nose in offense. "Bastien may have locked your magic away, but believe me, child, he did not destroy it completely."

"Destroyed, locked away, what difference does it make?" said Mallory. "I can't use it. I can't do anything to fix this. I can't help Armand."

"But *you* are a witch," Anaïs piped up, addressing Gabrielle. "Could *you* conduct the spell? To return Bastien to the underworld?"

"Not by myself," said Gabrielle. "It would require Armand to be still for a period of time. Unconscious or . . . otherwise incapacitated. And it would require a candle. And all five rings, including mine, so it's a good thing the two of you never sold it off. And . . . I'm sure I'm forgetting something. It's been a very long time."

"That sounds rather achievable," said Fitcher. "I think perhaps we can help each other. That is why you wished to summon us in the first place, isn't it? To rid the House Saphir of this dreadful spirit?"

"Yes," said Mallory. "But I cannot pay you. And neither, it seems, can Armand."

"I can," said Anaïs. "I would gladly give up my god-gift, if you can make use of it."

"I cannot *take* it from you," said Fitcher. "You would need to come with us, to help break my own curse when the time comes."

"Then the choice is half fig, half grape," she said, swallowing. "But I've always wanted to go on an adventure."

Fitcher drummed his fingers, studying her. Then he nodded. "Done. In return, we shall rid you of this devil."

"Anaïs, are you sure?" Mallory whispered, grabbing her hand. "You don't have to—"

"I do," she said. "You and I brought this monster back. We must find a way to end this." She gnawed on the inside of her cheek. "But if we go back so soon after Armand tried to kill you, dragging along a couple of monster hunters . . . won't Le Bleu be suspicious? Surely he'll know that we've returned for him, and he'll try to . . . er, sacrifice one of us as soon as he can get us alone."

"Then we shall have to act faster," said Fitcher.

"Besides," added Constantino, "we needn't tell him that we're monster hunters."

"What else are we going to tell him?" said Anaïs. "That you're a traveling circus?"

"No." Mallory glanced at the stagecoach. "I have another idea."

CHAPTER THIRTY-SEVEN

They returned on horseback, with the baukhauv pulling the large stagecoach in their wake and Gabrielle—a bird once more—flitting in and out of the trees that lined the road. Mallory imagined they were a sight coming down the drive. Their wagon wheels must have made enough of a racket, or perhaps Gideon, the stable hand, ran ahead to announce them, because by the time they pulled into the circular drive, the front door of the château had been thrown open. Armand stood on the steps, Yvette and Pierre crowding in behind him.

Mallory wished she could read Armand's mind, but his expression was closed to her. Surprised—yes. But she was sure there was something else. Something that made her pulse flutter beneath her skin. He was happy to see her again, she was almost certain. It was the *why* that eluded her. The *why* that made her wonder if she should greet him with a kiss or a knife to the jugular.

The last time she'd seen Armand, he'd had his hands wrapped around her throat, though the true Armand would have no memory of that.

Who was she speaking to now?

And which Armand had kissed her with such unfettered, unapologetic desire?

"Mallory," he breathed, coming down the steps as they dismounted from the steeds they had stolen two nights before. "Anaïs. We weren't sure . . ." He let the words hang, unfinished.

Mallory listed her head. "You weren't sure, what? That we would come back?"

He hesitated. "When you disappeared that night, we worried . . . I thought you had left forever."

The housekeeper's frown carved lines even deeper than usual into her face, and Mallory could easily imagine the conversation they must have had the next morning. *Nothing but liars and thieves, those witches. I told you they were up to no good, and now poor Julie is dead and they've taken two of our best steeds and a sack full of silver and humiliated you to boot. If you'd only listened to me . . .*

"We have a job to finish," she said, handing the reins to Gideon. "We went for reinforcements."

The coach's door swung open. Fitcher and Constantino emerged, their bodies draped with shapeless red robes that Anaïs had fashioned from a set of curtains and belted with beaded ropes. Though neither of them had chosen to shave their heads—not quite as committed to the role as Investigator Sophia Blaise had been—they nevertheless played the part of loyal acolytes to the Seven surprisingly well, approaching the house with serene, measured steps. Even Constantino had managed to mold his suggestive grin into something resembling piety.

"Count Saphir," said Mallory, "may I introduce Initiates Fitcher and Constantino of the Order of the Fallen Veil. After what happened to Julie, I felt it would be wise to have a representative of Velos to assist with our . . . predicament. Anaïs and I rode to the temple north of Grevinny to request their aid."

"Blessed morn," said Fitcher. "We grieve for the soul of the victim and offer our condolences. Should anyone of the household require blessings, we shall happily bestow them."

"I . . . thank you," Armand stammered, bewildered. "And welcome. We are . . . honored to have you." He said it a bit like a question, looking from Mallory to Yvette, who had puffed up with pride. "We shall have guest rooms prepared."

Fitcher bowed. "Thank you for your generosity, but we have brought our own accommodations."

"Are you sure?" asked Armand.

"They're very particular," said Anaïs. "They only drink water purified by the holy spring of Eostrig, and sleep with blankets woven by those who are Hulda-blessed. It's really best to leave them to their own devices."

Constantino cleared his throat. "Though we would not refuse some of your finest wine."

A muscle jumped in Fitcher's jaw.

"All wines, as all harvests," Constantino added with a flourish of his hand, "are approved by Freydon."

"Of course," said Yvette. "Anything you require." She hesitated, before asking, with some unease, "What *do* you require?"

"Very little," said Fitcher. "But we wish to conduct our business as soon as possible. Has the deceased received her final prayers?"

"No," said Armand. "Traditionally we have buried our own here."

"We mean no intrusion," said Fitcher, "but with your permission, we shall see to the preparations of the body ourselves. As for her interment, has a grave been prepared?"

To this, Armand nodded. "She is to be buried in our family cemetery, in the northwest corner of the estate. I would be most grateful for your assistance. It was not a job I felt qualified for, and not one I wished to pass off to any member of my staff."

"Very good." Fitcher craned his head. "With no objections, we would like to proceed at sunrise."

"Sunrise?" said Armand. "Tomorrow?"

Mallory's pulse jumped. "Is that a problem?"

"I . . . no. Maybe not. But tomorrow is . . . It is the anniversary of the death of Bastien Saphir."

Mallory wondered if the murderer was peering back at her, even now.

She smiled coolly. "I doubt Le Bleu will have interest in a burial ceremony."

Armand's brow furrowed, as if he did not entirely agree with this statement.

"In the meantime," Mallory added, "the acolytes have agreed to assist with the monster infestation as well. Would you have time today to show them around the estate?"

ARMAND, FITCHER, AND CONSTANTINO EMERGED FROM the overgrown gardens four hours later. Though the day was cold, with a brisk wind coming from the west, Mallory sat on the terrace waiting for them, bundled up in furs that Armand had graciously provided. His hands had lingered cautiously as he settled a cloak across Mallory's shoulders. He'd looked like he desperately wanted to say something to her, but with Anaïs and the "acolytes" lingering a few steps away, he'd instead muttered something about a croque-mitaine in the creek, then hastily retreated toward the forest, Fitcher and Constantino in tow.

Now, as they returned, he seemed unwilling to meet her eye, and Mallory wasn't sure what to make of it.

Armand wasn't the only one avoiding her. As soon as she and Anaïs had finished setting up for the next day's ritual, sneaking about to avoid the servants' questions, she'd gone searching for Triphine, to apologize for abandoning her.

But Triphine was nowhere to be found. Probably sulking and cursing Mallory's name. She could hold a grudge longer than a kraken could hold its breath.

Strangely enough, she saw no sign of Lucienne or Béatrice, either.

"These are the best hunting grounds I've ever seen," said Constantino, taking the steps two at a time before dropping onto a low stone wall beside Anaïs. He unhooked a velvet pouch from his belt and tugged open the cord, revealing dozens of glass figurines within. They clinked together as he sifted his hand through them. Mostly salamanders and lutin, a couple of cats and owls that Mallory thought might be matagots. Some creatures were reptilian, others humanoid, one resembled a porcupine.

Anaïs picked up a speckled, spiral shell with tentacles erupting from its base. "Look, Mally. It's the thing that attacked us in our room."

"Lou carcolh," said Mallory, inspecting Constantino's haul. So many creatures—from fierce to docile, but all nuisances of one sort or another—so quickly reduced to pretty trinkets. "How did you find them all?"

"The count was a most helpful guide," said Constantino.

Armand made a dubious face. "I didn't do much but show them the trails and point out places a few beasts had been seen over the years."

"Yes, that's true. I was being generous. I did also have some unexpected assistance." Constantino dug out a stump of bound dry twigs from his pocket, their ends blackened. Mallory recognized the remains of one of the herbal smoke sticks she'd made with Armand's help. "Somebody has been spreading around madwort smoke."

"Madwort?" asked Anaïs. "What is that?"

"A plant that is practically bait for magical creatures."

Horror prickled at Mallory's skin. "What do you mean?"

"They're drawn to it, like cats to catnip."

"Or Stivalens to wine," Fitcher added, taking the bundle from him.

"That too," agreed Constantino.

"I can't imagine why anyone would be foolish enough to saturate the air around here with something so enticing," said Fitcher, sniffing the herbs. "But I don't think it was done with malicious intent. Juniper, pennyroyal . . . judging from the rest of these plants, my guess is they were attempting to work a petty spell to dispel evil spirits, but used madwort when they meant to use madderwort."

Constantino shook his head. "Amateur."

Armand's quizzical gaze slid toward Mallory, but she ignored him, not wanting to discuss her botched attempt at petty magic.

"I'm sure it's a common mistake," she muttered.

"The smoke should be cleared," said Constantino, taking a handful of arrows from his quiver to inspect their fletching. "We'll monitor the grounds for signs of any beasts we might have missed, but for now, I feel we've quite excelled at our responsibilities." He winked at Anaïs. "Praise to the Seven."

CHAPTER THIRTY-EIGHT

Yvette delivered a pot of tea and some pastries to their room early the next morning, though Mallory didn't know if Armand had asked her to do it, or if the housekeeper was actually warming up to them now that they'd brought representatives of her beloved Seven. Either way, Mallory found that she was too nervous to eat or drink anything, while Anaïs's nerves made her eager to devour everything on the tray. It was a symbiotic relationship.

The early afternoon sun was merely a rumor on the horizon when they met the rest of the household in the courtyard. A shroud of fog had crept in from the ocean, obscuring the distant vineyards on the hill and lending the air a damp, frigid quality.

They were a dismal procession as they went to collect Julie from the chapel. Her body still appeared frighteningly alive, her skin too soft and pink, preserved by whatever dark magic was stirring through the House Saphir.

Fitcher and Constantino played their roles well, whispering

prayers that sounded halfway authentic as they anointed Julie's skin with fragrant oils and placed silver coins over her eyelids. The group had fallen silent as they transferred Julie's body into the coffin and made their way steadily, silently through the gardens and into the forest.

The forest was too noisy, as far as Mallory was concerned, though probably it was her own anxiety making her pulse jump at every snap of a twig, every caw of a ruffled crow, every rustle in the shrubbery that lined the path. On this—the anniversary of Bastien's death—she couldn't help feeling anxious, expecting to see Monsieur Le Bleu following after them, gripping a bejeweled sword and wearing a wicked smile.

But when she glanced back, all she saw was swirling mist.

Armand, Fitcher, Pierre, and Gideon carried the ebony coffin between them, while Constantino went ahead, bow on his shoulder, to clear fallen trees and be alert for any monsters that might confront the ceremonial procession. Mallory, Anaïs, and Yvette followed behind the group.

Mallory noted that Armand was wearing the coat he'd worn on the tour, once fashionable, but now she couldn't unsee how the fabric had gone threadbare around the collar.

Somewhere, she knew that the sun was creeping over the mountains, but the light did not change so deep in the woods. Nothing but gray trunks and charcoal shadows in every direction.

She rather would have liked to draw it.

Le Bleu had been quiet since their return, a silence that felt more foreboding than fortuitous. There had been no plaintive whistling. No distant laughter. She and Anaïs had taken precautions the night before, locking the bedroom door and dragging a heavy trunk in front of it. Le Bleu might be able to get at them, but they would have warning if he used Armand to do it.

Even still, she had hardly slept, and in the end, her fears had been for nothing. It was as though Bastien were biding his time until nightfall, when the fountain would fill with blood and the true horrors would be unleashed.

He certainly had a flair for the dramatic.

They expected Le Bleu to be eager to conclude this sorcery business. Surely he would take any chance to coax Mallory away, perhaps even during the burial. To do that, he'd need to take possession of Armand again.

She was counting on it.

Up ahead, the gate's rusted hinges creaked, startling a flock of hedge sparrows from the trees.

Constantino held open the gate as the procession slipped inside. Moss squished beneath Mallory's boots. The air was thick with the smell of damp leaves and fall-blooming witch hazel.

As the sparrows dared to return, prancing about between the stones, the pallbearers picked their way over the uneven ground, to the grave that had been dug in the far corner of the cemetery.

Julie's coffin was laid onto the prepared ropes.

"Initiate Constantino," Fitcher said, hardly having to pretend to act the part of the devout acolyte, "please prepare the ceremonial drink."

Constantino graciously accepted the supplies that Anaïs had brought before stepping away from the crowd. While they waited, Pierre and Yvette gathered flowers, talking in hushed voices as they passed among the stones, and Gideon leaned against a statue of Wyrdith, using his hat to dab sweat from his brow. Anaïs lingered nearby, pretending to read the headstones even as her attention darted between Mallory and Armand. Mallory was certain her sister had not slept last night, either.

Despite their expectations, Armand had made no attempt to get Mallory alone. If anything, he'd largely been avoiding her—though when their eyes did meet, he seemed to be struggling, as if he had something he wished to say but couldn't find the words.

"Let us begin," said Fitcher. The sudden pronouncement, breaking the quiet, startled her.

Constantino had set cordial glasses on a silver tray. He passed them out to the gathered mourners while Fitcher recited some poetic diatribe about how the wine, which Armand had been happy to supply at Constantino's request, symbolized the river that would carry Julie's spirit into the land of the lost, and in partaking of this drink, they were promising to keep her memory alive in love and faith.

Something like that, anyway. Mallory wasn't listening. While Yvette sobbed and Pierre and Anaïs sniffled and Gideon looked like he would rather be anywhere else, Mallory watched Armand from the corner of her eye, searching for a hint that he knew the truth of what had happened. Searching for a sign that would indicate whether or not he could be trusted.

When Fitcher was finished, he raised his own glass, and as one, they tipped back their drinks.

The coffin was lowered into the grave. They took turns shoveling dirt on top. While they worked, Fitcher and Constantino maintained their ruse, whispering prayers over the body. They sung low, haunting chants.

As an official headstone had not yet been made, a slab of rock was placed over the fresh grave once they were finished.

"Now we shall leave her in peace, to find her own way by the light of Velos's lantern," said Fitcher.

Yvette placed a chrysanthemum on the softly churned dirt, and they began the melancholy journey back to the house.

Mallory was heading toward her sister when the brush of a tentative finger nearly had her leaping from her skin.

Armand drew back. "I'm sorry. I didn't mean to . . . alarm you."

"That's all right. Just . . . you know. Cemeteries tend to make a person nervous."

His frown deepened and Mallory cringed at her fib. Cemeteries did not make *her* nervous, and they both knew it.

He cleared his throat. "I was hoping I might speak to you. A-alone."

As he said it, twin splotches of pink bloomed on his cheeks. Was he thinking of their kiss? Or of how he'd tried to kill her?

Did he even know that he had tried to kill her?

The group was already halfway across the graveyard. Mallory's instincts told her to call out to them, to tell them to wait. They'd prepared for this possibility, aware that Bastien would likely take the first opportunity to get either her or Anaïs alone . . . to make his final sacrifice.

But if Bastien knew she suspected the truth, the entire plan could be ruined.

She forced a smile. "Of course."

They lingered behind. Anaïs turned back once, alarmed, but

Mallory offered a casual wave and hoped her sister interpreted it as *don't you dare go far.*

With a subtle nod, Anaïs followed the others beyond the cemetery wall and disappeared into the trees.

Mallory felt suddenly trapped with this high wall and iron gate, and nowhere to run or hide. This would not do.

"Mallory, I—"

"Where is Le Bleu buried?"

The words vanished from Armand's tongue. "Le Bleu?"

"You said he is not in this graveyard."

"Oh—no, he is not here. He was originally intended to be buried there, beside his wives." He pointed to a smaller crypt beside the enormous mausoleum. "But his son—my great-grandfather—did not think it was proper after what he had done. So it was decided that he would be buried outside of the walls instead."

Mallory recognized it for what it was—the ultimate sign of disgrace.

"Can I see?"

"I suppose." Armand chuckled quietly, giving a bewildered shake of his head. "You do have the strangest curiosities. You know that?"

"I have the same curiosities as everyone else. I'm just not afraid to say them aloud."

His lips quirked gently. "Yes, I know. It is one of the things I admire about you."

Before Mallory could unravel those words, he ducked out through the gate. When he headed in the opposite direction from the house, she hesitated for only a moment before she followed him.

CHAPTER THIRTY-NINE

Armand headed south along the cemetery wall. Following in his footsteps, Mallory searched the trees for movement, listening for crackling branches and scurrying footsteps. But if they were being watched, if her sister or Fitcher or Constantino or even Gabrielle in her guise of a common barn swallow were near, she saw no signs of them.

The cemetery was mostly built atop a hill, and soon they were descending on the other side, along the edge of a shallow ravine where a creek burbled among moss-covered stones. They had been trudging silently through the foliage for a few minutes when Armand pointed. "There."

Mallory spied the headstone beside a young alder tree. A short, nondescript fence surrounded the grave, which had long ago been overtaken with weeds. The stone itself was simple—nothing like the elaborate marble edifices in the cemetery, plainer even than those given to the farmers and the maids. It was crumbling—one corner broken off, the stone leaning at a dangerous slant.

When Armand did not move closer, Mallory gathered her courage and brushed past him. The hair stood on the back of her neck as she did so, her body overcome with a sense of vulnerability. She had not realized how instinctively she'd avoided turning her back to him, and now she felt his presence behind her like that of a prowling monster.

She was even more aware of the knife in her boot. She'd practiced reaching for it, extracting it. Her reflexes were primed. But would it be enough?

"Perhaps this is what his spirit is so angry about," she said, stopping beside the fence. "That he wasn't buried in his lavish crypt."

Armand made a low noise in his throat and Mallory shivered. He had followed her, and was so close she imagined she could feel the vibrations of his chest. "Let him be angry. He deserves no better."

Mallory lifted her attention from the grave. Scanned white birches interspersed with slim poplars. Bushes heavy with winter berries. The birds had begun to chatter in the faint morning light. Was Gabrielle among them? She had the strangest sense that they might be trying to warn her.

She exhaled and faced Armand. "You once told me that it horrifies you, knowing that you were related to a monster like him."

His attention lingered on the crooked grave. "I assume it would horrify anyone."

There was no veil over the words, no hint of exaggeration or shame. She had to believe he was being truthful.

Still, he seemed to struggle over whether or not to say more.

Mallory waited, attempting to breathe through the thundering of her pulse. Finally, he added, "As a child, I would scare myself. Whenever I got angry, I would worry that it was my nature—something deep inside me that I couldn't stop and couldn't avoid. If my anger could overtake me, then who knew what I might be capable of? Who knew if I could become a monster, too?" He grimaced, tugging at a loose thread on his sleeve. "My solution was to stop being angry. Whenever something was upsetting, or irritating, I would take that emotion and shove it down as deep as I could. I would smile through it all. Remain calm and stoic, no matter what I faced." He hesitated, his voice quieting. "I would never let the monster free."

Mallory recalled the face he'd made in the stables, when he'd caught her preparing to run away. The absolute rage that had overtaken him. The way he'd almost delighted in wrapping his hands around her throat.

There was a monster inside him—but it was not his own anger he needed to fear.

If she told him the truth, would he believe her? Gabrielle had said it was pointless. Armand was not in control. There was nothing he could do—not until they completed the ritual necessary to cast the spirit out.

He might not even believe her. For who would want to consider such a thing?

And right now, she needed him to trust her.

"I'm sorry."

She blinked. "Sorry?"

He drew away from her, like he was shrinking into himself. Shriveling into the coat that was a little too worn. Drawing into the shadows of the forest. "I've frightened you again. It's the last thing I want, but I can't seem to stop doing it."

Her heartbeat was as sharp as a chisel, cutting into her ribs. Maybe he remembered after all. The stable. His cruel words. "You don't frighten me."

He laughed—a sound that rumbled through her every nerve. "You're lying."

"I am not."

"Every time we're alone, you end up running away from me."

She swallowed. Perhaps that was true.

"And maybe that's for the best." He studied her face. "You know something. At first I thought maybe it was . . . in my room, when you . . . when we . . ." He paused to gather himself. "But after you left, I realized things had begun to change the moment Julie died. You looked at me differently. Like you didn't trust me, and like you had every reason not to." He lifted a hand to the side of his head. "Then you disappear, take two horses and run off without a word, and I wake up in the stables, a shovel next to me and a head that feels like it's been thrown into the winepress."

If he'd seemed fearful before, now there was a quiet dread creeping over his features.

"I've had time to think. About you. And about Julie. I always thought she was odd, because she'd often say things that made no sense. Or look at me in a way that was . . . secretive. I thought she was merely flirtatious, and I hoped that by ignoring her, it would pass, but then she would act so hurt, and it became a cycle of guilt and kindness that went on for months. And then, suddenly, she's dead. And you talk about her having some secret romance, and being given a wedding ring, and—" He cut himself off.

"You found the wedding ring in your room," Mallory whispered.

He startled. "You *did* see it. That's why you ran." He shifted forward, grabbing her hands, pleading. She tensed at the touch but did not pull away. "You have to believe that I would never have hurt her. I don't know how the ring got there. I have no idea who killed her or why, but it wasn't me, Mallory."

"But you forget things."

He fell quiet, startled.

"You don't know how you got to the stables. And there are other times, too, when you have no memory of how you got to a place, or why you are there." She wet her lips. "You do not know for sure what you were doing the morning that Julie was murdered. There is time missing that you can't remember. Isn't that so?"

Armand's pallor turned gray.

But with her certainty that she was right, she was struck with a new realization.

He'd mentioned what had happened in his room. The way she'd pushed him away when she saw the ring.

Armand remembered their kiss.

Mallory's breath hitched. It hadn't been Le Bleu, and it hadn't been her imagination. It had been Armand, the real Armand—and he had wanted her. *Her.* Strange Mallory, with her dark jokes and dark drawings and dark curiosities.

"Tell me the truth," Armand murmured.

For an instant, the truth was there in her mouth, on her tongue, threatening to spill out into the world where she could never take it back.

She yearned for him in a way that terrified her. The very sight of him ignited a fire inside her. His self-conscious laugh made her want to crush her mouth to his. The way he rattled off unfamiliar plant names did something to the chemistry of her brain.

It scared her. It scared her *so much*. Far more than bloodthirsty monsters or odious spirits.

But her messy, complicated, irrational feelings were not what they were talking about.

Tell me the truth.

His calloused hands tightened on hers like a drowning man grasping at a piece of driftwood. He looked devastated—because he must have already known, without her having to say it.

"You killed Julie," she breathed, as gently as she could.

Armand released her hands, drawing away.

"And you tried to kill me, in the stables. Anaïs hit you with a shovel."

He started to shake his head, but stopped. He pressed a hand to the top of a fencepost, squeezing the wood with whitened knuckles.

Mallory settled a hand on his wrist. "It isn't your fault—"

"Not my *fault*?" He tore away from her, stumbling back so quickly that he nearly tripped over a tree root before catching himself. "Great gods, Mallory, what are you doing out here?" He whipped his arm to the side, gesturing at the dense woods that surrounded them. "If I am a monster, then why did you come back? And why . . . ? You need to stay away from me!"

The birdsong fell quiet around them.

"I came back to help you."

"Help me? After I tried to—"

"*Yes*," she said, with as much force to the word as she could manage. Wishing he would just understand, without her needing to actually *say it*. "Even after *Bastien* tried to kill me, I came back. It was him. His spirit can possess you. He . . . he can take over your body. He is the one who manipulated Julie and killed her. Who attacked me. But he controls you to do it."

Armand's words fizzled to nothing, his mouth left hanging.

Mallory took a cautious step closer, relieved when he didn't back away. Though his expression was a cross between dismayed and horrified, he also seemed the tiniest bit intrigued.

"I came back because I had to know if . . . if you . . . possibly feel for me, what I . . ."

His lips parted father, but no sound came out. She had rendered him speechless.

She cursed inwardly, her face suddenly burning. If given a choice between facing another cheval mallet or having this conversation, she would have taken her chances with the horse. How did anyone do this? How could anyone express their feelings without wanting to throw themselves into one of those crypts?

And then Armand's attention dropped to her mouth, and some of Mallory's terror kindled into hope.

But, as if mortified that he was tempted to kiss her after all she'd told him, Armand pulled away again. She followed, staying an arm's distance until his back hit the trunk of an old maple, its autumn leaves painted vivid red.

"No." The word was strained, and somehow, Mallory did not feel the slightest sting of rejection. If anything, the word encouraged her.

"No?" she pressed.

"This is insanity," he breathed. A terse laugh erupted from him, like he couldn't quite believe he had to explain this. Like he couldn't believe he was having this conversation at all.

Neither could Mallory, truth be told.

"First you tell me there is this awful darkness inside of me, and I already tried to kill the first girl I have *ever*——" He stopped.

Mallory's eyebrows shot upward.

Renewed determination overtook Armand—touched with a hint of anger. Pushing away from the tree, he dared to step closer to her. Mallory held her ground. She wasn't intimidated. If anything, she wanted to grab him and pull him closer.

"I will not be responsible for hurting you, too," he said fiercely. "I want you to leave. Tonight. Leave, and never come back. Tomorrow I will turn myself in for the crimes I committed, and gods willing, I will be put into prison and no one will be in danger from me—or him—ever again."

Mallory felt her knees weaken. She smiled, hesitant. "That is the most romantic thing I've ever heard."

He glowered, like he wanted to shake some sense into her.

Or like he wanted to kiss her, and while Mallory had never been skilled at reading such signs, something told her she was getting good at reading *him*.

So good, in fact, that she knew at once when the effects of the tonic finally hit him. His skin paled. His gaze lost focus. He frowned, his breaths slowing. "What is . . ." His voice caught.

Realization flashed across his face—followed by confusion and, lastly, betrayal.

"Mallory . . . what did you do?"

"There may have been a sedative in your wine," she confessed.

"I actually got the idea from Bastien himself. Poisoned his wives before killing them, remember?" Realizing how awful that sounded, she hurried to add, "Not that I'm planning to kill you, I just—"

She didn't manage to finish before Armand collapsed into her arms.

CHAPTER FORTY

"That took long enough," Mallory grunted, lowering Armand's body to the ground.

"Sorry," said Fitcher as he and Constantino emerged from behind a wall of brambles. "He didn't drink much during the ceremony, otherwise it would have affected him sooner."

"Let's be grateful he didn't try to kill you," said Constantino. "As soon as this so-called Le Bleu knows what we're up to, things will get a lot more complicated."

Fitcher's expression was irate. "You were supposed to keep at least three paces between you two so Constantino could shoot him if he attacked you."

"Don't you see?" said Constantino. "It was impossible for her to resist his magnetic allure. At times I was sure I could see bolts of lightning flash between your very souls! I am most impressed, bellissima." Constantino nudged Mallory with his elbow. "You play the icy part well, but I see now there is a fire burning deep. It just required the right lover to stoke the flame."

"Please stop talking," said Mallory, "or I will vomit ceremonial wine all over your fancy boots."

Constantino took a step back, his grin teasing. "I am not fooled. You have a romantic's soul, no matter how you try to hide it."

She shot him a scathing look, before addressing Fitcher. "Where is my sister?"

"Keeping an eye on the staff. They each took a third glass when offered. Hopefully they made it back to the house before falling unconscious." He gave a sullen nod at Armand. "Shall we?"

Mallory walked ahead, carrying Armand's feet while Fitcher and Constantino—already tired from clearing fallen tree branches earlier—took turns at his head and shoulders.

By the time they reached the chapel, deep among the gardens, Anaïs had worked herself into a frenzy.

"Oh, thank the gods," she said, pulling Mallory into an embrace. "Did he try something?"

Mallory hesitated, unsure if confessing one's innermost emotions counted as *trying something*. "No. He just wanted to talk. How are the others?"

"We weren't even out of the forest before they passed out. I was able to find shelter for them under a pine tree." She nervously chewed her pinkie nail. "I hope they won't be too upset when they wake up."

Inside the chapel, Anaïs had pushed the benches against the walls, leaving an open space in front of the altar where Mallory's drawing portfolio was open to the page where they had written the detailed notes about every type of spirit possession Gabrielle and Fitcher had ever heard of.

Anaïs had also sneaked a chair out of the house while Armand and the "acolytes" hunted monsters. The chair itself had been tucked away in a salon that apparently hadn't been used in decades, and its damask fabric was frayed and moth-eaten.

As soon as they'd settled Armand's unconscious form onto the chair, Fitcher set to work strapping down his arms and legs with the belts and ropes they'd scavenged while Gabrielle—still a barn swallow—hopped anxiously back and forth on the altar.

They had barely finished when Armand coughed, head lolling heavily to one side. His eyes opened into a squint, trying to focus as he peered around the chapel, finally landing on Mallory. Confusion drew across his features. With a stunted exhale, his head fell against the back of the seat. "Mal . . . what—" He frowned then and looked down at his arms, held tight against the chair. "What's going on?"

"Congratulations!" said Constantino. "We are gathered here today to celebrate your exorcism."

TWO HOURS LATER, IT WAS APPARENT THAT THEY HAD been overconfident. Fitcher claimed to be a scholar of all sorts of magic—dark, petty, god-given, fae, sorcery. Though he had no magic himself, he had been certain that between him, Gabrielle, and the sisters' connection to Velos, they would quickly find a spell to break Bastien's hold over Armand.

Fitcher had prepared for three different exorcism rituals, and they had worked diligently to follow his instructions down to the finest detail. They had burned hazel and pine branches. Draped carved runes over Armand's neck. Anointed him with water that Fitcher insisted came straight from the delta of the Eptanie River, where Freydon was said to have bathed. They had collected blood from Armand's fingers. Saliva from his mouth. Hair from his scalp. They had chanted and sung and burned candles and held hands and tossed so many different types of herbs at Armand's feet that Mallory wasn't sure if they were trying to purify him or prepare him for a stew.

Nothing worked. There was no noticeable change, other than Armand being a little damp and stiflingly aromatic. What Fitcher had assured her would be a simple, everyday exorcism was proving to be more complicated. Either that, or . . .

"Are you *sure* he's possessed?" Constantino asked, sitting on the altar and letting Gabrielle peck sunflower seeds from his palm.

"Either he's possessed by a murderous ghost or he's a murderer," said Mallory. "For once in my life, I'm trying to be an optimist."

"I appreciate your confidence in me," Armand deadpanned.

Constantino gave Mallory a sympathetic look. "I believe in optimism, but, stellina . . . I do not think there is a ghost here."

"Would the two of you stop talking?" said Fitcher, who had become increasingly irate with every failed attempt. He was bent over a fae spell book he'd brought from his collection in the stagecoach, trying to parse the tiny handwriting, which he claimed was in an unusual dialect that required more time than usual to decipher. "We need a colt's foot for this one." He looked up apologetically. "Don't suppose there are any expendable horses in the stables?"

Anaïs gasped. "You will not!"

"I'm no expert in fae magic, like you are," said Armand, his sarcasm evident, "but could it possibly be referring to coltsfoot, the plant?"

Fitcher bent back over the pages. "Actually, yes. I think it might."

Armand rolled his eyes. "Leaves or flowers?"

"Er . . . leaves?"

"Good, because it won't bloom again until the spring, though I have some dried petals in the kitchen. But you can find fresh leaves in the conservatory. Coltsfoot is in a glazed yellow pot in the northeast corner. Its leaves are shaped like a lily pad, softly scalloped on the edges, bright green but tinted gray on the underside. They smell a bit like sweet vinegar."

Fitcher signaled to Constantino, who seemed more than happy—relieved, even—to take off on the mission to secure said plant.

As the door swung shut, Armand sighed in exasperation, staring up at the cobweb-cluttered beams that crisscrossed the vaulted ceiling. He had taken the whole exorcism thing in stride so far, even commenting on occasion as different pieces of his own life fit into place, and curious experiences began to make sense. He insisted that he, more than anyone, would love to eradicate his great-great-grandfather before Bastien could harm anyone else.

But Mallory got the feeling that this desperate attempt from a fae grimoire could be their last. If this failed, they would have to assume that Le Bleu was not possessing Armand at all—at least, not at the moment. In which case, they would have to exorcise the spirit from the house itself.

And as far as Mallory could tell, no one had the faintest idea how to do that.

Gnawing on her knuckle, Mallory glanced at Armand—and caught him watching her. His hooded eyes held a sadness that struck her heart as surely as one of Constantino's arrows.

If he was a monster, then he was frighteningly adept at hiding it.

She sighed. She would never know what was true and what was false, not until this ordeal was over. Not until Le Bleu was gone for good, and she could trust that when she peered into Armand's eyes, it was Armand looking back at her.

"This whole time," he said slowly, "this is what you've thought of me."

She self-consciously folded her arms across her chest. "Not the *whole* time."

"No? Did you begin to suspect I might want to kill you before or after I actually tried to kill you?"

She wasn't sure how to explain to Armand that it wasn't personal. "I generally assume most people want to kill me," she admitted. "You'll recall that I did think you were attacking me when you arrived for the tour."

"Of course. So, literally, from the first moment of our acquaintance, then. I've been trying to court you, like an absolute fool, while you feared for your life."

At this, Mallory guffawed, which she quickly realized was not the best knee-jerk reaction she could have had to this confession.

Fitcher and Anaïs, no doubt embarrassed on her behalf, awkwardly busied themselves with trivial tasks.

"I only feared for my life occasionally." She scratched at the itchy fabric of her collar, not daring to admit that his romantic interest in her was one of the most suspicious things about him.

"Only occasionally," Armand repeated, discouraged. "How illuminating. Because unlike you, I've spent every moment since we met searching for ways to see you, to talk to you. Wondering what might make you want to stay after the job was finished. Trying to convey how much I enjoy your company, how much I—" He let out an unruly laugh—a little flustered, a little angry. "There were times I thought maybe it was mutual, but in actuality . . . you were . . . what? Being nice, so I wouldn't *murder* you?"

"Don't be ridiculous," she snapped. "We both know I'm not that nice."

"No, we *don't* both know that. Mallory—"

"Also," she interrupted, "don't act as if you weren't lying to me this whole time."

He started to shout, his arms straining against the ropes. "I didn't know I was being possessed!"

She stood over him, hands fisted on her hips. "But you knew you were bankrupt!"

Surprise flashed across his features, and he jolted back against the seat again, anger evaporating.

"Three thousand lourdes, that's what you promised me." Mallory jabbed a finger at him. "Three thousand lourdes to finish this job. Money that you don't have. And oh! Take this precious medallion as proof of my good intentions, Mallory. It's priceless! Use it as collateral! Clearly, you have no reason to doubt *me.* I'm a *fancy count.*" She dug the medallion out from her collar and yanked it off over her head. She threw it into Armand's lap, pleased at how he flinched. She bent forward, snarling. "What was your plan, exactly? Let me and Anaïs deal with your ghost problems, then call in the investigators and have us shipped off to jail?"

"Of course not."

"No? Then what? Because we clearly weren't getting any of those coins you promised us."

"I was desperate," he said. "I needed help and didn't know where else to go. I hoped once the ghost was dealt with, we could hire new staff, the vineyards would be tended to again, after a few years the winery would be profitable—"

"A few years? What were we supposed to do until then, while we waited for you to get your affairs in order?"

"I don't know! Stay with me?" He looked almost pleading. Almost hopeful. "Once you were here, I hoped that . . . I didn't want you to leave."

"That isn't your decision to make."

"I know. I would have told you."

"When? After we got rid of Le Bleu? How about the monsters? How about—"

Anaïs loudly cleared her throat. "Perhaps," she said mildly, pressing a hand on Mallory's arm, "this would be a good time to tell Lord Armand that we are not actually—"

Mallory yanked her arm away. "It most certainly would *not* be a good time."

Anaïs drew back. "All right. Maybe later, then."

"Tell me what?" Armand asked.

"Nothing," they said in unison.

Eyes darkening with suspicion, Armand continued, "Why are you here if you knew I couldn't pay you and that Bastien wants one of you dead?" He shook his head. "Why did you come back?"

Mallory's heart was a deafening staccato beat in her ears as she stared down at him. After a moment, she lifted her chin and proclaimed, "Because it was the right thing to do."

Fitcher choked, clapping a hand to his mouth. Even Gabrielle let out a disappointed whistle.

"What?" she snapped at them.

With an equally unconvinced smirk, Armand asked, "And now for the real reason?"

"*Because*," she said forcefully, "you have some foul, manipulative spirit living inside of you, controlling you like a puppet master, making foolish girls swoon at your feet, and I find that intolerable. I will stop him. And when we are finished here, I will let the world know that I was the one to defeat the infamous Monsieur Le Bleu." She smiled wickedly. "It will be very good for business."

"In theory, I'll have had something to do with it," said Anaïs. "And Fitcher, and Constantino . . ."

"Not the point," said Mallory.

Armand was watching Mallory with thoughtfully narrowed eyes. "Are you one of the foolish girls in this scenario?"

"What?"

"The ones who supposedly swooned at my feet. Are you including yourself?"

She bristled, unable to tell if he was mocking her. "Don't insult me."

"Is that . . ." The wrinkle pinched between his brows. "Do you think it was him? Bastien? This whole time?"

She didn't respond.

A bellowing laugh escaped from Armand. "Oh, it just gets better. Not only did you think I might try to murder you, but you also assumed that my pathetic attempts at romance were *the ghost*."

"Given the situation, I do not think it implausible that Bastien could have been manipulating me . . . through you."

Armand leaned forward, as much as he could against his restraints. "And yet, as far as we can surmise, he is not here. Not right now. So, Mallory. Do you believe it is Bastien talking to you at this moment? Saying that you are both the most clever and the most frustrating person I've ever met? And that when this is over, I *don't want you to leave*."

Though her pulse raced, Mallory slipped a step away from him. "That's the problem, isn't it? I don't know how to tell."

Armand released his breath in one disgruntled huff. "I didn't expect courting a girl to be easy, but I didn't think I would be *so* bad at it."

"You aren't," she said. "It's just that *he* was so very good at it."

"Actually," said Fitcher, daring to intrude on a conversation he'd respectfully avoided thus far, "given that Savoy blood was already spilled in service to the spell, Monsieur Le Bleu does not require another marriage vow—not so long as his final sacrifice is either you or your sister."

"I know that," Mallory growled.

"I'm pointing out that he has no reason to try to seduce you. He only has to kill you."

Bristling, Mallory said, "Maybe he enjoys toying with his prey."

Fitcher grinned sardonically. "Or maybe it was Armand after all."

"What a novel concept," Armand said. "Maybe I'm not possessed. Maybe I just *like* you."

"You—*he*—tried to strangle me."

"Well, clearly I was possessed *then*."

"So you see the confusion!" Throwing her arms into the air, Mallory stomped away and slumped down on one of the benches.

She was grateful when Constantino returned carrying a bundle of leaves. "Is this the right one?" he asked, holding it up.

They looked at Armand, who nodded.

Fitcher set aside the grimoire, his expression clouded.

"Great. What do we need to do? Grind it up? Burn it? Weave the strands into his hair?" Constantino studied Armand's head. "I think it's long enough . . ."

"Nothing," said Fitcher with a drawn-out sigh. "There is no point."

"Excuse me?"

"I am sorry for the effort you went through to obtain this ingredient, but I believe this is a waste of our time. Bastien is not here."

Armand swiveled his head toward Fitcher. "How do you know?"

"Because I know that *is* the right plant," he said, "as I've found a detailed illustration of it in the grimoire. If you were being controlled by Bastien, you never would have admitted as much, as I have to imagine that Bastien does not *wish* to be expelled from the vessel he has chosen."

Armand wrinkled his nose, mystified. "That's it, then? I have spilled my heart out for this past hour. I have"—he tried to raise his arm, but settled with gesturing with his fingers—"confessed, not only to Mallory but to a room full of strangers, that I am utterly smitten with her. And yet, *this* is when you choose to believe that I might actually be me, and not some hundred-year-old murderer? Because I correctly identified some leaves?"

"Sometimes the simplest tests are the most accurate," said Fitcher. "I believe he has been telling you the truth."

Armand let out an annoyed snort, and Mallory wondered if he would still have any warm feeling toward her when this was over.

"But what does that mean?" said Anaïs. "That *Armand* tried to strangle Mallory, by his own will?"

"No," said Fitcher. "It would seem that Bastien can choose when to inhabit his vessel—"

"Please stop calling me that."

"And when to be separate from him."

"But if he isn't here now," said Constantino, "then where is he?"

Gabrielle let out a racket of excited tweets, then stopped suddenly and shook out her wings. A moment later, she emerged from the bird's form, a woman once more—naked and perched on the altar with wide, darting eyes. "But this is a good thing!"

Armand yelped and shoved at the floor so hard that the chair toppled over backward. He landed with a pained grunt. "Who is she?" he yelled.

"That's Gabrielle Savoy," said Mallory. "It's a long story. What do you mean, this is a good thing?"

Constantino gamely helped Armand upright again as Gabrielle shunned the robe that Fitcher offered her and excitedly explained, "We feared we would have to disentangle Bastien's spirit from Armand's, but as that is not the case, we can proceed with the dissolution of the spell. His dark magic, left unfinished, is what has kept me tied to this world. It is what has tethered the spirits of his other wives to the rings that were used in his ritual. But if we finish the ritual ourselves, we can loosen the binds of this magic upon the house and not only free his victims, but also cast the monster himself back to Verloren."

"Finish the ritual?" said Mallory. "You mean, the one in which one of us gets sacrificed?" She gestured between herself and Anaïs.

"One-two-three, not it," said her sister.

"As our goal is not immortality," said Gabrielle, "no further sacrifice is required. We need only to untie the threads of magic that are holding him here, holding all of us—and summon Velos to claim what is rightfully theirs."

"Oh, right, we'll just summon the god of death," said Constantino. "So simple."

Gabrielle's head twitched to one side, then the other. "It is not difficult magic to open a gateway into the land of the lost. I have done it many times." She peered at Mallory. "*You* have done it, too."

Mallory shivered. "That turned out to be a mistake."

"This time, I will help you." Gabrielle gave her head a shake. "If this is to work, we are going to need those rings."

CHAPTER FORTY-ONE

Armand seemed both frustrated and resigned when it was decided that he would not be untied while they went to obtain the wedding rings, and he only got a little flustered when Mallory had to undo his belt to take the house keys.

Gabrielle refused to return to the house while Bastien might be inside, so she and Anaïs stayed behind to watch over Armand, while Mallory, Fitcher, and Constantino carried out the mission. A light rain had started to fall, shrouding the house in a gloomy mist. The sky was dark violet. Somewhere above the cloud cover, the sun sank toward the horizon.

The house was eerily still as they slipped in through the terrace doors. Mallory led them through the battery of parlors on whispering feet, through the library, up the grand staircase.

As expected, the door to Armand's suite was locked, and it took her a few tries to find the right key on the ring. Inside, the air felt cold and silent. No fire had been lit, and the curtains were pulled shut. Nevertheless, being here again conjured a host of memories that Mallory preferred not to think about as she crossed to the vanity and crouched down, feeling around for the hidden hook.

She stilled.

The hook was there, but it was empty.

She got down on the floor and searched the underside of the vanity.

The rings were gone.

She sat up. "They aren't here."

Watching her skeptically, Constantino asked, "How did you ever find them under *there* in the first place?"

Ignoring the question, Mallory started rummaging through the vanity drawers, the armoire, the writing desk, every nook and cranny of the room. She discovered a dented pocket watch, a handful of galets, a wax seal, and inkpots and quill pens and tallow candles and buttons and linen shirts that smelled like peppermint and growing things—but she did not find the four wedding rings.

She cursed, continuing to dig through the last drawer of the writing desk even after she was positive the rings weren't there, when suddenly the drawer slammed shut of its own accord, pinching the tip of her finger.

With a cry, Mallory reeled back, clutching her hand to her chest. The fingertip throbbed as she looked up. Malevolent blue eyes were reflected in the darkness of the window.

She spun around, pressing back against the desk. The villain was in the doorway, barring their exit.

Fitcher and Constantino swiveled at her sudden movement. "What is it?" Fitcher asked. "Is he here?"

Bastien Saphir rubbed one finger down the length of his beard. "Are you searching for something?" His mouth curled tauntingly around the words.

"That *hurt*," Mallory spat.

"You poor darling," he cooed back at her, sauntering closer. "Do you know, this is an important day for me, and yet . . . no one seems to be around to celebrate the day of my death. The house has been so peculiarly peaceful." His attention slid toward Fitcher and Constantino. "I am beginning to wonder if you have been plotting against me."

Out of the corner of her eye, Mallory saw Constantino shift—slowly, slowly peeling the bow from his shoulder. Though he could not see the spirit himself, he was watching Mallory closely, trying to discern Bastien's location.

"So paranoid," said Mallory, skimming away along the far wall, trying to drag Le Bleu's attention away from the archer. "It isn't always about *you*. We had a burial this morning, as you know."

"I am sure my honored wife was sad to miss it. I trust you said very thoughtful things in her absence."

The way he could so easily mock Julie after he had manipulated her, tortured her, *murdered* her made Mallory want to draw her knife and impale his heart on the blade, but she resisted—tightening her hands into fists. "Julie is still here?" Even as she asked it, she realized—of course Julie was still there. Tethered to her ring like the others.

But she hadn't seen any sign of the wives since her return, not even Triphine, who was usually impossible to be rid of.

Where were they?

"Is that why you came back? For her? I am sure she would be most flattered." Bastien slinked closer to Mallory, almost close enough to touch her, and she tried to tell herself that he could not harm her, not in this form. He needed the strength of a mortal human to do anything more than brush a cold finger on her skin. He needed Armand.

He was just a spirit. Just a ghost. Smoke and nothingness. Even if he made himself corporeal for a moment or two, no doubt she could overpower him.

But when he took another step closer and the overwhelming aroma of oranges accosted her, she could not keep herself from shrinking away.

"Did you seek to give rest to my beloveds?" he said, half jokingly. "To help them find eternal peace? I did not take you to be so chivalrous." He reached forward, his fingers teasing the buttons at Mallory's throat.

She recoiled from the touch.

The bow snapped.

Bastien dissolved, like a cloud of squid ink in water. The arrow thunked into the wall.

Even unable to see the ghost, Constantino had sent the arrow straight through the side of his head.

Constantino snatched another arrow from his quiver and nocked it on the string. "Did I get him?"

"You got him," Mallory breathed, watching the slimy black tendrils vanish into the air.

Then a laugh, coming from everywhere, all at once. Fitcher and Constantino both ducked from the noise.

"You should not have done that," Bastien sang.

In the next moment, the house—so still, so serene—was thrown into chaos. The windows shattered. A fire flared to life in the hearth, burning an unnatural blue. And the wooden floorboards opened up beneath their feet and swallowed them whole.

CHAPTER FORTY-TWO

Mallory screamed as she fell.

But it was barely a blink, not even enough time to know what was happening, before fabric wrapped around her wrist and yanked her to a stop with such force she thought her shoulder might have dislocated.

She, Fitcher, and Constantino had fallen straight through the floor of Armand's bedroom suite, and then through the floor of the game room directly beneath it, and now they were dangling like fish on a line over the kitchen on the ground floor.

The curtains of Armand's four-poster bed had stopped their fall, whipping out faster than the tentacles of the lou carcolh to grab each of them in midair.

Mallory's thoughts were still spinning when the fabric released them and they crashed to the stone below. Pain reverberated up Mallory's leg and she dropped to one knee. Every bone felt like it had been pounded on with a hammer.

A cacophony of groans and snapping wood roared through the walls as the curtains snaked back up to the bedroom and the floorboards over their heads pieced themselves back together, though wood remained splintered and iron nails jutted through the beams.

It felt as though the house was about to collapse on top of them.

"Everyone all right?" asked Fitcher, voice strained as he checked himself for injuries.

"No!" Constantino bellowed. "I most certainly am not." He rolled off the table he'd landed on with a grunt. His whole body was trembling. "What in the name of Velos just happened?" He spun on Mallory. "You could have told us that he can control *the house*."

"I did!" she shouted. But then hesitated. "Didn't I? Look—I didn't know he could do *that*."

The bolts holding a hanging rack of copper pots to the ceiling gave way, sending lids and pans crashing to the floor. More blue fire erupted from the bread oven, spewing out of its cavernous mouth.

She kicked at the door that led to the servants' halls, surprised when it swung easily open, crashing into the wall. "Come on!"

They rushed past the coal store and the scullery, the butler's pantry, the larder, the cupbearer's room, while the walls shook and sconces flickered with that same eerie blue flame. It felt like the walls themselves were being torn apart, stone by stone.

As they passed the stairs that led down to the cellar a new sound breached the noise.

Screams.

Mallory froze. She whipped around, staring into the black depths of the stairwell.

A trap. It had to be a trap.

Or . . . the wives.

Where the ring goes, the spirit goes.

Fitcher shouted her name, gripping her arm. "How do we get out of here?"

She shook herself free. "The rings. I think they're down there."

"Not an option," said Constantino. "I've been in my fair share of wine cellars, and they are almost always a dead end. If we go down there, there'll be no way back out."

The screams grew louder. Pleading. Panicked. Tortured.

At the far end of the hall, an earsplitting crack. A thunderous roar. A wall imploded—plaster and mortar and limestone blocks caving inward. The devastation rolled toward them, the wall collapsing in massive chunks, a wave of destruction. Dust clogged the air.

They twisted around in time to see the kitchen door slam shut—and catch fire. The wood flared greenish blue. A surge of heat filled the corridor.

"On second thought," said Constantino, "I never turn down a chance to see a good wine cellar."

They rushed down the steps, descending into the deepest part of the house. The glow emanating from above cast the oak door in shades of blue and silver.

Mallory's lungs felt crushed in a vise as she reached the bottom step and placed her hand to the solid wood. The door pulsed like a living thing, steady and warm. A beating heart. As if it were happy that she had come back. No, not happy. Eager.

She licked her lips. Tasted the briny, metallic stench of blood on the air.

The door was locked. The air sizzled like the inside of an oven, and Mallory fumbled for the ring of keys, trying to separate the one with the ornate bow molded into heavy brass. It slipped into the lock. The mechanism inside took hold.

The screams beyond the door grew louder, but above the shouts—the telltale click.

She yanked the key from the lock and pushed the cellar door open. They crowded into the blackness beyond. Fitcher slammed the door shut in their wake, so loud it startled Mallory into dropping the key. They were suddenly blocked off from the heat of the flames, and Mallory distantly wondered if they'd just entered their own grave.

But the air in the cellar was blissfully cool and strangely quiet. Here there were no collapsing walls. No crumbling stones. No flames. Even the screams had stopped.

Instead of noise, this room was filled with a stench that invaded Mallory's nose and caught in her throat. Thick and cloying and metallic.

Mallory dropped to her hands and knees to search for the key. The floor was wet. She gasped and sat back on her heels, feeling her skirts. There must be a leak in one of the wine barrels.

Lights flickered on overhead. Two burning oil lamps hung in the center of the room, illuminating teetering racks of oak barrels, their edges stained red.

Not with wine.

There was blood everywhere. Oozing from the corked holes, splattered across the stone floor.

Mallory snatched up the key. The metal was sticky with blood, and she tried to rub it off on her skirt, but no matter how she scrubbed, it did not come clean.

Constantino placed a hand on her shoulder. "Bellissima," he whispered, "look."

She hobbled to her feet, her breaths coming in desperate spasms.

The cellar door itself was bleeding. Thick crimson drops cascaded through the crack around the doorjamb, coating the wood, spreading a sticky puddle across the floor, mingling with the splatters in the room.

Words began to appear in the blood, as if written by an invisible finger, their letters sharp and distinct.

>BE BOLD
>BE BOLD
>BUT NOT TOO BOLD

Even as the words were scrawled, the blood continued to fall, slowly devouring the message to make space for more writing to appear.

>LEST YOUR BLOOD
>SHALL RUN COLD

No sooner had they been completed than the words were swallowed by the cascading blood.

"I think the mean ghost is threatening us," Constantino whispered.

Fitcher dragged a finger through the blood on the door. "It is only a powerful illusion," he said, holding up his finger to smell it. The face he made suggested to Mallory that he wasn't convinced by his own theory.

She peered down the towering rows of barrels, where the cellar disappeared into shadows. This cellar was a cave, but sometimes caves led to other caves. Sometimes there was light at the far end of a tunnel. Maybe they were not trapped.

Tucking away the bloody key, she took the knife from her boot and cut away a strip of fabric from the hem of her ruined skirt. She grabbed a bottle from a nearby case, yanked out the cork, and dumped out half the wine onto the blood-slicked floor, ignoring Constantino's whine of dismay. She tucked the strip of cloth into the bottle, letting the top hang out like a wick.

Once the wine in the bottle had climbed up to the top of the fabric, Mallory prayed to whichever god had dominion over fire and held the bottle up to the crackling blue flame from one of the lamps. The fabric caught—burning as pale as moonlight.

Fitcher raised an eyebrow. "I would not have thought wine would contain enough alcohol for a makeshift lantern."

"Fortified wine," Mallory explained. "Ruby Comorre is wine mixed with brandy."

"A beverage after my own heart," said Constantino. He went to grab a second, unopened bottle, but hesitated at Fitcher's stern expression.

They started through the cellar. The blood seemed to be a living thing, following in their footsteps. Occasionally a cork would loosen on one of the barrels and more blood would gush forth.

The cave had a gentle downward slope, and Mallory sensed that they were burrowing ever deeper into the earth beneath the estate. Farther away from fresh air and the outside world. Farther away from Armand. Farther away from Anaïs.

Her heart clenched. What if all this was a distraction—a way for Le Bleu to drag Mallory away from her sister? What if Anaïs was his target now? Her blood would do just as well to fulfill the required sacrifice . . .

Mallory had to get out of here.

Ahead, the light caught on a wall, and Mallory worried they'd reached a dead end until she saw it was a doorway. A gate of heavy wrought iron stood open, framed by two brass sconces, each one shaped like the skeletal bones of a hand holding a lantern aloft.

Mallory lit the sconces. The light, though dim, revealed a room smaller than the inside of the stagecoach. Rough walls hewn from stone. A solid iron door opposite to her, crossed with studded iron bands.

A body dangled in each of the room's four corners. Triphine, Lucienne, Béatrice, and Julie—the holes in their chests gaping open, heads lolled forward. Their arms were raised overhead, their wrists tied with rope and secured to metal hooks that hung from the ceiling. The words carved into their skin glistened red. *Echtraus* and *greischt.*

Trust and *betrayal.*

Mallory told herself it wasn't really them. These forms were solid—not the wispy, barely corporeal figures of spirits. And while their bodies may have been preserved by magic, she knew they were also buried in the cemetery. She'd seen Julie laid to rest that very morning.

Fitcher was right. This was an illusion, intended to terrify them out of their senses.

Well, applause to Bastien, because it was working.

A series of footprints made crisscrossing tracks back and forth around a pentagon-shaped table in the center of the room, its top inlaid with a woven pattern of ebony and pearl. A scabbard lay across it, holding a familiar slim-bladed sword.

At four of the table's five points, a wedding ring had been placed in a small porcelain dish.

Mallory had nearly forgotten their entire mission, their purpose for coming back into this house in the first place. They needed the rings to complete the ritual, to end the spell and return Bastien back into the arms of death.

She knew it could be a trap. She knew it could be an illusion.

But she set down her makeshift lantern and drove forward anyway. As her fingers seized the first ring, the scream of grating iron echoed through the chamber, so shrill that Mallory ducked, pressing her hands to her ears.

Fitcher and Constantino cried out. The gate had come alive and bent around them, trapping them against the stone walls. Mallory threw herself at the bars, yanking and pulling. She had visions of the gate squeezing her companions, crushing their bones, bars cutting into flesh—but the gate had solidified once more.

"It's all right," said Fitcher. "He needs to kill you, not us."

"That isn't a comfort."

"Mal . . . lory . . ."

Mallory spun around, heart in her throat.

Julie's eyes were open. Her skin was ashen. A drop of blood clung to one side of her mouth.

"Help..."

"Great gods," Mallory whispered, horrified at the pain etched onto the girl's features. Gripping her knife, she made quick work of cutting the ropes that bound Julie's wrists to the hook, ready to catch her body when she collapsed.

But when Julie fell—her body slipped right through Mallory, landing on the stone floor. Her form no longer that of a living person, but once again with the vague haziness of a ghost.

The other wives remained motionless, suspended in time.

The shadows at the edges of the room began to shift, drawing inward. Mallory knelt beside Julie, who was crooning in pain, wishing she could do something to comfort the girl, but she couldn't even lay a hand upon her shoulder.

"I'm sorry," she whispered, overcome with sudden, maddening guilt. This was her fault. "I'm so sorry."

The shadows converged into an inky figure that rose into a slender column, slowly taking form. Mallory was not surprised when Monsieur Le Bleu stood before her again, though she noted that he was more unkempt than before. His blue-tinted beard had grown wiry and long, his hair unruly, deep wrinkles carving themselves into the planes of his once-handsome face.

Mallory stood to face him.

"Oh, fabulous," Constantino muttered. "He's back again, isn't he?"

"Do you still think to plot against me?" Bastien said. "Or have you begun to realize how futile that would be?"

Mallory drew on every ounce of courage as she faced him. "What are you going to do?" She scoffed. "You might be able to crush me under rubble or incinerate me with your creepy sorcerer fire, but if you want a proper sacrifice, you need to drive that sword through my heart. And you can't do that. Not without Armand."

"Oh, I don't have to kill you, Mallory Fontaine." His grin widened. "You are going to do that for me."

CHAPTER FORTY-THREE

"Sacrifice myself?" She let out a peal of anxious laughter. "You really are mad."

"Once you are dead," he went on, as if she hadn't spoken, "the pieces will be in place. I had hoped you'd make this easy for me, and you never fail to disappoint."

She ground her teeth. He could threaten all he liked, but Bastien had not yet made his fifth sacrifice, and he did not have Gabrielle's ring.

He hadn't won, not yet. She searched for a way out. There was that other door, iron and ominous, but Bastien was blocking her path, and she couldn't leave Fitcher and Constantino down here.

Could she?

A voice told her that she could. She would leave them at the first chance she had to save herself. She barely knew these two men. She owed them nothing. She would choose survival, as she always had.

And yet . . . she wasn't sure if it was true.

Julie grimaced and curled into a ball, hands pressed over the wound in her chest. She let out a sob, as if she were dying all over again.

The sound frayed the ends of Mallory's nerves.

Bastien strolled around the table, caressing each ring with a tip of his finger as he went. He paused when he reached the bowl that had held Julie's. "I will be needing that back."

Mallory squeezed the ring tighter in her fist, delighting in how the stone cut into her skin. It was a small rebellion, but one she would hold on to for as long as she could. "You'll have to take it from me."

His chuckles turned boisterous. "Yes. That is the plan. Except . . . you were right." He reached for the sword on the table, but his hand passed right through it. "A Savoy is within my grasp, but without a mortal body to act for me, what can I do?" He clicked his tongue thoughtfully. "But I am patient, and sooner or later, your sister will have to set Armand free. Unless you intend to kill him, you will not be able to keep me away forever."

She choked back the bile in her throat, wishing she could do more than glare at him.

"Unless," he said, drawing out the word in a quiet hiss, "you are willing to bargain with me."

"I'm not," she said through her teeth.

"Do not be hasty. You have not heard my terms."

She snarled. Beside her, Julie shuddered.

"Sacrifice yourself," he said, his tone so light that he might have been asking her to put on a kettle for tea, "and I will have no need to claim your sister."

"What's going on?" said Fitcher. "What is he saying?"

"He wants me to sacrifice myself," she said. "To save Anaïs."

Fitcher snarled. "Don't listen to him. He can't be trusted."

"I know that," Mallory snapped. Even though . . . she was considering the deal. Weighing her choices, of which there weren't many.

It was true that Anaïs could not keep Armand tied up forever. When she freed him, Bastien could so easily slip back into Armand's body. Could so easily catch Anaïs off her guard.

Either way, he would have his fifth sacrifice.

But if Mallory took her own life, this still wouldn't be over. Bastien required the fifth ring, even now on Anaïs's finger back in the chapel.

Which meant that the spell wouldn't be completed yet. There would still be time for the others to stop him.

"You're doing all this, for what?" she said, stalling for time. "A little bit of immortality? So you can rule over a crumbling wine empire again?"

Bastien cocked his head, evidently entertained by the question. "My descendants have not been as ruthless as I was, and Armand in particular has been a great disappointment. But once I am alive again, I will reclaim our standing. Soon, Ruby Comorre will again be the most desirable wine in Lysraux." He smirked at Mallory's skeptical expression. "You did not think it was an accident—did you?—when the competition disappeared, leaving only Saphir estates to provide the world with its favorite vice."

Mallory frowned. Saphir wines had always been highly coveted—for generations, the only terroir that could grow their particular grapevine. In Bastien's time, their vineyards alone had survived, unscathed by drought, blight, and fire that had ravaged other crops.

"You were sabotaging them," she said.

"What is the point of being a sorcerer," he said, almost jokingly, "if you cannot destroy your enemies? Of course, none of this makes any difference to you. You will be dead. But your sister will be free to go."

Mallory ground her teeth until her jaw ached. "What would I have to do?"

"Mallory, no!" shouted Constantino. "You can't."

Bastien raised an eyebrow at Mallory. "A sword driven through your heart. Very simple."

"And you promise to leave Anaïs alone?"

"You have my word. I will not require her death, only the ring. Once Armand is within my control again, that will be easily obtained."

She shuddered to think of him possessing Armand, stealing Anaïs's ring off her finger—knowing her sister would not give it up easily. She thought of the wives' dismembered fingers, which Bastien had cut from their bodies after their deaths.

But she could not escape. Could not run. Could not kill him.

With a shudder, Mallory stepped toward the table. Gripping Julie's ring in one hand, she unsheathed the sword with the other.

Bastien shifted backward, as if to give her space. She was glad to put the table between them as she weighed the sword in her hand—even knowing that he could pass right through it if he wanted to.

Distantly, she could hear Fitcher and Constantino yelling at her, but she wasn't listening. They couldn't help her. She was alone with the monster, and she had no weapons with which to fight him.

"You promise," she whispered, weighing the sword in her hand before slowly angling the tip at her heart.

Bastien's eyes burned as blue as the torches. "You have my most solemn vow."

She knew beyond doubt that he was lying. He cared nothing for vows. Not the ones made to his wives, and certainly not the one made to her.

Then—a scream. Though less a scream than a savage shriek. Julie arose from the shadows and launched herself at Bastien. She knocked him against the wall and, with a strength Mallory would not have expected, wrapped the remains of the rope that had bound her wrists around Bastien's throat.

Mallory gaped, dumbfounded, as the rope tightened. Julie yanked Bastien against her. He was so much taller. So much broader. He drove one arm back to try to dislodge her grip, but Julie held firm, hatred making her face almost unrecognizable.

"You did this to me, you awful brute!" she wailed. "You did this!"

And though Mallory half believed Julie might actually decapitate the murderer with nothing but a bit of rope—she was outraged enough for it—Bastien soon got the upper hand. Grasping Julie's arm, he twisted so hard a bone snapped. Julie screamed and fell back.

Despite her pain, Julie threw herself at him again with clawed fingers.

Which was when Mallory realized . . . they were both ghosts. Which meant that Julie could touch him. Julie could *hurt* him.

She scanned the room, but the other ghosts were still in their undead, slumbering state. Why had Julie awoken? Why had she—

The ring warmed in her grip.

Mallory dashed forward, weaving in and out of the brawl as she cut the ropes binding each of the women's corpses from the hooks. One by one, they tumbled to the floor, heavy and still. Once they were free, Mallory reached for the dishes on the table—knocking one of them over as she grabbed the rings, stealing them from whatever magic spell Bastien had prepared.

Immediately, a change came over the wives. The illusion of physical bodies shed for the hazy illumination of spirits. Their eyes snapped open.

At the same moment, Julie was thrown against the table, which she slipped through, landing beside the gate where Fitcher and Constantino wore identical looks of bewilderment.

"What is happening?" Constantino whispered.

"Ghosts," Fitcher whispered back. "I would assume."

"Help me," Mallory said as Triphine picked herself up off the cellar floor with a look of disgust. "Help me, please. Help Julie!"

They gathered their wits, shaking off the dregs of magic that had held them in their undead stasis. But then—they did help. With more fury than Mallory thought possible, Le Bleu's victims converged—nails and teeth and elbows and battle cries and vengeance—and when Mallory was certain they would literally tear him apart . . .

Bastien vanished.

The four women fell back, snarling and panting, a blackish substance that might have been blood on their hands.

The iron bars holding Fitcher and Constantino released them. They stumbled forward, dragging in breaths of air.

"Care to explain what's going on?" Fitcher asked.

"The wives," Mallory panted. "They attacked him."

"Is he dead?" asked Constantino.

"I don't think so. He . . . ran away."

Mallory squeezed her fist around the four rings. She had to get back to Anaïs, to Gabrielle, to Armand. They could end this. Truly end it.

"Where does that door lead?" Constantino gestured to the iron door at the far side of the room. "Is it unlocked?"

It wasn't, but when Mallory inserted the cellar key—no longer sticky with the illusion of blood—it opened.

Half expecting something useless, like a secondary murder closet, Mallory was surprised to see a ladder leading upward. A metal platform rested at the base, attached to ropes on the walls.

"A dumbwaiter," said Fitcher. "That must be how they brought the wine barrels down here."

He picked up the sword and returned it to its sheath. Constantino left his bow on his back.

Mallory was tucking her knife back into her boot when she heard a quiet click. She noticed Fitcher examining his odd golden pocket watch. The needle was spinning, spinning . . .

A shadow crossed Fitcher's face, and he slammed the pocket watch shut.

Constantino raised an eyebrow.

"I shouldn't have looked," Fitcher said gruffly. "May Wyrdith favor us."

Though he had played the part of the acolyte, Mallory felt it was the first real prayer she'd heard him utter.

With a glance around at the wives—who stood watching her, bleeding, exhausted, and tousled—she pocketed the rings, grasped the rungs of the ladder, and started to climb.

CHAPTER FORTY-FOUR

Cobwebs clung to Mallory's hair as she climbed upward into darkness. Her arms shook the higher she went, but after perhaps thirty feet, her hand struck a wooden surface. With some effort, she managed to find the edge of the panel and shove it to the side.

Dim light filtered in, catching on the dust motes and a long-legged spider that quickly scurried into the shadows. Fresh, damp air greeted her, smelling of rain and dirt and the fervent charge of lightning on the horizon.

She climbed out of the hole. She was behind the potager, where the top of the dumbwaiter had, at some point, been buried beneath a compost heap. The gray sky had grown dark since they'd entered the house.

Fitcher and Constantino stumbled out behind her. They surveyed the house. Mallory expected to see it engulfed in blue flames, but it was intact. There was no sign of the fire in the kitchen that had sent them scurrying into the cellar. It had been an illusion after all.

But part of the roof really had caved in above Armand's suites. Perhaps Bastien was willing to damage the house, but not destroy it completely.

They slipped out of the garden. As they were passing the terrace, the stones cracked beneath their feet. Mallory was launched forward, barely catching herself before she crashed to her knees.

With a frazzled look at each other, they started to run. Through the overgrown lawns, where vines and brambles grabbed at their ankles. Where the ground trembled and topiaries shaped like nymphs tried to stop them as they bolted past.

Bastien made one last effort to block their path, a horrifying figure screaming with guttural rage as he emerged from the trunk of an ancient oak. Mallory tripped. She fell to the ground, rolling a couple of times before coming to a stop, her body bruised and throbbing. With a growl, she yanked her knife from her boot and threw it at Bastien's visage. The blade sank into the wood. The tree shuddered. Bastien's ghost reeled back and disappeared.

Fitcher hauled Mallory to her feet. They did not stop running until they burst into the chapel and slammed the door shut so hard the entire building shook. The three of them fell panting against it.

Anaïs had lit the candelabras around the perimeter of the room, giving it a warm, flickering glow. Armand still sat tied to the upholstered chair, with Anaïs cross-legged on the floor in front of him, having laid out a spread of Wyrdith cards. Recognizing the Acolyte card and the Harvest Moon, Mallory at first assumed her sister was attempting to read his fortune. But then she noticed the betting pool of acorns that lay between them and realized they were playing Enigma, a gambling game that many considered blasphemous.

Anaïs and Armand both gawked at Mallory, Fitcher, and Constantino—torn, bloody, bedraggled, sweating, and livid. So very livid.

"That ghost," Mallory gasped, "needs to go."

Anaïs laid down her cards. "What happened?"

Armand added, "Where did Fitcher get a sword?"

Mallory didn't even know where to begin. Honestly, she'd forgotten about the sword.

Unstrapping it from his back, Fitcher hastily passed it to Anaïs, who eyed it with distaste. "We'll explain later," he said. "Mallory, the rings?"

She dug the four wedding rings from her pocket and stormed across the room, jutting a finger at the small bird with ruffled feathers. "Lots of help you were. We could have used some magic."

With an annoyed squawk, Gabrielle transformed into a human again, gripping the black-and-white feather like a weapon of her own. "I was watching over the prisoner."

"Well, guess what? Le Bleu isn't here to possess him right now. But he is certainly in possession of the house. And not just the walls. Oh no, he controls the floors, too. And the ovens. He can make *blue fire*. We were completely unprepared!"

"Mallory." Anaïs settled a hand on her arm. "It's all right. You got the rings. We can end this."

Mallory glanced at Anaïs's hand and Gabrielle's ring—passed down through generations.

On the altar, they had placed a single candle, already burned down to a nub, inside a glass lantern. A pentagram had been drawn in chalk around the candle and decorated with flowers and herbs. Mallory laid the rings around the sigil. Anaïs pried Gabrielle's ring from her own finger and laid it on the fifth point of the pentagram.

"Should I be doing something?" Armand said. "Actually . . . if we know that I'm not currently possessed, maybe—"

"No," said Mallory. "We're not untying you. Bastien knows where we are and what we plan to do. He will possess you again the first chance he gets."

The wives appeared then, their hazy forms climbing up from the center of the rings that had been placed around the pentagram, their figures shimmering but whole.

"We tried to find the brute," said Julie. "He's become a part of the house again."

Mallory conveyed this to the others, informing them the wives had arrived.

Gabrielle snorted. "He cannot hide from me."

Lucienne shrieked giddily. "Gabrielle, is that you? It's been so long! You look . . ." She trailed off, cheek twitching, before she took in Gabrielle's thin, naked figure, feathery hair, twitching movement. "Like you could use a drink."

Whether Gabrielle couldn't hear the ghosts or she simply chose to ignore this, she moved to stand beside the ring that had once been hers. "We can begin."

"What do the rest of us do?" asked Mallory.

"Nothing. Bastien is held by the same dark magic that he has bound us with. Once I summon him into this circle, his spirit will be trapped inside this candle and no longer able to invade the minds and bodies of others. We need only hold him, and when the flame can burn no longer, the death of the candle will snuff out his spirit as well, and the monster will be reclaimed by Verloren."

"Must we wait for the candle to burn out?" asked Mallory. "Or can we . . ." She mimed pinching the wick with her fingers.

"Once he is here, the circle is not to be broken," said Gabrielle. "Do not be impatient."

"Is this going to hurt?" asked Triphine. "I've had a bit of a sore throat of late, and I don't want it getting worse."

"Hush," said Lucienne as Gabrielle began to chant.

Mallory recognized the words from the old language, the same she had recited to open the door to Verloren and summon her ancestor when she was a child. The spell that had brought Le Bleu back to this world.

It began to storm outside, rain pounding at the roof of the chapel, coming down so hard on the stained glass that Mallory worried it might shatter. The candles flickered, as if a wind had coursed through—though Mallory felt nothing but her own shudder.

The flames flickered again, and this time they went out, all at once.

Gabrielle's chanting grew louder.

Anaïs gripped Mallory's hand.

Armand looked worriedly at the door. Fitcher tapped restlessly at the closed pocket watch. Constantino thumped an arrow into his palm.

Outside, lightning flashed—brightening the chapel in one blinding instant, thunder shaking the walls.

When it passed, the candle on the altar had burst to life with a single tall flame—burning blue.

Anaïs's grip slackened with surprise.

Gabrielle fell quiet, the blue flame dancing in her dark eyes. "He is here."

Mallory inched closer to Armand and crouched beside him. His hand flexed in welcome, and she took it, squeezing tight, her pulse pounding.

The candle was so small—barely more than a wick and a coin-sized ball of tallow. Surely it would not take long to burn out.

After everything, to see the great Monsieur Le Bleu reduced to that tiny, inconsequential flame felt strangely anticlimactic. And perhaps too easy, though she reminded herself that, actually, it had not been easy at all.

The flame brightened and Mallory imagined Bastien, with all his stubbornness and will, fighting the fate that threatened to claim him.

"How do we know for sure that he is trapped in that candle?" Anaïs whispered, sounding a little wistful. "It seems too small to hold him."

Armand squeezed Mallory's hand tighter.

Anaïs took a step closer, still clutching the sheathed sword, head cocked as she peered into the blue flame. She stilled, her brows knit. "Something is wrong."

Mallory tensed. "What do you mean?"

Gabrielle did not react. She and the wives were locked in a trance—their bodies motionless, their focus latched onto the blue flame.

Mallory stood. "Anaïs, what is it?"

Her sister hesitated. "Bastien is here," she said slowly. Thoughtfully. "But . . . he is not trapped." She was motionless, listening.

Lightning flashed again, illuminating Anaïs's face—and the slow, cruel smile stretching across her mouth.

Backing away from Mallory, Anaïs drew the sword from its sheath, turned to the altar, and drove the blade into Gabrielle's back.

CHAPTER FORTY-FIVE

The windows shattered. The likenesses of seven gods rained through the chapel in shards of colorful glass, a sandstorm of reds and blues. Mallory felt the sharp bits pelting her skin, but she barely winced. She could not look away from the nightmare before her.

Gabrielle reached for the altar, her hand knocking her ring onto the floor, then fell to her knees.

Anaïs released the sword, leaving Gabrielle impaled on the blade. She met Mallory's gaze for one brutal moment. One haunting, terrible moment, when her sister's eyes shone an unnatural, brilliant blue.

Then Anaïs leaped through one of the broken windowpanes and disappeared into the storm.

With horrified yells, Fitcher and Constantino raced after her.

Mallory took a step as if to follow, but hesitated. Her mind was whirling with the impossibility of what had just happened.

Anaïs, a murderer.

Anaïs, *possessed*.

She dropped beside Gabrielle, a trembling hand on her great-grandmother's back. She didn't know if she should pull out the sword or not. She didn't know what to do. She didn't know how things had gone so wrong, how she had been misled. Every step, every choice—

A hand gripped hers. She met Gabrielle's eyes, glossy and impossibly black.

"Tell me what to do," Mallory pleaded. "How do I fix this? How do I save you?"

"He has . . . his fifth . . . sacrifice," Gabrielle said. Blood mixed with saliva began to drip from her mouth. "He has won."

"No! I don't believe that." Her vision blurred. "There must be something . . ."

"Velos will still . . . want him back. He can be bound. With magic. The house . . ."

Tears slipped down Mallory's cheeks, cutting trails through the dust and dirt caking her skin, but she hardly felt them.

"I can't bind him," she whispered. "I am not a witch."

"You are a Savoy." Gabrielle's face twitched in that strange, birdlike manner. She spoke with her head cocked to one side, never addressing Mallory straight-on. "He cannot take away what you are. You must . . . trust . . . yourself." Her last words came in stunted gasps. Her hand squeezed one last time, then fell limp. She shuddered forward, her body suspended on her knees. Her blood dripped down the length of the sword, splattering on the floor.

Mallory looked at her palm. Gabrielle had tucked the black-and-white tail feather into her fist.

She launched to her feet. Tears blurred her vision, and she let out a scream of fury, the sound tearing out of her—feral and vicious. She would see Le Bleu dead. She would destroy him, for all he had done, for all the pain he had—

Swiping at her eyes, she sniffled once, then dragged her emotions back inside as she spun toward Armand. Tucking the feather behind her ear, she reached for the straps on his arms and started unbuckling him from the chair.

"Mallory," he breathed, "are you—"

"We're not talking about it," she said, sniffling again. "We're going to get my sister back."

Before Armand could roll out his joints, Mallory sprinted from the chapel in the direction Anaïs had gone.

The storm had died down to a soft drizzle. She expected to have to search the entirety of the mansion, but drew to a sudden stop when she reached the circular drive and spotted Fitcher and Constantino side by side, each of them still and open-mouthed. At first Mallory worried they were caught in some sort of enchantment, but then she realized, disheartically, that they—like her—had no idea what to do. They couldn't attack Bastien, not while he inhabited Anaïs's body. They had to find a way to exorcise him first. But how could they set up the ritual now?

Before them, Anaïs stood on the edge of the fountain, staring up at the massive stone stallion. Utterly expressionless.

The fountain gushed thick and red. Blood poured from every corner, falling over the pedestal and stones. Mallory had read about the phenomenon so many times, from so many witnesses, that she had yearned to see it for herself. But now the reality of it churned her stomach.

"How?" Mallory yelled, stomping closer. "And when, and . . . and *why*?"

Anaïs turned to face her.

"It's quite simple, really," she said, and while it was Anaïs's voice, the inflection she recognized as Bastien. "Some herbs are repellent to spirits, while others draw us in. Royal skullcap is particularly effective. Whenever a mortal has it in their system, it becomes so easy for me to whisper a quick incantation and . . . sneak inside."

"Royal skullcap." Armand's voice came from behind Mallory. "The herb I take to help me sleep. I've been taking it since I was a boy—"

"Since you were twelve, approximately," said Anaïs—no, *Bastien*. "When I returned, I knew I would need a human host to assist me. It was easy enough to frighten my young heir into a few months' worth of nightmares. I knew you would be keen to find a solution among the herbs you had already developed such an affinity for. Soon, you were given peaceful rest . . . and I had access to your malleable mind. When you started brewing tea for this lovely little witch, well . . . as I said. So simple." Her grin widened and she laughed. "Gabrielle's heart has stopped. She is dead, finally."

Her eyes rolled back into her head and, without warning, Anaïs fell backward into the fountain.

Mallory cried out and ran to the edge. The pool of blood churned and gurgled. Her sister was not visible beneath. Mallory screamed her name and was about to throw herself in after her when a figure broke through the surface. Wearing a cloak of crimson, the figure rose upward. Mallory froze, horrified, at the sight of the demon she remembered from her failed séance all those years ago—needle claws and drooping arms and glowing blue eyes.

As the blood dripped away, the figure morphed into that of a man. Count Bastien Saphir I. Monsieur Le Bleu. Anaïs, unconscious, was draped across his arms. He set her onto the lip of the fountain. Mallory could not tell if she was breathing.

Bastien stepped out of the fountain, solid, strong, and mortal. He surveyed the mansion, then started toward the door, his strides purposeful and elegant.

An enraged scream clawed out of Mallory's throat. "Is that it?" she yelled. "All those deaths, for what? So you could live again? Be the lord of a manor that's falling apart around you? No money, no family. You have nothing. You did this for nothing!"

Bastien paused, his form silhouetted by the house's towering columns, the leaded windows. He raised his arms to his sides, fingers outstretched.

For a moment, nothing happened. And then it was as though a shroud of magic descended over the château. The roof that had caved in shuddered and righted itself. The bricks from a fallen chimney re-mortared into a tidy tower. Cracked windows were sealed. Black soot faded from the white limestone blocks. Missing finials atop the gable dormers grew out of molten iron and solidified. Broken balustrades and fallen gutters and missing tiles were mended, until everything was pristine and dignified. When he was finished, the house appeared both ancient and immaculate.

Bastien turned to face them, his mouth twisted into a haughty grin. "I am afraid there is not room for two lords of the House Saphir. Young Armand, it would seem that you are no longer useful to me."

"Not room?" Mallory shrieked. "It's a big house. You could find the space."

"As for you, little witch," he continued, as if he hadn't heard her, "as I rebuild my estate, it will not do to have rumors circulating that could damage my reputation."

"Oh, that's rich," said Mallory. "Everyone knows that Bastien Saphir is a murderer."

Bastien craned his head, studying her. "But *Armand* Saphir is a young count with a prominent title. A charming if reclusive bachelor who suddenly finds himself needing to enter high society and find for himself a suitable bride." He grinned maliciously. "How fortunate that so few members of society have had occasion to meet my descendant. So as you see, it really will not do for you to live."

Mallory gaped, horrified by this monologue, when the telltale twang of a bowstring struck her eardrum. An arrow hurtled toward Bastien—driving straight into his chest.

Bastien stumbled backward, then dropped to one knee.

"One negative about being mortal," growled Constantino. "It makes you easier to kill."

Bastien's form shuddered, then exploded into shadows. Mallory expected to see a figurine of the count tumble onto the house's front steps, a new addition for Constantino's box.

Instead, the shadows coalesced again. First into that same long-limbed beast that had crawled from Verloren, then slowly into the form she recognized as Bastien Saphir.

It was only seconds until he stood before them again.

As if nothing had happened.

He took hold of the arrow and snapped it from his flesh. With a passing glare at Constantino, he threw the broken shaft to the ground. With an arrogant lift of his chin, Bastien flicked his fingers. The doors yawned open in welcome and, once he had passed through, slammed shut in his wake.

"That—that didn't work," Constantino stammered, throttling his bow as if the weapon had betrayed him. "Why didn't that work? I'm blessed by *Tyrr*."

"Blessed to capture monsters," Fitcher said darkly. "But he is once more a man."

"Men can die," said Constantino. "That should have killed him!"

"And if he's alive again," Armand said quietly, "how is he still controlling the house?"

"He was always a powerful sorcerer," said Mallory, bending over her sister to feel for a pulse. A collection of glass souvenirs tumbled from Anaïs's pockets, spilling onto the cobbles. Mallory blinked at the tiny monster figurines. A salamander, a lou carcolh, a cheval mallet . . .

Tokens from Constantino's haul, which she assumed her sister had taken when he wasn't paying attention. Her penchant for pretty, unusual things . . .

"Are those mine?" said Constantino. "Did she steal those from me?"

Ignoring him, Mallory leaned her ear against Anaïs's chest, relieved to hear a faint heartbeat. "She's alive."

She sat back on her heels, trying to think. *Think.* Five vows, five sacrifices, five betrayals of trust . . .

And now that sorcerer, that murderer, that monster . . . was immortal.

An earsplitting crack drew her attention back to the fountain.

The horse and rider were moving. The horse's front hooves pawed at the air and let out a bellow. The count in the saddle swung his sword in an arc overhead.

Mallory screamed. Constantino jumped forward and scooped Anaïs into his arms, pulling her off the lip of the fountain.

The stone horse surged off its pedestal, splashed through the pool of blood, and stampeded toward them. Its hooves pounded through the puddles left from the storm and crushed one of the glass figurines, inches from where Anaïs's head had been.

Barely missing Armand's neck with his swinging sword, the rider pulled back on the reins, swiveling the horse to face them. Though cast in stone, the rider's passive expression had become hostile.

But Mallory found her attention diverted to something just as horrifying and . . . fantastical.

Where the horse had crushed the small figurine, a beast was emerging. Eight feet tall, with claws and fur and fangs and . . .

"Is that . . ." Armand whispered.

"The voirloup?" she said in disbelief.

"Oh, right," said Constantino, still cradling Anaïs's unconscious body. "They do that."

The count heeled the sides of the horse, who broke into a gallop, charging for them again. They scattered in different directions.

"You know what would be useful right now?" Constantino yelled. "If one of us could magically transform into an enormous bear!"

Fitcher glowered at him. "It doesn't happen on command."

"I know that! But it should!"

The rider whirled around and chased after Armand, face contorted with rage.

But as the horse drove past the voirloup, the beast roared and leaped, knocking the rider off his steed. Both rider and horse fell—and shattered. Marble and debris flew across the hard pavers of the courtyard.

The voirloup landed hard on its side, startled that its prey had not been edible flesh.

Mallory froze. If the voirloup saw her running, she knew it would give chase.

Suddenly regretting not taking the sword that had killed Gabrielle, Mallory faced the beast. Her hand searched for the knife, before she remembered throwing it at one of Bastien's apparitions.

Cursing, she took a slow step back, her gaze pinned to the voirloup as it lifted its muzzle and released an agitated howl. When it was done, it stared at Mallory, watching her with hungry yellow eyes.

She spied Armand, on the other side of the voirloup. "Oy, mangy beast!" he shouted, waving his arms in an attempt to pull the monster's attention away from Mallory.

No use. The beast prowled closer, slobber dripping from its maw.

Then, suddenly, Anaïs awoke, screaming. She looked around—at Constantino, who still held her in his arms, to the voirloup, to the blood-filled fountain, then screamed again, louder this time.

"Er . . . I'm just going to put you down now," Constantino said, before he unceremoniously dropped Anaïs into a garden bed. Her scream turned into a bewildered, slightly affronted grunt, while

Constantino slung his bow off his shoulder, grabbed an arrow from the quiver—

The voirloup pounded closer. Mallory's vision went white. The monster was mere paces away when the bowstring snapped, sending the arrow into the voirloup's shoulder. Golden light flashed. The beast's momentum carried it forward, even as its body degenerated into a small glass figurine once again. Constantino caught it midair. For a moment, he stood unmoving, fist raised like the monument of an honored warrior.

Then, without warning, Constantino collapsed down onto his rump, his expression dazed. "I would like to be done with all this now," he breathed.

Giving herself a shake, Anaïs scrambled on her hands and knees toward Mallory. "What . . . what is . . . ?"

"A lot's happened," Mallory said. "Do you remember anything?"

Anaïs shuddered. "The ritual. We were in the chapel, and the candle was lit, and . . . and that's the last I remember."

Mallory looked at the chunks of stone that had been thrown from the fountain's pedestal when the horse broke free. She spied the fire-breathing salamander that she'd tried to steal her first night at the château.

"He . . . he can still be bound. Trapped. In the house. That's what Gabrielle said." She blinked up at Armand. "Isn't that what she said?"

"I . . . don't really remember, precisely. So much was happening."

Coughing against the dust in her throat, Mallory reached up

and touched the feather behind her ear. "Gabrielle tried to bind his spirit to the candle. It didn't work, but maybe that's because he was possessing Anaïs at the time. Now that he has his own body back, I don't think he can possess people anymore. And we are no longer trying to get rid of a ghost. We are trying to get rid of a sorcerer."

Armand held her gaze, his hair damp from the rain and clinging to his brow. He accepted her statement with a slow, encouraging nod, even though she could tell he didn't fully understand what she was saying. *She* wasn't sure she understood what she was saying. But she knew enough about petty magic to hope that she was right.

Gabrielle could not complete the binding spell.

But maybe . . . maybe she could. If she had her magic.

"With a big enough flame to hold him, and the right spell . . . maybe . . . ?"

"Yes," said Armand. "Whatever you're thinking, yes. Tell me what to do."

She peered up at the house.

She wasn't Gabrielle. She wasn't her mother. She wasn't a witch. She couldn't do this.

But she *had* to do this.

"I need the rings," she whispered. "The wedding rings. They're in the chap—"

"Here," Armand interrupted. "Everyone kept talking about them like they were important, so . . ." He held out his hand, revealing five rings in his palm.

CHAPTER FORTY-SIX

"This isn't safe for you," Mallory said as her toes searched for the ladder's next rung.

Somewhere in the darkness beneath her, Armand responded, "This isn't safe for either of us, but I'm not letting you do it alone."

They reached the bottom of the steep passageway.

Even the cellar was changed. The cobwebs had mysteriously vanished. The bars of the gate that had bent to hold Fitcher and Constantino had been straightened and reset into an elaborate design of wine grapes hanging from spiraled vines.

"I've never been down here before," Armand murmured as they left the room with the ritual table and started down the underground cave where wine barrels were stacked three-high on shelves that had been miraculously cleansed of every speck of dust.

She faced Armand. "I'm sorry if this will be difficult for you."

He looked amused by the comment. "In case you hadn't noticed, I don't exactly share my ancestor's passion for Ruby Comorre." He hefted the pickax on his shoulder, the one they'd found in a gardening shed. "All of them?"

Mallory took a sledgehammer in both hands. "As many as possible."

They attacked, steel and iron smashing into the oak barrels. The wood splintered easily. Gallons of wine splashed across the floor, drenching their shoes and filling the room with an aroma that was too sweet, too cloying.

Mallory was surprised how good it felt to destroy something—especially something of Bastien's—and judging from the way Armand's face glowed as they made their way through the cellar, she suspected he felt the same.

They were done too quickly.

"Next?" Armand said.

Hefting the hammer, Mallory crossed to the cellar door. It swung open under her touch.

The house was eerily quiet as they ascended the stairs, hauntingly so after the disaster they'd wreaked in the cellar.

They sneaked into the cupbearer's room and started uncorking the bottles that filled the shelves. They dumped some in the hall and down the steps. They emptied others in the kitchen, where she paused to grab a knife from a wooden block.

Armed with as many uncorked bottles as they could carry, they slipped out into the banquet hall.

The house remained perfectly still and . . . *beautiful*.

Armand sucked in a surprised breath. The mansion was as exquisite as if a staff of hundreds had spent weeks preparing it for a ball of royal proportions. Every candle and lantern burned, casting a jocund glow throughout each room. The floors had been polished to a mirror sheen. Aromatic bouquets of flowers in porcelain vases adorned every alcove—most of them not even in season.

It occurred to Mallory that Bastien didn't need wealth. He had sorcery. He had *everything*.

Arrogant bastard.

"Where is he?" Armand whispered.

Mallory shook her head. "He'll come to us once he figures out what we're doing. But by that point, the carrots will be cooked. It will be too late for him to do anything about it."

Armand finished dumping out a bottle of wine on the hallway carpet. "I don't like how easy you make it sound."

"Me either," she agreed.

They reached the main vestibule. Mallory had to trust that by now, Fitcher, Constantino, and Anaïs had finished placing the rings into the designated pentagram outside the house's walls. This room would be as close to its center as they could get.

Grabbing a silver candlestick lit with a single taper, she sat cross-legged in the middle of the floor and pulled Armand down in front of her. She could still recall the rules of witchcraft she had learned from her mother, though she'd long believed it was useless for her to even attempt to use petty magic.

As for the ritual itself, it would forever be etched into her memory.

If there was a drop of magic in her bones, in her blood, in her *soul*, she needed it now. Now.

"You do know what you're doing, right?" Armand said, watching as she sketched out the symbols across the tiles.

"Now you decide to doubt me?"

"I just feel obligated to mention that the candle idea didn't work out so well earlier."

"This is going to be a little different." She cleared her throat. "I can do this."

After a short silence, punctuated by the scratch of chalk, Armand said, "I do love how you always sound so confident, even when I suspect you have no idea what you're doing."

Refusing to let this comment distract her, she handed him the knife. "I need three drops of blood inside the circle. Saphir blood."

To his credit, he didn't hesitate to drag the blade across the tip of his finger. Three drops welled up on his skin and dripped down beside the candlestick. She was relieved when the flame continued to burn a steady orange.

As her mother had told her, back when she was too young to truly understand the meaning of her words, fire was a conduit between the mortal world and Verloren. After the others put the rings in place around the house, she would use magic to tether Bastien to its walls so he couldn't escape. Once the fire burned out, he would have no choice but to return to the underworld.

At least, that was the idea.

She took Armand's hands, unbothered by the blood on his skin, and caged the candle between them.

The words of the spell had never left her, though Mallory had not uttered them again after that night so long ago. They came whispering back, the song she'd created for them sliding easily from her tongue. She had spent hours poring over her mother's spell books. She remembered the power she had felt tingling in her fingertips. She could still feel the absolute certainty she'd had in her abilities, her lineage, herself.

Mallory Fontaine. A witch, through and through.

It was overshadowed by the seven years of emptiness that had followed. Seven years disconnected from petty magic. Seven years of guilt and resentment and anger, of being nothing more than a fraud.

She tried to shove those thoughts away, thinking instead of Gabrielle's words, and trying so very hard to believe them.

He cannot take away what you are.

At first, nothing happened. Mallory felt her fragile hope start to disintegrate. She held tight with both fists, squeezing with every ounce of faith she had.

She was Mallory Fontaine.

Descended from Gabrielle Savoy. Daughter of Noele Fontaine. Her sister was Velos-blessed, and dammit, *she* had magic, too. She always had. She always would. She was a witch. She was—

The windows shook. The walls trembled. The lock on the entry door was thrown and bolted shut.

Pain burned through Mallory's chest, emanating from the scar at the base of her throat. She gasped. Her lungs tightened. The words would not come.

Armand's hands enclosed hers, warm and strong.

She swallowed and spoke again. Her tongue became heavy. Every word threatened to choke her. But as she finished the seventh recitation of the spell, a sudden blackness yawned open between them.

A hole. A cavern. A doorway into nothing.

Mallory didn't want to be surprised—but she was. She was *astonished*.

It was working. Her magic was actually working.

Then the candle flame turned blue.

"Mallory . . . Mallory!" Voices called to her—first from far away, but growing steadily closer. Triphine, Lucienne, Béatrice, Julie . . . Gabrielle. "Mallory, it isn't safe. He's coming, Mallory, he's coming, you can't—"

The voices became screams . . . then fell silent.

Mallory peered around. The wives were surrounding her, their bodies hung from chandeliers and curtain rods, their throats slashed.

An illusion, she told herself. The wives were long dead. This was not them.

She glanced at Armand, wondering if he could see them, too, but Armand's head was slumped forward. His eyes closed.

"Mallory Fontaine."

Monsieur Le Bleu stood on the stairs, still solid and human—if an immortal sorcerer could be considered human.

"I am attempting to make this a respectable estate once more, and here I find you and my useless progeny pouring my finest vintages onto the carpets." He sighed. "Do you honestly think you are going to lure me back into that hole?"

Mallory grabbed the knife and forced herself to stand. "I don't have to lure you into anything. I just can't let you leave. And lucky for me . . . you already did the hard work on my behalf."

His eyes narrowed.

Her fist tightened on the knife handle.

"Julie was killed in the trophy hall. Gabrielle in the chapel. Lucienne in the tower and Béatrice in the conservatory. And . . . you. You were killed at the fountain. Funny, isn't it? Five deaths. Five sacrifices. And if one were to draw them on a map, they would make almost a perfect pentagram. Which, if my spell holds, means that five spirits can never again leave this place. Including yours."

She couldn't help glancing at Triphine—alone not included in the spell, and yet, still captured by Bastien's dark magic. Though she was hanging from the ceiling, Triphine's eyes were open, watching her.

"Forgive me," Mallory whispered.

Then she pulled her arm back and threw the knife, striking the priceless vase on the vestibule table. It wobbled and fell, shattering to pieces on the floor. Velvety black roses were flung across the marble tiles.

Bastien stared at them, and she was glad to see that she had, at least, surprised him. "Now you're just trying to annoy me," he muttered.

"No. I'm trying to distract you."

Mallory grabbed the candle from the center of the circle and threw it onto the wine-soaked carpet. She held her breath and—

Nothing happened.

Well, that wasn't entirely true. The flame extinguished.

Her jaw fell. No, no, *no*.

Bastien smirked. "I do enjoy a good monologue. Unfortunately, one needs actual magic to back up a speech like that." His grin dissolved as he thundered down the stairs and grabbed the knife she had thrown. Then he was upon her, yanking her arm, hauling her body against his.

When he raised the knife, preparing to drag the blade across her throat, Mallory let her instincts take charge. She reached over her shoulder and took hold of his arm, before bucking her hips backward. It was a bit of déjà vu, tossing Bastien to the floor as she had once tossed Armand. He landed with a pained grunt.

Perhaps he couldn't be killed, but if his breathless cough was any indication, he could certainly be hurt.

Mallory snatched the knife from him while he was still laid out on the floor and drove it into his heart.

He snarled at her, before his body dissolved into wisps of black smoke.

Having no idea how long she had before he returned, Mallory took the tiny salamander ornament from her pocket and threw it as hard as she could at the floor. It shattered, and like a lizard from an egg, a shiny, slimy salamander emerged from the wreckage. It flattened its sticky little toes onto the tile floor, momentarily transfixed as it took in its strange new surroundings.

Then it scuttled toward the fireplace.

"Hold it!" Mallory leaped forward, landing on her stomach with a grunt and a jolt of pain that vibrated up her spine. Her hands clasped around the salamander, trapping it. "I need you!"

Scooping the creature into her fists, she spun around, arms outstretched, and aimed the annoying little pest at the nearest patch of wine-soaked carpet.

When the salamander did not immediately comply, she growled and stuffed its sharp little face into one of the tumbled rosebuds.

The salamander stiffened. Pulled back. Squirmed.

Then it sneezed. A blast of orange fire burst from its mouth.

The carpet ignited. Flames flared upward and billowed down the corridor, toward the kitchen and cellar.

Heat surged through the room. The salamander squealed. As soon as Mallory dropped the creature, it disappeared through the narrow crack beneath the entryway door. As the heat singed Mallory's skin, she threw open the lock and yanked on the door handle.

The door did not open.

Vision going white with panic, she yanked harder, rattling the door in its frame.

It refused to budge.

She ran toward the door to the parlor.

It slammed in her face.

She approached the doorway to the drawing room. A chandelier dropped from the ceiling, directly into her path.

She spun around.

"Armand! Armand, wake up!" She hurried to the window and tried to throw up the sash. That, too, refused to open. Grabbing a heavy bookend off a nearby shelf, she threw it at the glass—but she might as well have thrown a daisy at it. The window stayed intact, proof that Bastien was still there. Perhaps not visible, but perfectly in control of the house. And he was not going to let her leave.

The black void was still in the center of the floor when she smacked Armand hard across the face. His head rocked back, eyelids fluttering. She hit him again, because the flames were growing larger by the second and he was not waking up fast enough.

"Up, get up," she yelled, pulling his arm.

He groaned, attempting to shake off the dregs of unconsciousness as she hauled him to his feet. The stairs loomed before them. She did not want to go upstairs. Every instinct told her she was condemning both Armand and herself to a smoldering death. But she had no other choice.

Armand stumbled after her, stealing glances at the fire roaring below. "Did it work? Is he gone?"

"Not yet. We need to find a way out of here." On the second story, she tore through parlors and salons, Armand on her heels.

"We were just in the entryway," he cried as the smoky air stung their eyes. "Where are you—"

She stopped and faced him. "Bastien doesn't want us to leave. He is trying to trap us here. No doors, no windows. How do we get out?"

Alarm flashed across his face. They had made it to a hall filled with portraits of his ancestors, their blank eyes watching. She spotted the painting of Triphine perched on a settee, her newborn son bundled in her arms. Bastien stood behind her, a hand on her shoulder. No doubt he was meant to look the doting husband, but Mallory saw him as he was. Domineering. Cruel. Already plotting her murder.

Soon this painting would burn.

They all would.

An explosion shook the house, shuddering through the walls. At the far end of the gallery of rooms, the floor groaned and caved in, quickly engulfed as the flames grew higher.

"I think the fire reached the cellar," mused Armand.

Bastien's rough voice echoed at them from every wall. "You are still in my castle, Miss Fontaine."

Every painting now bore his face—not only the family trio with Triphine and their son, but so many of Armand's ancestors. Now they all depicted the same sharp cheekbones, the gemstone eyes, the navy-blue beard.

"You will not escape. You will end this spell, or you will burn with me."

"If that's what it takes," she hissed. "I will die before I set you free."

Hatred seared the air around her.

"Yes," he said coldly. "You *will*."

CHAPTER FORTY-SEVEN

Armand grabbed Mallory's hand and dragged her thoughts away from the paintings.

They charged past guest suites and music rooms, gaming halls and libraries.

The air felt like an oven. Smoke filled her lungs. They climbed another staircase. Mallory grew dizzy with the spiraling steps, no longer sure what the point was. There was no escape. They were running deeper into his clutches.

They reached the tower. Armand climbed the ladder before offering her his hand.

"Come on!" he yelled when she hesitated.

Mallory started up after him. The rungs cracked beneath her, but Armand's hands wrapped around her wrists. He pulled her onto the tower floor. The opening in the floor slammed shut, sending up a plume of dust.

Though they were in the open air again, black smoke was

billowing from every corner of the house, and steam from the faint drizzle of rain arose from the smoldering walls.

Climbing to their feet, they approached the rail, where they could take in the inferno that surrounded them. Flames had devoured more than half the building, surging through chimneys and windows, sweeping closer with every second that passed. Though it had not yet reached the roof directly beneath the tower, Mallory felt the embers singeing her cheeks.

She saw her sister standing with Fitcher and Constantino near the fountain that still glistened with blood. Though Mallory could make out the shape of her name on her sister's mouth, she could not hear her screams above the raging fire.

The walls shook suddenly as a thunderous crash was heard below. She grabbed a pillar, wrapping both arms around it to steady herself.

"There!" cried Armand, pointing at the house's pitched roof, each side steeply sloped and dotted with chimneys and the dormer windows that jutted out from the attic. But she didn't care about that. Her attention was caught by the ground, so far below that it swam in her vision. Dizziness overtook her, and she slid down, her entire body trembling.

She needed to get out of this tower.

She couldn't get out of this tower.

"There's a trellis on the wall over there." Armand crouched in front of her, grabbing her shoulders. "Beneath that dormer. We only have to climb a short way to get down. The fire hasn't reached that side of the house yet."

"No," said Mallory. "I am not climbing out onto a roof."

His fingers dug into her. "You have to."

She cursed up and down and inside out, every curse she could think of, as her brain struggled to find another option, any option.

And she knew, with sudden certainty, that she was going to die in this house. She would be Bastien's final victim. Someday, another con artist would give tours and satisfy their guests' dark curiosities with tales of how Mallory Fontaine had burned in the tower of the House Saphir. Or how she had plummeted to her death. They would show a drawing of her skull, smashed on the pavers below. Blood spilling from her ears—

"Mallory, look at me."

She did.

"All you have to do is trust me," he said. "Can you do that?"

She didn't know. A part of her whispered that it would be easier to succumb to the fire than to risk a fall. Part of her knew that her limbs would never cooperate if she forced them to climb over that ledge, with the ground so very far away . . .

"Mallory." His voice was strained now, pleading. "Please."

She swallowed, her saliva tasting of smoke, and forced a shaky nod.

He yanked her to her feet before she could change her mind. "I'll go first," he said, already slinging one leg over the rail. "Follow behind me and do exactly what I do. And *don't look down*."

Smoke was blackening the sky as Armand swung his other leg to the rooftop. He waited for her to follow, her knuckles white as she clutched the rail, her arms already trembling. One leg went over and then the other, searching for the lip between the balustrades.

There was a small step down to the roof. Armand reached up a hand to steady her.

It was impossible. There was no way. She would never make it. She was going to fall. She was going to die.

"One foot at a time," he coaxed. "I've got you."

"Don't," she said through gritted teeth, "tell me what to do."

A pause, before he said quietly, "I wouldn't dare."

She exhaled through her nostrils. Her eyes stung. Tears blurred her vision.

But one foot came down. And then the other.

"Good. I'm going to bend down now, like this."

She followed the movement, having to pry her own fingers from their death grip on the rail in order to lower herself onto hands and knees, straddling the crest of the roofline.

"Now we're going to crawl in this direction. Slowly. Are you breathing? Don't stop breathing."

She *had* stopped breathing, and wasn't sure how he could tell.

She filled her lungs, then coughed to dispel the smoke. The air had grown hotter. Another crash from inside rocked the house.

"Maybe we shouldn't take it quite so slow," Armand said. He was below her on the roof, having put his body between her and the sharp descent.

It was so steep. And the fall was so far.

As she inched backward because she was too terrified to attempt turning around, she thought of Gabrielle, who had fled to this very tower when she had escaped from Bastien, who had transformed into a bird and flown away to safety.

It was a trick she might have taught Mallory while she was still alive. If Mallory had still been a witch. If Bastien hadn't stolen her powers from her.

No. Not stolen. He had locked her magic away somehow.

Locked it away behind that ghastly hourglass tattoo, a mockery of Velos's gift. He hadn't stolen it. He couldn't have. She'd finished the spell, hadn't she? She'd opened the door to Verloren. She'd bound him to these walls.

He cannot take away what you are.

But in that moment, Mallory hated Gabrielle Savoy. She hated petty magic. She hated god-gifts and sorcerers and these damned slippery roof tiles. She half crawled, half scooted toward the nearest dormer, Armand's voice coaxing her forward inch by tedious inch. She tried to ignore the stinging wind that threw her hair into her face, and the way her fingers were cramping, and her sister's cries barely heard over the din.

The tiles bucked beneath her, trying to throw her off.

Mallory cried out and threw her body flat against them. Armand pressed his body over hers while the tiles bucked again, beating out a jumbled rhythm, and suddenly the roof was pounding and clapping like an enormous piano. Clay cracked and shattered. The nearest chimney groaned, the stonework collapsed, and Mallory did not know if it was Bastien attacking them or the fire or both.

One of the roof tiles lifted, like the mouth of a monster preparing to clamp down on her hand.

Mallory screamed and let go, but Armand wrapped an arm around her, holding tight.

"We're almost there," he said. "Keep going."

She didn't know if she believed him. But as he shifted away from her, tugging at her side, she went with him. Every muscle shook and ached as they started down from the peak, down the wet slope of the roof. When her foot slipped, Armand caught her.

When her foot had nowhere to find purchase, he pressed his own thigh against the sole of her boot, supporting her.

They reached the dormer.

The window had broken, leaving its edges lined with shattered glass. Flames were devouring the attic inside.

"Keep crawling backward," Armand said, shouting over the fire's roar. "Stay with me."

They moved together, his body sheltering hers as her knees hit the edge, her feet dangling into nothingness. She whimpered, and started to climb back up, but Armand gripped her waist, stopping her.

"The trellis is right below us," he said, and she could tell he was making every effort to keep his voice comforting and level. "It's going to feel a little scary, but you can reach it, I promise." His mouth pressed into the back of her hair. "Put your hand over here. I will not let you fall."

She let him guide her hand to a gargoyle that jutted out from the gutter. She didn't think it would bear her weight, and yet it did.

Armand scooted back. "I'm touching the trellis. Keep coming back, just a little farther."

Her skirt dragged against the tiles as she scooted down, her feet flailing for purchase.

"That's it. You're almost—"

Wood splintered. Iron screeched.

Armand cried out.

He could have grabbed her as the trellis crumbled beneath him, grabbed her and pulled her down with him—but he didn't.

"Armand!" His name was whipped away on the burning wind.

The roof tiles loosened and Mallory nearly lost her grip, her body swinging off the roof, dangling by one desperate handhold.

She looked down.

Armand was in a heap, three stories below.

Not moving.

"*Armand!*" With a desperate sob, she threw up her other hand to grab the gargoyle, her feet clambering against the side of the wall. She was losing strength, her feet flailing, the ground a million miles away. And Armand . . . Armand was . . .

"And now, Miss Fontaine?" came Bastien's voice, seething through the mouth of the gargoyle. Its stone eyes glowed like spectral gems. "End the spell. Free me from this prison, and I will save you."

"No!" She slammed her eyes shut, tears leaking from beneath her eyelids.

"I am the only one who can save you," he roared, his fury making the fire flare brighter, incinerating everything.

She wouldn't. She would never. She would die first. This would end with her.

"Mallory!"

She opened her eyes and dared to look up.

The ghosts were there—all five of them, kneeling at the edge of the roof.

Her heart lifted, but it was a brief hope. Ghosts could not help her.

"Listen to me," said Gabrielle, staring at her with those bottomless black eyes. "You know this spell. I watched you as you studied it, memorized it. Now, repeat. *Verzolar involaris, arausch flischwalen, arausch fligeto.*"

Mallory gaped at her. Her fingers started to slip.

"Repeat it!"

"*Verzolar inflo*—"

"*Involaris.*"

"*Involaris*—"

"From the beginning, Mallory! *Verzolar involaris, arausch flischwalen, arausch fligeto.*"

"*Verzolar involaris, arausch*—"

The gargoyle sneered. A growl vibrated through its stone throat.

"—*flischwalen, arausch* . . ."

Its maw opened; its teeth grew long as razors.

She screamed and let go. ". . . *fligeto!*"

Mallory fell. Flailing arms and absolute terror and a vision of her own death in her eyes.

And then, suddenly, she flew.

Mallory didn't feel the change. Didn't know how, exactly, it happened. Only that one second she was falling and the next she was gliding away from the house on open wings, smoke and flames billowing behind her.

She felt free. Like she could climb to the very top of the sky.

Then she remembered Armand, and she plummeted back to the ground.

CHAPTER FORTY-EIGHT

For a moment, Mallory feared that she might never be human again. But as soon as her small, scaly feet touched the wet ground and she willed herself back to normal—the magic faded and she stood in her body once again, a little off-balance and still trembling with the rush of fear and adrenaline and the nearness of certain death, but alive and herself.

To her unbridled relief, Armand's eyes were open when she dropped to her knees beside him, his lashes fluttering in a daze. He had landed in a garden bed full of young, fragrant lavenders. The foliage had helped to break his fall—though Mallory could see the pain etched onto his features.

"You," he said stiltedly, "make for a very pretty bird."

She sobbed, bending over and pressing her forehead to his chest. He raised one hand to her hair, trying to brush it back from her face, but his fingers caught in her knotted tangles.

"Barn swallows are disgusting creatures," she said. "I thought for sure I'd be a hawk."

Armand wheezed a halfhearted chuckle, then winced in pain.

"Come on," she breathed, sitting up and gripping his hand. "You need to stand. The fire . . ."

Though he groaned and hissed in complaint, he allowed her to help him stumble to his feet. She suspected a broken rib or two from how he hunched to one side, but he accepted her support, and together they hobbled away from the house. The others met them halfway across the garden. Fitcher and Constantino flanked Armand, taking his weight onto their shoulders as Mallory fell into her sister's arms.

When they were safely away, they stopped to watch the flames devour the House Saphir. The blaze grew so bright that Mallory had to shield her eyes, squinting into the fire as the house was consumed. It was not a slow death. Mallory listened for the screams of Count Bastien Saphir I, but the roar of the fire was too loud. Nevertheless, as the inferno ran out of fuel, as the house succumbed and caved in on itself, there was a moment when the flames burned vibrant blue. As they eventually died down and smoldered, smoke and ash dancing on the wind, she knew that the spirit of Monsieur Le Bleu was no longer in this world.

Mallory wasn't sure when the wives joined them, but at some point she noticed their figures, hazy in a half circle by the garden, watching the house burn. Lucienne toasted the ashes of the house with a bottle she must have had stashed away somewhere. Then, one by one, the ghosts flickered from existence: Lucienne and Béatrice linked arms as they quietly vanished. Julie cast a mournful gaze at Armand, who could not see her, before the wind stole her away. Gabrielle was watching Mallory and Anaïs, smiling a soft, proud smile, as the rain and mist claimed her.

Only Triphine remained, clutching her blue shawl. At first, Mallory did not understand why she hadn't vanished with the others. But then she remembered that this time, it was *her* spell that was tethering these spirits, not Bastien's. The magic she had worked, the ritual she had enacted, had not involved Triphine, who had been killed miles away, in Morant. Her spirit was not tethered to this house. Not like the others. Not like Le Bleu.

"All that wine, wasted," Constantino murmured, drawing her attention away from the lonely ghost. The first words to be spoken in what felt like ages.

Armand, dirty and bedraggled and so very, very handsome, peered at him. "I own a winery," he said simply. "There's more wine."

Constantino smiled.

A shocked wail invaded their little coterie. Yvette, Pierre, and Gideon stumbled from the forest, where they had been sequestered and sheltered after drinking the drugged ceremonial wine. Their mouths were agape as they stared at the smoldering ruins of the château.

"What . . . what *happened*?" Yvette panted, dropping to her knees in mournful prayer.

Exhausted, dismayed, hardly able to believe she was still alive, Mallory felt a giddiness burble up inside of her. She knew her timing was terrible. She knew it wasn't appropriate. She knew any member of high society would chastise her for such dreadful behavior.

And yet, she started to laugh.

Armand turned to her, surprised.

Then his eyes crinkled at the corners, and soon, he was laughing, too.

CHAPTER FORTY-NINE

"I think I have scurvy," said Triphine, feeling around the inside of her mouth. "This tooth feels like it might be getting loose." She leaned dramatically against the fireplace mantel. "This one will be the death of me for sure."

"Would only that were true," Mallory muttered.

Triphine sent her an irate look. "I beg your pardon?"

"I said, *I wish there were something I could do*," adjusted Mallory. "Perhaps you should try that new tea Armand has been working on. Supposedly it can help fevers, chills, sore throat, stuffy nose, dizziness, heart palpitations, itching, delirium, skin rashes, numbness, body aches, inescapable crabbiness . . . and, *interestingly*, toothaches. It's almost like it was made specifically for you."

Triphine squinted at her a long, *long* moment, before giving a quiet harrumph. "Maybe I will."

Mallory shook her head, watching the ghost float up the staircase and disappear into her bedroom. With Bastien gone and the spell for which Triphine had been sacrificed completed, her spirit was no longer trapped in this world. No longer tethered to her wedding ring. She could have gone to Verloren with the others after all.

But she'd chosen to stay, and Mallory was beginning to think that, despite all her complaining, Triphine was actually quite happy here.

Mallory would never admit it, but she was actually quite happy to have her.

She returned to arranging the cabinet of merchandise she and Armand had ordered, including salamander figurines and potted plants grown from cuttings from the Saphir estate's own conservatory. The first *official* tour of the House Saphir, Morant, was scheduled for that evening—a half hour past sunset—and while she wasn't exactly nervous, she wanted everything to go well.

The house had changed significantly since she had given the tour to Armand and the investigators. She and Armand had worked tirelessly to fix the holes in the roof, the broken windows, the crumbling plaster. With Yvette's help, they had eradicated every cobweb, expelled every bat, evicted every rodent. They had cleaned and waxed the floors until they shone like mirrors. Replaced the broken lanterns, repaired and rehung the torn drapes, filled the common spaces with secondhand furniture—much of it purchased with a bottle of Saphir wine and a Wyrdith card reading.

Mallory was getting pretty good at reading the cards, in fact. It was one of the many roles she had easily slipped into. She was her mother's daughter. Mallory Fontaine—medium, apothecary, fortune teller.

Well, Armand was much more adept at the art of preparing herbs, roots, and flowers for medicines and spells than she was, so perhaps he was the true apothecary. Either way, it was a service that the people of Morant were happy to pay for.

The investigators had come for her when she and Armand had first returned to Morant. But what could they possibly arrest her for? All those people who called her a fraud? Just rumors and lies.

Mallory Fontaine *was* a witch, a master of petty magic. The same as her mother and grandmother and great-grandmother—the famous Gabrielle Savoy herself. It had taken some time to prove her legitimacy, but now, even Investigator Louis Garneau was one of her regular customers, requesting a monthly dose of emerald brittlegill potion. She thought it best not to inquire why.

It was not a bad living that she and Armand had carved out for themselves, and they even had some money tucked away, thanks to the sale of the vineyards and winery—a merchant from Chablac had been thrilled to purchase such historic land. Perhaps someday they would hire a larger staff. Pierre and Gideon had both chosen to find other employment in Comorre, to stay close to their families, and it was a lot of work for Yvette alone. It could be nice to have a chef, or a maid, or even a gardener. Though Mallory and Armand were in no hurry. If the house was in a bit of disarray, the garden a tiny bit overgrown . . . well, they weren't running a bed-and-breakfast. They were running a haunted house, and a little mayhem was good for business.

She heard the opening of the front door and went to meet Armand in the entryway, where he was removing his boots and jacket. He beamed when he saw her—the look bringing the same flutter to her stomach that it had a hundred times before.

"You have a letter," he said, holding out a piece of parchment, stamped with a wax seal. "From your sister, I presume."

Mallory grabbed it eagerly. Anaïs's letters were one of the great highlights of her life these days, detailing her travels as she, Fitcher, and Constantino made their way across the country—living her very own real-life adventure.

"They've reached Stivale," she said, recounting the letter to Armand as she meandered back toward the study. "Constantino has promised to take her to a masquerade, and she is hoping they'll have an opportunity to see the floating city of Caprietti, though Fitcher is eager to move on to Piermo. Evidently a borda has been terrorizing the countryside."

"What's a borda?"

"No idea. But other countries do have entirely different monsters than we have here."

"Sounds like a nightmare." Armand smirked. "I guess we'll have to go visit someday."

Laughing, she sat down at the writing desk and smoothed her sister's letter out before her to finish reading it.

> You should see the fashion here! I'm beginning to see where Constantino got it from. I'm planning to buy myself the most extravagant gown I can find the moment I can afford it.
>
> Fitcher has not said anything more about my god-gift, though their business does frequently involve not only monsters but

corpses and ghosts. Though I dread being called on to use this abysmal curse, I draw strength in knowing that it may help bring justice to the deceased.

I hope that your life in Morant is as fulfilling, dear sister, though I know it is not half so exciting.

I do love and miss you so.

Yours, Anaïs

Mallory had just finished reading when a warm kiss on her neck sent pleasant tingles dancing across her skin. After Bastien's demise, the wound on her chest had finally healed, the scar fading to pale pink, almost nonexistent. She had even begun to wear gowns that revealed her throat, her clavicle, and even—how dare she?—a hint of décolletage.

She shut her eyes, luxuriating in her shiver of pleasure as Armand kissed his way from her neck to her shoulder, his fingers brushing the strap of her dress . . . before she turned and smacked him on the arm.

"Go away," she said, trying to hide her breathlessness. "I have to write back to my sister."

His eyes glittered as he cupped her face in both hands. "Are you going to tell her our news?"

She scowled at him. "I'm considering it."

He pressed a kiss to her mouth, teasing and slow. "By all means," he murmured, pulling away, "don't let me keep you."

It took a fair amount of effort for Mallory to keep from calling him back as he left the study, her skin flushed.

She grabbed a piece of parchment and a quill, dunking it into the inkwell.

Dear Anaïs, as it should so happen, I have news of my own to share . . .

As she wrote, her engagement ring glinted in the light from the candle that burned on the desk.

The love was real. The trust was unbreakable. But the ring? Cheap brass beneath a thin layer of silver plating, the sapphire nothing more than shiny blue glass.

But no one else would ever have to know.

ACKNOWLEDGMENTS

From the start of my career, readers have been asking what other fairy tales I may someday want to tackle, and "Bluebeard" has long been one of my top answers. The tale itself is gory and horrific and strange . . . so naturally, it's one of my favorites. I'm thrilled to finally have written this book that's been tugging at my brain for more than a decade. To that, I want to start by thanking *you*. Reader, your support—for me and this book, but also fairy tales and ghost stories in general—means the absolute world to me. I am honored that you trusted me enough to pick up this book and spend your time going on an adventure together, and I truly hope you enjoyed the journey as much as I did.

We authors might be solitary beings, but we are not alone in the creation of our books, and I am endlessly grateful to the many people who have helped make *The House Saphir* a reality, including:

My stalwart agent, Jill Grinberg, and the team at Jill Grinberg Literary Management—Lisa Barelli, Katelyn Detweiler, Sam Farkas, and Denise Page.

My wonderful editor, Liz Szabla, and the team at Macmillan Children's Publishing Group: Johanna Allen, Robby Brown,

Sara Elroubi, Jean Feiwel, Carlee Maurier, Megan McDonald, Katie Quinn, Morgan Rath, Dawn Ryan, Gaby Salpeter, Helen Seachrist, Naheid Shahsamand, Jordin Streeter, Mary Van Akin, Melissa Zar, and Kim Waymer.

My fastidious copyeditor, Ana Deboo, who helped this story sparkle.

My talented illustrator, Andrew Davis, and designer, Rich Deas, for creating such jaw-dropping cover art.

My brilliant critique partner and friend, Tamara Moss, whose input always serves to not only improve the book, but also to make me a better writer.

My assistant and friend, Joanne Levy, who has bettered my life and career in countless ways.

My graphic designer and friend, Taylor Denali, for creating gorgeous book merch, swag, and art for social media, and generally making me look like I know what I'm doing.

My phenomenally talented and supportive writing group—Lauren J.A. Bear, Kendare Blake, Martha Brockenbrough, Cookie Hiponia Everman, Arnée Flores, Shanna Germain, Tara Goedjen, Donna Barba Higuera, Corry L. Lee, Alison Kimble, Kelsea Koops, Nova McBee, Lish McBride, Margaret Owen, Sajni Patel, Rori Shay, Rain Sullivan, J. Ann Thomas, and Brianna Tibbetts. (And probably more will be added to the group after I submit these acknowledgments, so thanks to all my new and future friends, too!)

And of course—Jesse, Delaney, Sloane, and all my family and loved ones. These past few years have been exceptionally hectic (even for me), and it would be impossible to fully express how much your love and support means to me. I couldn't do it without you.

MORE FAIRY TALE RETELLINGS BY MARISSA MEYER AWAIT...

Cursed by the god of lies, Serilda has a talent for storytelling.

When one of her tales reaches the devastating Erlking, she is locked away in a castle dungeon and ordered to spin straw into gold, or be killed for lying.

In despair, Serilda unwittingly summons a mysterious young man, who agrees to help her – for a price. But love wasn't meant to be part of the bargain.

Unbreakable curses have tied Serilda and Gild to the castle forever.

The Erlking is plotting to capture a god and be reunited with his banished lover, but his quest for vengeance could alter the mortal realm forever.

Serilda and Gild must thwart his plans, free his enslaved ghosts and solve the mystery of Gild's name – as long as their love can sustain them . . .